Charlotte Smith

Portrait of Charlotte Smith by George Romney (1792)

Charlotte Smith

A Critical Biography

Loraine Fletcher

First published in hardcover 1998

First published in paperback 2001 by
PALGRAVE
Houndmills, Basingstoke, Hampshire RG21 6XS and
175 Fifth Avenue, New York, N.Y. 10010
Companies and representatives throughout the world

PALGRAVE is the new global academic imprint of
St. Martin's Press LLC Scholarly and Reference Division and
Palgrave Publishers Ltd (formerly Macmillan Press Ltd).

ISBN 0–333–67845–1 hardback (*outside North America*)
ISBN 0–312–21587–8 hardback (*in North America*)
ISBN 0–333–94946–3 paperback (*worldwide*)

This book is printed on paper suitable for recycling and
made from fully managed and sustained forest sources.

A catalogue record for this book is available
from the British Library.

The Library of Congress has cataloged the hardcover edition as follows:
Fletcher, Loraine.
    Charlotte Smith : a critical biography / Loraine Fletcher.
      p. cm.
    Includes bibliographical references (p.) and index.
    ISBN 0–312–21587–8 (cloth)
    1. Smith, Charlotte Turner, 1749–1806. 2. Women and literature–
–England—History—18th century. 3. Women authors, English–
–18th century—Biography. I. Title.
    PR3688.S4Z63 1998
    823'.6—dc21
    [b]
                           98–15157
                               CIP

10   9   8   7   6   5   4   3   2   1
10 09 08 07 06 05 04 03 02 01

Printed in Great Britain by Antony Rowe Ltd, Chippenham, Wiltshire

For Mary Green

Contents

She chose rather to speak first of Books of a lighter kind, of Books universally read and admired, and that have given rise perhaps to more frequent arguments than any other of the same sort. 'You have read Mrs Smith's novels, I suppose?' said she. . . .

'Catharine'

Charlotte Smith: a lady to whom English verse is under greater obligations than are likely to be either acknowledged or remembered.

William Wordsworth

Acknowledgements

Like everyone interested in Charlotte Smith, I am most of all indebted to Judith Stanton, who has spent many years collecting and annotating her letters, now at The Indiana University Press. I should like to thank her for permission to quote from these letters, for her research into Smith's finances from publication and the Trust, and for many enjoyable conversations about the life and work. Many thanks also to Joan Catapano and The Indiana University Press for sending photocopies of these letters and for permission to quote from them. I was lucky in having Barbara Hardy as the supervisor of my thesis, which has provided a basis for the commentary on novels and poems. John Lucas has kindly given permission for the inclusion of material published in *Critical Survey* and in *Writing and Radicalism*.

Barbara Thompson and Sarah Wimbush at the Courtauld Institute supplied the pictures of Smith and Henrietta O'Neill. Alastair Laing of the National Trust has recently identified O'Neill as the sitter and given permission to reproduce her portrait here. The William Hayley, William Cowper, Frances Burney, Mary Wollstonecraft and Jane Austen portraits are reproduced by courtesy of the National Portrait Gallery. The portrait of Tom Hayley as Robin Goodfellow is reproduced by courtesy of the Tate Gallery. Chichester, Worthing and Weymouth Libraries, Weymouth Borough Council and the Guildford Muniment Room have responded promptly and helpfully to enquiries. I should also like to thank Iris Williams for medical information from British and American journals of psychiatry, Janet Moult, Kate Devaney and Mike Bott at Reading University Library, and the staff at the Bodleian. Plates of 'The Female Exile' and 'The Forest Boy' are reproduced from *Elegiac Sonnets* (2799 f.3156) by courtesy of the Bodleian.

Kath Whiteley and Pam Brain of Brains Typography, Reading have been endlessly patient and efficient in typing, providing camera-ready copy, and assisting with the Index for what has always turned out to be not quite the final version.

List of Plates

Cover design: front, portrait of Charlotte Smith by George Romney

Frontispiece: Romney portrait of Smith

1. 'The Infant Otway' by Thomas Stothard, from *Elegiac Sonnets*, 1789

2. 'On some rude fragment of the rocky shore' by Thomas Stothard, from *Elegiac Sonnets*, 1789

3. Henrietta O'Neill by William Hoare (Stourhead House)

4. William Hayley by Romney

5. William Cowper by Romney

6. Tom Hayley as Robin Goodfellow by Romney

7. 'The Female Exile' by Harriet, Countess of Bessborough, from *Elegiac Sonnets* Vol 2, 1800

8. 'The Forest Boy' by Richard Corbould, from *Elegiac Sonnets* Vol 2, 1800

9. Frances Burney by Edward Burney

10. Anna Seward by Romney

11. Mary Wollstonecraft by John Opie

12. Jane Austen by Cassandra Austen

Introduction

At thirty-eight, Charlotte Smith left her husband and relied on her writing to support herself and her children; she became at once the most popular English novelist of her time. She wrote ten novels and a collection of novellas between 1788 and 1802, and before, during and after these years she also published poetry and children's books. Popularity and prolixity then are no particular recommendations now, but she has better claims to be remembered: a witty, vigorous prose style and a talent for satire and political analysis. *The Old Manor House*, especially, is a profound and beautifully articulated novel. Though she sometimes felt, under pressure to fill her three, four or five volume quota, that she 'loved novels no more than a grocer does figs,'[1] she also gained some freedom and pleasure through her career, which spans an exciting decade. For many English intellectuals in the 1790s, the first three years of the French Revolution offered a possible model for change in England. Corrupt old institutions and economies, it seemed, might at last be swept aside for a New Jerusalem built by ordinary, not especially privileged people. Charlotte Smith belongs with the group of writers who were called by their detractors 'Jacobins', writers who wanted radical reform or revolution. They included Mary Wollstonecraft, William Godwin, Helen Maria Williams, Robert Bage, Thomas Holcroft, Elizabeth Inchbald and Mary Hays.

She was the first novelist to take as her setting a castle or great house intended to be read as a precise emblem of England. Questions raised by her plots about who should own the great house and how it should be run are questions about England's ownership and government. In this she influenced Jane Austen and the later development of the novel. Mansfield Park, Chesney Wold, Howard's End, Wragby Hall, Darlington Hall and many other fictional houses testify to the lasting usefulness of the metaphor. She was a poet before she was a novelist, and her heroes and heroines are often poets themselves, sensitive to language and ill-at-ease among the matrimonial schemers, raffish aristocrats and corrupt lawyers and clergy

1

around them. Hers are poems and novels of Sensibility, a word that implied sympathy with suffering, a tendency to impulse and rashness, a contempt for traditional forms, love of nature and a taste for literature, painting and music. Her landscapes are sharply and lovingly observed, and mirror her central characters' states of mind.

For her early life I have drawn on three accounts by contemporaries, two of them anonymous. The series *British Public Characters* was an early *Who's Who?* without the class bias. It gave fairly extensive biographies of men and women eminent in their professions. Charlotte's is in the 1800–1 issue, and runs to twenty-two pages. It is a reflective appraisal, the work of an accomplished fellow-writer. The manner is conceptual, poems are quoted in full, and more attention is paid to the achievement than to detail of the life. The writer is warmly partisan, has had several long interviews with the subject, and knows her work well. This piece is by Mary Hays, feminist and friend of Mary Wollstonecraft, author of *The Memoirs of Emma Courtney* and other novels. In 1803 she published *Female Biography*, an interesting example of early revisionist history, containing the lives of nearly 300 distinguished women.

Charlotte's fullest obituary appeared in *The Monthly Magazine* of April 1807, six months after her death. The obituarist is evidently familiar with the *British Public Characters* account, but some details are different, the focus is on the subject's difficult life as much as on her writing, and the style is more journalistic. This is probably by Richard Phillips, who had known Charlotte personally and commissioned work from her. He was the publisher of both *British Public Characters* and *The Monthly Magazine*.

There are many other contemporary and near-contemporary comments on her life and work, but the most useful biographical source is a memoir by Catherine Dorset, Charlotte's sister, contributed to Sir Walter Scott's *Lives of the Novelists* published in 1821. Catherine had read the *British Public Characters* and *The Monthly Magazine* narratives. She probably wrote with them open beside her, as there are echoes of both in her memoir. Younger by only a year than her sister and an author herself, she is certainly best qualified as a source of information. But she was recalling events sometimes fifty or sixty years back when she was still at school while Charlotte was already 'out' in society; soon after that, both were married and often living at a distance from each other. More conventional than her sister, Catherine attempts to explain away Charlotte's revolutionary politics and to defend the family decorum in a changed moral climate. This is nonetheless an affectionate and intimate memoir, running to thirty-eight pages.

In the twentieth century, Florence Hilbish's *Charlotte Smith: Poet and Novelist,* her doctoral thesis published by the University of Philadelphia Press in 1941, is admirable and thoroughly researched, much of it devoted to biographical criticism, which inevitably attracts accusations of naïveté now. But it is, I think, the right approach to Charlotte Smith, and one she herself invited by her frequent use of autobiographical material. All subsequent writing on this subject is deeply in debt to the pioneering work of Hilbish in the 1930s.

I have also drawn on Judith Stanton's splendidly annotated collection of the Letters, soon to be published by The Indiana University Press. Many are to publishers, and provide a fascinating insight into the author's working conditions – 'chained to her desk like a slave to his oar',[2] as William Cowper put it – and her finances. They give a sharp sense of her day-to-day preoccupations over the last eighteen years of her life, and I have extracted longer passages than is usual in a biography, as the edition is not yet available.

A few paragraphs from early letters survive because they were preserved in the *British Public Characters* account or in Catherine Dorset's memoir. But most of them are lost. Though she wrote poetry from a very early age, this is lost too, and she published nothing until she was thirty-five. So a sense of her development as child, adolescent and young woman is hard to reach. The first part of this book is a necessarily tentative reconstruction with, I am aware, too many mays and perhaps. But when she at last began to write novels she used, more than any other author I know, autobiographical material scarcely disguised, projecting herself, her father, courtship, husband, marriage, children, friends and enemies into her fiction and expecting readers to recognise the dramatisation – as they did.

So I have felt free, like Hilbish, to rely on her later fictionalisations for her young self. Geraldine's crossing the Channel in *Desmond*, the exile of the Staffords to Normandy in *Emmeline*, Mrs Woodfield's childhood in *Rural Walks*, Adelina's and Leonora's courtships and marriages in *Emmeline* and *The Letters of a Solitary Wanderer*, Laura's loss of her baby in *The Young Philosopher*, fill out what cannot now be known with certainty about Charlotte's thoughts and feelings. They are of course retrospective and biased. But any biography must be so, and it is more interesting to have the fictionalisations of the subject than of the mere biographer. 'Exile' combines episodes from the novels with a narrative based on the three external sources I have mentioned. The fictional situations I choose are those she wanted her readers to recognise as her own. I have allowed myself a little latitude, basing on the novels some provisional conjecture that future research may correct or endorse: I do not know, for instance, exactly where the Turner sisters met their future stepmother, or whether Charlotte had a midwife for her last baby, though I would guess she probably did.

In making these connections, however inadequately, I have had no sense of looting or distorting her work but rather of using material she provided for one of its intended purposes, and I have tried to show what comes from external sources and what from her own narratives. After her late thirties when she was becoming famous, many of her letters were saved. Here it is possible to move from fragile reconstructions to an evaluation of her writing with quotation from these wonderfully acerb and embattled letters. The last six years of her life are the most fully documented, but I have given more space to the years when she was writing novels, the late 1780s and 1790s.

Choosing a name to call her has been a problem, and sets a register for the book, which is not intended only, or mainly, for specialists in this period, but as a general, accessible introduction to her life and work avoiding the obfuscation of academic language. A surname is unapt for a child; she came to hate her husband's name and sometimes in her fifties signed herself 'Charlotte Smith', then put a line through 'Smith'. To adopt her patronymic is no better. Though she loved her father, his inadequacy when she most needed him had disastrous consequences. So I have opted for 'Charlotte' throughout. This may seem unprofessional, and certainly runs counter to the impersonality of much current criticism. But part of Charlotte's professionalism was to offer her readers an unusual degree of intimacy through author-representative characters and direct address. It is an intimacy that still speaks to us two hundred years later, as I hope the reader will feel, and so will find 'Charlotte' neither intrusive nor patronising.

1

Exile

On a cold evening in October 1784, Charlotte Smith was waiting at the embarkation point near the Ship Inn at Brighton to board the packet to Dieppe. Her nine children, their ages ranging from sixteen down to two, were with her. They had spent several days at The Ship waiting for the wind to change; now a steady gale was blowing from the northeast. Harriet, in her mother's arms, cried as they huddled together on the shingle, their possessions packed up in boxes at their feet. In the gathering dark they watched as lightermen began loading French and English passengers into the rowing boats that were to carry them out to the packet. Charlotte was taking her children to join their father Benjamin, who had been released from the King's Bench Prison that summer. He was living in Normandy to escape his creditors, who could have him sent back to jail for debt if he returned to England.

Her only servant, lent by her brother, had never crossed the Channel before and was almost crying with fright. Charlotte Mary her fifteen year old, usually the most sensible of the children, looked nervous as she watched the great shining Poseidon-figures of the lightermen wade into the water in their sea-boots, carrying passengers as casually as sacks. Even the three boys in their teens stopped boasting about what they would do in France. There was still time for Charlotte to change her mind. With the obstinacy that never deserted her she pulled the children's cloaks tightly round them and warned the men to be careful. They were carried in raised arms, scared but more or less dry, through the high surf to one of the rowing boats. Charlotte herself, holding tight to Harriet and five months pregnant, was more cumbersome, but her lighterman was used to heavier loads and delivered her into the boat without much difficulty. In the dusk she made the usual quick head-count while the servant was set down beside her and their boxes were loaded. With a furious crash the boat put off from the shingle and the spray splashed over them on their way to the packet a hundred yards out. The decision was made.[1]

It was a perverse decision, as she knew while she was making it. By now she resented Benjamin's demands on her and had no wish to join him. He had rented a dilapidated chateau between Dieppe and Rouen, picked out for him by some gambling friends he had just met, its only recommendation that a couple of Scottish noblemen had been renting it previously. Charlotte might have stayed with her brother at Bignor in Sussex where she had grown up, and looked to her own relations for support in the wake of her husband's bankruptcy. Instead she was taking her children deep into the Normandy countryside, where according to stories of returning English travellers, decent accommodation and even efficient servants were increasingly hard to find; there were rumours that the strikes and bread-riots of ten years back were likely to break out again. More worrying still, the maid with her had no skill in midwifery, and Charlotte knew she had little chance of finding in a remote French village the trained male *accoucheur* upper class Englishwomen expected when they went into labour.

But Benjamin had written, ordering her to join him and bring the children, and she could not make up her mind to disobey, or encourage the children to disobey. She knew he would be involved in further financial difficulties without her. She and the children could live much more cheaply in France than in England, she thought. She had no legal right to keep his children – or for that matter herself – from him. To do so would cut her off forever from all those wives whose self-esteem rested on their ability to endure. If she still loved him, she knew, she would not have felt this need to be a complete martyr to duty and follow wherever it led: she could consider her own and the children's interests as well as his. But though Benjamin had thrown away whatever affection she once felt for him, she must fulfil to the letter all that her social circle seemed to expect of her. And in circumstances as difficult as the Smiths', there was a certain relief in handing over all responsibility to one's husband, even a husband as feckless as Benjamin. Underneath the resolve to be blameless, though, and not just blameless but exemplary, a counter resolve was growing. She constantly fantasised about leaving him.

With the gale behind them, the crossing was fairly quick, only seventeen hours, though the appalling noise of a ship in sail and the violent pitching allowed them little sleep. There was no sign of Benjamin at Dieppe, but to Charlotte that was not unexpected, though the children were disappointed. Her French was excellent;

she chose a coach from the hire firm on the quay, the only vehicle big enough to take the whole party and their boxes. The licensees insisted on adding another pair of horses to the two pair already harnessed, as they were a party of eleven, and charged accordingly. It was useless for Charlotte to point out that Harriet was a baby, Lionel and Lucy seven and eight, and the other children hardly of adult weight. The regulations were clear, *madame* would be defrauding King Louis of the taxes due to him without the extra pair. She was too seasick to argue and within an hour they set out again towards Rouen. In a letter to a friend she wrote:

> My voyage was without accident; but of my subsequent journey, in a dark night of October through the dismal hollows and almost impassable chasms of a Norman crossroad, I could give a most tremendous account. My children, fatigued almost to death, harassed by seasickness, and astonished at the strange noises of the French postillions, whose language they did not understand, crept close to me, while I carefully suppressed the doubts I entertained whether it were possible for us to reach, without some fatal accident, the place of our destination. In the situation I then was [ie, pregnant], it was little short of a miracle that my constitution resisted, not merely the fatigues of the journey, with so many little beings clinging about me (the youngest, whom I bore in my arms, scarce two years old), but the inconveniences that awaited my arrival at our new abode, in which no accommodation was prepared for my weary charges.[2]

There was nothing romantic about the crumbling old chateau she reached after the long journey. Benjamin had bought for five times its value all the furniture the vacating Scottish tenants did not want, but there was still a shortage of beds and bedding; every room was damp and cold, and many without glass in the windows. Charlotte was too tired and angry to pretend much pleasure in seeing her husband again. But even these bleak surroundings gave the children the excitement of novelty. They were happy to be with their father, the older ones relieved he was still out of prison. They helped gather together what mattresses and blankets they could find, arranged them close to the small fires in two of the rooms, and gradually settled down for the night with their clothes piled over them.

Next morning she began to assess her surroundings. The few servants included in the rent appeared sullen and suspicious. Several large rooms were occupied by cages of canaries. Benjamin's latest project was to recover a fortune through breeding them; his concern for these birds had prevented him from meeting his wife and children at Dieppe. The servants had no intention of cleaning the cages or the floors of the rooms where they were allowed to fly. That October saw the onset of one of the coldest Normandy winters in memory. Charlotte learned at once there was a severe shortage of wood; all wood belonged to the King, was heavily taxed, and could only be bought legally through his contractors at Dieppe, their nearest market town twelve miles away. The local peasants paid no attention to this law, however, and took any wood they could find. Through the windows she could see the trees for miles around pollarded till they looked like poles. Eggs, milk and green vegetables were unobtainable in winter, and meat expensive.

But there was enough fruit in the walled orchard to last the winter and she directed one servant to begin picking and storing it. Benjamin was glad of an excuse to ride into Dieppe with another who could do the marketing. The cook was impressed with the need to make bread enough for them all. Her accent was the least impenetrable among the servants; she tried to tell Charlotte a complicated story about how the green corn had been cut down in the blade that spring by government agents, to keep up prices, but Charlotte could not believe such a thing possible, and ignored it.

Charlotte Mary with the four older boys, William, Braithwaite, Nicholas and Charles, explored the castle. Augusta, who was ten and like her mother, the only one who did not resemble Benjamin in features or colouring, with Lucy and Lionel formed the second, younger group. They were more wary of their surroundings and kept close to their mother on the first day. But the older children were used to caring for the smaller ones. Harriet was too young to be left unsupervised for a moment, but the English maid, once over her journey, proved herself a resourceful nanny.

At intervals Charlotte could hear bells, and the cook explained there was a church and a small monastery about two miles away on the Seine, just beyond the nearest village. A few days after her arrival she walked through the castle grounds in that direction, hoping to make contact with some local people who could supply her with cheap rabbits and perhaps with cheese. The land around seemed almost entirely uncultivated. Benjamin said nothing to warn her against walking on her own, and none of the stories she had heard about France prepared her for the desolation she found. The village was a scattering of miserable shacks, a few emaciated goats and dogs wandering between them. Heaps of night soil lay everywhere, and even on such a cold day few of the hovels showed signs of fire. While she hesitated, villagers appeared in their doorways to stare sullenly at her. When she began to retrace her steps, a group of older women in rags and thin sabots followed, caught up and surrounded her. They fingered her thick cloak, patted her belly and joked in a dialect too broad for her to catch as they eyed the lace at her neck longingly.

She was shaken, as much with a sensation of incredulity as with fear. All her life she had been used to the deference of English servants and estate workers. As the fierce, dirty faces closed in on her, it was like witnessing the reversal of a natural law, almost as if animals had suddenly begun to speak and assert their anger. Summoning all the *hauteur* at her disposal, she ordered them to stand aside, broke through them and hurried towards the castle. Luckily they did not follow. Once safe in her gloomy drawing room she could acknowledge the inhumanity of her feelings while admitting that in the same circumstances she would feel the same repugnance. After that she went out for exercise only in the orchards close to the house, and warned the children to stay within sight of the windows.

As well as she could in these surroundings, when their first preoccupations were food and keeping warm, she re-established her daily routine of hearing the younger children read from the few books she had brought for them and encouraging the older ones to write and draw. She also found time to write herself. A sonnet, headed 'Written on the seashore, October 1784' gives some sense of her apprehension. The heading asks us to consider it a spontaneous outburst of feeling, and it probably was begun on the Sussex seashore before she left. But it must have been completed later when she was far inland, in France:

> On some rude fragment of the rocky shore,
> Where on the fractured cliff the billows break,
> Musing, my solitary seat I take,
> And listen to the deep and solemn roar.
> O'er the dark waves the winds tempestuous howl;
> The screaming sea-bird quits the troubled sea:
> But the wild gloomy scene has charms for me,
> And suits the mournful temper of my soul.
> Already shipwreck'd by the storms of Fate,
> Like the poor mariner methinks I stand,
> Cast on a rock; who sees the distant land
> From whence no succour comes – or comes too late.
> Faint and more faint are heard his feeble cries,
> Till in the rising tide the exhausted sufferer dies.[3]

Death was much on her mind that autumn. The canary birds died off in the cold, to Benjamin's rage, and the children amused themselves in composing comic or pathetic epitaphs. He embarked on an affair with the girl who helped the cook in the kitchen, a girl the same age as his eldest daughter. Charlotte had long ceased to quarrel with him about his intrigues, but she noticed with distress that Charlotte Mary was now old enough to understand the kitchenmaid's air of contempt for her mother. She wondered whether her daughter talked to the boys about their father, but could never bring herself to begin the subject.

She was now approaching her twelfth confinement. At thirty-five she was still fairly strong. But she knew the chances of death, high at the first childbirth then decreasing, began to rise sharply again after the seventh or eighth. Her mother had had three babies in three years and died of the last. She did not need to be the daughter of a gambling man to understand the risk she faced. She could only wait, disguising her anxieties as much as possible from the children, but finding some outlet for them in a sonnet where time and nature are her enemies.

'On some rude fragment of the rocky shore' allows her to distance and control her fears. There is nothing specific or female about them. The speaker is sexless in the octave, becoming male-defined with the simile of the shipwrecked mariner in the sestet. The storm metaphor is a well-worn one from centuries of mainstream male writing. In her early poetry as in much women's writing in the eighteenth century, female sensibility is channelled into male form and imagery. The shadow of a man falls between the woman writer and her experience, but as Cora Kaplan says, the difficulties of a supposedly 'common' language which in fact excludes women can be made into strengths.[4] The imagery of drowning, of waves breaking on the shore, gets its unusual force here from Charlotte's anticipation of the familiar moment when her own waters would break, and a few hours must decide whether or not she survived. If she did not, her children's prospects were desperate. The new baby, if it was born at all, would die off like one of the canaries. The others, left to Benjamin, might never get back to England, and she could not imagine what would become of them in Normandy.

It was useless to talk to him about sending them back to her brother or sister. Her proposal of going back alone to have the baby and returning later he met with a direct negative. He refused to take her coming labour seriously, and in any decision about the children law and custom gave him absolute authority. A respectable woman's

children belonged to her husband. To deny that was almost to deny
their paternity. Her depression was compounded by the thought
that she had acted foolishly in coming at all, that in playing the
martyr role of the good wife she had been a very bad mother. In these
last months of 1784 she had time to think back to the events of her
early life, and the misfortunes that had brought her to Normandy.
Her thoughts are lost to us, but as some small compensation we have
the benefit of a much longer retrospect, and knowledge she could not
have then of how her experience would inform her writing.

*

She was born on 4 May 1749, the first child of Anna Towers and her
husband Nicholas Turner, in the Turners' town house in King Street,
just off St James' Square. From his father and an elder brother who
died in 1747, Nicholas had inherited two prosperous estates, Stoke
Place near Guildford in Surrey and Bignor Park on the Arun in
Sussex, as well as smaller properties. His sudden accession to his
brother's inheritance allowed him to please himself, and he married
Anna, who had only a thousand pounds, for love, when they were
twenty-seven and twenty-one respectively. They were an attractive
couple. *The Monthly Magazine* in its obituary for Charlotte described
Anna as being 'as distinguished by the graces of her mind as by a
person of exquisite beauty', and though something must be allowed
for the arts of obituary, Charlotte always remembered her as beautiful and loving. Nicholas is described here too as 'a man of very
superior talents, remarkable for the brilliancy of his wit, his power of
conversation and a peculiar vein of humour which rendered him the
delight of society.' Six weeks after Charlotte's birth they were back at
Stoke Place, where she was baptised on 12 June. Anna preferred the
country; she had perhaps chosen to be confined in London for the
benefit of the best medical advice, and returned to Stoke Place as
soon as possible. Two more babies rapidly followed, Catherine
Anne, then Nicholas. Anna died giving birth to the latter while
Charlotte was still only three.

In losing their mother, the three babies effectively lost their father
also, at least for five or six years. Nicholas put his children into the
care of his wife's unmarried sister Lucy Towers and left England to
try to forget his bereavement in travel and in a new social life abroad.

In the memoir of her sister written many years later, Catherine does not mention his leaving them. But as Mary Hays, the author of Charlotte's biography in *British Public Characters* puts it:

> when a blow so cruel falls on a man of lively passions, and thus destroys his domestic happiness, many evils ensue from the eagerness with which temporary forgetfulness is sought by mixing with the world.

This loaded comment hints at the gambling and extravagance that ensued, and their consequences for the Turners. But materially the children lacked for nothing when they were young, and they had a devoted mother-substitute in Lucy Towers.

They lived at Bignor Park when they were not at school and this house and its surrounding landscapes were recreated in many of Charlotte's novels and poems. Sussex often provides the setting for the isolated speaker of her sonnets, and in a poem of 1793, *The Emigrants*, she recalls summer days when the three children lived most of their time out of doors. She was free to explore the Downs and seashore, and to play beside – and in – the tidal reaches of the Arun:

> There (where, from hollows fring'd with yellow broom,
> The birch with silver rind, and faery leaf
> Aslant the low stream trembles) I have stood
> And meditated how to venture best
> Into the shallow current, to procure
> The willow herb of glowing purple spikes
> Or flags, whose sword-like leaves conceal'd the tide
> Startling the timid reed-bird from her nest . . .[5]

The passage suggests how absorbing these Sussex landscapes were. It resembles the lines in Wordsworth's *The Prelude* where the child makes 'one long bathing of a summer's day',[6] Charlotte too traced to such early experiences the growth of her individuality and impulse to write.

Lucy Towers shared the majority view of her contemporaries about girls' education. Much reading, especially of fiction, was bad for them, as was the academic course of study suitable for boys. Learning was unattractive in a woman. Her aim was to bring up her nieces to be socially accomplished, to have the widest choice of marriage partners and to marry 'well'. Perhaps she tried to live through them, and certainly Charlotte came to resent her conventional standards. But it was no part of her plan to turn her nieces into rouged and corseted dolls. Charlotte rode a donkey and fished her father's ponds with the estate workers, up to her knees in mud. The sisters were not expected to learn the practicalities of cooking or plain sewing, as their rank made it unlikely they would need such skills. Music and dancing were the important acquirements. Charlotte was never accomplished musically because she never bothered to practice much, but she learned her first dancing steps from a fashionable master as a small child on the dining room table, and loved it.

At six she went to school in Chichester, probably boarding by the week and coming home at weekends. Her first notable talent was for drawing, and she was allowed to have lessons two or three times weekly with the painter George Smith, who lived in Chichester. The son of a local cobbler, he was then in his early forties and rather famous as a landscape artist in the style of Claude and Poussin. Though Charlotte was still so young, she was intellectually and aesthetically very precocious. Smith taught her to see landscape feelingly, to appreciate not just physical features but the atmosphere that gave them meaning. But her short sight discouraged much practice in this form. Her gift was for close studies of flowers and leaves. Botany was then becoming an important part of girls' education; her detailed, coloured line drawings were the artistic expression of an interest in botany that found scope in the great local variety of plant life, on the chalk Downs, in the beechwoods, on the seashore and along the banks of the Arun. It was a passion that lasted all her life, and matured into a philosophy.

Later she claimed she could not remember a time when she could not read, and at six or seven she was beginning to write poetry. One early poem she still recollected vividly in her fifties, an elegy on the death of a pet dormouse. Here her sense of loss for the dead mother and absent father evidently found some relief in a subject of manageable size. None of her childhood verse survives.

At eight she moved with Lucy and Catherine to the London house, returning to Bignor in the holidays. Nicholas arranged for his daughters to go to a fashionable school in Kensington, giving them the advantage of the best masters in preparation for their eventual introductions into London society. It is not clear when he returned to England, only that he lived 'some years' abroad after his wife's death in 1751. He may have directed his daughters' education from a distance. But he was back by the time Charlotte was nine, and delighted with the children he discovered, especially his eldest, whose cleverness and vivacity looked likely to equal his own. His son was now enrolled at Westminster School, and the whole family spent much of their time in London. Nicholas needed the stimulus of fashionable company, parties and gambling.

At her Kensington school Charlotte was successful and popular, though often homesick for Sussex. She was the best dancer, the best actress, and often took part in French or English plays, or was called on for 'recitations' when her father had friends at the London house. She acquired French early, and hers was very good by school standards, though she felt afterwards that more time should have been spent on languages. Perhaps she had Italian lessons here too; certainly she was proficient in Italian later, and read Petrarch and Metastasio with pleasure. At Kensington she continued to write poetry; Catherine remembered verses on the death of General Wolfe, written in 1759 when Charlotte was a few months short of eleven. The Seven Years' War was then involving all Europe in a struggle for control of North America and India. From the age of six she would have been aware of the possibility of a French invasion, and with Bignor so close to the sea and the beacon on the Downs ready to be lit, she felt all the excitement of personal risk and a large local stake in the outcome. As well as dying a hero, James Wolfe was reported as saying he would rather have written Gray's 'Elegy in a Country Churchyard' than taken Quebec. From every point of view he must have seemed an irresistible subject for an elegy of her own.

A schoolfriend describes the impression she made at this age, eleven or twelve, in an account contributed later to Catherine's memoir:

> In answer to your enquiry, whether Mrs Smith was during our intimacy at school superior to other young persons of her age, my recollection enables me to tell you, that she excelled most of us in writing and drawing. She was reckoned by far the finest dancer, and was always brought forward for exhibition when company was assembled to see our performances; and she would have excelled all her competitors, had her application borne any proportion to her talents; but she was always thought *too great a genius* to study. She had a great taste for music, and a correct ear, but never applied it with sufficient steadiness to ensure success. But however she might be inferior to others in some points, she was far above them in intellect, and the general improvement of the mind. She had read more than anyone in school, and was continually composing verses; she was considered romantic, and though I was not of that turn myself, I neither loved nor admired her the less for it. In my opinion her ideas were always original, full of wit and imagination, and her conversa-

tion singularly pleasing; and so I have continued to think, since a greater intercourse with society, and a more perfect knowledge of the world, has better qualified me to estimate her character.

The word 'romantic' seems to imply literary, imaginative and original in her schoolfriend's vocabulary, and is an interesting early usage if it was applied to her at school. Her friend may be imposing a familiar word in the 1820s back on her recollection of Charlotte in 1760, or Charlotte may have seemed interesting enough at school to prompt her friends to find an unusual term. One can believe that her exceptional qualities were already visible at eleven or twelve to a clever friend.

Her father and her aunt had different attitudes to her reading novels. Lucy positively forbade them, and tried to plan Charlotte's day when she was home for the holidays so as to leave no time for them. Charlotte was not so easily managed. In her novels and children's books, many characters are author-representative, plainly intended to be recognised as versions of the writer herself. One of these is Mrs Woodfield, the mother and teacher in Charlotte's first children's book, *Rural Walks*, written in 1794, whose experience may be taken as very close to Charlotte's memories of her own. I quote this passage at length because it is so revealing about Charlotte's early adolescence, and interesting in its mixed emotions about the novel, typical of eighteenth-century readers:

> When I was a girl, I had nobody to direct my reading; and being a good deal at a solitary house in the country, I fell upon all sorts of books that lay about, and many that nothing but the rage for reading, with which I was devoured, would have tempted a young person to look into. By this means I acquired, at a very early age, a great deal of desultory knowledge; and I was contented without reading novels, for there were none in the house I inhabited; and at that time every little country town had not a circulating library, as they have now. I found, however, exquisite delight in the little narratives which are scattered here and there in the *Spectator, Guardian, Tatler, World, Rambler, Adventurer*, etc., and I read them with such avidity and interest, that I believe I could now repeat every one of them with tolerable correctness. Soon after I was eleven years old, I was removed to London, to an house where there were no books, and where my whole time was taken up by attendance of masters from morning till night. But I found out by accident a circulating library; and, subscribing out of my own pocket money, unknown to the relation with whom I lived, I passed the hours destined to repose, in running through all the trash it contained. My head was full of Sir Charles, Sir Edwards, Lord Belmonts, and Colonel Somervilles,

while Lady Elizas and Lady Aramintas, with many nymphs of
inferior rank, but with names equally *beautiful*, occupied my dreams.
My relation soon perceived that I was thinking of something very
different from my music and my arithmetic (for my drawing I never
neglected), and a poor squirrel and some birds I kept were formally
accused by my masters, as being the cause of my neglect, by occupy-
ing a great part of my time. I was threatened with the perpetual
banishment of my unfortunate favourites, if any more complaints
were made; and I redoubled my diligence that my menagerie might
not suffer, nor my secret studies be detected. It happened, however,
that before I could derive any benefit from this partial reformation I
was caught in my clandestine reading by my aunt, who having sent
me to practice a different lesson on the harpsichord, remarked, for
the first time (though the circumstances had often happened before)
that she did not hear it. She therefore fancied I was gone to play with
my squirrel, instead of conquering the piece of music; and descend-
ing softly into the room, the door of which was open, and which was
just opposite to the place where I sat, she found me with my elbows
on my knees and in my lap were three greasy looking books, on one
of which I was so intent, that I did not see her till she was immediately
close to me. I was sharply questioned as to the means by which I came
by those books, and the servant, who had been employed to procure
them for me, was severely reproved. My future communication with
the circulating library was prohibited and my father was told of my
misdemeanour. Instead, however, of being angry, he only told me,
that the more I read the better he would be pleased; but he wished I
should not waste my time in reading indiscriminately all sorts of
books, but that I would let him see what I was going to read. He
blamed me, however, for doing anything clandestinely; and forbade
my having any books in the future, which were not approved either
by him or one of my friends [ie, relations]. In consequence of this, I
read, among much other more profitable reading, a great number of
novels; and though I certainly did not derive much advantage from
them, I think the only harm they did me was giving me false views
of life.[7]

Mrs Woodfield is deprecating about the novels she read and their
effect on her. She is however a character in a book intended for girls
just entering their teens, and written at a time when novels were
often regarded as time-wasting if not positively damaging, likely to
awaken a precocious interest in men and sex. The omniscient narrator of Charlotte's novels also often shows her heroine looking through
a novel with contempt.

It took Jane Austen to make the case for them as part of a liberal
education in her polemical outburst in *Northanger Abbey*, probably
begun only about five years after the above passage, though not

published until 1817. Austen's heroine Catherine Morland and her friend Isabella Thorpe

> shut themselves up, to read novels together. Yes, novels: for I will not adopt that ungenerous and impolitic custom so common with novel writers, of degrading by their contemptuous censure the very performances, to the number of which they are themselves adding – joining with their greatest enemies in bestowing the harshest epithets on such works, and scarcely ever permitting them to be read by their own heroine, who, if she accidentally take up a novel, is sure to turn over its insipid pages with disgust. Alas! if the heroine of one novel be not patronised by the heroine of another, from whom can she expect protection and regard? I cannot approve of it. Let us leave it to the reviewers to abuse such effusions of fancy at their leisure, and over every new novel to talk in threadbare strains of the trash with which the press now groans. Let us not desert one another; we are an injured body. Although our productions have afforded more extensive and unaffected pleasure than those of any other literary corporation in the world, no species of composition has been so much decried. From pride, ignorance, or fashion, our foes are almost as many as our readers. And while the abilities of the nine-hundredth abridger of the History of England, or of the man who collects and publishes in a volume some dozen lines of Milton, Pope, and Prior, with a paper from the Spectator, and a chapter from Sterne, are eulogized by a thousand pens, – there seems almost a general wish of decrying the capacity and undervaluing the labour of the novelist, and of slighting the performances which have only genius, wit, and taste to recommend them. 'I am no novel reader – I seldom look into novels – Do not imagine that I often read novels – It is all very well for a novel.' – Such is the common cant. – 'And what are you reading, Miss –?' 'Oh! It is only a novel!' replies the young lady, while she lays down her book with affected indifference, or momentary shame. – 'It is only *Cecilia*, or *Camilla*, or *Belinda*;' or, in short, only some work in which the greatest powers of the mind are displayed, in which the most thorough knowledge of human nature, the happiest delineation of its varieties, the liveliest effusions of wit and humour are conveyed to the world in the best chosen language. Now, had the same young lady been engaged with a volume of the *Spectator*, instead of such a work, how proudly would she have produced the book, and told its name; though the chances must be against her being occupied with any part of that voluminous publication, of which either the matter or manner would not disgust a young person of taste . . .[8]

Even as a mature writer Charlotte never achieved quite the intellectual confidence of Austen in the genre they both loved and developed. For her, novels give 'false views of life', that is, they raise expectations about love and marriage that will seldom be fulfilled. Charlotte is forcing herself to take Lucy's point of view in the *Rural Walks* passage; but she vividly conveys her own young craving for fiction.

Both Charlotte and her sister Catherine became writers of children's works and experts on girls' education. Both were critical, later, of the education they received. Trends in teaching change so fast that each generation is scathing about the superficiality of a few years back, and convinced of its own recent enlightenment. But Charlotte's time in school and out of it was well spent, especially for a writer. Even her neglected musical accomplishments remained a source of pleasure. Dancing, particularly country dancing, was as good for health as competitive sports. She was free to wander alone, as few children would be now, in the neighbourhood of Bignor Park. Not that children were safer in the eighteenth century than later, far from it, but the social position of the Turner girls would have seemed a protection within a few miles of Bignor.

She read Shakespeare extensively, and other poets including Otway and Collins, and profited greatly from the luck of drawing lessons with George Smith, as her poems and novels were to show. Her study of botany, later assimilated into her interest in Rousseau's teaching, lead to other scientific interests, for instance in fossils and 'remains', and so to the interest in local history evident in 'Beachy Head'. The schools they attended encouraged – or at least did nothing to wreck – the development in Charlotte, her unknown school friend, Catherine and other capable pupils, of a sophisticated prose style. Charlotte had a strong motive for learning to write well when she was very young, if she corresponded with her father. Much of her reading was random and self-directed, but that is the case in a good student at any time. The only thing seriously wrong with her formal education was its brevity.

While she was acquiring it, her father's financial difficulties were becoming too serious even for him to ignore. The years abroad had turned his gambling habit into an addiction, and probably most of his ready money was lost before he returned to England. In 1761 when Charlotte was twelve he sold Stoke Place, probably in some alarm at the way his affairs were going, to Jeremiah Dyson, remembered now as the generous patron of the poet Mark Akenside, author of *Pleasures of the Imagination*. He also sold or mortgaged several smaller properties. It is unlikely his estates had been carefully managed while he was abroad. But nothing could stop him playing for high stakes, or curb the lavish style of a man accustomed to servants, clothes and horses in profusion, and conscious of the admiration his wit entitled him to in London society. Though not an aristocrat he had aristocratic tastes and expectations.

The sale of Stoke Place brought £15,500. But though he paid off his debts, he was soon in debt again. Charlotte was taken out of school in 1761, perhaps because school fees presented an obvious area of economy rather than from any educational principles in her father or Lucy Towers. She was unaware of these financial problems. Her dresses were as expensive as ever, and the pursuit of accomplishments was still encouraged at home. Soon she was enjoying all the excitements of a young woman coming out in London. Catherine writes in her memoir:

> At twelve years of age she quitted school, and her father, then residing part of the year in London, engaged masters to attend her at home; but very little advantage could have been derived from their instructions, for she was at that early age introduced into society, frequented all public places with her family, and her appearance and manners were so much beyond her years, that at fourteen [*British Public Characters* gives thirteen] her father received proposals for her from a gentleman of suitable station and fortune, which were rejected on account of her extreme youth. Happy would it have been if reasons of such weight had continued in force a few years longer!
>
> With so many objects to engage her attention, and the late hours incident to a life of dissipation, her studies (if they could be so called) were not prosecuted with any degree of diligence or success. As if foreseeing how short would be the period of her youthful pleasures, she pursued them with the avidity natural to her lively character; and though her father was sometimes disposed to check her love of dissipation he always suffered himself to be disarmed by a few sighs or tears. Her passion for books continued unabated, though her reading was indiscriminate, and chiefly confined to poetry and works of fiction. At this time she sent several of her compositions to the editors of *The Lady's Magazine*, unknown to her aunt.
>
> It is evident that Mrs Smith's education, though expensive, was superficial, and not calculated to give her any peculiar advantages. Her father's unbounded indulgence, and that of an aunt who almost idolised her, were ill-calculated to prepare her mind to contend with the calamities of her future life; she often regretted that her attention had not been directed to more useful reading, and the study of languages. If she had any advantage over other young persons, it must have been in the society of her father, who was himself not only an elegant poet and a scholar, but a man of infinite wit and imagination, and it was scarce possible to live with him without catching

some sparks of that brilliant fire which enlivened his conversation, and rendered him one of the most delightful companions of his time; yet when the short period is considered between the time of her leaving school and her marriage, and that his convivial talents made his company so generally courted, that he had little leisure to bestow on his family, she must rather have inherited than acquired the playful wit and peculiar vein of humour which distinguished her conversation.

In Catherine's prose style the sub-Johnsonian meets the Evangelical. We can still feel the waspishness of the younger, less favoured, not-'out' sister. But her high moral tone is adopted for generous reasons too. By asserting the strict principles of one sister, she implicitly endorses those of the other. And by being a little critical occasionally, Catherine can more convincingly defend Charlotte in the areas where she thought defence most necessary. The edge is unmistakable here too in her comment on the little time their father had for them. By her sixties, Catherine had thought hard both about early marriage and his irresponsibility. Though the memoir in places seems cautious and anti-intellectual, Catherine is recognising here, and regretting, the human and academic loss that came from the very early sexualisation of girls. Mary Wollstonecraft and Charlotte herself wrote about that damaging, socially-endorsed precocity in their work on female education. But these sober thoughts came only with maturity. At twelve and thirteen, Charlotte dressed, talked and danced like a woman; she sounds drunk with the excitement of doing it all so well. She was fourteen in May 1763, when the unknown admirer's proposal, though rejected, brought the probability of her early marriage to the forefront of Nicholas' and Lucy's minds.

Meanwhile his friends were urging on Nicholas the ideal recourse of single men in financial straits: to find an heiress and marry her. He was very handsome, and still in his forties. Heiresses, or at least their relations, expected wealth for wealth but it should, his friends argued cheerfully, be possible to find one prepared to pay for so much charm and talent. Such accommodations, if not quite taken for granted, were not unusual. His sister-in-law was acquiescent; unlike her elder niece she was not romantic. Since her sister's death she had directed Nicholas' household, without scandal. His marriage would disrupt her life as much as her nieces', but she knew it was useless to remonstrate.

A friend's wife knew a Miss Henrietta Meriton, living in Chelsea, whose father had recently died leaving her in control of her own finances. She was reputed to have £20,000 and valuable property. Now in her late thirties, she had led a sheltered life because of her father's fear of fortune-hunters, her social circle restricted to the families of his business associates. Nicholas was introduced and she fell desperately in love. The events of that year when Charlotte was fifteen are referred to with reserve in Catherine's memoir, and reconstructed in detail in Charlotte's later fictionalisations, in Adelina's story in her first novel, *Emmeline, the Orphan of the Castle*, published in 1788; and in Leonora's story in a collection of short novels, *The Letters of a Solitary Wanderer*, published in 1802, or some 38 years after the events described. Though these fictions must be treated with caution as records, they are evidently intended to explain Charlotte's relationship with Miss Meriton and its conse-quences. Leonora's story in *The Letters of a Solitary Wanderer* is especially circumstantial. The *British Public Characters* account makes clear that Nicholas married solely for money, while Catherine does not. The sources between them provide a painful insight into the financial currents and marital customs of the mid-century.

Lucy met Miss Meriton several times and saw nothing objection-able in her brother-in-law's intended asset. She was prepared to smooth over the awkwardness of marital negotiation. She tried to impress on her nieces the importance of winning Miss Meriton's approval, now their father was thinking of marrying again, and urged them to behave respectfully when they met her as if to their future mother. Charlotte felt a stab of disgust at this insensitive suggestion. Her memories of Anna, idealised now over eleven years, were still clear. The financial aspect of the matter was difficult to spell out to the sisters, but Lucy implied that Miss Meriton would save Nicholas from his financial worries. It is unlikely her hints conveyed much to Charlotte. She had had to think about money when Stoke Place was sold, and had felt angry about its passing to a new owner. Her grandfather had bought it in 1718. But she had always preferred Bignor Park, and in the excitement of leaving school and coming out she repressed the memory of this strange event. Now, more unpleas-ant things were happening. Her curiosity about Miss Meriton was intense, though what she could gather was not encouraging. As yet there was no positive engagement; Miss Meriton's relations had been approached and some half-hearted efforts of courtship made by Nicholas. Mostly, though, objecting to anything that bored him and rather ashamed of himself, he left his society friends to court her by asking her to their houses.

One morning Lucy took Charlotte and Catherine, who was allowed a day off school for the purpose, to visit Miss Meriton. It was a short journey, but the coach carried them from the fashionable environs of King Street, where aristocratic and genteel money was lavishly spent on entertaining and in the gambling houses around St James' Square, to the district adjoining Cheyne Walk on the River, where old Mr Meriton had made a fortune in the grocery trade. In the coach, both girls were anxious, Charlotte resentful. The years of separation from her father and reunion just as she was beginning to grow up had released powerful feelings of possessiveness. They went out together in the evenings with Lucy, and enjoyed each other's social success. He sent her into fits of laughter when he mimicked her suitor's embarrassment on discovering her age, and teased her about her dancing partners. None of them could compare with him. But perhaps she also had some hopes of Miss Meriton. She was, she thought, not bigoted about family. Some of her school friends were more cultivated than their parents; Miss Meriton's name sounded like a heroine's in a novel and she might prove to be as distinguished a woman as her father deserved, might even take the place of the mother Charlotte still missed and who had never been replaced by her sensible aunt.

If she had any such fantasies they ended a few minutes later in Miss Meriton's over-furnished drawing room. When the sisters had made their formal curtsies down to the carpet and Miss Meriton and Charlotte took their first long look at each other, their dislike was mutual and permanent. Miss Meriton saw – not the shy, bookish little girl she expected, but a confident and beautiful young woman, critically surveying her. What Charlotte saw and her reflections on that sight may best be understood through Adelina's first-person account of her meeting with her future stepmother in *Emmeline*. She saw

> a tall, meagre person, with a countenance bordering on the horrible, and armed with two round, black eyes which she fancied beautiful, [who] had seen her fortieth year pass, while she attended on her papa . . . Rich as her father was, he would not part with anything while he lived; and, by the assistance of two maiden sisters, had so guarded his daughter from the dangerous attacks of Irishmen and younger brothers, that she had reached that mature period without hearing the soothing voice of flattery, to which she was extremely disposed to listen. My father, yet in middle age, and with a person remarkably fine, would have been greatly to her taste if he could have gratified, with better grace, her love of admiration . . .[9]

Much of our sympathy now must be with the unfortunate Henrietta Meriton. The control custom gave to fathers over their daughters enabled any degree of psychosexual disturbance to flourish in the guise of parental responsibility. Released too late from her father's claustrophobic régime, she was miserably aware she was courted for her money but lacked the self respect to refuse Nicholas. There was nothing she could have done to conciliate Charlotte and Catherine. However little Charlotte knew about money, she probably knew something about sex. Though some families could preserve an unenquiring daughter's ignorance, intelligent girls did not grow up to be quite sexually uninformed as they often did a hundred years later. The frankness of eighteenth century habits and manners would make such an outcome difficult.

She read *The Lady's Magazine* whose editor 'Mrs Stanhope' never published her poems. It was a lively compilation of stories, verse and English news about fires, murders and muggings, each monthly edition containing 'A Succinct History of the Present War', a detailed and admirable piece of reporting. Some degree of sexual knowledge is taken for granted, as no similar publication aimed at young as well as older women could afford to do in Victoria's reign. Charlotte went to plays, including risqué Restoration revivals. The plots of the novels she read turned on episodes of seduction, attempted rape and violent passion. If the 'Sir Charles' she includes in Mrs Woodfield's account of early novel reading is Sir Charles Grandison, she had read Richardson, whose books are saturated in sexual feeling. Novels were not explicit, but the knowledge they offered could be supplemented with observations of the animals mating in the country, and in town with the wild surmises of a fashionable girls' school. Nicholas' marriage was not likely to be seen by her in its merely domestic, still less in its financial aspects. Her charming, popular father who had loved her best since his return to England would go to bed with this horrible woman. The thought was ludicrous, but her perpetual impulse to giggle scarcely concealed the anger underneath.

As the Turner family began to meet Miss Meriton almost daily, Charlotte's manners deteriorated. As she fictionalises it through her representative Adelina, Charlotte was then

> full of gaiety and vivacity, and possessed those personal advantages, which, if *she* [the future stepmother] ever had any share in them, were long since faded. She seemed conscious that the splendour of her first appearance would be eclipsed by the unadorned simplicity of mine; and she hated me because it was not in my power to be old

and ugly. Giddy as I then was, nothing but respect for my father prevented my repaying with ridicule, the supercilious style in which she treated me. Her vulgar manners, and awkward attempts to imitate those of people of fashion, excited my perpetual mirth; and as her dislike of me daily increased, I am afraid I did not always conceal the contempt I felt in return.[10]

Even when Charlotte puts this crisis into her novels many years later, when she had thought much about social injustice to women, there is no trace of pity for the Miss Meriton figure. Hatred went too deep for kinder revisions, though Miss Meriton was as much as herself the victim of Nicholas Turner's destructive egotism.

Perhaps her bad behaviour was consciously intended to frighten off the intruder. If so she underestimated her adversary and her father's need for money. His choices by now were limited. He could go to prison for debt, but he might remain there many years. The town house was rented, but he could sell the Bignor Park estate; Nicholas had the spendthrift's usual inflated sense of family and could trace the Turners back to a William Turner made Esquire in the household of Henry VI. He felt an embarrassment worse than the prospect of prison at the thought of proving so bad a steward to his son. Or he could marry Miss Meriton; if alternative, more attractive heiresses briefly crossed his mind, he knew it was too late to change.

Soon he had gone through the necessary professions of esteem, as alive as his daughter to a sense of the ludicrous, and formally asked for her hand. She accepted, but through her relations she made it clear to Nicholas and Lucy that the marriage would not take place until Charlotte ceased to live with her father. Miss Meriton had managed to convince herself that Nicholas' elder daughter was the only obstacle to her happiness. Catherine, always more compliant than her sister, was still at school and could stay there a few years longer. Young Nicholas at Westminster was destined for Cambridge and a church living his father was holding for him. They were not a problem. Charlotte was intolerable.

Catherine ascribes to her Aunt Lucy rather than her father the undertaking to find Charlotte a husband. She writes:

> In 1764, Mr Turner decided on a second marriage, and his sister-in-law contemplated this event with the most painful apprehensions for the happiness of that being who was the object of her dearest affection, and who, having hitherto been indulged in every wish, and even every caprice, was ill prepared to submit to the control of a mother-in-law [stepmother]. Without reflecting that the evil she anticipated with such feelings of dread would probably only exist for

a short period (for it was unlikely a young lady who was so generally admired would long remain single), she endeavoured, with a precipitation she afterwards had great reason to deplore, to establish her by an advantageous marriage, and her wishes were seconded by some officious and short sighted relations . . .

This places the blame for the marriage on Lucy alone rather than on Miss Meriton and on Nicholas' acceptance of an ultimatum. Catherine's memoir however is more distanced and reserved in some ways, especially where Nicholas is concerned, than either *British Public Characters* or Charlotte's account in the novels of her young self, which have the stamp of authenticity. Whoever might be most responsible, Lucy, Miss Meriton, Nicholas or Charlotte herself, her father's engagement was disastrous for her.

Among Nicholas' recent acquaintance was Benjamin Smith, the younger son of a wealthy West India merchant and Director in the East India Company, who had come from Barbados to settle in London. Benjamin was twenty-three, good-looking and potentially rich as a partner in his father's firm. He was struck by Charlotte's beauty and her popularity among the young men he considered fashionable. She had only a £3,000 dowry, but he did not need to consider that. The two young people were introduced; Charlotte did not dislike him – at least there was no other young man she preferred. With presents and flattery she was gently coerced into an engagement in the summer after her fifteenth birthday.

Nicholas married Miss Meriton. Their wedding was listed in the October 1764 issue of *The Gentleman's Magazine*: 'Nicholas Turner of Bignor Park Sussex Esq; to Miss Meriton of Chelsea: £20,000.' The public prints were in their way as crude then as now. Lucy rented a little house for herself after Nicholas' wedding, and Charlotte stayed with her for a few months. They were joined by Catherine in the school holidays. On 23 February 1765 when she was still two months short of sixteen Charlotte was, as she put it bitterly in a letter long afterwards, 'sold, a legal prostitute'[11] to Benjamin Smith.

However fair an analysis of arranged marriage this may be, she only arrived at it later. It seems unlikely she felt prostituted at the time, and there is some evidence that she married willingly. Only two people had doubts about the couple's compatibility. Her uncle, William Towers, pointed out their marked difference in character and education, but his views were ignored. And before he met her, Benjamin's father Richard Smith was not pleased to hear of his son's interest in her. He thought she was too young. He would certainly have known or quickly found out that Nicholas was deeply in debt. As a self-made man who had worked hard all his life, he had no time for the spendthrift ways of the landed, or in Nicholas' case increasingly unlanded, gentry. He was suspicious of all he heard about Charlotte's expensive education and literary tastes. He would have preferred his son to choose a practical young woman from a successful trading family who knew the value of money.

But his first meeting with Charlotte changed his mind. Knowing his feelings in advance, she set out to charm him and succeeded. His social circle was very different from the Turners' and from his bachelor son's, and he had probably never met a talking, funny, fashionable girl before. This first meeting is noted in *British Public Characters* and the memoir. It seems to suggest that Charlotte was actively engaged in smoothing the way for the marriage, though it may only show that like all fifteen-year-olds she wanted to prove she was not too young for anything. Benjamin was of age and did not legally need his father's consent, but Richard kept the firm's money under his own control as far as he could, and his approval was important.

Unknown to the Turners, he had been anxious for his son to marry for two or three years past. Benjamin was entirely unlike his father, and had so far lacked any purpose in life. He had no interest in business. When he was supposed to be at the warehouse he was more often at the races or a boxing match. He had no interest in books or a profession either. He had an enormous fund of volatile good spirits and was unable to concentrate on anything for more than a few minutes. Latterly he had been mixing with a smart set of young men who encouraged his contempt for trade. He drank and gambled and already, Richard suspected, had fathered several illegitimate children. Marriage might help him settle down, and once he was the father of a family, he would have a motive for working harder. Richard gave his consent, and though he continued suspicious of the accomplishments and the way Charlotte wasted her time reading and writing, he remained fond of her all his life. So she gained a father, if a gruff and prejudiced one, just as she lost Nicholas.

In *Emmeline*, Adelina is naïve and passive when Mr Trelawny, the representative of Benjamin, proposes to her. He is unused to educated upper class young women, and so appears more innocent than he is. Adelina says:

> with an infinite number of blushes and after several efforts he made me in due form an offer of his hand and fortune. I had never thought

of anything so serious as matrimony; and indeed was but just out of the nursery, where I had never been told it was necessary to think at all. I did not know very well what to say to my admirer, and after the first speech, which I believe he had learned by heart, he knew almost as little what to say to me; and he was not sorry when I, in a great fright, referred him to my father, merely because I knew not what answer to give.[12]

Later she reflects that 'the prospect of escaping from the power of my mother-in-law [stepmother] and of being mistress of an affluent fortune instead of living in mortifying dependence on her, might have too much influence on my heart.'[13] Mr Trelawny marries Adelina merely because she is considered beautiful by his friends, and becomes boorish and neglectful as soon as they are married, accusations Charlotte was to bring against Benjamin. Her agreement to the marriage must have been, if not altogether consciously, a response to her sense of betrayal by Nicholas. And if she represents her young self as naïve in *Emmeline*, she had a right to do so. However sophisticated she might seem, and indeed in some ways really was, she had no experience to judge a young man like Benjamin; the adults around her acted with great selfishness or stupidity.

Nicholas' marriage separated him from both daughters, as Catherine often stayed with Charlotte in the school holidays. In the fictional version of these events in *The Solitary Wanderer*, Leonora's stepmother, the Miss Meriton figure, dominates her husband so forcibly that he dares not show affection for the children of his first marriage. Again, this puts the blame for the father's inadequacy directly on the stepmother. We may guess the new Mrs Turner had plenty to bear too if Nicholas, with access to ready money again, soon made no more effort than his daughter to disguise his contempt. Nothing more is known of him after his marriage, except that he died 'some years' [*British Public Characters*] before 1776.

While they waited for their apartment over his father's great warehouse in Cheapside to be newly decorated and furnished, Charlotte and Benjamin stayed with his sister Mary Berney and her husband William, in one of those curiously intimate and familial marital arrangements before it became the custom for the newly married to go away on their own. At first Charlotte was not at all unhappy; Benjamin's high spirits and unpredictability amused her. The importance she gives to sex in *The Old Manor House* does not suggest any aversion in her own experience. By her account as well as her sister's, her dissatisfaction with marriage came on later as she learned more about him and as she grew more mature, while he did not.

The rooms over the warehouse, though large, were dull and sunless. Richard had done his best for her in expensive furniture, but he and his wife had no taste at all, she thought, and the contrast of style, where everything had to be bought new, with the elegance of Bignor and the King Street house gave outward form to the contrast in habits of mind she was already becoming aware of. The Turners and the Smiths belonged to quite different cultures but the Smiths, though they knew this, saw none of her difficulties in assimilating to theirs. Cheapside was one of the filthiest areas in the City. The night soil removers who came in the early mornings from the suburbs with their carts were never sufficient to deal with such a thickly populated area. Negotiating the street outside was a severe trial. In summer typhoid often struck here first, and the atmosphere of the apartment was worse with the windows open. She had never realised how important fresh air, grass and trees were until she lost them.

An immediate problem was Benjamin's stepmother Elizabeth Smith, Richard's second wife whom he had married in Barbados as a widow. She was constantly ill and demanding, and disapproved of Charlotte's lack of domestic skills. Catherine quotes a letter written when Charlotte could have been no more than sixteen, as Elizabeth died soon afterwards. This is therefore the first piece of her writing that survives:

> I pass almost every day with the poor sick old lady, with whom, however, I am no great favourite; somebody has told her I have not been notably [i.e. with domestic skills] brought up, (which I am afraid is true enough), and she asks me questions which, to say the truth, I am not very well able to answer. There are no women, she says, so well qualified for mistresses of families as the ladies of Barbados, whose knowledge of housewifery she is perpetually contrasting with my ignorance, and, very unfortunately, those subjects on which I am informed, give me little credit with her; on the contrary, are rather a disadvantage to me; yet I have not seen any of their paragons whom I am at all disposed to envy.

Richard and Elizabeth lived in Islington, so Charlotte had to be driven four or five miles for the benefit of these lectures. Catherine describes her as listening to the elder Mrs Smith 'with apathy and disgust', yet Charlotte writes temperately here. She wanted her marriage to be happy and was prepared to adapt her habits and curb her impatience with Benjamin's relatives. Her last sentence implies that her social life, what there was of it, was spent with families who had made their money in the West Indies, or with successful London merchants, and that she did not much like them. At great City dinners of turtle, among great City wives with the loot of Empire on their backs, she felt herself a different species. She was of course a snob, impossible that she should be otherwise, and so from a different standpoint were the people she was meeting. When she listened to the men talking amongst themselves she heard a new language that often irritated but sometimes made her laugh, like the 'drawbacks' that meant money returned on dutiable exports, or 'bottomry', a loan payable against the value of a ship. If she had found a companion and friend in Benjamin she could have got a lot of fun out of her new surroundings. Catherine writes that she could still occasionally 'give way to the sportiveness of her fancy.' But most of the time she felt an exile in the hated sound of Bow Bells.

Though far fonder of her than his wife was, Richard too expected her to spend her time in domestic duties, in family visits and supervising the servants. He even disliked visits from her old school friends, probably recognising that they made her more dissatisfied with Cheapside. Catherine writes:

> He was a worthy, and even a good-natured man, but he had mixed very little in general society – his ideas were confined, and his manners and habits were not calculated to inspire affection, however he might be entitled to respect and gratitude. He had no taste for literature, and the elegant amusements of his daughter-in-law seemed to him as so many sources of expense, and as encroachments on time, which he thought should be exclusively dedicated to domestic occupations; he had a quiet, petulant way of speaking, and a pair of keen, black eyes, which, darting from under his bushy black eyebrows the most inquisitive glances, always appeared to be in search of something to find fault with; so that whenever the creaking of his 'youthful shoes well-saved' gave notice that one of his domiciliary visits was about to take place, it was the signal for hurrying away whatever was likely to be the subject of his displeasure, or the object of his curiosity. If any of her friends and acquaintance happened to call on her, he would examine them with a suspicious curiosity, which usually compelled them to shorten their visits, and took from them the desire of repeating them. His lady, who was at that time in very ill health, exacted the constant attendance of the family, and a more irksome task could hardly have been imposed on a young person.

On Catherine, in Cheapside for the holidays, these new scenes and characters, so different from what the sisters were used to, made a vivid and disagreeable impression. Her sister's position was humiliating, for all her wealth, and Cheapside an odd setting for the romantic, intellectual Miss Turner as her schoolfriends had known her. Richard gave Charlotte and Benjamin an allowance of £2,000 a year, £900 of which was for household expenses, an enormous sum at a time when it was possible to live decently on a tenth of that. Nevertheless Benjamin constantly overspent his income, and used Charlotte as a go-between to extract more from his father. Consequently she often took the blame for his extravagance. Richard's ploy of engaging his son more in the business by placing him above the warehouse soon proved to be a waste of money. Her relationship with her father-in-law was a difficult one, especially at first. But she did justice to his rough kindness and sense of responsibility.

And yet he had made his money out of the slave plantations of the West Indies, and like many of his business associates was turning his thoughts to the enormous wealth of India, now more safe for trade with the Seven Years' War over and the seaways open again. The East India Company had been established in the early seventeenth century, and was the main agent of British Imperialism in the East, importing cotton, silk, indigo, saltpetre and spices. After the mid-eighteenth century, tea was the principal import, its cultivation financed in India by the opium trade. The Company was organised into a court of twenty-four Directors who were elected annually. Between 1757 and 1774, while Richard was a Director, it effectively decided British government policy in India, giving Richard and his City colleagues political influence in London.

He had run his own plantations in Barbados, and still bought and used slaves there, though now through his overseers. There is no evidence he engaged in shipping slaves across the Atlantic, though in England even as early as this, ownership of or part-interest in slavers was often acknowledged only among others in the same trade. But if he was too cautious to engage in the high-risk business of shipping, his fortune came from West Indian sugar and cotton whose production depended on the supply from Africa. This was the case with many of the fortunes made in the eighteenth century including, probably, Mr Meriton's. As Charlotte gradually learned more about the family she had married into, she learned some disturbing things about the generation of wealth. Elizabeth Smith took ownership for granted; the firm management of slaves was one of the housewifely skills she and her female acquaintances prided themselves on in Barbados, and which Charlotte heard so much about. The family brought five slaves with them when they moved to London, to wait on the children. Richard bequeathed these people and their descendants to relatives in his will, along with the household linen and plate.

Charlotte probably learned little from Richard himself. He was uncommunicative about business, especially with women. But Benjamin was indiscreet with everyone. He told her about the thirteen inches width allotted to women, sixteen inches to men, on the specially designed slave decks where they were chained except for a brief daily period of exercise. He told her how the crew were encouraged to rape the women repeatedly on the voyage so they would be pregnant with mulatto children, and worth more, when they were auctioned. He told her how often bodies were thrown over the side when disease broke out. Sometimes they died for no apparent reason, he said. About forty-five in a hundred did not survive the voyage, on an average run. Sometimes the whole cargo was lost. Occasionally they broke loose and killed the crew, so the investors lost their ship as well. But on a good run, immense profits could be made. Benjamin talked to captains of slavers and was fascinated by their stories. They were not the sort of men to be welcome even in Elizabeth Smith's drawing-room, however, and Charlotte never met one. But she learned a lot in these two or three years of her mid-teens when she lived above the warehouse, and made some painful connections.

She had always taken for granted that the world was divided into rich and poor, masters and servants. Now she had to think about trade, which depended on slavery. She was a spoilt child in some ways, but her early loss gave her at least a wish to sympathise with other people's pain. She wondered what it must feel like to be chained, to be sold at auction, and knew it was beyond her imagining.

It is beyond ours too. Beginning sporadically in the late fifteenth century, slaving had become a major European industry by the 1760s. The British model was triangular: cheap manufactured goods were shipped to West Africa and exchanged for slaves, who were transported to the West Indies or America; sugar or cotton replaced them on the home journey. Toni Morrison estimates the numbers who died prematurely as a result of American slavery overall at 'sixty million and more' in the dedication of her great novel *Beloved*, which comes closer than any history could to conveying some sense of what the trade inflicted. European historians give different figures for the numbers taken in West Africa. Norman Davies in *Europe: a History* suggests fifteen million, with four to five million dying in the barracoons or on the Middle Passage. In England, meanwhile, merchant banks and shipping companies flourished, commercial families married their children into the nobility and gentry, country house façades were torn down and Palladianised and the lines of famous romantic gardens laid.

Charlotte and Catherine, perhaps Nicholas too, were living on the money made through slaving. The more she thought about it the more it seemed that everybody was. Her childhood at Bignor felt far away and irreconcilable with this new knowledge. She wondered why some people had the right to own others, and began to question things as they were, the economic basis of society. But she had to keep her thoughts to herself. Benjamin was proud of his wife's good looks and social superiority, but he had no taste for philosophical speculation and grew sullen if she attempted it.

She found she was pregnant a couple of months after her wedding. Now there was something to look forward to and some purpose to her life. Benjamin was often away leaving her alone, except for the servants, over the great warehouse. He disliked his stepmother as much as she did, and had less regard for his father, but he expected her to spend days sitting or driving out with them while he was in the country with friends, or crossed to France for a change with betting men and their mistresses. His marriage had given him no greater steadiness or aptitude for work.

A first confinement was always a matter of apprehension, but Charlotte had plenty of courage and felt only moments of anxiety. Lucy, we may guess, was with her, and the best medical help available. It was more painful than she expected, but with the birth of a son that was soon forgotten in the pride she felt: he was beautiful, he at once showed himself witty and intelligent, he made up for everything, the beginnings of her disappointment with Benjamin, her dismal surroundings. There is no record of the baby's date of birth or of his name.

Though this was not Richard's first grandchild, as Benjamin's elder brother and sister had children, it was the first grandchild he saw almost every day. He would take his chocolate in Charlotte's dressing-room when he arrived at the warehouse and listen to her sketching out great futures for the baby. She nursed him herself;

Anna had put her out to nurse but Charlotte had strong feelings about the importance of maternal nursing, especially in the first few months. She had plenty of milk and the baby thrived. She meant to nurse all her children, she said.

In the summer of 1766, Elizabeth Smith died. She had been ill and querulous for the eighteen months Charlotte had known her, so she could feel no grief, though she was sorry for Richard. He was shaken by his wife's death though it had long been expected, and worried more about his own health. Used to Barbados for most of his life, he had never adapted to the English climate, and even on summer days would wrap himself in his red dressing gown and surround himself with medicaments. He expected Charlotte to accompany him on long 'airings' in his carriage among the brick kilns and stagnant ditches of Islington. Charlotte, soon pregnant again, would let her baby stay with Richard sometimes. It was the only comfort he seemed to feel, and a relief to her too. There was always a streak of Nicholas in his daughter and she probably did not take easily to full-time responsibility even when she had servants to do the work.

Benjamin himself was certainly no comfort to his father in his old age. Richard wanted him to take over more of the day-to-day running of the firm, but Benjamin was more apt to spend money than make it. Some insight into his pursuits at this time can be gained from a relatively affectionate portrayal of him as Alexander Elphinstone in his wife's third novel, *Celestina*:

> He was wild, eccentric and ungovernable: sometimes rode away to races when he ought to have been settling with the grocers . . . sometimes got into scrapes with his old school fellows, and was found at the watch-house [equivalent of a police station] instead of in the counting-house; or if he attended those solemn meetings at which the price of freight or the quality of Osnaburghs[14] was discussed, he turned the venerable persons of the old merchants and grocers into ridicule; and while they thought he was making calculations, was frequently drawing caricatures of them in all their majesty of wig, upon the leaves of his memorandum book.[15]

The side of him that appealed to Charlotte before their marriage and held her exasperated fondness for a year or two afterwards is recalled here twenty-five years later: the irrepressible high spirits, the flippancy and talent for mimicry. These were traits she shared with him when they were both young. But she was forced to mature fast while he never changed, except to grow bad-tempered, and his lack of interest in books or ideas, his inability to feel deeply or concentrate on anything for long were quite frightening to her as she grew older.

Her second baby was due that spring. Nursing, for her, never had any contraceptive effect, and her first son was only a year old when she was preparing for her second confinement. In the week before she went into labour there broke out in Cheapside and among the household over the warehouse what the *British Public Characters* account calls 'the malignant sore throat', probably diphtheria or a virulent streptococcal infection. The servants, her little boy and presumably Benjamin came down with it; only Charlotte escaped the infection. On 30 April 1767, the day she gave birth to a second son, or on the day following, her first child died.

Social historians sometimes attempt to construct the past as another world altogether. High infant mortality rates, it has been argued, made death something that parents were acculturated to accept, if not easily, at least without the lifelong grief they feel now. It has been estimated that in thickly populated areas half of all babies in the mid-eighteenth-century died before they were two. If we look at passages in Charlotte's novels about the death of a baby or a child, we can see that it was no easier then than later. Most women who lost their children have left no record of their feelings, and bereavement is in fact a condition impossible for writing to describe. But as late as 1798 in her last novel, *The Young Philosopher*, Charlotte tries to convey the sense of a baby's loss as starkly as she had felt it so long before. The heroine Laura Glenmorris, who is seventeen, has to bury her baby with the help of her maid, Menie:

> With Menie's assistance, at an hour when the rest of the household were asleep, I wrapt up my poor dead baby in the best linen I had, and Menie having procured me what answered the purpose of a coffin, I deposited him in it without shedding a tear – I could not shed tears . . . and having made . . . as deep a grave as we could, I placed in it the lifeless object of so many, many months of fond solicitude . . . and having done so in speechless anguish, which I now shudder to recall, I cast a last look on the grave, and suffered myself to be led back to my room, returning to my bed with no other sensation than the hope that I should rise from it no more.[16]

Laura's circumstances are very different. Women often did not attend an interment, and Charlotte's confinement would have made it impossible for her to be present in any case. But to write this she is remembering when she was seventeen, and saw her first child's coffin leave the house.

Under the shock of bereavement her milk failed to come in adequately, so the newborn baby's life was soon in danger too. But he survived, and was named Benjamin Berney. Perhaps her milk was just sufficient to keep him alive, or perhaps a wet-nurse was hastily found. But his health was never good, and she attributed this to the deprivation of his first few weeks. His frailty made him a constant source of anxiety, though he was to be the closest to her of all her children when they were young.

Acute depression followed the death, and her loathing of Cheapside could no longer be disguised even from her father-in-law. He suffered at the loss of his grandson, needed company constantly, and was reluctant to consider her moving out of London. Since Charlotte's marriage Lucy had continued to visit her niece, probably, from what we can guess of her, during the infection and its aftermath too. Richard had been a widower for nearly a year. Elderly hypochondriac as he was, Lucy now took her long bias in favour of matrimony at all costs to its logical conclusion, and married him. Their marriage articles were signed on 15 May 1767. We might infer, cynically, that his wealth was the main consideration. If she had the same small dowry as her sister, and invested it, she could only have afforded a tiny rented house, hard to adapt to after the years of reckless profusion enjoyed by everyone under Nicholas' roof.

But perhaps her decision was, rather, another proof of her love for Charlotte, however little Charlotte felt for her. She had lost her main purpose in life with the removal of her nieces from their fath :r's house. She knew by now how foolish she had been in encouraging Benjamin as a suitor. At her marriage sl:e became the necessary companion to Richard, releasing Charlotte from what father and son took for granted as a daughter-in-law's role. She might also hope to ensure in her new position that however infuriated Richard became with his son, the interests of Charlotte and her child would not suffer. But though by Catherine's account she almost idolised Charlotte, she aroused little feeling apart from irritation in her niece. Her misjudgment, the misjudgment of a small practical mind, at the time of Nicholas' engagement was something Charlotte could not easily forgive.

The Monthly Magazine's account says that Charlotte's grief seriously endangered her health. Richard, soon to be married again, was willing to buy her a small house in Southgate, then a village outside the London smoke. Here she had the luxury of time to herself and a home out of the foetid atmosphere of Cheapside, among the trees and gardens that she knew now were necessities to her. Benjamin was to be based in Southgate and travel in to work every day. But his

incomprehension of his wife's character and interests was turning to
resentment. Sometimes he did not come home at all; work was an
excuse to stay in London part of the week, though Charlotte knew he
was unlikely to be working.

She was already pregnant with her third son when she moved to
Southgate with her husband and Benjamin Berney. As with the first
baby there is no record of William Towers' date of birth or christen-
ing, but he must have been born in the first six months of 1768.
Her fourth child and first daughter, Charlotte Mary, was christened
on 2 May 1769 at St Faith's Church. She was to be the favourite among
all Richard's many grandchildren. Braithwaite, the last baby to be
born at the Southgate house, was christened on 19 July 1770. The
British Public Characters account says that Charlotte's family increased to three children while she was here, but this must be
inaccurate. Some confusion is understandable, as she had eight
babies in the first nine years of her marriage. Charlotte and Benjamin
had four children living with them at Southgate.

At about the time they moved Catherine, who had left school at
sixteen, met Michael Dorset, a captain in the army, and married in the
following year. Catherine was eighteen, and had the advantage of
freedom from family interference. Charlotte's was not an envious
character. She had too strong a sense of her own mental superiority
to want to change places with anyone, and she was happy for
Catherine; but she felt the difference in their luck.

It is particularly difficult to reconstruct these Southgate years.
Outwardly they were uneventful, but as Charlotte reached twenty
and had time to consider how she had been so easily thrown away,
her bitterness grew. She had four small children to look after, and
though she had servants provided by Richard and Lucy, she was not
content to be a mother by proxy, as many middle and upper class
women in the eighteenth century were. Her children's books take for
granted that mothers will spend part of every day teaching their
younger children.

But in addition to this, Catherine says, at Southgate 'she became
mistress of her own time, and was enabled to employ it in the
cultivation of her mind.' She began to collect a library while she was
here. Mary Hays in the *British Public Characters* account is careful to
defend her from the charge often directed at a reading woman, that
she neglected her duty as a mother:

Her studies, however, did not interfere with the care of her children; she nursed them all herself, and usually read while she rocked the cradle of one, and had, perhaps, another sleeping in her lap.

What she read is not specified, but 'the cultivation of her mind', given Catherine's views, suggests it was not only or mainly novels. By the time she wrote *Desmond* and *The Banished Man* she knew something about European history. Perhaps it was here she began to learn Italian, and to read more plays and poetry.

Some of Shakespeare's phrasing passed so deeply into her consciousness she was unaware she was quoting him. While at Southgate she continued to write poetry, as she always had, to impose some form and limit on regrets for her lost freedom, regrets everything around her urged her to suppress altogether.

But she was beginning to speak more openly of her unhappiness to her sister. Catherine writes:

> The result of her mental improvement was not favourable to her happiness. She began to trace that indefatigable restlessness and impatience, of which she had long been conscious without comprehending, to its source, to discriminate characters, to detect ignorance, to compare her own mind with those of the persons by whom she was surrounded.
>
> The consciousness of her own superiority, the mortifying conviction that she was subjected to one so infinitely her inferior, presented itself every day more forcibly to her mind, and she justly considered herself 'as a pearl that had been basely thrown away.'

Hilbish, apparently regarding the last comment as absurdly arrogant if attributed to Charlotte, attributes it to Catherine. But the quotation is evidently Charlotte's and sounds like a reference she made more than once. It is not a direct allusion to the Biblical text, 'Cast not your pearls before swine' but rather to a passage at the end of *Othello* when the hero has killed Desdemona and alludes to that text when he compares himself to one

> whose hand
> Like the base Indian, threw a pearl away
> Richer than all his tribe.[17]

The reference is unexpectedly comic in its application of 'Indian' and 'tribe' to Benjamin.

It is a revealing quotation if she was seeing herself as another Desdemona, Benjamin as another Othello. She had become much more conscious of mortality after her baby's death, and recognised each yearly childbirth as a risk. She knew that Benjamin's nights in London had nothing to do with work; he was too volatile and indiscreet to be able to deceive her. So she knew she was at risk from gonorrhoea as well as death in labour. If she died, the children's best chance would be Catherine. But Benjamin would not let them go. He would marry again, and at the thought of the stepmother he might provide for her children, Charlotte felt almost as angry as she felt six years before when she thought of Miss Meriton. But though the *Othello* quotation suggests an underlying fear that one way or the other Benjamin would kill her, she knew by now how helpless she was.

Catherine quotes a letter from Charlotte to a friend where she describes in retrospect this period of her life:

> No disadvantage could equal those I sustained; the more my mind expanded, the more I became sensible of personal slavery; the more I improved and cultivated my understanding, the farther I was removed from those with whom I was condemned to spend my life, and the more clearly I saw by these newly acquired lights the horror of the abyss into which I had unconsciously plunged.

It is impossible to date this letter, but it suggests that by the time she was living in Southgate she had made the common late-eighteenth-century link between women's subjection in marriage, and slavery. But perhaps she also saw a disparity between these two conditions, and the extremism of her language attempts to offer justification for the comparison. The adjective 'personal' with its strong eighteenth-century connotation, 'of the person' or body, suggests that it is the repeated pregnancies and perhaps marital sex that she sees by this time as enslavement. If it appears that she takes up the concept of marital slavery rather easily from her generalising remarks here, she may be concealing plenty that entitles her to her metaphor. However, it must be remembered that this is retrospect, and probably distant retrospect, written when she needed to represent her marriage as entirely wretched since this was then the only acceptable excuse for ending it.

Catherine, concerned as usual with propriety, goes on after quoting the letter:

> Impressed with this fatal truth, nothing could be more meritorious than the line of conduct she pursued. Whatever were her opinions or her feelings, she confined them to her own bosom, and never to her

most confidential friends suffered a complaint or a severe remark to escape her lips.

This sounds rather like Henry Austen's comment, also for public consumption, that his sister Jane 'never uttered a hasty, a silly or a severe expression',[18] and may be equally open to doubt. Catherine's standard of female merit was one Charlotte would fail to meet when she confided her opinions and feelings about her husband to the wide readership of her novels. Catherine wants to make the point that there was a time when her sister was willing to suffer in silence, however strident she became later.

But though Charlotte's relationship with Benjamin was by now very unhappy, he was not always provoking, perhaps because he was often elsewhere, and she was not always miserable. She had plenty to sadden her, and she had probably always had a depressive streak. But she also had the humorous vein that often accompanies a melancholic temperament. She had the ability to absorb and endure, and to live at least two mental lives at once. She had the great resource of reading and writing, of escape into a private world. Catherine refers to her friends at Southgate, and here the word may indeed mean friends rather than relations, herself and Lucy. Though Benjamin Berney was often ill, and less active than his brothers and sister, his exceptional intelligence gave her pleasure, as did the development of all the children. Whenever, later, she represents a woman in an unhappy marriage, the bond with her children is unusually close.

She was soon pregnant again; the family was increasing too fast for the small Southgate house. Richard wanted his grandchildren nearer to himself and Lucy. He at least was happily married. He was surprised by Lucy's understanding of business and placid temper. She was an oracle on bringing up children. For the last five years he had never stopped hoping that Benjamin would turn into a serious, capable businessman. He thought that a house in Tottenham might he preferable to one south of the river, bringing Benjamin's residence closer to the warehouse again, though he must have remembered that even living above the warehouse had done nothing previously for Benjamin's business acumen. Of this move Catherine writes:

> It was hoped that by removing nearer to London, Mr Smith would be induced to pay a stricter attendance on his business than he had hitherto done; and with this view his father purchased for him a handsome residence at Tottenham, where it was hoped he would

retrieve his lost time. But his habits were fixed, he had no turn for business, and never could be prevailed on to bestow more than a small portion of that time on it, which nevertheless hung so heavy on his hands, that he was obliged to have recourse to a variety of expedients to get rid of it. Hence fancies became occupations, and were followed up with boundless expense, till they were relinquished for some newer fancy equally frivolous and equally costly.

The move was a wretched one for Charlotte: she lost her Southgate friends and no longer made the effort to talk to people she considered hopelessly 'City'. Catherine notes that at this time her natural vivacity seemed extinguished by the monotony of her life. Three more children were born at Tottenham. Hilbish's long correspondence with the incumbents of the parishes where the Smiths lived turned up the following baptismal entries at All Hallows Church:

> Nov. 4th 1771 Nicholas Hankey Son of Benjamin and Charlotte Smith. Charles Dyer Son of Benjamin Smith Esq. and By Charlotte his wife Feb 27th 1773.
> Anna Augusta Daughter of Benjamin and Charlotte Smith June 18th 1774.

Charlotte's second daughter was named for her maternal grandmother but usually known as Augusta. She took after Anna in looks, and was a cheerful and affectionate child from her earliest months.

Richard's respect for Charlotte's abilities increased as she grew older, and he talked to her more about the business. Now she was back in London close to the hated warehouse once more, she did not refuse to give him what help she could. Like his clerks she learned about scrips or certificates of stock shares, Omnium or the aggregate of all parts of a loan, and tares and trets, allowance for the containers and incidentals of packing in calculating a cargo's net weight. Catherine writes:

> Her father-in-law was in the habit of confiding to her all his anxieties, and frequently employed her pen in matters of business. On one occasion she was called on to vindicate his character from some illiberal attack, and she acquitted herself of the task in a very able manner. This little tract was published, but not being of any general interest, has not been preserved. The elder Mr Smith has frequently declared, that such was the readiness of her pen, that she could expedite more business in an hour from his dictation, than any one of his clerks could perform in a day: and he even offered her a considerable annual allowance, if she would reside in London and assist him in his business, which he foresaw would be lost to his family after his death. Obvious reasons prevented the acceptance of

this proposal, which, singular as it was, affords a strong instance of the compass of her mind, which could adapt itself with equal facility to the charms of literature, and the dry details of commerce.

Among the obvious reasons were her large family, and her resistance, as a woman from the landed gentry, to working as a clerk. She may have considered that any money she earned would be legally Benjamin's, and could give her no degree of independence. And she may also have felt disgust with the sources of Richard's wealth, and her own. His implied intention to make her rather than his son eventually the head of the firm shows his capacity to think beyond the customary. He had changed in his attitude to the woman's role, or she had changed him. The dichotomy Catherine assumes between the 'charms' of literature and the 'dry details' of commerce was to be challenged in her sister's novels, with their interest in economics and ways of making money.

Richard was becoming less active, and his worries about the firm's future remained unresolved. His elder son, also named Richard, had been no more interested in business than Benjamin. Richard bought for him a living as a clergyman. However, one of the few things known of Benjamin's brother is his resolution never to expect a son of his to become a clergyman. We can infer that he was not very happy about his vocation, and perhaps that his parishioners were not very happy about it either. He and his wife had a young son and daughter. Benjamin's sister Mary had three children by her first husband. After a brief widowhood she had married a lawyer, Thomas Dyer. All the grandsons were too young for Richard to consider as possible successors in the business, and he recognised at last that Benjamin would never have the necessary application.

He began to consider ways of realising some of the firm's assets and putting more money into government bonds, to secure the grandchildren's education and provide them each with a lump sum at twenty-one. He also took back the nominal, as well as actual, management of the firm, releasing Benjamin from partnership, and allowed him and Charlotte, to her great delight, to move to a house with a hundred acres in Hampshire previously used as a centre for the firm's cattle-breeding enterprises. She had always wanted to bring up her children in the country, and hoped that life on a small estate with a farm to manage would provide Benjamin with an absorbing occupation and remove him from his dangerous and wasteful town friends. Her dream of Benjamin as gentleman farmer was in its way as absurd as Richard's dream of his son as sober businessman; but in late 1774 or early 1775 they moved with the seven children to Lys Farm in the village of Hinton Ampner near Bramdean. It was to be her longest residence in any one place after her marriage.

Her removal to Hampshire brought some pleasures, most of all in open countryside, in walking, and collecting wild flowers and plants again. She was away from Cheapside and the sound of Bow Bells, mixing in society she liked; she always felt more at home among gentry families; she clung to some remnants of the old self that felt threatened in the Smith household. Her children now had the freedom to explore the countryside, as she had as a child. When the Smiths moved to Hampshire she was twenty-five and, her sister says, 'in the meridian of her beauty', though adding that she had lost much of the former lightness of her figure. Catherine quotes a few lines of a deservedly obscure poem or verse drama that reminded her of her sister at that time:

> In the sober charms and dignity
> Of womanhood, mature, not verging yet
> Upon decay, in gesture like a queen:
> Such inborn and habitual majesty
> Ennobled all her steps.[19]

Pompous though this is, it suggests a spirit quite undiminished by the past ten years of continuous pregnancies and intellectual isolation. Catherine continues, of the life in Hampshire:

> if she had not more actual happiness [than in London], she had occasional enjoyment; she had better and more frequent society; she was better appreciated, both on account of her talents and her personal attractions.

Benjamin 'launched into farming with more avidity than judgment' according to Mary Hays in *British Public Characters*, buying land unnecessarily and making expensive alterations to the house. It probably first began to be known not as Lys Farm but Brookwood Park, the name it bore in the nineteenth century, during the Smiths' time there. The garden especially was an interest to both Charlotte and Benjamin.

It was the great age of garden design and of the passion for literary and picturesque landscapes. At Stourhead in the next county the merchant banker Henry Hoare had already laid the path around his lake with its classical statuary, temples and grotto. The visitor moves anti-clockwise, encountering first the Temple of Flora with its inscription over the portal from Book 6 of the *Aeneid*: 'Procul, o procul este, profani' (Keep off, keep off, all you unhallowed ones). Only the aesthete and classical scholar, the quotation semi-seriously proclaims, can appreciate such a garden. Stourhead is a refuge from the vulgar, from the business world that funded it. But Hoare was a man of some feeling, and perhaps a few black or white shadows from that world did indeed intrude in the evenings, and need warding off.

The grotto forms the 'descent to Avernus' with statues of Neptune and a nymph in the clear pools to which the visitor descends, drinks the water then reascends to daylight. A verse by Pope gives a voice to the fountain nymph:

> Nymph of the grot these sacred springs I keep
> And to the murmer of these waters sleep
> Ah spare my slumbers gently tread the cave
> And drink in silence or in silence lave.

Hoare and his designer William Kent imagined a Virgilian pastoral landscape as captured in paintings such as Claude's 'Ascanius and the Stag', and realised it in beechwoods, water, and plantings that break the view and open to frame new perspectives as the visitor circles the lake. Literature, painting and horticulture coalesce to form constant surprises, and reference to a classical golden world. Given Charlotte's early interest in Claude she would be eager to see Hoare's much-discussed garden in its first intelligent beauty, and she probably had an invitation there.

Hoare's daughter Susanna had married Charles Boyle, Viscount Dungarvon, son of John Boyle, Earl of Orrery. Their only child Henrietta was, at least by 1787, Charlotte's close friend, and the friendship may have begun much earlier. Since Charlotte's life was disrupted after 1783, it seems likely they met before that. Henrietta married John O'Neill of Shane's Castle, County Antrim in 1777. Either before or after her marriage she might have invited Charlotte to visit Stourhead when she was staying with her grandfather, who had already lost three of his four children while Henrietta was very young, and quarrelled with her father. But he was devoted to her. Charlotte's youngest daughter Harriet may have been named for Henrietta. 'Harriet' was a common variation and one Charlotte used for her friend.

Though the beechwoods were still in their teens and the design more raw than it looks today, Stourhead perhaps gave the Smiths the impetus to banish Richard's cattle to the middle distance and embark on their own landscaping. Charlotte's interest is evident in *Emmeline*, in Mrs Stafford's constructing walks bordered with flowering shrubs through the copses at Woodfield, which seems to represent Lys Farm or Brookwood. The Smiths did not have the advantage of water in the landscape since the house is too high, but they probably began the tradition of rare plantings in shrubs and trees that still continues at Brockwood, as it is now called. If their plans were more modest than Hoare's, they were still too costly for their income. Charlotte, expensively brought up and half-justifying these outgoings, which she could not in any case prevent, tried to convince herself that the benefit to Benjamin's health and morals was worth the cost.

Outwardly, to callers and casual acquaintances, her life was prosperous, even splendid. 'At a delightful place near this spot [Bramdean] Charlotte Smith passed the brilliant years of her early life',[20] wrote Mary Russell Mitford. Mitford, however, born in 1787, belonged to a later generation and heard about the Smiths from her mother. It was this acute observer of the Hampshire social scene who also passed on to her daughter her impression of the young Jane Austen as 'the prettiest, silliest, most affected, husband-hunting butterfly.'[21] Evidently Charlotte could still glitter at parties and wear her troubles lightly. When a friend suggested that Benjamin's expensive enthusiasms could be safely directed to religion she said, 'Oh, for Heaven's sake don't put it into his head to take to religion: he'll instantly set about building a cathedral.'[22] Another daughter, Lucy Eleanor, was born the year after they settled at Lys Farm, in April 1776.

Richard's health, always precarious, was now deteriorating rapidly, she knew from Lucy's letters. She wanted to visit Islington to show him and Lucy the new baby, but the illness of Benjamin Berney prevented it. She was distressed her father-in-law was so weak, and almost as sorry as Lucy when he died on 13 October 1776. By then she would not leave her son for the funeral. In spite of the great disparity of age and education, she and Richard had been allies from the start, even friends. They had shared feelings for Benjamin that were part protectiveness and part rage. Richard had cared about her children and come to respect her intelligence. She knew she would have reason to miss him.

When his will was read she was relieved to find each of her children provided with an annuity for maintenance and education, and a lump sum on marriage or coming of age. It was a complicated will, she thought. Some of the Trustees Richard had appointed to see his wishes for all his grandchildren carried out complained they could not understand it, and she was not surprised. She was touched to learn that Richard had made her an executor, with Benjamin and Lucy, though when she read it all through again she was no clearer than the Trustees about some of the provisions. But she was too sick with worry about her son to puzzle over the wording of the will that November, and as Benjamin did nothing about it she put it to the back of her mind for the moment.

Benjamin Berney had not benefitted as she hoped from his two years in the country. She had looked to him as a future friend and companion, Catherine says. He died at ten of a 'gradual decline', probably tuberculosis, in the May following Richard's death, when Charlotte was five months pregnant with her next child, Lionel. If he resembled Charlotte at the same age he was formidably well-read, the more so from the physical debility that made him less apt to spend time out of doors. Catherine writes, 'His delicate health from his birth had particularly endeared him to his mother, and she felt this affliction in proportion to her extreme affection for him.'

Charlotte drew on memories of bereavement, I have suggested, in Laura's story in *The Young Philosopher*. In *Celestina* (1791) Sophy Elphinstone experiences the death of a slightly older child than Laura's baby, though still too young to talk. In this fictional scene, Sophie has her husband with her and her sister close by, as Charlotte probably did when Benjamin Berney died. When she wrote this she had lived thirteen years after the death:

> – he died: and now I tell it with dry eyes, though, when it befell me, I thought no blow could be so severe, and that I could not survive it . . . yet I have lived now above ten years longer . . . and have learned that there are such evils in life as to make an early death a blessing. I was delirious, I know not how long, between the excess of my affliction and the opiates that were given me to deliver me awhile from the sense of my misery. In the meantime my sister sent a careful person to attend me, and saw me every day herself, though I no longer knew her, or anybody but Elphinstone, whose hand I held for hours, imploring him not to let them take my child from me.[23]

Like the fictional Sophy Elphinstone, Charlotte and Henrietta O'Neill used opium mixed with wine as a painkiller and tranquilliser. This was not unusual in the second half of the eighteenth century. In *Desmond*, published in 1792, Charlotte included a poem by Henrietta, 'Ode to the Poppy', of which the heroine Geraldine is

the supposed author. An Ode is a genre appropriate to escape from
rational restraint, with its varying line lengths and irregular rhymes,
so unlike the more usual contemporary form of the rhyming couplet.
It ends:

> Soul-soothing plant! – that can such blessings give,
> By thee the mourner bears to live!
> By thee the hopeless die!
> Oh! ever friendly to despair,
> Might sorrow's pallid votary dare,
> Without a crime, that remedy implore,
> Which bids the spirit from its bondage fly,
> I'd court thy palliative aid no more;
> No more I'd sue, that thou shouldst spread
> Thy spell around my aching head,
> But would conjure thee to impart
> Thy balsam for a broken heart,
> And by thy soft Lethean power,
> (Inestimable flower)
> Burst these terrestrial bonds, and other regions try.[24]

Henrietta and Charlotte, it would seem, both believed an opium
overdose was an easy form of suicide. Though Henrietta's life was
apparently much the happier and more successful, both evidently
spent quite a lot of time imagining such a way out. Charlotte was
obsessed with suicide at certain crises in her life, Benjamin Berney's
death being one of them. There is no account in her novels of an older
child's deathbed. Benjamin Berney of course knew he was dying, so
she had his grief and fear to alleviate as much as possible before she
could confront her own. She must have felt such suffering impossible
to recreate, even in her own often extremist fiction. Though she
believed in God, her religion lay in her sense of a spirit and a
permanence in Nature, and in her love for her children. Revealed
religion was not very important to her, and she had no consolations
to offer herself about an after-life, though she probably fell back on
such hopes to comfort her son. He was buried on 1 June, 1777.

Inevitably she went on with her routine of teaching the smaller
children to read, encouraging them to draw, and to read and write
poetry. She took them on long walks to study the different habitats
of plants and birds. Charlotte Mary and Augusta probably had
visiting teachers at Lys Farm. The boys may have had a tutor, or
perhaps have gone away to school at seven or eight, though it is
unlikely that Benjamin Berney was sent away. Benjamin's orphan
nephews and nieces, the children of his brother Richard and of his

sister Mary's first marriage often came to stay at Lys Farm. Of all Charlotte's children, Charlotte Mary enjoyed this the most. She would have suffered nearly as much as her mother from Benjamin Berney's death. They were close in age and both literary children. The five year gap between herself and Augusta with her brothers away must have made particularly welcome the visits of her dead Aunt Mary's two daughters, Dorothy and Mary Eleanor, who were a little older than herself.

Charlotte went through the county's social calendar successfully, even brilliantly, as Mary Mitford's mother remembered. But Benjamin Berney's lingering death revived all the ten year old grief for her first child, and frightened her, perhaps, with the prospect of pain still to come: Augusta sometimes looked as frail as her eldest brother had. Not only Catherine but friends and some acquaintances noticed the change in Charlotte; she was more melancholy and introspective.

The sonnets she wrote at Lys Farm in the late seventies and early eighties after her son's death are the first of her poems that survive. They are patchy, the banal and the unexpected coexisting uneasily in the same few lines. They blazon the author's capacity to suffer and to sympathise, traits that together were becoming known as Sensibility, a developed and conscious capacity to feel deeply. They notably lack the wit that was to emerge in her satirical prose, and because of this they can seem flat and embarrassing now, especially to the reader unused to any form of late eighteenth century verse. When irony gives the necessary edge to all speech and writing, when doltish ironies are better than none, Charlotte's style will seem highfalutin to many, and her grief mere posing. The sonnet she chose to come first in her first published collection begins:

> The partial Muse has from my earliest hours
> Smiled on the rugged path I'm doom'd to tread,
> And still with sportive hand has snatch'd wild flowers,
> To weave fantastic garlands for my head:
> But far, far happier is the lot of those
> Who never learn'd her dear delusive art;
> Which, while it decks the head with many a rose,
> Reserves the thorn to fester in the heart.[25]

The privilege of being a poet, to unweave her image, must be paid for in a greater sensitivity to pain. The literary reference is to Lear, 'fantastically garlanded with wild flowers' when he appears mad and destitute in Act Four and – in the last line quoted, though less obviously – to Philomel, singing out of her recollected rape and mutilation. The sonnet is self-dramatising and self-referential; taking the writer and her writing as its principal subject, it forms a manifesto for the rest of the collection.

It cannot be claimed she wrote solemnly because all female poets wrote solemnly at that time. Much eighteenth century women's verse is wry and self-mocking, or wittily aggressive. Anna Barbauld's 'Washing Day'[26] says, implicitly, 'there is poetry and then there is what women do.' Nevertheless Barbauld's self-directed irony is part of a positive resistance: the production of the poem itself upsets the assumption that poetry and washing do not mix. Mary Collier, on the same subject, is less playful. She worked as a washerwoman for most of her life and forces her genteel reader in the drawing room to acknowledge the relentlessly long hours and bleeding hands of the woman doing the household work in the basement. Her 'The Woman's Labour: an Epistle to Mr Stephen Duck', as much as any single poem by Wordsworth, reclaims the stuff of common life for poetry in the eighteenth century.

The virulent misogyny of male verse like Swift's 'Strephon and Chloë or The Lady's Dressing Room' (which made one lady instantly throw up her dinner) did not go unopposed. The anonymous Miss W. in 'The Gentleman's Study' goes well beyond Swift in her attack on the physical *grotesquerie* and repulsive habits of the opposite sex. More squeamish readers of *Eighteenth-Century Women Poets* are advised to skip this one. Lady Mary Wortley Montagu's 'The Lover', though it mocks men as more interested in their reputations for scoring than in sex, is rueful and self-mocking too. All these poets are humorous in different ways. But there was only the most sketchy tradition of specifically female poetry in the eighteenth century. Much that has been lovingly retrieved now was then unpublished and inaccessible, or published in small print runs and hard to find. The mainstream, that is, the published, admired and available, was male.

Charlotte usually avoids the sociable and self-mocking; she took herself seriously enough to risk solemnity. Her verse is confessional, but the confessions are nebulous and refined. Her introspection does not deny economics, but it denies the mundane. Her affiliations are with male writers, with James Thomson and Thomas Gray. These are poets of Nature, especially Thomson in *The Seasons*, a series of Keatsian landscapes inset with harmonising human figures published in 1721 and seldom out of print in the following hundred years.

Thomson aimed to create the Claude or Poussin landscape in poetry, his aesthetic the Horatian tag 'ut pictura poesis' (as is painting, so is poetry).

Stuart Curran, the editor of Charlotte's *Poems*, describes her as the first poet in England whom we could in retrospect call Romantic. It is true her poetic persona is a lonely figure whose moods are reflected in the setting, and her poetry was to influence Wordsworth and Coleridge, who acknowledged the debt, and Byron and Keats, who did not. But Thomson could be called Romantic too, or Gray in his 'Elegy in a Country Churchyard', or Pope in his lyrical manner, in their self-presentations or their natural landscapes. Charlotte's poems will be neither better nor worse for the label, and to apply it to the early sonnets is in some ways a disadvantage to her, as it draws attention to her political conventionality at this point. Wordsworth's characters in *Lyrical Ballads* are the poor and outcast, who have an uncanny way of disconcerting reader-expectations. In Charlotte's early sonnets, sensibility in grief is restricted to the better-educated, and there is an embarrassing surplus of the 'Blest is yon shepherd' theme:

> Blest is yon shepherd, on the turf reclin'd,
> Who on the varied clouds which float above
> Lies idly gazing . . .
> Ah! *he* has never felt the pangs that move
> Th'indignant spirit . . .
> Nor *his* rude bosom those fine feelings melt,
> Children of Sentiment and Knowledge born . . .[27]

This is as blinkered as one would expect from a minor poet of the early 1780s. There is no impulse to challenge the Augustan hegemony of witty or at least educated politeness.

But she could sometimes imagine the rural poor in a less patronising way. In 'To Sleep' she writes:

> Clasp'd in her faithful shepherd's guardian arms,
> Well may the village girl sweet slumbers prove;
> And they, O gentle sleep! – still taste thy charms
> Who wake to labour, liberty and love.[28]

Except perhaps for 'charms', one of the more irritating buzz words of the late eighteenth century, she discards, like Wordsworth later, tired poetic diction. The stereotypical shepherd of innumerable pastorals, including her own in Sonnet 9 above, has turned into something nearer a real shepherd. But this is still a rosy and distancing view of village life. Perhaps George Crabbe remembered with amusement 'To Sleep' and the alliterative, triple-abstract line quoted above. In 'Prisons', Crabbe's peasant boy Edward sleeps the night before he is to be hanged until

> the watchman on his way
> Calls and lets in – truth, terror and the day.[29]

The nightingale's song as symbol of the poet's is a traditional Petrarchan and Miltonic conception; but Charlotte's two sonnets on the nightingale, 3 and 7, were also read by Keats. Her nightingale unlike his 'light-wing'd dryad' is more closely identified with a suffering woman, with Philomel. She was raped by Tereus, who cut out her tongue so she could not relate her injury, but instead wove her story into a tapestry. The sestet of Charlotte's Sonnet 3 runs;

> Pale Sorrow's victims wert thou once among,
> Tho' now released in woodlands wild to rove?
> Say – hast thou felt from friends some cruel wrong,
> Or died'st thou – martyr of disastrous love?
> Ah! songsters sad! that such my lot might be,
> To sigh, and sing at liberty – like thee![30]

Keats' lines in the 'Ode to a Nightingale'

> Where but to think is to be full of Sorrow . . .
> Where youth grows pale and spectre-thin and dies . . .

seem a reminiscence of this. Charlotte's two nightingale sonnets have been discussed in separate articles by George Whiting and Burton Pollin. Jackson Bate and Claude Finney have noticed her more general influence on Keats' development.

The sonnets give little sense of a world beyond the speaker; she feels pleasure in flowers or moonlight for a moment but reverts solipsistically to her own suffering, looking back at the past with regret. Sonnet 2, 'Written at the Close of Spring' is a good example. Anne Ehrenpreis points out in her introduction to the OUP edition of *Emmeline* that this or one like it is the sonnet running in Anne Elliot's mind in *Persuasion* as she walks to Winthrop:

> The garlands fade that Spring so lately wove,
> Each simple flower, which she had nurs'd in dew,
> Anemonies, that spangled every grove,
> The primrose wan and harebell, mildly blue.
> No more shall violets linger in the dell,
> Or purple orchis variegate the plain,
> Til Spring again shall call forth every bell,

And dress with humid hands her wreaths again. –
Ah! poor humanity! so frail, so fair,
Are the fond visions of thy early day,
Til tyrant passion, and corrosive care,
Bid all thy fairy colours fade away!
Another May new buds and flowers shall bring;
Ah! why has happiness – no second Spring?[31]

As always with her description of flowers, species are named; she does not leave them as undifferentiated 'garlands', and they are lightly anthropomorphised. She constantly links the mood of speaker to setting, which is usually the Downs, woods and rivers of Sussex. Mitford wrote to Elizabeth Barret that she 'never took a spring walk without feeling Charlotte Smith's love of external nature and her power of describing it.'[32] Yet for many modern readers the delicacy of the octave is spoiled by the apostrophes and aphorisms of the sestet. For a modern taste, an immediate improvement can be made merely by taking out the exclamation marks, so averse we are to the surprised and declamatory; unfortunately, her tendency in revising was to add the screamers.

Anne Elliot has been remembering, as she walks, a number of poets' lines on autumn. After she hears the man she loves talking intimately to another women, she cannot immediately fall into a quotation again, 'unless some tender sonnet, fraught with the apt analogy of the declining year, with declining happiness, and the image of youth and hope, and spring, all gone together, blessed her memory.'[33] That 'blessed', not a word Austen could use casually, suggests how much Charlotte's poetry meant to some of her readers, in Austen's judgement, even as late as 1816 when she was writing *Persuasion*. Anne's thinking of a sonnet identifies Charlotte as the poet in the text. The form was neglected when she first began in the late 1770s to preserve her writing. She thought it 'no improper vehicle for a single Sentiment',[34] and her sonnets do encompass a single setting, a single tone: typically, there is no shift of subject or mood between the octave and the sestet in her Elegiac Sonnets as there is in her models, Shakespeare and Petrarch. But in *Persuasion* the 'ploughs at work and the fresh made path spoke the farmer, counteracting the sweets of poetical despondence and meaning to have Spring again.' It is the narrator's response to the elegiac and inward-looking tone. Charlotte was particularly associated through the 1780s and nineties with the revival of this form, and Anne, a literary heroine, is thinking of her.

The only other serious contender for a place in Anne's mind is William Lisle Bowles, whose *Fourteen Sonnets* published in 1789 and reissued with additional poems ran to nine editions or reprintings in the 1790s and early nineteenth century, almost as many as Charlotte's. But there the speaker is male, mourning the death of a young woman, and Bowles has no lines so close to Anne's consciousness as Charlotte's. Later when Anne wonders whether she is to be 'blessed with a second spring of youth and beauty',[35] her consciousness returns to the last line of Sonnet 2, but this time with the hope that her experience will differ from Charlotte's speaker.

A preoccupation with death and especially with suicide runs through these sonnets. In five of them, Geothe's Werther is the speaker, and presented without irony. They are only loosely related to *The Sorrows of Young Werther* (1774), which had become a cult book by the late seventies, with spin-offs in Werther teacups and yellow britches. Werther was exciting because of his active defiance of established society, his attempt to assert his individuality even through suicide rather than adapt to convention. In Sonnet 23, Werter (as she spelt it) addresses the North Star as it shines on the sea, imaging the coldness of the death she half longs for:

> Or in the turbid water, rude and dark,
> O'er whose wild stream the gust of Winter raves,
> Thy trembling light with pleasure still I mark,
> Gleam in faint radiance on the foaming waves![36]

The attraction and terror of stormy seawater, quite absent in *The Sorrows of Young Werther*, runs through her poems and novels. She must have read Edmund Burke's *A Philosophical Enquiry into the Sublime and Beautiful* (1757). For both of them, the great but terrible scenes of nature fill the mind with grand ideas and turn the soul in upon itself.

In a sonnet more clearly rooted in economic fears, the speaker watches her children playing. This was probably written in 1781:

> Sighing I see yon little group at play,
> By sorrow yet untouch'd, unhurt by care;
> While free and sportive they enjoy today
> Content, and careless of tomorrow's fare.
> O, Happy age! – When Hope's unclouded ray,
> Lights their green path, and prompts their simple mirth;
> E'er yet they feel the thorns that lurking lay,
> To wound the wretched pilgrims of the earth,

Making them rue the hour that gave them birth,
And threw them on a world so full of pain,
Where prosperous folly treads on patient worth,
And, to deaf pride, misfortune pleads in vain!
Ah! for their future fate how many fears
Oppress my heart, and fill mine eyes with tears![37]

Like the shepherd in Sonnet 9, the children are distanced and conventionalised. But even in her weaker poems, there is metrical delicacy and flexibility: she never writes doggerel. She avoids the Petrarchan form with its break, new rhymes and shift of subject after the octave and uses instead, at the hinge, an unexpected rhyming couplet – earth and birth, here – so that there is no change of mood but a sense of continuation and relentlessness.

Slight personifications such as folly and worth, pride and misfortune are survivals of the powerful conceptualising manner of Pope and the Augustan satirists of the earlier eighteenth century. Hope, the presiding genius of childhood, is more fully personified. As Stella Brooks points out, there are a number of fragile figures in the sonnets representing youth, love, security or hope; they 'are painted with the lightest touch, but then allowed to fade as their inadequacy, like that of their creator, in the face of intractable social and economic problems, is acknowledged.'[38]

Assertion of the writer's powerlessness and marginality is nonetheless assertion. She has the confidence to assume that her depression, economic vulnerability and fears for her children are no improper subjects for one of the most historically privileged genres. Her affiliation is with Gray here, whose 'Elegy in a Country Churchyard', published in 1750, was perhaps the most popular poem of the next half century. His speaker marks out his apartness both from the muscular peasant world and the world of politics and fame. His alienation – his encrypted homosexuality, Daniel White convincingly argues – becomes the poem's subject and provides its graveyard's best epitaph:

Here rests his head upon the lap of Earth
A youth to Fortune and to Fame unknown.
Fair Science frowned not on his humble birth,
And Melancholy marked him for her own.

Large was his bounty, and his soul sincere,
Heaven did a recompense as largely send:
He gave to Misery all he had, a tear,
He gained from Heaven ('twas all he wished) a friend.[39]

Charlotte appropriates his aesthetic in her Elegies, placing herself in the foreground alone and at odds with peasantry and wealthy alike, as with the smiling or sublime landscapes. Her proclaimed powerlessness is at odds too with the role she seizes as woman poet. She can imply, as Gray does, 'Here lies the author', and mandate the reader to seek the hidden biography.[40] Writing gave her an independent source of happiness in all but the worst misfortunes; even in the worst, it asserted her sense of self and ensured her survival.

Mary Hays' *British Public Characters* account, Catherine's memoir, and Charlotte herself in her Prefaces represent her as forced into publication reluctantly, to raise money for her children and because her work had appeared in mutilated form already. This may be so. But it was a claim genteel writers made then, that family duty forced them to become professionals, or that they were coerced into publication by overzealous admirers – 'Obliged by hunger, and request of friends',[41] as Pope bitchily puts it – or because their work had already appeared in distorted versions without their consent. Publication was an especially bold step for a woman. Charlotte may always have hoped to publish her poems at some time for her own sake, and because she thought they were worth it. But in 1784 she was desperate to raise some money. And here it is necessary to return to Richard's will, the Smiths' finances and their lives at Lys Farm.

Richard's will[42] had been made after careful thought but without the help of a lawyer. He had estates and properties in the West Indies, the largest being two plantations in Barbados, and in England and Scotland. He had stock in the East India Company, Consolidated Annuities (Consols), government bonds and mortgages on estates in England and Barbados. The relatives he wanted to provide for were Lucy, Benjamin (his only surviving child), Charlotte, and his many grandchildren. His elder son Richard and his daughter Mary predeceased him by four years and one year respectively. His grandchildren were Richard and Mary Gibbs Smith, the orphan son and daughter of his son Richard; the eight grandchildren by Charlotte and Benjamin, of whom Charlotte Mary was the acknowledged favourite; by his dead daughter Mary's first marriage he had three more grandchildren, Robert, Dorothy and Mary Eleanor Berney; by her second husband Thomas Dyer she left two sons, who are not individually named in the will, and a daughter, Maria Dyer, whom Richard also favoured over her brothers.

When he was making his will, Richard evidently confronted and tried to deal with his main problem, which was to prevent Benjamin from realising the firm's assets and spending all the money before the grandchildren came of age. He also wanted to provide small annuities for some of his servants, and fulfil a promise he had made to leave a bequest to Poplar Hospital. He had a stepdaughter, Mary Crowe Robinson, the daughter of his second wife Elizabeth's first marriage to Nathaniel Crowe of Barbados, whose heiress she had been. As far as is known, Richard and Elizabeth had no children together. Mary was married to a rather prominent personality in the House of Commons, now about fifty, whose career sheds an interesting light on eighteenth-century social mobility.

This was John Robinson, who was born at Appleby in Westmorland where Richard owned property. Robinson was articled as a lawyer's clerk to Wordsworth's grandfather, his second cousin, but meeting the heiress Mary Crowe, perhaps through his dealings with Richard, he quickly married her and used her dowry to advance a political career. He was considered a steady, clever man of business by Sir James Lowther, who became his patron, but he switched parties when Lord North offered him the post of Secretary of the Treasury; Lowther challenged him to a duel, which Robinson declined. His supporters were known as Robinson's Rats. Sheridan, attacking bribery and its main instigator in the House of Commons would respond to shouts of 'name, name', by looking fixedly at Robinson on the Treasury Bench and exclaiming, 'Yes, I could name him as soon as I could say Jack Robinson.'[43] It is surprising Richard trusted such a man; but in his last year or two he became over-impressed by social position and lost much of his former judgment. He lent £20,000 without securities to an absconding baronet, and never recovered the money.

The small bequests to servants, in some cases for 'rare and singular attendance' on him in his illnesses, the bequest to Poplar Hospital, the division of household goods and plate, are plainly written and unproblematic. All too clear also are the bequests of his black servants to different members of the family. He appointed Lucy, Benjamin and Charlottle as joint executors, an unusual mark of confidence in the women when executors were usually male.

For Lucy, 'my dear wife Lucy', he added a second annuity additional to the settlement made on her in her marriage articles in May 1767, emphasising that this was an addition to, not merely an endorsement of, the earlier settlement. He also recommended that she should 'direct the education' of Charlotte Mary and some of the other grandchildren including the Berney sisters, but noting that he did not 'intend that she should be at any expense therein.' Perhaps he hoped that she would make her home at Lys Farm and that most of the orphan grandchildren as minors would live there. She seems to have stayed in Islington, however, where the Berney girls joined her, paying 50 guineas a year for their board; Charlotte Mary went on extended visits there. He left the guardianship of all the orphaned grandchildren to Benjamin.

Richard's estate amounted to about £36,000 after some outstanding debts were paid and after the baronet's depredations. His aim was to ensure that each grandchild had investments large enough to pay interest for maintenance and education, and to realise a sum of at least £1,000 each at marriage or at twenty-one, whichever was the soonest. He appointed as Trustees relatives and friends of the family, to see that his directions on how and when money should be paid to the grandchildren were carried out. These were John Braithwaite, presumably young Braithwaite's godfather in 1770, Joseph Deane and Deane's two sons, Monkhouse Davidson, Thomas Dyer his widower son-in-law, the Revd Samuel Nott, Edward Chamberlayne, George Whatley and John Robinson. The last two were added in codicils. The Trustees were allowed to release a grandson's share early if it was required for entry into a business or profession. A thousand pounds was a dowry worth having, though not overly tempting to rogues, or it would provide a decent but not lavish maintenance for a granddaughter who did not marry. The two children of Benjamin's dead brother already had money settled on them following their father's death, so their share in Richard's will was smaller; he was at pains to make clear his reason for leaving them less than their cousins. However, as with the Berney and Dyer children, he was anxious that the aggregate of their money should yield enough annually to maintain and educate them; if the Barbados estate, from which they already benefited, should yield less than this, the shortfall should be made up from capital left in the will.

Charlotte Mary and Maria Dyer were intended to receive ultimately more than their brothers, £1,500 each at marriage or majority. If the living in Richard's gift, the perpetual avowdson of St Mary's Islington, vacated by his son Richard's death, were ever to be wanted by one of Benjamin's sons, that son was to pay Charlotte Mary the whole value of it, £1,000. Richard also tried to guard against loss to the other grandchildren if Richard Smith III ever successfully claimed the entire Barbados estate by right of primogeniture. Augusta's position is ambiguous. No doubt from an oversight,

Richard only stipulated, in one of those crass provisions making a will so often entails, that if Charlotte Mary died Augusta would get her sister's share. The new baby, Lucy, whom Richard had never seen, was left her annuity and the £1,000 capital sum. Any further children born to Benjamin were not separately provided for unless all his children then living had already died; he presumably expected Benjamin to put money aside for any future children himself.

Provision for the grandchildren was more complicated and open to interpretation than this brief summary can suggest; the will runs to nineteen pages and is extremely confusing, as contemporary experts agreed. But in general, after contingencies affecting Richard and Mary Gibbs Smith were allowed for, the Berney and Dyer children were ultimately to receive two fifths of the estate, Charlotte and Benjamin's children three fifths. The latter were less well provided for, and the family was still increasing. Thomas Dyer was only in middle age, so he might be expected to provide more for the Dyers. His father the baronet was prosperous; ultimately the baronetcy, through the deaths of Dyer's elder brother and elder son, descended to Dyer's second son Thomas. Mary Crowe Robinson and her daughter, also Mary, who in 1781 married Henry Neville, Earl of Abergavenny, received ten guineas each for mourning rings, sums which probably did not please John Robinson in 1776.

The bulk of the estate went to Benjamin for his lifetime, with strict instructions about paying the children's and servants' annuities promptly and fully. The Trustees were exhorted to ensure that this was done. Benjamin had to pay off debts owed by the firm, and call in money owed to it. He was also required to pay Thomas Dyer, under severe penalties if he failed to do so, £2,500 still owing to him as part of his late wife Mary's marriage settlement. Presumably Dyer had left it in Richard's control as an investment in the firm. Richard suggested in the will that Dyer might leave it there for a few years longer, but acknowledged that it was legally Dyer's and must be paid when asked for. Suspecting that Benjamin would want to sell off assets from the firm and invest in land, Richard tried to pre-empt him by providing that the agreement of the other two executors, Lucy and Charlotte, was needed before he could make such investments. Some provisions though fair for their time would be hard to accept, as in any will. Benjamin, for instance, inherited the Appleby estate in Westmorland for his lifetime, but at his death it would go to Richard Smith III, reasserting the order of primogeniture.

Richard was notably generous to Charlotte. She was to inherit a third of Benjamin's life interest if he predeceased her, the other two thirds to go to her children. Her share would go to her children when she died or if she remarried. But even if she remarried, she was allowed two hundred pounds a year for life, the magic sum necessary, in Richard's view, for freedom from want and a small measure of independence. It is a pity she never got it. The annuity however may have been dependent on all her children dying first. This is another of many ambiguities.

The will is complex but not perhaps impossible to unravel, though it would have needed active executors to observe all its directions. The codicils Richard nervously added, contradicting provisions in the will proper, the number and the nature of the Trustees appointed, and the character of his son, all conspired to negate his wishes. As if foreseeing trouble, he urged all parties to behave with love and affection for each other, and avoid disputes. There is a final proviso that:

> in case any of the parties interested shall attempt to disturb the Family peace by Commencing a Suit at Law or in Equity against my Executors or otherwise I do hereby revoke all and every such legacy I may have bequeathed him her or them by this my Will and declare the same to be void.[44]

Nevertheless, he left a legacy that broke up his family.

By the time the will was read, Benjamin was engaged in his new role of gentleman farmer. His responsibilities as executor and guardian to so many children were formidable; the duty of prompt payment of the annuities to Lucy, the servants and his nephews and nieces he carried out irregularly or not at all. To pay annuities into accounts for his own children probably never entered his head. He made excuses to put off paying the £2,500 to Dyer; the penalty for withholding this was £5,000. The access he gained to Richard's money plunged him into new expenses, especially in further enlarging the house, which in turn involved engaging new servants. The threat of disinheritance, the one restraint on Benjamin in his father's lifetime, was now removed. His two co-executors were powerless to stop him. He was also spending money settled on Charlotte in her marriage articles. She had no legal rights that could not be easily negated by a husband, as Catherine notes in the memoir. She adds that Lucy, 'weak and infirm, was easily overruled by cajolery, or less gentle means.' The Trustees could not agree on the meaning of parts of the will, and refused to act.

A portrait of Benjamin as Mr Stafford, immediately recognised by readers who knew the Smiths, appears in *Emmeline* and gives an account, however subjective, of him while at Lys Farm. In this novel Charlotte put herself and Benjamin into Adelina and Trelawny, and also into Mrs and Mr Stafford:

> Mr Stafford was one of those unfortunate characters who having neither perseverance or regularity to fit them for business, or taste and genius for more refined pursuits, seek in every casual occurrence, or childish amusement, relief against the tedium of life. Tho' married very early, and tho' father of a numerous family, he had thrown away the time and money which should have provided for them, in collecting baubles, which he had repeatedly possessed and discarded, 'till having exhausted every source that that species of idle folly offered, he had been drawn, by the same inability to pursue proper objects, into vices yet more fatal to the repose of his wife, and schemes yet more destructive to the fortune of his family.[45]

One of these schemes, in Mr Stafford's case and possibly in Benjamin's, was the process of manuring land with old wigs, on which a treatise had recently been published.

Yet Benjamin had abilities, and in 1781, four years after his father's death, was prominent enough to be appointed High Sheriff for Hampshire. The expenses incurred by this however may have contributed to ruin him. In the portrait of Mr Stafford, Charlotte suggests the effect of financial losses: that his temper grew worse as his property decreased. The bad temper she describes in *Emmeline* may have been accompanied in real life by a marital violence impossible to include in a novel she hoped would sell well but without injury to her reputation. She would have suffered more attacks from the critics if she had revealed the worst of her marriage in print. In a letter written many years later on 25 January 1804, she recalls how, at this time,

> once in his coach going to dine at Lord Clanricarde's he threw a large bunch of keys at me and hurt me on the breast, without any provocation but my saying we should make Lady Clanricarde late, and put her out of humour. I could have brought another person, a relation of mine, who would have taken the most solemn oath that she has seen him strike and kick me, and once at table, throw a quatern loaf at my head without provocation at all but the phrenzy, for so it seemed at the moment.[46]

Catherine hints at violence in his manner to Lucy. If we accept Verney in *Desmond* as a portrait of Benjamin, his attitude to his children was sometimes scarcely better, at least in Charlotte's memory of it by 1792. After Lionel's birth she did not become pregnant again for five years; this may reflect the couple's increasing dislike and estrangement, or simply that they were less fertile now they were in their thirties. Another daughter, Harriet, was born in 1782.

The year the Smiths moved to Hampshire was the year of the American colonists' rebellion, and war. For John Robinson, Benjamin and their entrepreneurial friends, war meant lucrative contracts for supplying the army and navy abroad. Robinson may have helped Benjamin to his position of High Sheriff of Hampshire in return for Benjamin's help with electioneering in the county. Benjamin had never been interested in politics before, but under Robinson's influence he entered enthusiastically into vote-raising for a ministerial candidate against an independent. Charlotte used her skills for the first time, and the last, to support what we would now call a conservative candidate; this pamphlet, unfortunately, has not survived.

Her economic and social interests were still inseparable from Benjamin's. But just as when she was living over the warehouse, her thoughts were running in the opposite direction from those of her immediate circle, as appeared later. Benjamin, his friends and many of the Hampshire county families could cultivate an easy indignation against the American rebels, assert their patriotism and enjoy the money their contracts made them. Charlotte grew up during a run of British military successes and the expansion of Empire, and as a child responded emotionally to news like Wolfe's capture of Quebec. But her patriotism was very unlike the outraged arrogance of the pro-War party in 1775 and 1776.

Lord North, she learned, the Prime Minister – though he would never consent to answer to the title, claiming there was no such thing in the British constitution – was reluctant to prosecute the American war. George III insisted on it. The bets of her husband's friends on how soon it would be over, their only fear it would be over too soon, disgusted her, like their discussions about how they could cut the cost of army provisions. Later, she dramatised her own learning process about the American War of Independence in *The Old Manor House*. Written in 1792, it is a historical novel set in the 1770s. Her hero, Orlando, goes to America with the British Army to fight the rebels, and on the voyage out finds himself thinking seriously for the first time about military glory. In school he has been taught to admire the kings and generals of antiquity and English history who led their armies personally:

> There was something great in their personal valour, in their contempt of death; and he did not recollect that their being themselves so indifferent to life was no reason why, to satisfy their own vanity, they should deluge the world with human blood. There were, indeed, times when the modern directors of war appeared to him in a less favourable light – who incurred no personal danger, nor gave themselves any other trouble than to raise money from one part of their subjects, in order to enable them to destroy another, or the subjects of some neighbouring potentate. Nor had he, after a while, great reason to admire the integrity of the subordinate departments, to whom the care of providing for troops thus sent out to support the glory of their master [George III] was entrusted. The provisions on board were universally bad; and the sickness of the soldiers was as much owing to that cause as to the heat of the climate. Musty oatmeal, half-dried pease, and meat half spoiled before it had been salted down, would in any situation have occasioned disease; and when to such defective food, their being so closely stowed and so long on board was added, those diseases increased rapidly, and generally ended fatally. But it was all for *glory*. And that the ministry should, in thus purchasing glory, put a little more than was requisite into the pockets of contractors, and destroy as many men by sickness as by the sword, made but little difference in an object so infinitely important; especially when it was known (which, however, Orlando did not know) that messieurs the contractors were for the most part members of parliament, who under other names enjoyed the profits of a war, which, disregarding the voices of the people in general, or even of their own constituents, they voted for pursuing. Merciful God! can it be thy will that mankind should tear each other to pieces with more ferocity than the beasts of the wilderness?[47]

In a footnote to an earlier part of this chapter Charlotte adds sardonically, 'It has lately been alleged in defence of the Slave Trade, that Negroes on board Guineamen are allowed almost as much room as a Soldier in a Transport – Excellent reasoning!'[48]

The American War ended ignominiously for the British in 1782. In March Lord North resigned as First Lord of the Treasury and Chancellor of the Exchequer. John Robinson lost his position as Secretary to the Treasury. Benjamin lost his contract. He had incurred further debts as High Sheriff, and had still not paid the money owing to Thomas Dyer, or the Berney and Dyer children's annuities. Dyer resorted to a lawsuit to recover his late wife's money; other creditors, seeing Benjamin on the verge of bankruptcy, hurried to put in their claims. In December 1783, Benjamin was arrested at Dyer's suit and sent to the King's Bench Prison in London for debt and for embezzlement of his father's Trust fund.

The details of the negotiations Charlotte undertook to get him out are not clear, and the evidence in some respects is contradictory. She may have sold Lys Farm, or it may have been forcibly taken over by the bailiffs. As Hilbish discovered, the entry of assessment in the Hinton Ampner Vestry Book for 1784 states that 'Mr Shakespeare, Esq., is assessed for the lands of the late Benjamin Smith, Esquire.' Benjamin was very much alive, though in prison, and this is perhaps a mistake for Richard Smith, the actual owner of Lys Farm till his death. However, Richard had died eight years earlier. It may simply mean that Benjamin was the recent occupier of the house. Mr Shakespeare may have bought it from Charlotte, acting for Benjamin, or from Benjamin's creditors.

The *British Public Characters* account is emotive but deliberately vague; Benjamin and Robinson were both still alive when this was written:

> On a subject of so much delicacy it would be improper to dwell; those who witnessed Mrs Smith's conduct, both while she apprehended the evils that now overtook her, or while she suffered under them, can alone do her justice, or can judge, at least as far as a single instance goes, whether the mind which feels the enthusiasm of poetry, and can indulge in the visionary regions of romance, is always so enervated as to be unfitted for the more arduous tasks and severer trials of human life. Neither the fears of entering into scenes of calamity, nor of suffering in her health, already weakened, prevented her from partaking the lot of her husband, with whom she passed the greater part of seven months in legal confinement, and whose release was, at the end of that time, obtained chiefly by her indefatigable exertions. But during this period some of her hours were spent at the house in Hampshire, which was now to be sold, under such circumstances as those who, in that sad hour, deserted her, are now as unwilling to hear of as she to relate them.

This may suggest that she was allowed to collect some of her own and the children's belongings from Lys Farm before the bailiffs arrived. Catherine says only that the estate in Hampshire was sold, but not in what circumstances. She goes on:

> Mrs Smith never deserted her husband for a moment during the melancholy period of his misfortunes and perhaps her conduct never was so deserving of admiration as at this time. When suffering from the calamities he had brought on himself, and in which he had

inextricably involved her and her children, she exerted herself with as much zeal and energy as if his conduct had been unexceptionable – made herself mistress of his affairs – submitted to many humiliating applications, and encountered the most unfeeling repulses. Perhaps the severest of her tasks, as well as the most difficult was that of employing her superior abilities in defending a conduct she could not have approved.

It is not clear how much of Benjamin's seven months in jail she spent with him. Wives were not necessarily expected to accompany their husbands, but prisoners had little food fit to eat unless a relative brought it in daily. She put her children into the care of her brother Nicholas, who had inherited Bignor Park when their father died and was now a clergyman. Catherine was also living at Bignor Park, or close by, while her husband was still in the army. The Dorset children, Lucy, four at the time of Benjamin's arrest, and Charles then aged two, were baptised in Holy Cross Church there.

Perhaps Benjamin ordered Charlotte to join him, as he did when he wanted her in Normandy. But pride alone might determine her not to desert him now. Any marriage is much too complicated for general statement, but the Smiths' marriage and sexual relationship is especially hard to fathom. As she knew, Benjamin had been sent to England aged three, confined in the hold. It might have damaged him permanently. If, as seems probable, he suffered from what is now called Attention Deficit Disorder, he could not, rather than would not, concentrate on business or domestic matters even when it was obviously in his interest to do so. Charlotte, knowing this, must have felt a constant pity and concern mixing with her resentment. 'She was in love with me once,'[49] he said many years later, and though this, reported back, provoked furious denials, there may be some element of truth in it. With nine children at Bignor, she had every excuse for absenting herself throughout his imprisonment. But she stayed with him often during the early months of 1784, and in May fell pregnant again in these grim surroundings.

In *Ethelinde*, written six years later, she describes the feelings of a woman entering a prison and the scenes she came to know well that winter. The heroine and her father enter the lobby of the prison, where two or three turnkeys wait to admit visitors, then they

> ascended the stairs, and were in the first entrance. The fierce and stern faces of the keepers who filled it, the noise of riot and wrangling from other figures, who were by the gloomy light discovered among them, all gave a new shock . . . as the men who surrounded her

> looked with inquisitive and attentive eyes into her face, she was
> terrified ... [Then they] proceeded across the space in which the
> dwellings of the imprisoned are built. The night was cold and wet;
> the rain, or rather an heavy fog, fell murky and gloomy on a few
> wretched-looking persons, who were carrying their scanty suppers
> from the place where they had been making their melancholy market;
> yet in the place where liquor is sold, the voice of merriment and even
> of riot was heard, that aggravated rather than relieved the dismal
> appearance of the wide court, which, as it was extremely dirty,
> Ethelinde did not cross without being wet quite through her feet.[50]

The numbered cells in this account are arranged around a dark stone
staircase. Each cell has only a small tent bed and a chair. Charlotte's
visits there would have been very uncomfortable.

But some of her time was spent at Lys Farm, and at Bignor with
the children. A sonnet headed 'Written in Farm Wood, South Downs,
in May 1784' must have been composed during a visit to them:

> Spring's dewy hand on this fair summit weaves
> The downy grass, with tufts of Alpine flowers,
> And shades the beechen slopes with tender leaves
> And leads the shepherd to his upland bowers,
> Strewn with wild thyme; while slow-descending showers,
> Feed the green ear, and nurse the future sheaves!

The cyclical processes of Nature have no healing power for the
speaker:

> Ah! what to me can those dear days restore
> When scenes could charm, that now I taste no more![51]

The elegiac tone in all these poems stems from memories of childhood, particularly painful when she revisited Bignor after perhaps a
twenty year interval.

But much of her time that winter was spent in London, sleeping
in the King's Bench. Her first thought was to raise money to pay their
debts, and she decided to try to sell her sonnets. A friend and former
neighbour when she lived at Lys Farm was Bryan Edwards, who was
to become well known in the 1790s when he published *The History of
the British Colonies in the West Indies*. He was a voracious reader and
enthusiastic about her poems. She sent him as many as she could
collect together early in 1784. Some had to be retrieved from other
friends. He encouraged her to approach the publisher Richard Dodsley
in Pall Mall.

The British Public Characters account says that Dodsley's reception
of her

which impressed itself on her memory, was by no means liberal or flattering. Slightly regarding the manuscript he assured her, that for such things there was no sale, that the public had been satiated with shepherds and shepherdesses, and that he must decline offering money for the manuscript. To this he added, whimsically, that he should not object to print the poems – when, should any profit arise, he might take it for his pains, and, should there be none, there would be no great harm done.

Charlotte declined this offer, and went back to the King's Bench more humiliated than ever. She tried Messrs Dilly in the Poultry, near Cheapside, again without success. She then plucked up courage to send the sonnets to William Hayley, a poet and patron of poets, who lived at Eartham in Sussex, about six miles from Bignor. They had never met, though they had acquaintances in common including John Sargent the local MP, who was himself to publish a volume of poems, *The Mine*, in the following year. Hayley had published *The Triumphs of Temper* three years earlier, a winsome, mock-epic definition of the Ideal Girl in rhyming couplets which was extremely popular. After consulting Sargent, she asked Hayley's permission to dedicate her poems to him, if they should be accepted for publication. He agreed, and with a famous name for her Dedication, which refers to him as 'the greatest modern Master of that charming talent, in which I can never be more than a distant copyist', she returned to Dodsley and this time let him have the poems without advance payment.

Under the title *Elegiac Sonnets and other Essays by Charlotte Smith of Bignor Park, Sussex*, a title that throws a pleasing drapery over her status and residence at the time, they were printed in Chichester and published in early June 1784 in Chichester and London. The *British Public Characters* account tells us that 'the immediate success of this thin quarto edition more than justified its author's confidence', the confidence, that is, to let Dodsley have it for nothing on the gamble that it would sell. However, it paid little at first, Benjamin was still in prison, and more humiliating negotiations with creditors and the Trustees to Richard's estate were necessary to release him.

She visited Thomas Dyer, ignoring all rebuffs while she tried to persuade him to wait a little longer for the £2,500. A strong antipathy had developed between her and Dyer, 'detestable, cream-coloured Dyer'[52] as she called him. Perhaps it had been latent for a long time. He met his wife and the rest of the Smith family not long after Charlotte and Benjamin married. In *Emmeline* the shifty lawyer who clearly represents Dyer makes sexual advances to the heroine. Perhaps the sight of Charlotte at sixteen in the first year of her marriage infuriated him from the start. By this time he seemed to take a delight in her reduced circumstances. He was contemptuous of Benjamin, who had put him off with reassurances for so long. On the other hand he had little hope of payment while Benjamin remained in prison. Charlotte also visited the notorious John Robinson, waiting for hours in his anteroom then enduring his insulting manners while she discussed her husband with him. They finally agreed, at Robinson's suggestion, that in return for Dyer's releasing Benjamin from prison, Robinson and Dyer's elder brother, by now Sir John Dyer, should take over the executorship of Richard's will with two subsidiaries, Edmund Boehm and Richard Atkinson, through a legal process established where an executor was deemed incompetent to act. This may have been their object from the first, in having Benjamin arrested.

Certainly they offered only a brief reprieve. Benjamin's temporary release from Dyer's suit did not release him from the debt or from his liability for the unpaid annuities to the nephews and nieces. And his other creditors would begin to hope again when they heard he was out. Nevertheless, it felt like triumph to Charlotte.

During Benjamin's time in prison, she talked to other lawyers as well as the Dyers and Robinson. She perhaps talked to other prisoners and their wives and thought about the law, especially as it related to debtors. She could see her father's gambling losses, mercantile profits based on the savage gamble of slave running, Benjamin's winning and losing his army contract, Robinson's rise then loss of office, as equally the operations of chance. Wealth was the lucky outcome of someone else's misfortune, though the gambler at cards did not depend on war and death to make his money. Still, she could not comfortably sink Benjamin's misdemeanours in a sense of the general corruption. He had embezzled his father's Trust fund; his spending was an addiction worse than her father's gambling and equally beyond cure. Her false position as his wife merely made her hate the lawyers more. Hays in *British Public Characters* says that 'the experience she acquired during these seven months of the chicanery of law, and the turpitude of many of its professors' prompted and justified the treatment of lawyers and the law in her novels.

Nicholas had taken a house for his sister's family close to his own at Bignor Park. He and Charlotte knew that Benjamin would have to go abroad if she could not persuade the creditors to wait. The negotiations for transfer of the executorship took up the whole of June, but at last, after another long day of waiting and more insults from her brother-in-law and step-brother-in-law, in the first queasy stage of pregnancy, she saw Dyer sign the document releasing Benjamin. The *British Public Characters* account says that:

> After a day of excessive fatigue, which had succeeded to the most cruel solicitudes, Mrs Smith experienced the satisfaction (the deed of trust having been signed) of beholding her husband released from his confinement, and accompanied him immediately into Sussex.

The account quotes a letter from Charlotte to an unnamed friend, describing that day. It may have been written from Sussex in the summer, or perhaps from Normandy in the following winter, and it conveys her relief vividly:

> It was on the second day of July that we commenced our journey. For more than a month I had shared the restraint of my husband, in a prison, amidst scenes of misery, of vice and even of terror. Two attempts had, since my last residence among them, been made by the prisoners to procure their liberation, by blowing up the walls of the house. Throughout the night appointed for this enterprize, I remained dressed, watching at the window, and expecting every moment to witness contention and bloodshed, or, perhaps, be overwhelmed by the projected explosion. After such scenes, and such apprehensions how deliciously soothing to my wearied spirits was the soft, pure air of the summer's morning, breathing over the dewy grass, as (having slept one night on the road) we passed over the heaths of Surrey! My native hills at length burst upon my view – I beheld once more the fields where I had passed my happiest days, and, amidst the perfumed turf with which one of those fields was strewn, perceived, with delight, the beloved groupe, from whom I had been so long divided, and for whose fate my affections were ever anxious. The transports of this meeting were too much for my exhausted spirits. After all my sufferings I began to hope I might taste content, or experience at least a respite from calamity.

Letters like this suggest the natural buoyancy of her temperament. They are also helpful for the new reader of late-eighteenth-century works who needs to get her eye in. The over-refined and overwritten, by twentieth century standards, is entirely compatible with the experience and record of immediate danger. We are forced to shift our notion of what is authentic about tone: not necessarily the laid back, in the age of Sensibility.

Her 'respite from calamity' was brief. Dyer was still threatening, as were the other creditors. Benjamin must have had some money left, or the Smiths could not have lived in Normandy as long as they did, but it was not enough to pay his debts. Charlotte's *Elegiac Sonnets* sold well in London, and in Sussex the volume would have turned her into a celebrity if she had remained there long. *British Public Characters* says that

> the profits of the work, in its progress, relieved the writer from those solicitudes for her children which had weighed down her spirits, and enabled her to look forward with fortitude to the period which should disembarrass their father's affairs.

But in that summer of 1784, the profits could only allow her to pay the rent and feed her children. And though she had more confidence now to tackle Dyer, Robinson and the other creditors, she was less successful than before. They had, perhaps, only used her to gain the executorship. From *Emmeline* we can infer that she tried to release money from her own marriage settlement to help Benjamin, but her Trustees refused to allow this. It is not clear what she asked of Benjamin's creditors, but it seems she tried to persuade Sir John Dyer and Robinson as Trustees to realise assets from Richard's estate to pay her husband's debts. This they refused – and they were of course right, whatever their motives, as Charlotte must have seen. Richard had always intended to leave his property in such a way that Benjamin could not get his hands on money intended for the grand-children, though probably even Richard had not foreseen his son's arrest. Benjamin dared not stay in Sussex for more than a few weeks, knowing that Dyer could have him re-arrested. Charlotte went with him to Dieppe, since he knew no French, and took lodgings for him in the town; she was there only one day, returning on the same packet before her absence could be noticed.

She stayed on with the children in the house at Bignor Nicholas had taken for her. From the tone of Catherine's and Mary Hays' accounts, one might expect her to be quite disheartened if not entirely broken down by so many misfortunes. But whatever her anxieties, she was following the sales of *Elegiac Sonnets* eagerly, excited by her sudden emergence as a successful author. She was curious about William Hayley, whose patronage had given her the confidence to publish at her own expense. So far she had only corresponded with him. A letter from Hayley to his wife gives an odd, unexpected sighting of her on 28 September. He wrote:

... First let me say, did you hear yesterday, that a post-chaise was sent for to convey a lady, suddenly taken ill at Eartham, to her own home? So it was; and this sick lady was no less a personage than the elegant poetess of Bignor Park. About one o'clock, I was surprised by an exclamation from Nurse, 'Lord, sir! there are three strange ladies in the garden.' – 'Find out who they are.' My ambassadress, however, did not return, but bustled about the poor invalid; and when I descended to make further inquiries, I found the veteran Charlotte Collins, with Mrs. Smith and her daughter, in a piteous plight, in the parlour.

Our tender sister of Parnassus had been seized with spasms in her stomach, which had obliged her to quit her horse, and creep, like a poor wounded bird, through the garden.

I played the physician with some success; and by a seasonable medicine soon restored the sick Muse. The chaise had been ordered in their first alarm, and as it could not arrive till between four and five, I insisted on their taking a poetical dinner, to which they consented after many apologies.

The fair invalid was sufficiently restored to survey all our walks, and the chaise arriving, they departed between five and six.[53]

It seems unlikely the stomach pains were genuine. She made a quick recovery. She could have had herself formally introduced to Eliza Hayley through some such literary mutual friend as Charlotte Collins. But she may have felt embarrassed to suggest it, given Benjamin's recent imprisonment. Instead she rode six miles along the overgrown Roman way to Eartham when four or five months pregnant, with her friend and Charlotte Mary, and briefly suffered or faked an illness in the grounds that forced the housekeeper to ask her in. This housekeeper, or 'Nurse', Sarah Betts, was the mother of Hayley's former mistress, now living in a cottage in the village, who had also been one of the household servants and born him a son: Thomas Alphonso was three, acknowledged by his father and accepted as part of the family by Eliza. Hayley referred to all his female literary friends as his Muses.

It is an amusing and rather touching glimpse, even through Hayley's quizzical prose, of the three Charlottes in the garden, one of them fifteen and the other two acting like it. Charlotte was desperate to be known in literary circles, to have new and intellectual company. The manipulative cheek – as it probably was – she shows here agreeably counters the wan Lady of Signal Sorrows that is Hayley's image in his bland epitaph for her. But she was not to enjoy her new status as Sussex Poet for more than a few weeks. Benjamin, never

quiet for long, soon made English friends in Dieppe. At their suggestion he hired a ruinous château some twelve Norman miles on the
way to Rouen. 'And thither,' writes Mary Hays grimly, 'was Mrs
Smith, with her children, directed to repair.'

*

Looking back from her Normandy exile, she saw the last as a
particularly difficult year: Benjamin's arrest, prison, the loss of her
beautiful house and of that familiar social landscape of friends and
acquaintances whose goodwill she took for granted until trouble
came, and most of them dropped her. Only the two years when her
first son and Benjamin Berney died had brought her closer to breakdown. But having survived the deaths of two children, no mere
financial or social losses could harm her permanently, though rage
still seized her at the thought of Dyer's and Robinson's insults. And
then there was the great irrefutable fact that her poems were published; it was a pleasure nothing could spoil. She wanted to be back
in England to hear what people were saying about them, wanted
letters that would tell her.

Henrietta O'Neill now spent most of the time in Ireland. Charlotte
Collins lived near Midhurst and read all the latest publications; she
was the daughter of a clergyman who had educated two sons of the
Earl of Bolingbroke; later she married the elder and became Lady
Bolingbroke. This may explain Hayley's sarcastic 'veteran': she was
much older than the boy she meant to marry. She and Charlotte were
intimate enough, judging from the concerted attack on Hayley,
for Collins to keep Charlotte informed about sales and readers'
reactions.

Recently Charlotte had been able to talk to Bryan Edwards, but
though he read poetry his real interests were exploration and history.
She had been ill-at-ease in some of their conversations. He was an
advocate of slavery, a subject that made her feel ashamed; the
Abolitionists were to find him a dangerous opponent in the nineties.
He had lived in the West Indies and spoke with all the authority long
residence seemed to confer. Charlotte, without such experience and
married into a planter's family, was far less equipped to oppose him
than Clarkson or Wilberforce. Now she felt confident enough to
write her own experience and her beliefs. She had established,
though tentatively, a presence and a personal history in the sonnets
and she could imagine writing even about her struggles with the
lawyers, or about prison. In fact, she recognised with some amuse-

ment, a background of prison would make her literary persona all the more romantic and all the more saleable. The sardonic vein, missing in her poetry, seldom deserted her in life. She knew she could not have taken the risk of publication, especially at her own expense, without Benjamin's arrest.

So far *Elegiac Sonnets* had not raised as much money as she hoped – the printing had first to come out of her profits – but within a few weeks of arriving in France she would have heard, from Nicholas or Catherine if not from Charlotte Collins, that a second edition was due out before the end of the year. And one of them would surely have sent her an account of *The Monthly Review* of November 1784. Here her reviewer discusses the merits of the Italian form compared to what he sees as the formality and uncouthness of most English sonnets. He is probably referring to Shakespeare and Milton. He goes on, 'Plaintive tenderness and simplicity characterise the sonnets before us.'[54] In the age of Sensibility, these were terms of praise. The opening sonnet, 'The partial Muse', is quoted in full, as is 'The Origin of Flattery', a satire in rhyming couplets after Hayley, described by the reviewer as beautiful, sprightly and elegant. Quotation in full of course marked the incompetence or laziness of the reviewer, but it could make a better advertisement than genuine evaluation. The November *Monthly Review* helped her second edition to sell out too.

She was a woman who always had to have something to read when she sat down: old numbers of *The Gentleman's Magazine*, old farriers' manuals would be better than nothing. She found a few volumes left by previous tenants, all in French, and looked through them without expecting much. One of the dingiest, its edges worn down by fifty years' handling, caught her attention in the first pages. In the November evenings when the children had gone to bed she would wrap herself up to read, by the light of the meagre fire, *Manon L'Éscaut*.

In L'Abbé Prévost d'Exiles' novel, the Chevalier Des Grieux throws away career and reputation for a fifteen year old he meets in an inn yard. Manon sometimes tricks Des Grieux, sometimes other, richer lovers in her pursuit of wealth and security. Writer and reader are on Manon's side all through two volumes. The elderly aristocrat Gevres de Malleville tries to buy Manon. While Des Grieux poses as her country-bumpkin brother, she takes the money and jewels de Malleville hands over, makes the excuse that she needs to use a chamberpot, and the couple slip away. De Malleville gets his revenge by having her sent to prison on a *lettre de cachet*, but Des Grieux rescues her, shooting a prison porter to get her out. Des Grieux's family and friends cannot persuade him to give her up. His irrational passion, her feckless charm are set against the dark background of castles and prisons controlled by a tyrannical aristocracy. She never gets pregnant. Finally she is arrested and transported in chains to New Orleans where Des Grieux follows her and where she dies young, regretting her infidelities and still loved by him. Her death adds the necessary pathos and, as the punishment of vice, the obligatory but unconvincing moral.

For Charlotte the book offered more than a brief escape from her impossible role of caterer and teacher in exile. Prévost's secret sympathy with so wild and criminal a heroine appealed to all the feelings women were brought up to suppress. There was no English novel quite like it. She wondered if she could imitate the understated style, so unlike her own, and do justice to the elegance of the original. She began to make a translation in the evenings, absorbing herself in plot and tone, thinking about phrasing in the day time and writing by firelight when she should have been asleep.

Some things would not do for an English reader. In Prévost's novel Des Grieux, and more surprisingly his respectable friend Tiberge, regard the murder of the prison porter as the mildest of misdemeanours. Tiberge praises the generosity of a priest who sees the killing but will not add to Des Grieux's problems by informing the police. The story is told through first person narrative by a fictional, sympathetic onlooker, and by Des Grieux's narrative, so it is hard to distinguish Prévost's attitude. But it seemed to Charlotte that in France in 1731, and probably still – she remembered the gaunt fierce creatures in the village – the life or death of a peasant was entirely insignificant. But she had to recognise in fairness that this was often the case in England too, that young boys and girls were hanged for stealing a few shillings or a piece of irresistible finery from a market stall. She was careful where she went on hanging days, and never looked at such things. Only the tone of literature was more refined in England, she thought, not the tone of life, the way things were, which was often as cruel as in France. Still, she changed the passage about the porter; he recovers, and her young lovers seriously harm nobody but themselves.

Even more than Prévost she manipulates the reader to take a sympathetic view of Manon, whom we see first in chains on her way to New Orleans, disarming the disapproval we might feel later as her trickery is revealed. Charlotte translates:

> Such was the beauty and elegance of her face and form, that neither the deep depression she appeared to be under, not the dirt and dust with which she was cover'd, could conceal it; and she inspired me at once with pity and respect. While she turn'd from the gaze of vulgar curiosity as much as her chain would admit, there was in her countenance and attitude such an air of dignity and modesty, that it was difficult to believe she could ever have deserv'd the terrible punishment under which she was suffering; and the expression of grief and terror impressed on features delicate, regular and animated, made her the most interesting figure I had ever seen.[55]

The passage in Prévost translated word for word reads:

> Her depression and the dirt of her linen and clothes could so little spoil her appearance that her sight filled me with respect and pity. She remained silent, turning as much as her chain would allow to hide her face from the spectators' eyes. The attempt she made to hide was so natural, it seemed to come from modesty.[56]

Charlotte is warmly expansive where Prévost is effectively spare. This is typical of her *Manon*. The heroine's beauty and elegance, her dignity, her grief and terror, and the vulgarity of the spectators' stares appear only in her version. She has a more palpable design on the reader than Prévost, and more insistently suggests the incongruity of Manon's punishment.

At Christmas some old friends, debt-exiles like themselves, arrived to share the freezing and ill-provisioned castle for a week. Charlotte seized the opportunity to try out her new translation on them. There is no record of what they thought, but she decided that winter to turn her ability, if she survived, to prose fiction. Poetry was far the more prestigious form, but it was largely male-oriented. The novel was often female-authored and sometimes centred on a female consciousness. It also paid better. Frances Burney had made herself famous and eventually rich with *Evelina* in 1778; Charlotte might do the same. *Manon* gave her a plot that delighted her, tired as she was with being always responsible. She knew other women would enjoy it too.

In January she would have begun to prepare for her confinement, sending the children and servants out to scour the outbuildings and country around for burnable wood, old gates or old doors, so one room at least could be kept warm for two or three weeks. Charlotte Mary made baby clothes out of the few petticoats the girls had with them; Charlotte tore old sheets into strips and gathered together extra bedding. The midwife made her way through the snow from Dieppe in a farm cart at the end of the month. It must have felt like the arrival of the executioner to Charlotte. This woman with the English maid and Charlotte's own experience would have to do. Charlotte Mary, her mother was determined, would keep out of the room. Benjamin was quite solicitous in this last month, now it was too late to risk going back. Every evening when the children went off to their makeshift beds, she wondered if she would ever see them again, Catherine records. It was more bitterly cold than ever; the snow was over a foot deep and underneath it the ground too hard even to take a spade.

Something may be guessed about this confinement, from her temperament and altered circumstances. When her waters broke at last, her spirits suddenly rose. With the waiting over she had the battle to fight, and she had never lacked energy. To her surprise the midwife wanted her to walk up and down the room as the pains grew stronger, and in a kind of recklessness Charlotte went along with whatever the woman said. She felt as if she walked miles that night between the fire in the grate and the fire in the window pane against the white outside, trying not to cry out, knowing her eldest daughter was in the passage listening. She went into the last stage more quickly than she expected, and only just had time to get back on the bed before the head was out, then the whole baby, then, to her almost equal relief, the afterbirth. It was a boy; the midwife held him up to Charlotte's eyes in the firelight, then cut the cord, wrapped him and handed him to his mother. His crying filled the room. She wrapped the afterbirth, helped Charlotte squeeze her bladder dry again and pinned her linen carefully round her. She had been extraordinarily kind and deft, Charlotte thought, as she lay back against the thin bolster laughing weakly, while the tears still ran down her face. He was alive and so was she.

The first day was a celebration as she put him to the breast, dozed, and woke each time to the same new sense of safety. When the sheets and mattress were taken away – burn them, she said, to the cook's disbelief – the midwife allowed Benjamin to come in, then the children. A new baby, though no miracle, was always an interest. She and Benjamin agreed to call him George. For Benjamin, conformist in his politics if in nothing else, it was the King's name. Looking out at the frozen snow, remembering the picturesque Claudean landscapes of her first, best drawing teacher, Charlotte was glad to have another

George Smith. Charlotte Mary, the only one of the children who knew how frightened she had been, would not be parted from her and slept in her clothes on the floor beside the bed.

By the following day Charlotte's milk had come in and the baby nursed eagerly. Benjamin set out on horseback to Dieppe for provisions. With the baby tucked into his cradle, a padded desk drawer on the table, and Charlotte Mary asleep beside her, Charlotte slept too; George woke her once in the night, and she fed him then drifted into sleep again in the knowledge of a birth safely over.

When she woke it was light and a strange chanting noise was coming from the passage. The door swung open and a procession of monks, one of them carrying a cross, filed into her bedroom. She could only lie and stare in amazement as they looked closely at her, then in the desk drawer. One of them stepped forward and picked George up while another helped wrap him in a cloak. Charlotte could not believe she was awake. The one holding George addressed her in a dialect she did not understand, then they made to leave, taking George with them. She screamed out loud and swung herself clumsily off the bed, trying to get between them and the door, but she was still bleeding profusely and too weak to stand. Two of them took her arms and lifted her back on the bed, then they all went out; their chanting struck up again as they went down the passage. Attracted by all the commotion the older boys, Augusta, the midwife, and the servants were soon in the room; the boys and Augusta quickly grasped what had happened and with Charlotte Mary ran after the procession. The servants refused to interfere. They explained that the good fathers wanted to baptise George.

Charlotte could hardly take this in. The weather was well below freezing. None of her babies had ever been out of the house in such cold. She begged the servants to bring George back, but it was out of the question, they said, to dispute with the fathers, much less oppose them by force. They left, the cook telling her to calm herself and there would be no harm done. The midwife sat beside the bed to wait with her.

When the children caught up with the procession they realised there was nothing they could do that would not make things worse. William was grown to his full height, Braithwaite and Nicholas were growing fast, but there were at least eight monks. They had waited until Benjamin was out of the house. The boys could not win in a fight, and George might be more damaged than from the cold. They followed the procession, in spite of shouts and gestures from the monks for them to go back, for two or three miles in the snow, through the filthy village until they reached the parish church beside the monastery. Here they waited outside, and after twenty minutes saw the procession emerge again, George audibly still alive. The monks turned towards the castle, and Braithwaite ran ahead to tell his mother they were coming back.

Charlotte was lying as they had left her. She had waited almost two hours before Braithwaite returned, and it was another half hour before George was carried back through the door. A monk handed him to her, smiling with hateful benignity. She hugged the baby to her as the children settled themselves around her.

Benjamin grew sullen when he heard what had happened. He knew the children should return to England when Charlotte was well enough to travel, even if he could not go with them.

In Catherine's memoir, which gives a brief account of this episode, she describes the clerics as priests not monks. In *Emmeline* the Normandy countryside is sparsely populated and only one *curé* is mentioned; this landscape is clearly based on Charlotte's experience. It seems more likely that in a rural area a group of monks from a nearby monastery would arrive together than a group of parish priests. Catherine says only that after George's birth, Charlotte

> was astonished by the entrance of a procession of priests into her bedroom, who, in defiance of her entreaties and tears, forcibly carried off the infant to be baptised in the parish church, though snow was deep on the ground and the cold extreme. As not one of her children had ever been exposed to the external air at so early a period of their existence, she concluded her boy could never survive this cruel act of the authority of the church; he was, however, soon restored to her without having sustained the slightest ill consequence.

But Charlotte took a long time to recover. Her exile and helplessness were brought home to her in the most intimate way when the fathers abducted her baby from her bedroom. There was nothing she could do to punish these bigots, who would rather risk killing George than let him live unbaptised.

*

These six months abroad were critical in the redirection of her life. She could look at her whole history from another perspective. Benjamin cared no more about her than before, despite her going to prison with him, working to release him, and joining him in France.

He took it all as his right. She felt more bitter about that than about his liaisons with the servants. She could scarcely have a harder life than she had endured in the past fourteen months; even going into service would be less exhausting. But there would be no need for such dramatic measures. Her poems would continue to sell, she could add to them, publish her *Manon* translation, write a novel and support the children until Richard's will was settled, when they would have plenty to live on. Charlotte Mary was growing more anxious every day as she watched her father and mother; the other children would be affected too as they saw more of Benjamin in the narrow surroundings of poverty. His violence to herself would intensify, and this was the reason she always gave for the separation. A woman seemed to be defying both God and Nature if she declined to go on reproducing. Austen thought separate bedrooms sensible to reduce the risks her sisters-in-law ran; but she never had to make that claim for herself. Charlotte, though she never says so, was probably determined to avoid a thirteenth confinement. She had been lucky with George, but at thirty-five she had at least ten childbearing years ahead, and she could not be lucky for so long. Her children, if they lost her, would not have even a home to grow up in. Whatever the secrets of her relationship with Benjamin, to stay with him was to have sex with him, and she would no longer risk it. The decision to leave him was probably made before she returned to England. All that remained undecided was when and how to do it.

2
Writing to Live

The three eldest boys, William, Braithwaite and Nicholas, went home first, taking the packet then the stage. They returned to the house at Bignor, and as soon as she was well enough Charlotte followed with Charlotte Mary, the younger children and the luggage, including her almost-finished *Manon* translation. Benjamin stayed in France. She meant to make one more effort to persuade Dyer and the other creditors not to have him re-arrested if he returned. Spring had come by the time she took the packet once more. She felt immensely relieved to be back and yet disoriented too. In *Montalbert* she describes Rosalie's arrival in Chichester after long absence abroad, among familiar sights and sounds again:

> as she passed through that town and sat at the door of the inn, while the horses were putting to, a thousand recollections crowded upon her mind. The objects formerly so familiar to her, brought back the days of Rosalie Lessington, and the strange vicissitudes that had happened since seemed rather like the fictions of romance than reality . . . while she indulged these mournful thoughts she did not venture to show herself, lest she should be known . . . she now rejoiced that she was going a distance from these her old acquaintance, whose notice and intrusion it was improbable she could have escaped had she remained at any place within their reach; a consideration which had confirmed her resolution of going into the eastern part of the county.[1]

But Charlotte could not so easily escape her old acquaintances, with the attendant embarrassments and explanations. That sense of fracture between young and later selves is developed more fully in *The Emigrants*.

She had to go to Brighton to negotiate with creditors, and to London, no longer to a shared single bed in a prison but to lodgings. She seems never to have considered her many journeys, taken alone by the stage, as dangerous or exceptional. Later her daughters too travelled alone without much anxiety, as do her heroines. Perhaps unexpectedly, she was successful in gaining Dyer's agreement to an amnesty. It must have occurred to him and even to Robinson that forcing ten children, their relations, to live abroad in extreme poverty would do them little credit; and Charlotte was no longer merely a bankrupt's wife but a poet with a growing readership sympathetic to her economic problems. So Benjamin came back and joined his family at Bignor.

They did not stay with her brother in Bignor Park House itself, though it was large enough to take so many children easily. Henrietta Meriton Turner had by now married again and was Mrs Chafys, so if she ever lived there with her stepson, she would not have been there still in 1785. But though Nicholas helped Benjamin earlier, he may have begun to see the Smiths' demands as exorbitant. During Benjamin's imprisoment, Mary Hays writes in *British Public Characters*, when many friends fell away, 'her brother only never relaxed in his tenderness and attention towards her, or in such acts of friendship as he had the power of performing towards her husband.' Charlotte must have told Hays this. But once she began to discuss her marriage, her possible claims on Nicholas may have alarmed him. He may have objected to so many children, or thought that once they moved in he would never get rid of them. It is not clear when he married, though by the nineties he had at least one son in his teens. He was an active clergyman, as such things went then, with a parish at nearby Fittleworth, and an occasional writer on agricultural subjects. He probably did not get on well with Benjamin. Each of the siblings, Charlotte, Catherine and Nicholas, had periods of hostility towards the other two.

Charlotte may have confided in her brother an intention to leave Benjamin and live at Bignor Park House again. It would be strange if she did not consider that. She had always loved the place. The law of primogeniture fell hardest on her as the eldest child; her novels attack the injustice of the claims of eldest sons. She seems to have inherited £2,000 to add to her £3,000 dowry on the death of her father, who left Catherine an income from the rents of Bignor Park. But if she moved in without Benjamin, even as a visitor, Nicholas' position would be awkward. He could not be seen to condone separation, legal or informal. Divorce would be still more embarrassing, but luckily for him divorce was out of the question. Charlotte had no grounds for divorcing Benjamin. His infidelities, even if they could be proved, did not constitute grounds, and his violence was not violent enough either. Nicholas evidently intended to keep out of the Smiths' domestic battles as much as possible.

At Bignor she revised her translation of *Manon*. Charlotte Mary
perhaps first took on here what was to be her special job of making
the fair copy of the finished work. Charlotte was ambitious in her
choice of a publisher, and by now had Hayley's guidance. She
decided against Dodsley, who had been so rude about her poems and
from whom she hoped soon to transfer them. Thomas Cadell was
Hayley's publisher and the head of a respected firm that had produced Johnson's *Lives of the Poets* and Gibbon's *Decline and Fall of the
Roman Empire;* he was also a gentleman in manner, which was
important to Charlotte. He accepted the two-volume *Manon* and
printing went rapidly ahead.

These were idyllic times for writers, when a long complex manuscript arrived at the publishers, was hand set in type, back to front,
by the printer's devils, so called because they were often smothered
in ink, and the copies were sewn, bound and could be in the
bookshops six to eight weeks later. It cannot have been so enjoyable
for the typesetters, working against the clock for minimal pay; their
literary intelligence must have been remarkable. *Manon Lescaut, or,
The Fatal Attachment* was in Cadell's shop in the Strand a few months
after her return to England.

Whether the Bignor house proved too expensive, too close to
Nicholas or Catherine, or too small for all the children, the Smiths
soon moved nine miles away to the village of Woolbeding just
outside Midhurst. Sir Charles Mill, a friend from Benjamin's days as
High Sheriff and one of the few Tory county people who kept up the
Smiths' acquaintance, lent them his family house there. Impoverished as she often was after 1784, Charlotte at least made up for her
Cheapside days by living in some of the most beautiful places in
Southern England. Woolbeding House, gold stone and sheltered,
stands next to All Hallows Church with the river flowing through
meadows behind it. Thomas Otway's father had been Rector of the
parish in the 1650s, and Otway grew up in Woolbeding, 'a circumstance', *The Monthly Magazine* says, 'which rendered it classic ground
to Mrs Smith and inspired those beautiful sonnets in which his name
is so happily introduced.' In 'To Melancholy. Written on the banks of
the Arun, 1785' she wrote:

> When latest Autumn spreads her evening veil
> And the grey mists from these dim waves arise
> I love to listen to the hollow sighs
> Thro the half-leafless wood that breathes the gale.
> For at such hours the shadowy phantom pale,

Oft seems to fleet before the poet's eyes;
Strange sounds are heard, and mournful melodies . . .
Here, by his native stream, at such an hour,
Pity's own Otway I methinks could meet . . .[2]

The title, as so often in her *Sonnets*, claims spontaneity for the writing. The speaker is glimpsed in a painterly chiaroscuro, and dissolves into her setting; it is hard to tell who is the poet and who the phantom. Otway's violent, titillating blank verse plays *The Orphan* (1680) and *Venice Preserved* (1682) were popular in their own time and continued to be performed in the eighteenth century. In 'Pity's own Otway' she claims him for the age of Sensibility. He appealed to her as macabre analyst of extreme psychopathologies and as the stricken deer of romantic aesthetics, dying young and destitute in spite of his genius.

At Woolbeding House she added other sonnets to her collection, including free imitations of Petrarch and Metastasio. She renewed her acquaintance with Eliza Hayley, John Sargent and Charlotte Collins. Through Hayley she met George O'Brien Wyndham, Earl of Egremont; to them and other friends and acquaintances she addressed complimentary sonnets, intended to add to the next edition a social context with the graceful amenities of the epistolary poem. But this tone is embarrassing. Her dislike of John Robinson does not seem to have extended to his daughter, or perhaps Charlotte was being diplomatic on her return: her sonnet celebrating the Countess of Abergavenny's wedding anniversary is less inert than others of the type. More interestingly, she began to construct in her sonnets a literary cartography for Sussex as Henry James Pye had done on a larger scale in 'Faringdon Hill', flagging the landscape with poets.

While she was correcting and annotating the third and fourth editions of the *Sonnets*, William, now seventeen, was preparing through Robinson's patronage to leave England for a job with the East India Company in Bengal. The Company had changed since Richard's day. It was no longer so powerful or autonomous but closer to a branch of the Civil Service. Preliminary training was sometimes given in England, and William may have left home the year before; he sailed in February 1786 and arrived in Bengal by the end of that year. As 'writer' his duties were mainly clerical and legal. The position had good prospects of promotion, and William was well-connected as Richard's grandson. But of course the risks were high. Charlotte invested in an expensive version of the medicine chest that travellers to India took as frail insurance against the climate. She had to acquiesce in his leaving; only in the colonies or the army or navy could penniless young men hope to make money. The children were still not receiving the maintenance or allowance for education that Richard had intended. And William was eager to go. He was ambitious, confident, determined not to stay at home as a charge on his parents. He promised he would send money back when he began to earn something above his immediate keep. If Charlotte was anxious, she also had reason to be hopeful for him.

But the reception of her *Manon* translation was disastrous. Living out of literary London as she mostly did, she made the mistake of asking Cadell to send a copy to George Steevens, an editor of Shakespeare and an influential and irascible critic. Steevens strongly objected to its moral tone. Charlotte admits in her prefatory remarks that 'notwithstanding all her errors and failings, the picture of Manon is too captivating'[3] but maintains, like Prévost in the original preface, that the work is moral because the heroine's sins are punished. Steevens was not mollified by this, and of course Charlotte was being disingenuous. The book, as she knew, was capable of disturbing many 1780s readers, but this unfortunately included Steevens.

Catherine comments on this episode in her memoir, and transcribes the letters. As he had already bought a copy, he returned the presentation copy to Cadell, and wrote to the editor of *The Public Advertiser*:

> Sir,
> Literary frauds should be made known as soon as discovered; please to acquaint the public that the novel called *Manon L'Escaut*, just published in two volumes octavo, has been twice before printed in English, once annexed to *The Marquis de Bretagne*, and once by itself, under the title of *The Chevalier de Grieux* – it was written by the Abbé Prévost about 40 or 50 years ago. I am, Sir, your old correspondent
> 'Scourge'

Steevens' letter was fraudulent in itself. Charlotte had never attempted to pretend that her *Manon* was other than a translation, so no plagiarism was involved. But the printer Dennett Jacques, a Chichester associate of both Dodsley and Cadell, was alarmed, and contacted Cadell. He then wrote to Charlotte:

> I have seen Mr Cadell, who was apprehensive that the reviewers would lay hold of this letter, and that such an assertion would be of ill consequence, not only in regard to the sale of the book, but to himself, as the public would consider him as endeavouring to

impose on it, and his reputation might be injured. I take the liberty of repeating this to you, because, as I assured Mr Cadell, the circumstance [that there had been earlier translations] was as unknown to you as to himself. The sale is at present at a stand.

Catherine writes about the matter at length, concerned that her sister 'was severely censured for her choice as immoral.' She claims Charlotte had no choice, confined as she had been in France, 'which induced her to employ a mind qualified for worthier purposes on such a work.' Translation was a form of literary business favoured by women authors, especially as a first step to professional authorship; but it was the more incumbent on a woman to choose an uncontroversial text. Steevens might have been less energetically hostile had there been a man's name on the title page. Catherine was a friend of Charlotte Collins, who also knew Steevens well; when he died in 1800 he left her a legacy of £500. After his death Collins, by that time Lady Bolingbroke, confirmed to Catherine that Steevens and 'Scourge' were identical; he behaved similarly to David Garrick years before, and later to Hayley. Collins showed Catherine a letter from Steevens to herself where he gave his response to *Manon*. It reads, in part:

> I am beyond measure provoked at books which philtre the passions of young people till they admit the weakest apologies for licentiousness; and this story is so managed, that one cannot occasionally withhold one's pity from two characters, which, on serious reflection, ought every way to be condemned.

His reluctant susceptibility to the novel's sex appeal was probably in its backlash responsible for the violence of the letter to *The Public Advertiser*, which effectively strangled *Manon* at birth. Generously, Charlotte wrote to Cadell at once asking him to withdraw the work rather than risk his firm's reputation. A letter from her to an unnamed recipient, probably also Charlotte Collins, soon afterwards, gives a strong sense of her chagrin and embarrassment. She speaks of Steevens' asperity in treating the book as literary poison and confirms she was ignorant of any earlier translations:

> I will venture to say, they are not to be found in any catalogue of the circulating libraries; and perhaps are only known to those who would take the pains to seek after such trumpery.

By that designation she colludes, sadly, with Steevens' and Catherine's view of Prévost's novel. But some copies of her *Manon* were sold in the following year, the two volumes cheaply bound as one and without her name or Prévost's on the title page; this was reviewed in

the *Monthly* by a critic who assumed a male translator; his response
was a more temperate version of Steevens.'

She was tough enough to turn, in the next paragraph of the letter
in which she discusses Steevens' strictures, to plans for a fifth edition
of the sonnets:

> I have the pleasure to add, that the last edition of the *Sonnets* is, as
> Jacques informs me, so nearly all sold, that it is high time to consider
> of another edition, which, however, I shall not do hastily, as I intend
> they shall appear in a very different form as to size and correctness,
> and I think I shall be able to add considerably to the bulk of the
> volume.[4]

She had in mind an edition with illustrations, the considerable
expense to be met by subscription, writing on 3 June 1787 to Cadell
that 'many of my friends and several persons of high fashion' had
suggested this. It was not unusual. Novels as well as poetry sometimes appeared by subscription. She intended that he should be the
publisher; in the next eighteen months she was adding to the collection and encouraging friends and acquaintances to subscribe.

Benjamin spent most of his time in London or abroad again in the
two years Charlotte was at Woolbeding. It was the only way to avoid
the duns, and he had no taste for country living unless as squire on
his own land. So Charlotte was probably alone with the children
when in June 1786, by Catherine's account, most of the Woolbeding
household went down with a sudden 'malignant fever', perhaps
typhoid. As in Cheapside many years earlier, Charlotte was
unaffected. For three or four days and nights she nursed those of the
children and servants who were too ill to get out of their beds. After
thirty-six hours, Braithwaite died. At sixteen, he was the eldest boy
left at home. Nothing is known of him, or of Charlotte's reaction; she
had now lost three sons out of her twelve children, a common enough
occurrence, and no less terrible for that. Her efforts saved the rest,
Catherine says.

She embarked on another translation here, a selection from the
stories in Gayot (or Guyot, as she spelt it) de Pitaval's *Les Causes
Célèbres* (Famous Lawsuits), first published in 1735. It seems likely
she came across this vast rambling work too in the Normandy castle,
and concluding that nobody could have so much use for it as herself,
brought the thirteen volumes back in her luggage. The compilation
is based on real court cases; de Pitaval's narration is often confused
and his French obscure, full of medieval legal terms. Charlotte found
the rewriting tedious, and must have almost despaired when she

thought of the failure of her earlier, more distinguished translation, but she forced herself on and managed to fill three small volumes.

In a prefatory note she explained she had selected from de Pitaval those stories that 'might lead us to form awful ideas of the force and danger of the human passions'.[5] She was trying to cover herself against the charge of circulating immoral French literature again. Leigh Hunt, who later rewrote de Pitaval himself, considered she chose the best stories. They include 'The Pretended Martin Guerre', which is based on a court case in the Basque country in 1539. Martin leaves his wife Bertrande; an identical stranger arrives and lives with her for three years, when Martin returns. Twentieth century reworkings include a play, a musical and two films, the second, *Sommersby*, set in America's postbellum South and starring Richard Gere and Jodi Foster. These versions explore in different ways the situation's psychological and feminist potential. But subtleties like the feminist joke at the heart of *Sommersby* – the anxious impostor tries very hard to please the wife, which is how she recognises the imposture – are absent in de Pitaval's and Charlotte's story. Unlike the Jodi Foster character, Bertrande is a woman of 'timid temper' and 'weak understanding'[6] who is imposed on by everyone. The interest is in the oddity of the circumstance and the unreliability of perception and memory.

Charlotte calls 'The Chevalier de Morsan', a tale of transvestism, 'one of the most romantic stories the various occurrences of life ever produced'.[7] Margaret Charlotte Donc's father dies when she is fourteen and M. Robert, a notary's clerk who has worked for the family, proposes to marry her. Charlotte – for the narrator identifies closely enough to call her Charlotte throughout rather than Margaret – refuses, preferring to enter a convent. She is 'at an age when keen sensibilities made her feel all the misery of such a union', writes Charlotte Smith, adding, 'indeed, who can help shrinking from the view of wretchedness for which there is no remedy, from sufferings which can only terminate in the grave?'[8] Robert carries Charlotte off by force and marries her, but she escapes by dressing as a man and establishing a new identity as the Chevalier de Morsan. She is admired and socially successful, and the pretence is only discovered when she dies.

The narrator shows sympathy or humorous tolerance for all the female characters in unhappy marriages, however criminal they may be. In 'Madame Tiquet', Angelica has 'an understanding of masculine firmness'.[9] When she falls in love with another man, she tries to poison her husband's broth, and when this fails, has him stabbed. The narrator comments that, in Paris, priests

> were constantly shocked with the confessions of women, who acknowledged their having attempted the lives of their husbands; and that, to put a stop to such enormities, which had lately increased to an astonishing degree, it was absolutely necessary to make an example of Madame Tiquet.[10]

Angelica goes unrepentant to her execution, and the narrator comments sardonically that she was unluckier than many women who make similar attempts.

The stories are about the limitation of women's freedom, which was to become a major theme of Charlotte's novels. The law, the church and the aristocracy are more corrupt than those they control. In 'The Marchioness de Gange' the widowed heroine attempts to will her money to her mother rather than to her husband's family. Her brothers-in-law, the Abbé and the Chevalier de Gange, murder her, giving her the choice of sword, pistol or poison. Even by modern standards the murder scene is protracted and painfully detailed. This story was worked into a full length novel, *La Marquise de Gange*, by de Sade. Made to swallow poison, the Marchioness jumps out of the window, is struck by a pitcher thrown by the Abbé, and is pursued and stabbed to death. There is no poetic justice: the Abbé and the Chevalier remain untried and die natural deaths.

As the setting is French, the cruelty of the clergy can be attacked in anti-Catholic England with impunity. Aspects of French law like the *lettres de cachet* and French customs that limited the freedom of young people in their twenties are exposed. De Pitaval is much inferior to Prévost, and Charlotte was not sufficiently engaged with the original to produce her best work. But the stories evidently overlap with her own fantasies and feelings about marriage and the law. She was making apprentice attempts to define and celebrate liberty.

The Romance of Real Life was published early in 1787, and was unexpectedly popular. The marital and family breakdowns analysed in these court cases made absorbing reading, rather like the carnival offered by the tabloids now. She made £330 from the first edition, more than from one edition of any other work. It was enough to support her and the children for eighteen months or so.

Her resolve to separate from Benjamin had been deferred for several reasons: the removal from Bignor to Woolbeding, the need to raise enough money, the failure of *Manon* and the death of Braithwaite.

Benjamin was back in England in the spring of 1787; he had made no attempt to retrieve his position; admittedly it is hard to see what he could have done. Though Dyer had left him alone, he had many other creditors and was still harrassed by duns and unpaid tradesmen, one of them, John Silver of Winchester, threatening to seize even their beds in payment. In his disorganised way he was considering a visit to the West Indies, though he kept changing his mind. He still had relations in Barbados, and he may have wanted to see if the plantations could yield more profit. On 15 April 1887, two months after *The Romance of Real Life* was published, the couple separated, all the children choosing to go with Charlotte. They made an informed if not objective judgement of their parents' merits. The law would have given Benjamin custody in a formal separation. Most of the children were now old enough to recognise that their mother could not be expected to go on living with him. Catherine writes in her memoir:

> An increasing incompatibility of temper, which had rendered her union a source of misery for 23 years [in fact 22], determined her on separation from her husband; and, after an ineffectual appeal to one of the members of her family to assist her in the adjustment of the terms, but with the entire approbation of most of her most dispassionate and judicious friends, she left Woolbeding House, accompanied by all her children, some of them of an age to judge for themselves, and who all decided on following the fortunes of their mother.

Lucy must have been among the judicious friends who supported Charlotte's decision, regretting more than ever her haste so long ago. Discreet as usual Catherine gives no clue as to who failed to secure a legal agreement. Perhaps Charlotte asked Nicholas; it seems unlikely she would ask her lawyer relatives Dyer or Robinson for help. It is not surprising if he refused; he still had to work with his clerical colleagues. So Charlotte left without any legal settlement; Richard's will of course made no provision for a separation. Even when the difficulties were resolved and the money began to be paid, she could expect nothing for herself from his will unless Benjamin predeceased her. But except for Lionel, Harriet and George, born after Richard died, the children would soon start to receive their annuities, she thought, and that would be enough. She usually received £35 each January and July, the interest on her own dowry and bequest from her father, to which she had no direct access. Robinson was her Trustee, and this payment was completely at his discretion. If he decided he did not approve the purpose she wanted it for he would tell her, sneering, to 'exercise her admirable talents'[11] to earn more herself. But with the money from her translation coming in, she could act at last. Catherine writes that

> the summer of 1787 saw Mrs Smith established in her cottage at Wyhe, pursuing her literary studies with much assiduity and delight, supplying to her children the duties of both parents.

Wyhe, now called Wyke, is between Aldershot and Guildford, not far from the Turners' former estate Stoke Place. The area was familiar to her, and she may still have had acquaintances there. A cottage generally meant what we would consider a house rather than, as later, the dwelling of a farm worker.

By now Charlotte Mary was eighteen, well read and thoughtful, her mother's amanuensis. Nicholas was sixteen. He would spend less than a year at Wyke, soon following his brother into the Indian Civil Service, though initially based in Bombay. Charles was fifteen, and at Winchester like Lionel; presumably the sales from *Elegiac Sonnets* had been paying their fees. Charlotte was hoping Charles could take the perpetual avowdson of St Mary's, Islington which had been in Richard's gift. She could not bear to see another son go abroad. He would have to put in the necessary terms at Oxford first, though, and his expensive education would be prolonged. And he did not have £1,000 to pay Charlotte Mary, as Richard's will required. Augusta, now fourteen, was the family beauty and grown up already. Lucy was two years younger and unlike her namesake rather moody and reckless, judging from her later life. Lionel, aged ten, the only one who would be famous in his own right, was inclined to be difficult at school. Harriet was five, and had had little teaching in the last disrupted years. She liked to spend most of her time outdoors. The baby, George, was still Charlotte's favourite; he was '*tout à moi*',[12] she said, all her own, the only one who would scarcely remember Benjamin.

They were a formidable charge on her earning ability, especially as she intended to continue their educations as ladies and gentlemen; the girls would have the same tuition in languages and accomplishments as at Lys Farm, the boys would stay at Winchester. Though now reading radical authors, and soon to style herself pro-revolutionary, Charlotte had no notion of extending levelling principles into her own family. But they were no more her responsibility than they had always been, and they were clever, resourceful children. Except for Augusta, they all had some physical resemblance to Benjamin; she loved them nonetheless, and Catherine suggests her pleasure in reinventing herself as both mother and father.

What might seem to many contemporaries an equivocal and embarrassing position as separated wife and single mother gave her, as well as some regrets at leaving South Sussex, new confidence and energy.'Thirty-Eight', addressed to Eliza Hayley who was a year younger than herself, looks forward to the independent middle-age they ridiculed when they were young:

> In early youth's unclouded scene,
> The brilliant morning of eighteen,
> With health and sprightly joy elate
> We gazed on life's enchanting spring,
> Nor thought how quickly time would bring
> The mournful period – Thirty-eight.
>
> Then the starch maid, or matron sage,
> Already of that sober age,
> We view'd with mingled scorn and hate;
> In whose sharp words, or sharper face,
> With thoughtless mirth we loved to trace
> The sad effects of – Thirty-eight.
>
> Till saddening, sickening at the view,
> We learn'd to dread what Time might do;
> And then preferr'd a prayer to Fate
> To end our days ere that arrived;
> When (power and pleasure long surviv'd)
> We met neglect and –Thirty-eight.[13]

The 'we' is generic of course; at eighteen Charlotte was not so carefree. The verses are perhaps rather directive. Eliza was gregarious and in her husband's view extravagant. She would go to Bath on long visits and refuse to return; she spent much of her time away from home. By now her marriage was very unhappy, as Charlotte knew, though she probably attributed the absences to a silly love of public places rather than to what it really was, an aversion to her husband. The poem, if amusing, is conventional. Several more verses predictably describe the compensations Time brings in wisdom and learning; but the shift into a slightly different verse form makes an effective ending:

> With eye more steady we engage
> To contemplate approaching age,

And life more justly estimate;
With firmer souls, and stronger powers,
With reason, faith and friendship ours,
We'll not regret the stealing hours
That lead from thirty – even to Forty-eight.

It is a sociable poem, but Eliza's problems were beyond easy consolation. Two years later the Hayleys separated permanently.

In September Charlotte began writing *Emmeline* and worked steadily for the next eight months. But the autumn and winter did not pass uninterrupted by Benjamin. He seems to have acquiesced in the separation, and was busy with his Barbados plan. But he kept in touch with Charlotte and his children, and she had to suffer at least one more scene with him at Wyke.

Cadell had published *The Romance of Real Life*; her relationship with him was cordial and he was to publish her forthcoming novel as well as the subscription edition of *Elegiac Sonnets*. In the late eighties she began to correspond with him often and he kept many of her letters. She confided her domestic and financial problems, entangled as they were with her writing life, and a long letter to him is worth quoting fully for what it reveals of her precarious position after the separation. Benjamin was entitled even to the earnings from her writing, and on 14 January 1788, evidently not for the first time, she warned Cadell he might turn up in London and demand them. Benjamin had written to tell her he had already paid for his passage to Barbados and wanted to see the children before he left. She goes on:

> As I could not doubt an assertion so positive and as many of our joint friends to whom he had represented his sorrow at being parted from his 'dear Wife and children' thought I *ought* to comply with this request, I not only assented to it, but instead of sending his children to meet him at the Inn as he suppos'd I should, I hired a post chaise and met him myself at Godalming, desirous not only to convince him I had no malice against him, but to conceal his journey from his numerous creditors in Hampshire and Sussex – concluding he would only stay a day or two and then return to sail for the West Indies.
>
> But I soon found reason to repent my credulous folly. Tho' my house is so small & I have eight children at home & am therefore forced to put a tent bed up in my little Book room, he took possession of it & treated me with more than his usual brutality – threatening to sell the furniture, the Books, and every necessary which I have twice saved from the rapacity of his Creditors. This is the situation I have been in for three weeks; yet I have borne it with patience in hopes of obtaining what I at length got him to do, a deed providing out of my

fortune for his three Younger children born since the death of their Grandfather, who has given to the rest some provision. But within these two or three days a new fit of frenzy has seized him: he has broke open all my drawers where my papers were, taken away several sign'd receipts for the Sonnets (Of which Heaven knows what use he may make) and foul copies of many things I am writing, all of which he has taken with him; and he openly declared a resolution of demanding of you the money You hold of mine.

To day he is gone – to London, & there is reason to suppose may make immediate application to you. I now believe him capable of any thing and therefore, relying entirely on you, beg the favor of you if you have any apprehensions of his having the **power** to take the money that you will be so good as to pay it into the hands of your own Banker or any confidential friend; and on your informing me that you have done so, I will instantly forward to you a receipt in full of all demands. And I am informed that on your producing Such receipt to Mr Smith he can have no power to molest or trouble you. I shall be extremely uneasy till I hear from you or Mr Davies [Cadell's partner] on this matter As he appears careless of every thing & totally regardless of the infamy that must attend such an action. From his own account he is connected with persons in Town, who are engaged in the desperation of gaming houses, and I know not what – & from such a Man so acquainted, I and my family have every thing to fear.

Conscious of having done for him more than any other person on Earth would have done and in this last instance shewn a foolish reliance on his word which I knew worth nothing, I am now firmly resolved never again on any pretence whatever to see him & have no longer the least wish to keep terms with him, & I beg that if he calls at your shop as I find he has already done, you will give him no information whatever As to the Sonnets or any thing else . . .

I hope to hear from you by an early post and Am, Sir, yr obligd & obt hble Sert, Charlotte Smith

In fact Benjamin made no provision for the three younger children, and paid nothing towards the support of any. However distressing such scenes must have been, the separation at last allowed her to speak more freely of her difficulties with him. But it was years before she could allude to some aspects of his behaviour. Much later she accused him in a letter to the Earl of Egremont of 'the most gross violations of morality and decency before his daughters',[14] though she says nothing more specific. She may refer to crude advances to women servants, or guests, in front of his daughters; or to fullscale incestuous abuse – though 'before' rather than 'with' or 'towards' makes the latter explanation the less likely. She felt nothing but relief at getting rid of him.

That relief can still be felt in her first novel's raciness and ease. *Autumn at Wyke* saw the beginning of a long struggle to support herself and her children by writing. She expected then each coming year would be the last when she must 'live only to write and write only to live'.[15] Always before her was the prospect of a comfortable maintenance when the children's annuities began to be paid and she could revert to writing poetry alone, and not for money. As this will o' the wisp retreated the angrier she became but also the more doggedly determined not to be beaten by Dyer, his solicitor Anthony Parkin, Robinson and the allies they made even among her own family and friends. It was to be a struggle as heroic as anything her protagonists went through. She published 63 volumes, often long volumes, of prose fiction, and of poetry and children's books. She added poems to her *Elegiac Sonnets* editions through the nineties and wrote longer meditative blank verse poems, *The Emigrants* and 'Beachy Head', and at least one comedy, *What Is She?*. Her novels, apart from *The Wanderings of Warwick*, run to three, four or five volumes each as of course the longer the novel the more she was paid. Inevitably much of that work must be left unconsidered here, with much contemporary comment on its author in reviews and letters, and with the history of her posthumous reputation.

I will concentrate on her skill as a satirist, as a political commentator on the condition of England. This is I think the most interesting aspect of her fiction and the one that had most influence on later writers. The castles or great houses in each novel will be considered as indicating how she viewed tradition and the possibility of reform or revolution. The development of her ideas about national politics can be traced in the way she constructs her castles: the more radical the novel the more sinister and oppressive its castle. Fictional castles and prisons were also becoming recognisable as codes for a more specifically female confinement; Charlotte herself did much to focus this metaphor.

Her heroes and especially her heroines have a hard time in the ugly, competitive economy she describes. They are unclassed and isolated, unable to adapt to society's demands. They have little to live on and reject the security of a convenient marriage or of work that would contaminate them. The professions are closed as satisfactory vocations for her heroes. She had little respect for lawyers or clergymen, the former being merely the more active parasites, and the army is equally distasteful. Only a lucky, and clearly fictional, last minute legacy can make way for her happy endings: her narratives acknowledge that sensitive feelings are incompatible with success. Sense and reason untempered by strong emotion are the qualities of contrasted characters who have outlived their feelings, who are self-interested, unimaginative and materially successful.

The heroes and heroines are always readers, observers of their times, and often poets. Artistic or musical, with a love of nature, they are inclined to depression and thoughts of death. Often the heroines are actually or apparently illegitimate. Women, Charlotte saw by now, were inherently illegitimate, left out by the law. Strong feelings take effect on their bodies in tears, sleeplessness or faintness. The discourse of Sensibility derived partly from medicine; as John Mullan says, 'the best people become ill, their sensitivities visceral and privatised'.[16] Physical sensitivity to experience is a liability; nevertheless it is inseparable from sexual responsiveness: hence the sexiness always associated with Sensibility. I want to consider how her heroes and heroines embody virtue as feeling.

From the preface of *Elegiac Sonnets* to the end of her career, she made her sorrows a conspicuous subject. She addresses the reader directly in her prefaces, and uses recognisably autobiographical material, often admitting though occasionally denying in the preface that she is doing so. She increasingly focuses on middle-aged rather than on young heroines and makes them resemble herself. The reader who is aware of her age and personal history – and she constantly fostered such an awareness – identifies the author with a character. Making her heroes and heroines poets helps to free them from their fictional contexts and associates them with herself. By writing about the problems of writers, even when they are men, she achieves self-revelation. She encourages us to see her fictions as rooted in the facts of one woman's life, the results of financial necessity, but honest commentaries on the corruption of a society in which writer, heroine and perhaps reader are assumed to be victims. Reflexiveness emphasises didactic intention, suggesting that real solutions are needed for women's problems outside the novels as well as novelistic solutions for problems within them. I will briefly consider the autobiographical material in each novel, the self presentations that are meant to be recognised, the direct address in prefaces, and strategies for making common cause with her readers. Her ironic habit of mind made her a self-conscious writer who manipulates a range of literary stereotypes.

The first three courtship novels have much in common: clever, independent heroines, conflicting family interests, acceptance that marriage is a woman's goal but that she needs to use extreme caution in getting married, a more tolerant attitude to extramarital sex and divorce than is usually found in English novels of the eighteenth or nineteenth centuries, constantly shifting locations including mountain landscapes, and robust radical satire. From *Emmeline* to *Celestina* Charlotte was becoming increasingly radicalised. *Emmeline* questions contemporary patterns of courtship and marriage. *Ethelinde* shows more concern with the strange disposition of the goods of fortune; it is a novel about money. *Celestina* incorporates the French Revolution into its own narrative, and celebrates what seemed the model of a fairer system.

Later in her *Avis Au Lecteur* at the beginning of the second volume of *The Banished Man* (1794), Charlotte included a retrospect of the literary castles she created in the early part of her writing career. She lists them, derisively:

> For my part, who can now no longer build *chateaux* even *en Espagne*, I find that Mowbray Castle, Grasmere Abbey, the castle of Rock March, the castle of Hauteville, and Rayland Hall, have taken so many of my materials to construct, that I have hardly a watchtower, a Gothic arch, a cedar parlour or a long gallery, an illuminated window or a ruined chapel left to help myself. Yet some of these are indispensibly necessary, and I have already built and burnt down one of these venerable edifices in this work, yet must seek wherewithal to raise another.[17]

The last reference is to the Castle of Rosenheim, burnt down by the *sans-culottes* in the first volume of *The Banished Man*. Her self-mocking tone reflects her ambiguous attitude to her profession, half-enjoying her own ingenuity as a craftswoman and half-despising the form. But her comment shows she saw her imaginary castles as central to her fictions. In her first three novels the castle evolves from an impressionistic setting to a political metaphor.

Excepting Horace Walpole's *The Castle of Otranto* (1764) and Clara Reeve's *The Old English Baron* (1778), *Emmeline* is the first work of fiction to take the Gothic Castle as setting for the heroine. Mowbray Castle in Pembrokeshire is a picturesque place for Emmeline to grow up in Wordsworthian freedom:

> On those evenings in summer, when her attendance could for a few hours be dispensed with, she delighted to wander among the rocks that formed the bold and magnificent boundary of the ocean, which spread its immense expanse of water within half a mile from the castle. Simply dressed, (and with no other protection than Provi-

dence) she often rambled several miles into the country, visiting the remote huts of the shepherds, among the wildest mountains.[18]

She has a strong sense of local attachment. Leaving Mowbray Castle, she lingers over what she considers her last sight of it:

> The road lay along the side of what would in England be called a mountain; at its feet rolled the rapid stream that washed the castle walls, foaming over fragments of rock; and bounded by a wood of oak and pine; among which the ruins of the monastery, once an appendage to the castle, reared its broken arches; and marked by grey and mouldering walls, and mounds covered with slight vegetation, it was traced to its connection with the castle itself, still frowning in gothic magnificence; and stretching over several acres of ground: the citadel, which was totally in ruins and covered with ivy, crowning the whole. Farther to the West beyond a bold and rocky shore, appeared the sea; and to the East, a chain of mountains which seemed to meet the clouds; while on the other side, a rich and beautiful vale, now variegated with the mellowed tints of the declining year, spread its enclosures, till it was lost among the blue and barren hills.[19]

She sees nothing except the castle, but the whole scene is precisely described and we can see beyond her preoccupation and set the castle in its context. It is autumn, Emmeline is leaving, the castle is ruinous and we are not sure what importance it is to have in the scheme of the novel. Clearly it *is* important, not part of a quiescent landscape, but alive and vigorous. The verbs are energetic and anthropomorphic. The scene opens itself to 'reading', though Emmeline herself does not read it, through the walls that link monastery and castle, eliciting from the groundplan of the buildings a conceptual connection between medieval church and medieval secular authority still traceable in the society of the 1780s. The cultivated landscape has its enclosures, but the reader's focus has no specific limits, as the picture shades off into the distance. The impression society makes on the landscape is slight and imperma-nent when seen against the sea and the mountains. Such a landscape setting, more striking in 1788 than a scene correspondent to the central figure's mood or situation was to become in the later devel-opment of the novel, draws attention to itself as more than merely 'background'. Questions of the castle's ownership and of its possible renovation implicit in Emmeline's love for her home begin to take on symbolic importance and are linked to Charlotte's presentation of the social map.

The plot turns on questions of Mowbray Castle's ownership and the heroine's identity. Emmeline, apparently poor and illegitimate, is considered by her uncle Lord Montreville an unfit wife for his son, Frederic Delamere, and she is despised by Lady Montreville and her elder daughter. Inevitably it emerges that her parents were married, and she inherits the castle and a large sum of money. Like many eighteenth-century novelists, Charlotte can be absurdly inconsistent in her attitudes to privilege. Eleven years earlier, Frances Burney's *Evelina* successfully introduced the formula: the heroine's illegitimacy and poverty provide the satiric focus for the malice of other characters, who are disconcerted, and the reader's sense of fitness satisfied, when she is found to be the legitimate heiress. Burney's satire is conservative. Aristocratic values and the hierarchy are not seriously questioned. Lord Orville, whom Evelina marries, is the highest ranking person in the novel and a model of courtesy and conscientiousness. It is impossible to make much of a case for the radicalism of Charlotte's first novel either. Emmeline proves herself the heroine by her ability to upstage the most arrogant snobs in her family. When her uncle asks her what answer he should give to the steward Mr Maloney, who has offered to marry her, Emmeline suggests,

> that you are astonished at his insolence in daring to lift his eyes to a person bearing the name of Mowbray: and shocked at his falsehood in presuming to assert that I ever encouraged his impertinent pretentions.[20]

The crumbling castle has its library, and though this is damp and ruinous, and swallows fly in and out of the broken windows, some of the books are worth preserving. Emmeline is an autodidact; as a child she finds 'Spenser and Milton, two or three volumes of *The Spectator*, an old edition of Shakespeare, and an odd volume or two of Pope',[21] and the study of these forms the most important part of her education, after she has been taught to read and write by Mrs Carey. But already, in Charlotte's presentation of Mowbray castle, the library suggests that though the past and the established order of things contain valuable knowledge and wisdom, they also contain obfuscation and dead letters, only fit for the swallows to nest in.

But Emmeline's eventual inheritance of Mowbray Castle brings much needed new ideas and less formal manners to the old order. Kate Ellis points out that Emmeline and the hero Godolphin 'gently displace the undeserving representatives of the old aristocracy',[22] though Ellis considers the castle only as domestic space, as a representation of the family. Even in this first novel the castle should be read as imaging the organisation of the state, which needs rearrangement and new blood. The question of ownership is central to the plots of *Emmeline, Celestina, The Old Manor House*, and *Marchmont*. In *Emmeline*, the – apparently – legal owner Lord Montreville has allowed the building to fall into disrepair and seldom visits it. His son, Frederic Delamere, is flippant about opportunities to improve the estate, referring to the landscaping of Capability Brown when he says

> Upon my soul . . . I already begin to see great capabilities about this venerable mansion. I think I shall take to it, as my father offers it me; especially as I suppose Miss Emmeline is to be included in the inventory.[23]

Neither of them has earned the privilege they take for granted. Emmeline has better judgement and more self-possession than almost any other character in the novel, and this is an innovation. Sophia Western is comparable, but Sophia defers to Mr Allworthy, and the narrator of *Tom Jones* is more knowing than either. Charlotte's are not novels of 'education', of the type where a naive or erring heroine learns about life from an older male mentor. Emmeline needs no mentor, though she has an adviser in her friend Mrs Stafford; and there is no ironic distance between heroine and narrator. Her intelligence and energy make her a suitable owner to inhabit and renovate Mowbray Castle.

The building also functions as an extension of Emmeline's self, her shell and her body. In the early scenes when Delamere arrives, he means to seduce or rape his apparently illegitimate cousin. Charlotte drew on Richardson for scenes and conversations as freely as she drew on Burney. Delamere breaks the lock on her bedroom door in the turret, but she escapes through the winding corridors, which she knows better than he does. The model is Isabella's flight in *The Castle of Otranto*, but the metaphoric correlative of rape is introduced by Charlotte. Though Delamere denies any intention of rape, his violence as he enters her bedroom condemns him. Even the sentence construction is broken:

> The door, however, was locked. Which was no sooner perceived by the assailant, than a violent effort with his foot forced the rusty decayed work to give way, and Mr Delamere burst into the room![24]

Symbolic doors are violently broken in several of her works. In this episode, her Gothic castle becomes a code for physiology. Jane Spencer in *The Rise of the Woman Novelist* makes this point about Mowbray Castle. When Emmeline's retirement

> is broken by her cousin Delamere's inconsiderate courtship, the castle keeps her safe. She escapes from him by running through the dark passages which she knows well and in which he is soon totally lost. At this point in the novel, the impenetrable castle is being used as a symbol for the unviolated heroine.[25]

Mark Madoff in 'Inside, Outside' says that in *The Monk*, Matthew Lewis' Gothic shocker written eight years later, 'a locked room almost always defines a boundary between sexual repression and sexual rapaciousness'.[26] Emmeline's abduction by Delamere is based on Clarissa's by Lovelace, but Charlotte refuses to make her heroine a tragic victim.

When Delamere thinks she has had an illegitimate baby, she is less outraged than we might expect. She is shocked, but also relieved, since his mistake may free her to marry Godolphin, a captain in the navy who appears halfway through the novel after her conditional engagement to Delamere. Charlotte breaks the novelistic etiquette that a virtuous heroine must marry the first person she seriously considers as a husband, an innovation felt to be dangerous by some readers. They saw it as the thin end of the wedge. The heroines talk racily, and can laugh at their own heroic attitudes. When Emmeline is pursued by three eligible suitors, which was to become Charlotte's standard number, she remarks to Lord Westhaven:

> 'it is my fixed intention, if I obtain, by your Lordship's generous interposition, the Mowbray estate, to retire to Mowbray Castle, and never to marry at all.' Lord Westhaven, at the solemnity and gravity with which she pronounced these words, began to laugh so immoderately, and to treat her resolution with ridicule so pointed, that he first made her almost angry and then obliged her to laugh too.[27]

To remain single is ludicrous, however clearly Charlotte saw the abuses inherent in eighteenth-century marriage. She differed from Wollstonecraft, who ended her first novel with her heroine longing for a state where there is neither marrying nor giving in marriage. In a letter to a friend, Sarah Rose, on 15 June 1804 Charlotte was still regretful about the marriage-chance she had wasted when she was sold 'in my early youth or what the law calls infancy.'

That waste is revisited in the narratives of Lady Adelina and Mrs Stafford. Adelina, Goldophin's sister, is married off very young to Trelawny because her father is going to marry a rich and disagreeable grocer's daughter. It is of course Charlotte's story pushed a rung up the social ladder into the peerage. Trelawny is a racing man and a heavy drinker. Adelina has to endure his boorish relations; he soon loses interest in her, and she spends much of her time alone. The couple go to Ireland to visit her sister who is married to that rare bird in the English novel, an exemplary Irish peer, Lord Clancarryl. He and his wife sound like idealised versions of John and Henrietta O'Neill, and their beautiful house beside Lough Carryl, reconciling traditional and modern styles, like the O'Neills' Shane's Castle beside Lough Neagh. Charlotte may have visited her friend there before the crash in 1783. The Clancarryls have an exemplary domestic life, though we do not see much of it.

Coming back from Ireland Trelawny is so callous Adelina admits her love for her libertine admirer FitzEdward, who has been waiting his chance for some time, and who looks after her when her husband's crazy behaviour results in bankruptcy and the loss of her house; she manages to save a few valuables and leaves just ahead of the bailiffs. She gets pregnant by FitzEdward, and Emmeline and Mrs Stafford help her to have her baby in secret. Unusually for an eighteenth century novel, she does not die, though she goes mad for a while. She recovers in time to marry FitzEdward after her husband's convenient death.

Though *Emmeline* was very popular, this thread of the narrative worried more readers than the broken engagement. Mary Wollstonecraft had just lost her job as a governess, returned to London and begun reviewing, anonymously as was the custom then, for a new magazine the radical publisher Joseph Johnson had launched, *The Analytical*. She wrote of Adelina's seduction, despair and eventual marriage to her lover:

> we must observe, that the false expectations these wild scenes excite, tend to debauch the mind, and throw an insipid kind of uniformity over the moderate and rational prospects of life, consequently adventures are sought for and created, when duties are neglected and content despised. We will venture to ask any young girl if Lady Adelina's theatrical contrition did not catch her attention, while Mrs Stafford's rational resignation escaped her notice? Lady Adelina is indeed a character as absurd as dangerous ... Mrs Stafford, when disappointed in her husband, turned to her children.[28]

Wollstonecraft's own spectacular departures from the moderate and rational were still to come, but she is of course fighting herself here as well as Charlotte. She is funny and accurate about the melodramatics of the Adelina episodes, the

> hair freed from its confinement to shade feverish cheeks, tottering steps, inarticulate words, and tears ever ready to flow, white gowns, black veils and graceful attitudes.[29]

But it was Mrs C. Stafford whom readers identified with Charlotte. She is married to a husband who sinks into debt as a result of gambling and pointless improvements to his house. She is reluctant to complain about him, but her unhappiness is evident to Emmeline. Mrs Stafford's loss of Woodfield, her humiliating negotiations with the creditors and the Staffords' escape to Normandy closely parallel the Smiths' experience. Mrs Stafford rejects while Adelina accepts FitzEdward's advances; Charlotte was to use this schematic doubling throughout her career. Only Mrs Stafford's love for her children keeps her from taking the path Adelina takes. The reader is invited to sympathise with both, the knowing reader with the author's marital unhappiness and decision to separate. Charlotte's tolerant attitude to her fallen woman has something in common with the earlier, robust views of Fielding. Most of the women in *Tom Jones* are fallen, and survive. But her complicit tone is quite different from his ebullient Toryism. In *Emmeline* she questions marriage as lifelong sacramental institution: it should not have to be, if it has been engineered by the wife's family, or if the husband breaks his promises.

The poet Anna Seward, 'The Swan of Lichfield' as she was known, and one of Hayley's Muses, was more indignant about the novel than Wollstonecraft. Charlotte was now a favourite Muse, to Seward's annoyance, and she wrote to Eliza Hayley in a letter obviously meant for Hayley too:

> I have always been told that Mrs Smith designed, nay that she acknowledges, the characters of Mr and Mrs Stafford to be drawn for herself and her husband. Whatever may be Mr Smith's faults, surely it was as wrong as indelicate, to hold up the man, whose name she bears, the father of her children, to public contempt in a novel. Then how sickening is the boundless vanity with which Mrs Smith asserts that herself, under the name of Mrs Stafford, is 'a woman of first rate talents, cultivated to the highest possible degree'.[30]

While allowing that Charlotte was 'a fine woman in her person'[31] she also despised the 'everlasting lamentables . . . [and] hackneyed scraps of dismality'[32] of *Elegiac Sonnets*. But Wollstonecraft and Seward were in the minority. The *roman à clef* aspect of *Emmeline* was especially intriguing, as Charlotte knew it would be, providing fiction and autobiography in one and a forum where she could defend herself.

In her sonnets, as we have seen, her poetic persona is sensitive and melancholy; in *Emmeline* she gave the traits of her sonnet speaker to some of her characters. They are poets whose verses are transcribed in full and who are therefore partially freed from the narrative and associated more closely with the author. But as characters, they are set in a social context examined with irony and contempt. Charlotte tried to fuse sentiment and satire in her fiction and the attempt is interesting even if the fusion does not always hold. As each new edition of *Elegiac Sonnets* was published in the late eighties and the nineties, it gathered in poems from the novels. Adelina's sonnet catches the scenic pre-Turneresque light and shade readers by now associated with the author:

> Far on the sands, the low, retiring tide,
> In distant murmurs hardly seems to flow,
> And o'er the world of waters, blue and wide,
> The sighing summer wind, forgets to blow.
> As sinks the day-star in the rosy West,
> The silent wave, with rich reflection glows;
> Alas! can tranquil nature give **me** rest . . . ?[33]

Emmeline, the Orphan of the Castle was published in April 1788. The first edition of 1500 copies sold out at once, and a second was hastily prepared. Cadell voluntarily paid Charlotte more than he had agreed; and she made more than £200 from the first edition, fifty guineas a volume, and from the two further editions about £40 each. Later, in the nineties, Ann Radcliffe made £900 from *The Italian* and Burney £3,000 from *Camilla*, but these sums were exceptional. Charlotte was never so well paid, though if one takes into account the many reprinted and foreign editions, she sold more copies. Reviewers in *The Critical, The Monthly* and *The European* magazines praised the book, as did more eminent judges. Sir Walter Scott looking back in 1821 to his teens reminisced:

> We remember well the impression made on the public by the appearance of *Emmeline, or* [sic] *The Orphan of the Castle*, a tale of love and passion, happily conceived, and told in a most interesting

manner. It contained a happy mixture of humour, and of bitter satire mingled with pathos . . .[34]

Sir Egerton Brydges and Hayley praised its freshness and originality. She sent a copy to William and one for his senior officer in Bengal, and after the endless wait attendant on all correspondence with India, had the pleasure of hearing he had been promoted; she was always convinced that this was due to *Emmeline*.

She had broken off the writing to visit London on Trust business several times in the previous eight months. Once the novel was out she took a holiday with the O'Neills at their house off Portland Place, meeting new people as a celebrity at Henrietta's parties for her. Here she probably first met Georgiana Cavendish, Duchess of Devonshire, whose novel *The Sylph* was published ten years earlier in 1779. It is a lively and inventive if not especially witty study of aristocratic manners, with a strong reformist streak; she published anonymously, and her poems, which included 'The Passage of the Mountain of St Gothard' were as yet known only in manuscript. She had bought votes with kisses for Charles James Fox and the Opposition in the borough of Westminster in 1784. She and Charlotte evidently took to each other. Charlotte also met some of the society or literary people who were subscribing to the fifth edition of her *Sonnets*, including Elizabeth Montagu's Blue Stocking circle, which she thought formal and boring. She spent part of the time talking over possible illustrations for *Elegiac Sonnets* with Cadell. Though nothing had come of her meetings with the Trust lawyers, she could feel she had retrieved some of her family's former position by her own efforts.

One of *Emmeline*'s most passionate readers was a twelve year old called Jenny, who lived near Basingstoke. She was as intellectually precocious as Charlotte had been, and had no problems with the novel's vocabulary and complex sentences. She raced through it, desperate to find out if Emmeline would marry the impetuous Delamere or her more rational though devoted Godolphin. She was disappointed when Emmeline preferred Godolphin, and angry when the novel killed Delamere off in a duel at the end. Her brothers laughed about the craze, but she did not forget him. Two years later she was writing an alternative History of England in protest against Oliver Goldsmith's dull school history. Royal favourites, gay or straight, were sufficiently unsuitable subjects. She makes an atrocious 'carpet' riddle out of Robert Carr as James I's pet. Thomas Seymour, reputedly the young Elizabeth Tudor's first favourite, would she

knows have felt honoured to be beheaded had he known it would be
the fate of Mary, Queen of Scots. She runs on:

> This Man was on the whole a very amiable Character and is some-
> what of a favourite with *me*, tho' I would by no means pretend to
> affirm that he was equal to those first of Men Robert Earl of Essex,
> Delamere or Gilpin.

Gilpin was William Gilpin, whose *Observations Relative to Picturesque
Beauty Made in the Year 1772, On Several Parts of England, particularly
the Mountains and Lakes of Cumberland and Westmoreland* qualify him
for this company. All three men are inclined to rulebreaking and
romantic excess, Essex as courtier, Delamere as fictional suitor and
Gilpin as aesthete. In her 'Reign of Elizabeth' Jenny writes:

> This unfortunate young Man [Essex] was not unlike in character to
> that equally unfortunate one Frederic Delamere: the simile may be
> carried still farther, and Elizabeth the torment of Essex may be
> compared to the Emmeline of Delamere.

She is mocking the strained analogies of moralistic history, but she
did in fact prefer the wild and romantic to the prudent then, loving
Mary Stuart and hating Elizabeth Tudor.

Encouraged by her success, Charlotte planned another courtship
novel, *Ethelinde, or the Recluse of the Lake* which she began as soon as
she returned to Wyke. She was also working on a comedy, perhaps
the one that was eventually performed in 1799, *What Is She?* Charlotte
Bolingbroke had for the last two or three years been encouraging her
to leave the plangent nightingales alone and draw on the wit apparent in her conversation, though seldom in her poems, to write plays.
After a career as an actress Elizabeth Inchbald had begun in the
eighties to write or translate plays on social or 'problem' themes such
as unmarried motherhood, divorce and crime. Her *Such Things Are*
of 1788 contains a portrait of the prison reformer John Howard; her
best known play was to be a translation of August von Kotzebue,
Lover's Vows. Charlotte was evidently interested. There is little
dialogue in *Manon* or *The Romance of Real Life*, while *Emmeline's*
dialogue is pointed and extensive.

She discussed the demands of dialogue with Hayley and perhaps
with the elder George Colman, playwright and manager of the
Haymarket. While she was working on *Ethelinde* she wrote a scene
for Hayley describing an unexpected visit from John Lane of the
Minerva Press, who published and supplied what she considered
trumpery novels to the proliferating libraries that even small towns

now boasted. Her playful and plaintive tones are perhaps too easily elicited by Hayley's manner to his Muses. 'As you love a dialogue,' she begins, 'here follows one that passed this morning':

> Scene. *The poor novelist at her desk just about a chapter of Ethelinde. Enter her servant.*
> Ser: 'A gentleman wants you Ma'am below.'
> 'A gentleman! who is it? anybody of this place?' for I had seen from the window a vulgar fat man and heard a consequential rap.
> 'I don't know Ma'am, but I believe it is a stranger.'
> 'Ask his name & business.'
> *Exit servant. Enter again.* 'Ma'am, he says he can't leave his name or business but must speak with you.'
> I now concluded it was some dun on account of T. with which I have been so repeatedly plagued and harassed, and submitting to the interruption as patiently as I could, I went down with sad civility and an aching heart.
> *Scene the Parlor. A consequential red-faced pert looking Man Solus: Enter to him the unfortunate novelist.*
> Man: 'Madam! your obedient – my name is Lane – I hear you are writing a novel.'
> 'Well, Sir, sit down, Sir. Mr Lane the bookseller?'
> 'At your service, Madam. Novels are – as perhaps you know – quite my forte and, understanding you are about one, I called to know if you are disposed to deal for it!'
> Novelist: 'Whatever may be my intention, Sir, as to disposing of it, I am and have long been engaged to Mr Cadell.'
> 'I assure you Madam that – no disparagement to Mr Cadell – you wld not be hurt by giving him up for me. I will venture to say that where he will give you one hundred pounds, I will give you two.'
> 'I have no reason, Sir, at present to complain of Mr Cadell, nor any intention of leaving him.'
> 'Well, Ma'am, but the thing is this. Mr Cadell has made a great fortune. Now I have a fortune to make & for that there is reason d'ye see, I would give you twice as much as he will; by reason that a novel of yours just now would be worth any money to me.'
> 'I cannot listen Sir to any proposals for that in question, it is already disposed of.'
> 'I am very sorry to hear it. I hoped I might have got the preference – what you have enter'd into an agreement with Mr Cadell? I hope you have made a good bargain. Why I am told now that he gave you but £60 for the *Orphan of the Castle*.'
> 'You have been misinformed, Sir. The copyright of that is my own.'
> After a few more very impertinent enquiries & professions on his part, & what I thought necessary hauteur on mine, he departed,

but in about half an hour, a servant in a fine laced livery came
with a letter thus –

Madam –
Understanding the copyright of the Orphan of the Castle is yours,
wish to treat for 100 copies of same, as in consequence of my
extensive dealings & supplying all the libraries, can put them into
extensive circulation & will deal on such terms as you will find
advantageous & wait on you immediately as I leave the place at four
o'clock. Any future production in the novel way, flattered to be
remembered, which will oblige
your humble sevnt Willm Lane

Answer

Sir,
The copyright of *Emmeline* is mine. But I leave to Mr
Cadell the sale & all trouble & expense. On applying to him, you may
I apprehend have any quantity of the 3rd edition when it is published.
I have at present not the least intention to change my publisher,
having found Mr Cadell hitherto equally liberal & respectable.
I am , Sir, yr ob Sr C S.

There is something highly in character in this **dealer** in wit. He would
make a glorious figure in the farce we were talking of. But I am such
a proud fool that I feel humbled & hurt at being supposed liable to
his negociations & felt then all in a tremble about it. Somebody I
apprehend has told him how cruelly I want money, & he thought my
poverty wld make me eagerly grasp at his offers, & finding the first
fail, thought I cld not resist 40 or 50£ for 100 copies of Emmeline, by
wt means he cd get a sort of hold on me. But I think I have done right
in repulsing forever his pert advances. Alas! how unfit I am for the
common intercourse of common life, & how very unfit for all I am
forced to encounter.

The letter is headed only 'Friday evening', but is probably from the
autumn of 1788 after the second edition of *Emmeline*, when Lane
would have had time to consider its success and decide on outbidding
Cadell for the next novel. Clearly publication had not brought
financial security for the author.

The reference to 'T' is obscure, but he is probably a shopkeeper or
tradesman determined to be paid. Debts and duns were to remain as
much a part of her life as in the days of Nicholas and Benjamin.
Though she thought she was frugal, she was incapable of living like
a woman brought up to poverty; she spent, for instance, at least £40
a year on meat alone, justifying the expense by the common belief

that meat was necessary for growing children. She took it for granted that 'everyone' had a cook, a personal maid and two or three other servants.[35] As the publisher Joseph Johnson, driven to unusual asperity, later pointed out, her income would have been ample for most women, that is, for those not brought up to affluence. Johnson was remembering the careful management and few indulgences of the Everton farming family he came from. Charlotte found it hard to lower her standard of living.

And though she is worried by the dun, she is not as worried as she might be. Since she was known to be living apart from her husband, she could herself be liable to imprisonment for debt, though no tradesman would commit her without warning or without losing other customers' goodwill. But that Friday evening she was absorbed only in catching Lane's idiom, in making her reader cringe sympathetically with her at the class confrontation. She succeeded with Hayley; though the original letter is lost, he took the trouble to copy it out in his own hand.

The £180 she made, on Stanton's estimate, by the fifth, subscription edition of *Elegiac Sonnets* did a little to ease her financial problems. It was a beautifully produced and much admired volume, appearing on New Year's Day 1789. The 815 subscribers are listed at the beginning. They are family and friends, constellations of the nobility headed by the Duchess of Cumberland and of the clergy including the Archbishop of Canterbury. John and Henrietta had co-opted substantial sections of their families and the Irish peerage, and subscribed for a handsome ten copies each. Among distinguished literary women were Frances Burney, Elizabeth Carter and Mary Delany; the actress Sarah Siddons, voice coach to the Royal children, subscribed for two copies.

Five illustrations were added to this edition, the two most striking by Thomas Stothard. He was one of the finest illustrators of the eighties and nineties, adept at catching the mood of a text. The picture for one of the Otway sonnets is excessively cute; even at five, the approximate age of the child in the drawing, Otway probably looked less wholesome than this. The style is a comment on Charlotte's prettification of him into the sentimental phantom of the Arun. But Stothard's picture for 'On some rude fragment of the rocky shore' admirably catches this poem's and the whole volume's construction of Sensibility. Hayley urged Romney to contribute a drawing, and the picture may be based on a Romney design.

Blake, John Flaxman and Thomas Stothard were friends and drew together in the evenings in the early 1780s. Blake later wrote in one of his bitter epigrams:

> I found them blind, I taught them how to see
> And now they know neither themselves nor me.[36]

There is indeed a certain resemblance to Blake in the drapery. An elegantly dressed young woman, clearly a heroine, sits on the seashore. Behind her the storm is driving a ship onto rocks. She holds a book open in her hand, like the reader of *Elegiac Sonnets*, but her gaze is neither on the threatened ship nor on her book, but turned inward on her own sadness. The book held in the hand links reader with pictured heroine, herself the projection of Charlotte inside her volume.

One of her finest and most frequently anthologised sonnets, 'Written in the church-yard at Middleton in Sussex', first appears in this edition:

> Press'd by the Moon, mute arbitress of tides,
> While the loud equinox its power combines,
> The sea no more its swelling surge confines,
> But o'er the shrinking land sublimely rides.
> The wild blast, rising from the Western cave,
> Drives the huge billows from their heaving bed;
> Tears from their grassy tombs the village dead,
> And Breaks the silent sabbath of the grave!
> With shells and sea-weed mingled, on the shore
> Lo! their bones whiten in the frequent wave;
> But vain to them the winds and waters rave;
> **They** hear the warring elements no more:
> While I am doom'd – by life's long storm opprest,
> To gaze with envy on their gloomy rest.[37]

This apocalyptic Gothic goes well beyond the plaintive. The persona is fated, world weary and looks on death without flinching. Though 'Romantic' is almost meaningless as a term to label a shifting but always large group of disparate writers, never used to designate a literary period in the time to which it is applied, she is Byronic here. It was on this poetic persona that he drew for *Childe Harold*; she cleared the way for the pageant of his own bleeding heart, displayed for all Europe.

Ethelinde is more sombre than *Emmeline*, and shows wider reading in its analysis of late eighteenth century capitalism and Imperial ambition. The drift from the country into urban industry was, or at least seemed to be, accelerating. Charlotte was just over twenty when she first read Goldsmith's *The Deserted Village*. It is an elegy for a lost, idealised rural community, attacking the enclosures and new industrial money of the mid-century and the depopulation of rural areas. Goldsmith's lines on the systemic degradation of the working class are often quoted, never out of season:

> Ill fares the land, to hast'ning ills a prey,
> Where wealth accumulates, and men decay:
> Princes and lords may flourish, or may fade;
> A breath can make them, as a breath has made;
> But a bold peasantry, their country's pride,
> When once destroyed, can never be supplied.[38]

By the time Charlotte was thirty-eight, her own family was unclassed; William and Nicholas had left England for a profession she could only regard as legalised looting; it was quite uncertain whether they would ever return. Goldsmith's 'Far, far away, thy children leave the land'[39] had its personal resonance now.

But William Cowper's *The Task*, published in 1785, had a greater influence on the ideas traceable in *Ethelinde*. It is both intimate and civic, a meditation in six books on contemporary England and its breaks and continuities with the past. In 1793 she was to dedicate her own long blank verse poem *The Emigrants* to him, claiming she had read *The Task* almost incessantly from its first publication, and perceptively praising what she described as 'the felicity, almost peculiar to your genius, of giving the most familiar objects dignity and effect'.[40] Cowper too established a vulnerable personal presence inside his poem, a hint of his recurrent madness; for him, Christ is the healer:

> I was a stricken deer, that left the herd
> Long since; with many an arrow deep infixt
> My panting side was charg'd, when I withdrew
> To seek a tranquil death in distant shades.
> There was I found by one who had himself
> Been hurt by th'archers. In his side he bore,
> And in his hands and feet, the cruel scars.[41]

Here, and in his intransigent judgement on 'fallen' women, Charlotte could not follow. But his pithy, quirky celebration of rural pleasures, walks, plants and conservatories, his praise of liberty, his indignation at slavery and colonial exploitation made him an admired friend before she met him.

France, the old enemy, was increasingly the subject of English curiosity and *Schadenfreude* as its fiscal problems grew more desperate and its court supposedly more disreputable through the eighties. Cowper contrasts its judicial system with England's in his description of the innocent Bastille prisoner who makes a friend of a spider and counts the door studs to pass his time. He apostrophises the Bastille melodramatically:

> Ye horrid towers, th'abode of broken hearts;
> Ye dungeons and ye cages of despair
> That monarchs have supplied from age to age
> With music such as suits their sov'reign ears –
> The sighs and groans of miserable men!
> There's not an English heart that would not leap
> To hear that ye were fall'n at last . . .[42]

These were patriotic English sentiments in 1785, though not for long. But he comments quite as sharply on the irresponsibility of the English ruling class and the sense of impending disaster felt by ordinary people, most of them of course without a vote:

> 'Tis therefore many, whose sequester'd lot
> Forbids their interference, looking on,
> Anticipate perforce some dire event;
> And , seeing the old castle of the state,
> That promis'd once more firmness, so assail'd
> That all its tempest-beaten turrets shake,
> Stand motionless expectants of its fall.[43]

This metaphor of the state as a castle was to be given greater point and currency by Burke; but already Charlotte was beginning to make fictional castles centres of good and bad social organisation.

She uses her description of buildings more programmatically in *Ethelinde* than in *Emmeline*. There are two Gothic houses, two moral poles around which the novel is organised, though the scheme is complicated by the contrasted settings of the King's Bench Prison and the bourgeois household of the Ludfords, near Bristol. The first Gothic castle in the novel, Grasmere Abbey, is unlike her other Gothic houses. *Ethelinde* begins and ends at Grasmere; the Abbey is described in detail and as if in the process of assimilation into the landscape, with apple trees growing out of its buttresses. The surrounding Cumberland scenes and particularly Grasmere Water are described with a landscape painter's imagination.

There is no dispute about the Abbey's ownership; it belongs to Sir Edward Newenden, and is not a symbol of England's social system, but a refuge for those characters, Ethelinde, the hero Montgomery and Sir Edward himself, who are disgusted with what English society has become. Lady Newenden finds its temperature hard to bear, used as she is to the comforts of London, and her servants with their 'London assurance'[44] are appalled by its inconvenience. S.R. Martin writes:

> Charlotte Smith is still a good way from a 'symphonic' integration of nature, character and action, with landscape a continuous thread in the fabric of the novel contributing constantly to its tone. The Lake District descriptions come at the beginning of the first and towards the end of the final volume, but there are huge stretches in between of domestic and satirical material in which CS ignores the 'setting'.[45]

But Mrs Montgomery, the hero's mother, remains in her cottage beside Grasmere, and hero and heroine think longingly of the landscapes there or reminisce about them frequently. It is by contrast with Grasmere that the urban or social settings appear so sordid and unjust.

The second Gothic castle, the place of authoritarianism and hierarchy, is Abersley, the house owned by Lord Hawkhurst, Ethelinde's uncle, which she visits towards the end of the novel. Here Lady Hawkhurst invites Mr Harcourt to dinner to give her elder daughter Arabella a chance to entrap him, Ethelinde's brother Harry continues careless and contemptuous towards her and she feels an unwelcome intruder in the house where her father grew up. As the sun goes down, she finds in a remote apartment dark wainscotting, an arras, family pictures including one of her father, and old stone-framed windows through which she glimpses the family mausoleum where her father lies buried, half hidden by a rookery of elms.

Charlotte effectively deploys these Gothic trappings, not then hackneyed as they became later, to provide a single symbol for all the threats she has created for her heroine in the previous four volumes: the vulnerability to the blows of 'the world', the hostility of most of her family, poverty and confinement. She sets a scene where at her lowest point of anxiety and distress Ethelinde is struck by lightning as it flashes through an open window. This is how de Sade's heroine in *Justine or the Misfortunes of Virtue* (1791) dies: not only the social world but nature itself is the enemy of virtue. Though Ethelinde does not die, the lightning bolt marks her as a passive victim. The heroine never returns in triumph to Abersley, the home of her ancestors, and there is no sense of a possible rejuvenation of the old order, as there is in *Emmeline* and *Celestina*.

The concern with the provision of money for the hero and heroine is inseparable from Charlotte's analysis of society's economic basis. There is an interesting scene where the heroine's brother leaves for the West Indies and her fiancé for the East Indies on the same morning. Charlotte emphasises the cruelty of Empire even to its administrators; men leave their families for years or forever to pursue corrupting avenues to wealth, and often to die abroad. To some writers inherited money looked by contrast clean and enviable.

Perhaps more than in any other novel until George Gissing's *New Grub Street* (1891), anxiety about money is the theme. The seclusion and simplicity of the Montgomerys' Lake District cottage is a tempting solution, but to marry Ethelinde and have children Montgomery needs a larger establishment. He states the problem halfway through the novel:

> The peasant that traverses these bleak hills, and retires at night to his clayey and thatched cottage, is to me an object of envy. Alas! as I sat by the scanty embers of the shepherd's fire those two nights when you lay so ill in the adjoining cabin, how did I wish that we had both been born to a destiny as humble as his, and that even now you could learn to prefer the quiet comfortable cottage on the border of Grasmere Water, to long long years of separate misery, terminated perhaps by death, perhaps by affluence, for which we may find too late that happiness and health have been sacrificed.[46]

Montgomery is willing to risk loss of status for love, and finds competitive capitalism destructive of self-respect. But in the judgement of Mrs Montgomery and Ethelinde herself, young people must postpone marriage until the children's future can be provided for. Montgomery goes to the East Indies, but finds successful colonial adventurism incompatible with his sympathy for the Indians. The problem of ethical money-making is never seriously resolved, and of course it cannot be. As Charlotte knew by now, it was all tainted money.

Only a lucky prepossession for Ethelinde on the part of a rich and late-discovered relative of Mrs Montgomery provides enough for the couple, and the novel can end happily. A similar *deus ex machina* appears at the end of several later novels. A fudged happy ending is not unusual in the novels of the 1780s and 90s: we find it even in Bage's *Hermsprong*. Sir Walter Scott said of Charlotte's endings:

The hasty and happy catastrophe seems so inconsistent with the uniform persecutions of Fortune through the course of the story that we cannot help thinking that adversity had exhausted her vial, or whether she had not further persecutions in store for them after the curtain was dropped by the authoress.[47]

The reader is aware of the unlikelihood of the resolution, when the wealthy relative dies or the abandoned orphan turns out to be a legitimate aristocrat. The endings are in fact so unlikely that they make no attempt to deceive us: these are fictions, Charlotte implies, so the conventional endings do not compromise the exposure of poverty and social injustice. Her resolutions are obviously factitious, but the problems are honestly explored. And in her most sophisticated novels, *The Old Manor House* and *The Young Philosopher*, closure is entirely self-conscious.

In *Ethelinde* she emphasises the hero's and heroine's need for money rather than, as in *Emmeline*, the heroine's disdain for money and rank. Ethelinde is a more mature and socially conscious woman than Emmeline, and she can muse on injustice as Emmeline does not. The criticism of society is more explicit and central. The concern Ethelinde feels for the poor reflects the author's own view of the social order. Her thoughtfulness to servants saves her when she is in danger of rape by the drunken Tom Davenant, and two of Davenant's grooms risk their jobs to help her escape. But in the first two novels Charlotte idealises the servant or peasant class only occasionally: the shepherd wattling his cote whose help Montgomery tries to enlist when Ethelinde is thrown from her horse and concussed is not an example of simple rustic kindness. He is as unfeeling as his social superiors.

Ethelinde is Charlotte's most appealing novel in its depiction of Sensibility as a love for sublime and healing scenery. Charlotte creates in Grasmere an early-romantic Eden far from London's debased social world, though London comes to Grasmere. Ethelinde is the most sensitive of the three early heroines, the most pained by the world's vulgarity and in the Lake District she is placed in a sympathetic context that delighted the contemporary reader. It is possible Wordsworth eventually came to Grasmere by way of *Ethelinde*. He took Dove Cottage on an impulse, but he may well have been remembering consciously or unconsciously the white cottage with its square walled garden a little apart from the village, where Montgomery and his mother live. Later still he was to complain that tourists were interested only in the location of Grasmere Abbey.

Humorous peasants would point out unfinished sheepfolds as its ruin, presumably in the hope of a tip.[48]

The Abbey and its environs create a moral and emotional not just a physical setting. As the carriages containing the party from London drive beside the water, the descriptive language is striking and innovatory. Ethelinde sees 'the tall blue heads of the fells'[49] and 'an immense pile of purple rock';[50] the colouring defines a quality of the fading light. Charlotte had read Thomas Gray's *Journal in the Lakes*, and she might have visited Grasmere herself. When Ethelinde goes outdoors to avoid a battle between rival ladies, she finds an Eden at nightfall:

> It was now evening: the last rays of the sun gave a dull purple hue to the points of the fells which rose above the water and the park; while the rest, all in deep shadow, looked gloomily sublime. Just above the tallest, which was rendered yet more dark by the woods which covered its side, the evening star arose; and was reflected on the bosom of the lake, now perfectly still and unruffled.[51]

The unruffled bosom of the lake reflects Ethelinde's temporary serenity. As darkness deepens, Grasmere becomes 'spangled with stars.'[52] Her sensibility is romantic in her desire for solitude and her love for the Lakes scenery. Later that evening, tiring of cards and visitors she again

> went out unperceived, and taking with her that volume of Gray, in which he with the clearest simplicity describes this small lake, she pursued her way, now over 'eminences covered with turf, now among broken rock' till she reached the village which stands on a low promontory projecting far into the lake.[53]

Charlotte creates an exact literary context for her heroine, though Ethelinde is not herself a poet. She takes Gray's *Journal*, as if to check his description against her own perceptions, though she does not see nature through books, but freshly, as a relief from the irksomeness of the London set. Gray wrote, and Ethelinde read:

> The bosom of the mountains spreading here into a broad bason discovers in the midst Grasmere Water; its margin is hollowed into small bays with bold eminences, some of them rocks, some of soft turf that half conceal and vary the figure of the little lake they command. From the shore a low promontory pushes itself far into the water, and on it stands a white village with the parish church rising in the midst of it, hanging enclosures, corn fields and meadows green as an emerald, with their trees and hedges, and cattle fill up the whole space from the edge of the water.[54]

Gray notes with satisfaction that there are 'no red tiles, no flaming gentleman's house or garden walls.'[55] This is precise descriptive writing, but without the impressionistic and moonlight effects Charlotte brings to her scenery. Her passion for landscape dated like Wordsworth's from childhood, and like his was intensified by residence in the city. Placed against the ugliness of the social world she satirises, the power and beauty of the mountains and lake hold out to Ethelinde the promise of a different kind of life. As the heroine is introduced to the sublime setting and exposed to the triviality of fashionable invaders of Grasmere Abbey, she and the reader are alerted to injustices and economic inequalities. An appreciation of natural landscape is a touchstone of the heroine's sensibility, but such descriptions also emphasise the grandeur of England and so the importance of reform.

Observing the genius of the place, Sir Edward has constructed a cave-like recess on the fell above the Abbey, hung with ivy, and Ethelinde sits here to look over Grasmere Water and Montgomery's cottage. Crucial scenes in the novel take place at the cave, which forms a literary link between the taste for grottos and mannered rusticity in the garden, and the wilder scenery and human isolation of *The Prelude*.

The critique of established codes in the presentation of Grasmere is developed in the radical line Charlotte takes on sex and marriage. Mrs Montgomery's mother Mrs Douglas was left a widow dependent on her relatives' reluctant charity, with a baby to look after. This is a more extreme version of the 'odd woman' problem of the heroine, dependent on the charity of her relations. Charlotte's radicalism emerges in her creation of a 'fallen' woman whose lover remains faithful. Mrs Douglas is seen in Hyde Park by Lord Pevensey, whose wife is in an asylum. He makes her acquaintance, takes her home, and proposes to make her his mistress. She accepts, and against all the rules of the contemporary English novel lives faithfully with him, while he brings up her daughter Caroline as his own, until his death ten years later. Her grandson Montgomery can refer to this episode with sympathetic amusement, an attitude which is also the narrator's.

As in *Emmeline*, the unfairness of a legal system in which a couple can be imprisoned in marriage for life is explored, though here the husband is the victim. Sir Edward is rational as well as feeling. Though he discovers his marital incompatibility and love for Ethelinde, he acts scrupulously. He and Montgomery are both characters of a more extreme and tortured sensibility than even the heroine. Ethelinde has enough sense to avoid an immediate marriage and the 'group of lovely beggars'[56] that would result, and to wait until she and Montgomery can provide for children.

But Charlotte invests her heroes and heroines with scruples that prevent financial success. Montgomery is unable to toady to the politician Mr Royston or to Ethelinde's titled uncle, refuses, unlike Tom Jones, to accept money for sexual services, and is disgusted by his visit to India and the money-making there. Charlotte disliked the army as a solution to the financial problems of her heroes as of her sons. Mrs Montgomery's description of the battlefield just after the Battle of Minden in which Montgomery's father has been left for dead is a good example of Charlotte's ability in anti-war polemics. It is impossible for Montgomery to earn a living with integrity.

Ethelinde has common sense and fortitude, is less given to extravagant bursts of feeling than the men, and stops just short of frenzy at her parting with Montgomery, when

> struck forcibly with the idea that Montgomery was gone for ever, an idea which she had hitherto combated, she found herself strangely tempted to give way to shrieks, cries and all the agonies which despair extorts from the impatient sufferer under cureless misfortune.[57]

But though she controls herself, she can find a place in the world no more easily than he can. Love is a 'tyrannical and fatal attachment'.[58] Even Colonel Chesterville, Ethelinde's father, assumes that since Ethelinde's and Montgomery's love is mutual, 'to repress it must be fatal'.[59] A few characters have a more sardonic attitude to the feeling heart, and we appreciate the horsey eccentric Ellen Newenden's point of view as Ethelinde once more runs off in tears:

> At the bottom of the stairs, where Ethelinde arrived almost without knowing why she went, or whither she intended to go, she met Miss Newenden – 'Hey day!' cried the latter, 'what's the matter now? I never saw such a house in my life . . . it's altogether excessively wearing. Do have done with these perpetual lachrymals.'[60]

The language of Sensibility was already diffusing itself through the commercial classes. Charlotte creates a parodic poem she attributes to the literary son of a Bristol merchant:

> Lo! Sensibiliity with iron fang
> Doth on my palpitating heartstrings hang
> And more and more thy dulcet charms appear . . .[61]

But *Ethelinde* is witty too, not just the narrator; only rarely are Charlotte's novels unintentionally funny. And Ellen herself becomes a victim of her own sensibility, or sexuality, when she meets a man who despises her and courts her for her money.

The couple who most clearly represent the anti-sentimental point of view, Lord Danesforte and Maria Newenden, are cool, impassive and deceitful. Danesforte maintains his aristocratic *panache* even when he falls in a duel with Sir Edward over the latter's wife, saying 'with a smile that neither pain nor apprehension robbed of its acrimoney – "I believe, Sir, all your qualms on account of your wife may now be over – so far as relates to *me*".'[62] But Charlotte cheats when she suddenly disposes of Maria by suicide. She does not prepare for it. Ethelinde has earlier hoped that her own life 'which was not likely to be happy, would be short',[63] but there is no trace of Werther in Maria, and Charlotte employs a crude device of closure that breaks the gradations of sensibility and sense the novel mostly offers.

Ethelinde though less lively is more sophisticated than *Emmeline*, and most effective when author, heroine and reader understand about literary stereotypes. Ethelinde is a reader, though not a writer, and habitually measures her own behaviour against fictional models. When she falls in love at first sight with Montgomery, who has saved her from drowning, a favourite sub-category of rescue as a means of acquainting hero and heroine in earlier novels, she fears that

> to feel herself this strongly and suddenly attached to a person of whom she knew so little, was exactly that romantic infatuation which she had so often condemned as a weakness when it had occurred in real life, and as of dangerous example when represented in novels.[64]

Charlotte makes us aware she is enlarging the scope of the sentimental novel, and giving her heroine uglier, more sordid experiences than the average heroine has to endure. Money strikes at the roots of family affection, as Ethelinde discovers when she sees that her brother Harry is anxious to inherit the whole of their benefactor's estate, leaving nothing for her. Harry writes her a letter which makes plain that he does not want her to visit the house where he and Mr Harcourt are staying:

> Over this letter, which Ethelinde would not shew to Mrs Montgomery, she shed the bitterest tears which had fallen from her eyes since the death of her father. In all her other trials – in the comfortless society

of the Woolastons, and vulgar insults of the Ludfords – in her own indigent circumstances – even in the absence of the man she adored – there was something not unpleasing mingled with her sorrows. But here, in the neglect and ingratitude of her brother – of him whom she had so tenderly loved – for whom she had unrepiningly suffered – there was anguish, to the endurance of which her resolution was quite unequal. She saw in his behaviour to her more than neglect – she saw, with great reluctance, that while he could not well avoid giving her a cold and barely civil invitation, it was not his intention she should accept it.[65]

What is interesting here is Ethelinde's admission that there is something not unpleasing in the conventional novelistic trials she has already undergone. The society of the vulgar and arrogant, poverty, the separation from the lover, are standard situations in the novel of the time and as heroine Ethelinde knows such trials are to be expected. But the brother/sister relationship is usually sacrosanct in the eighteenth century novel, except in *Clarissa*, which breaks all the rules. The increasing antagonism of Harry, presented without exaggeration, threatens the heroine's sense of her identity, gives her a sense of shame, and sets up tensions between the 'real' world, the world of *Ethelinde*, and the conventional novelistic world with its standard trials. The heroine's perception shows Charlotte's consciousness of extending the scope of the sentimental novel into abrasive realism. Richardson had created a greedy, aggressive brother in James Harlowe, but Charlotte's Harry Chesterville is initially likeable, as Clarissa's brother is not, and his degenerating relationship with Ethelinde, which we notice before she does, is deftly handled.

Where rape is threatened, the possible destruction of the heroine's identity is linked to the destruction of written language. Charlotte probably took this idea from Clarissa's disjointed scribbling after her rape. Ethelinde's vulnerability is increased after her father's death. She goes to stay with Ellen, and her rejected suitor, Tom Davenant, arrives. Jealous of Montgomery, Davenant attacks Ethelinde, and offers her £600 a year to be his mistress. She escapes and locks herself in her room. At night she ventures out to gather up the pieces of Montgomery's letter which Davenant has collected from the post and torn up in front of her.

In Ethelinde's embarrassment at Harry's meanness, in the threat posed by the loutish Davenant, Charlotte acknowledges the etiquette of earlier novels and transgresses their limits to take in a wider and more unromantic range of experiences. At the beginning, we expect

Lord Danesforte to figure as the predatory threat to the heroine. His
name is Viking enough, and he has a good brand of mannered
aristocratic insolence. But Charlotte is more feminist, less collusive
with male power than Richardson or Burney. After Delamere she
never glamorises the would-be rapist or allows him to possess wit or
charm. The stylish Danesforte is deflected into an intrigue with
Maria Newenden, and Davenant's attempted rape of Ethelinde is the
result of drunken contempt.

Dramatic effect is achieved partly through a contrast of styles.
When Davenant meets Ethelinde and withholds her letter from her,
the language is brutally monosyllabic: 'with another oath, and with
something between a grin and a smile, he swore thro' his shut teeth
that he would compel what he asked, and if obliged to do so she
should never have her letter at all.'[66] Though this is not an epistolary
novel, the letter is part of Ethelinde's established identity as heroine.
Rape is the ultimate threat to the harmonious ending of the novel of
courtship, and the act is seen as a tearing of words also. When
Ethelinde goes to find her letter,

> the wind had dispersed it, and a few only of the largest portions
> remained on the spot. These she put into her bosom, and fancied that
> they acted as a talisman to sooth its throbbing anguish. The night was
> mild and calm; and as the moon now appeared through the fleecy
> clouds that gathered over the sea, she hoped if she waited a little it
> would afford her light enough to recover the remaining fragments of
> this precious manuscript. In this she was not deceived. In about half
> an hour a lovely clear moon was unveiled, and wandering in every
> direction round the spot she collected the remaining pieces.[67]

The words are put together again, and the threat averted, in a
moonlight scene like the one which opens the novel at Grasmere.

Mary Anne Schofield discusses Charlotte's acknowledgment that
her novels are indeed novels in *Masking and Unmasking the Female
Mind*. The metaphor of this title applies to a variety of episodes and
characters, to literal masquerades, to dressing as a man, to affecta-
tions, dishonesties and the release of aggression through telling a
story. She quotes the passage where Ethelinde reassembles the parts
of her letter, and is therefore closely associated with the author of the
fiction. 'So too,' Schofield writes, 'Smith pieces together the fabric of
her own story'.[68] This is well put, and emphasises the close connection between author and heroine.

But elsewhere Schofield assumes too readily that Charlotte's
learned women receive authorial support. A false counterpart to the

heroine, her cousin Clarinthia Ludford, is writing a novel. Schofield argues that the adventures of Clarinthia's heroine 'almost read like Ethelinde's own (at least with all the plot complications) or, even more to the point, like so much of the mid-century fiction. (I am reminded of numerous Haywood plots that could be synopsized thusly)'.[69] She wants to see Clarinthia the author as a self-projection of Charlotte though there is no resemblance between Clarinthia's plot and Charlotte's. Clarinthia reveals her conventionality, though a writer, by her simple plagiarism of standard episodes. Schofield writes that 'Clarinthia's own position as "a young lady of science" affords her a seriousness that in some ways Smith supports.'[70] But Charlotte's 'young lady of science' phrase is ironic, though it might be better for her if it were not, if she were willing to take the professional and intellectual aspirations of her Clarinthias and other learned young women more seriously. These inauthentic heroines are distinguished mainly by their unattractiveness to men. Clarinthia's literary ambitions and eagerness to engage in a clandestine love affair are parodic. She sees herself as another Clarissa and Danesforte as another Lovelace. Later, when she rejects her admirer Southcote because her father approves of him, she expects him to demonstrate 'one of those attachments, at once violent and hopeless, of which she has read so much,'[71] but instead he falls in love with Ethelinde.

Almost all Charlotte's young women then are the products of a literary culture and are affected by what they read, which makes her world and her women's minds convincing. Neither heroines nor anti-heroines can claim a monopoly of literary interests. Satire of novel-reading and writing in self-fictionalising characters like Clarinthia encourages the reader to take Ethelinde's troubles and adventures more seriously. Clarinthia is described as 'vain of her person, which was not above mediocrity, and vainer of her understanding, which was beneath it.'[72] This sort of sudden authorial sideswipe at a character is enjoyable, but the disapproval is not accounted for by anything Clarinthia is or says, except that she is rich. She too falls in love at first sight, is fond of her brother, is a reader and writes herself. Charlotte merely asserts that these traits are there only for display, though she gives Clarinthia much less intelligence than her heroine.

Ethelinde, or the Recluse of the Lake was published in the summer of 1789. During the writing, Charlotte was also preparing *Elegiac Sonnets* and correcting *Emmeline* for the second edition, which appeared in late 1788. During this year she had some misunderstanding with

Cadell over advance payment. She was increasingly inclined to think herself cheated, and secretly offered the copyright of *Ethelinde* to another publisher, George Robinson. But the difficulty with Cadell passed and he published it as agreed for fifty guineas a volume, or more than £260. Again the reviewers were enthusiastic, especially about the descriptions of the Lakes scenery. Only *The Critical* found it inferior to *Emmeline*.

By now Wollstonecraft was established as a regular reviewer for *The Analytical* and had just finished her own first novel, *Mary*, to be published by Joseph Johnson. She comments, of *Ethelinde*:

> Mrs Smith writes like a gentlewoman: if she introduces ladies of quality, they are transcribed from life, and not the sickly offspring of a distempered imagination, that looks up with awe to the sounding distinctions of rank and the gay delights which riches afford.[73]

She makes a good point here. Charlotte excels in her predatory minor aristocrats and was becoming increasingly adept at creating the casual upper-class brutality which appears in the Hawkhursts in this novel and the Molyneux in *Celestina*. Wollstonecraft however contrasted this authenticity with what she considered the factitious passions of the hero and heroine which, she claims, were taken from other novels.

Jenny probably admired *Ethelinde* most among Charlotte's early publications. She was writing short comic narratives herself now, parodying sentimental novels, but she took *Ethelinde* more seriously than these. She was fourteen when she first read it. Later when she had read one or two more of Charlotte's novels, she wrote a fragment called 'Catharine', an early attempt at a serious narrative, which includes the dialogue of two girls in their teens, Kitty Percival and Camilla Stanley, who have only just met:

> Kitty was herself a great reader, tho' perhaps not a very deep one, and felt therefore highly delighted to find that Miss Stanley was equally fond of it. Eager to know that their sentiments as to Books were similar, she very soon began questioning her new acquaintance on the subject, but though She was well read in Modern history herself, she chose rather to speak first of Books of a lighter kind, of Books universally read and admired, and that have given rise perhaps to more frequent arguments than any other of the same sort.
>   'You have read Mrs Smith's novels, I suppose?' said she to her Companion – 'Oh! Yes' replied the other, 'and I am quite delighted with them – They are the sweetest things in the world . . . ' 'And which do you prefer of them?' 'Oh! dear, I think there is no compari-

son between them – *Emmeline* is so much better than any of the others
. . . ' 'Many people think so, I know; but there does not appear so
great a disproportion in their Merits to me; do you think it is better
written?' 'Oh! I do not know anything about that – but it is better in
everything – Besides, *Ethelinde* is so long . . . ' 'That is a very common
Objection, I believe', said Kitty, 'But for my own part, if a book is well
written, I always find it too short.' 'So do I, only I get tired of it before
it is finished.' 'But did not you find the story of Ethelinde very
interesting? And the Descriptions of Grasmere, are not they Beautiful?' 'Oh! I missed them all, because I was in such a hurry to know the
end of it . . . ' then from an easy transition she added, 'We are going
to the Lakes this Autumn, and I am quite Mad with Joy; Sir Henry
Devereux has promised to go with us, and that will make it so
pleasant, you know.'

Camilla has never read any novel through to the end. Kitty has read
Charlotte's books, especially admired the description of the Lakes in
Ethelinde, and recognised how polemical her work is. Jenny uses
Charlotte as a touchstone of literary intelligence for her characters
here.

Charlotte was close to finishing *Ethelinde* on 18 June 1789 when
she wrote to George Robinson offering to sell the copyright. This
would not deprive Cadell, who already held the first three volumes,
of his profits from the first edition. Still, it was sharp business-
woman's practice, as she knew. She resented Cadell's refusing her an
advance. A postscript adds, 'I need not name to you I am persuaded
the necessity of secrecy, that in these cases being always understood.'
Of *Ethelinde*'s five volumes, she says, 'two are actually printed; the
third in the Printer's hands; the fourth ready and the fifth in such
forwardness that it will be very soon perfectly prepared for the
press.'

This was how she worked. Though she did not publish serially,
the demands on improvisation and memory were the same. Each
volume was copied and despatched to the publisher as it was
completed, so there was no possibility of polishing or revision.
Occasionally she leaves a loose end or forgets a character's name.
More often, as she recognised, she was apt to leave herself a lot to do
at the end in tidying up the plot and disposing of odd characters. Her
first volumes incline to a leisurely accumulation of background
detail, her last to much authorial shoving into place. But as her novels
increasingly acknowledge their own fictionality, the latter practice
becomes a strength, part of a radical nineties tradition: no solutions
to the problems raised are available in the current social system
except blatantly novelistic ones.

The Gothic house and its antitypes provide implicit political comment and controlling structures for her sprawling plots. But the ironist who is liberal or radical starts with a considerable disadvantage. Eighteenth-century satire is typically conservative, and the mode seems to demand an accepted set of values against which to measure the absurdities of contemporary fashions and customs. For Pope and Swift, as for Burney and Austen, the ideal is Christian and Tory, involving an acceptance of the providentially ordained forms of society, well-established duties, and the limitations of human reason. Elizabeth Bennet never stops to consider, as Charlotte's heroines might, whether she should marry Mr Collins and save the family estate. She knows that marriage is a sacrament; the point does not need to be made by her or the narrator. And Austen's conservatism links the Miss Steeles' lack of education, their lack of grammar and their lack of scruples.

Charlotte had no paradigm of Anglican order. Her religion was close to deism, and though her dissatisfaction with the established order was extreme, she had only the haziest ideas about how it might be changed. In her novels the rich, the religious and the elderly police the young and talented, so her heroes and heroines often cannot claim honesty among their virtues, because they need to deceive to preserve themselves. The lack of a consistent criterion of value other than Sensibility, that is, depth of feeling and a love of Nature, is her weakness as satirist; her strength lies in her depiction of 'the wonderful malignity of human nature,' a phrase which, like 'the inequalities of fortune' runs as a *leitmotif* with many variations throughout her work.

The letter to George Robinson was written from Brighton, where she would be based for the next three and a half years, though with many visits to London, to other parts of Sussex and Surrey and perhaps as far as Ross-on-Wye. Her restlessness was astonishing and increased as she grew older. I have not tried to chart every brief lodging and visit after she came back from Normandy; or to be more accurate, I have tried and failed in the effort to follow her. Travelling evidently gave her a much needed release from writing and worrying about the children, perhaps a new self on the road. She associated 'wandering' with literary inspiration and began to fear writer's block if she was stuck too long in the same place. Travel was notoriously rigorous, the other topic, with the weather, that could always be relied on for easy conversation. Outside towns the roads were unpaved, their upkeep the responsibility of the local landowner, who might or might not be public-spirited enough to keep them passable. And each time she went away, she had to find a married friend or relative to leave with the children. Charlotte Mary could not properly be left unchaperoned herself, let alone in charge of her siblings. Perhaps in the quiet of Wyke they could be left with the servants for a few days without raising unpleasant gossip. But in Brighton, standards had to be visibly maintained. When she went to London, she often took the older children with her.

Brighton was a rapidly expanding resort in the latter part of the century, with excellent libraries and interesting shops. Charlotte had memories of holidays here before her marriage, when she had been 'a gay dancer at Balls, and a lighthearted Equestrian on the Hills' and afterwards, when 'matrimony and misery came together',[74] she had brought children to convalesce here, and met Benjamin's creditors while he was in Normandy. The Prince of Wales was living at the newly restored and refurbished Marine Pavilion. His wife Maria Fitzherbert lived in a private house not far away. She was a Catholic and a commoner whom he had married in contravention of his father's Royal Marriages Act. His rival court in Brighton was now bringing new work and money to the town, which was a little cheaper than London, though more expensive than a country village. Probably Charlotte had had enough of country villages in the last two years; she was sociable, and gravitated towards lively company. There may have been more serious reasons for the move. Two years earlier she had complained of pain in her hands and difficulty in writing. This was probably rheumatoid arthritis, though she thought it gout, which ran in her family; it was to increase as she went into her forties. Brighton was famous for its sea-bathing and medicinal waters as well as for its fast and fashionable society.

Perhaps Charlotte Mary needed a change of scene as much as her mother. While Charlotte was finishing *Ethelinde*, and while she was making business overtures to Robinson, she wrote to Cadell asking for a £60 advance, giving as her reason that her daughter was in the way of marrying a gentleman of unexceptionable character and family if only Charlotte could manage to keep up appearances. Whether or not Cadell supplied the money, the marriage did not take place. Perhaps the prospective bride herself was not eager to rush into it.

For whatever mixture of reasons, to Brighton then she came in the summer of 1789 with all the children still at home, and took pleasant lodgings close to the sea. She meant to embark on a new novel here.

But it seemed almost a duty to accept an unexpected invitation from Henrietta to stay at Shane's Castle, which was in a beautiful part of County Antrim, and historically interesting: John O'Neill was heir to the oldest royal dynasty in Europe, though it was now disempowered. Henrietta was an amateur actress who had installed a private theatre and appeared in *Cymbeline* with Lord Edward Fitzgerald. She was a friend and patroness of Mrs Siddons, and considered by some critics equally talented. By now Charlotte had sent at least one play to an actor-manager, probably Sheridan, and had had no reply. The theatre was exceptionally difficult for a writer to break into. Even such a tireless networker as Hayley had discovered that. Inchbald succeeded partly because of her greater gifts as a dramatist but also because she had worked as an actress for so long. If Charlotte could have her play performed, even in a private theatre, it might impress the literary people with their London connections the O'Neills liked to invite every autumn. To take the children to Shane's Castle would defeat the object. She needed to get away from them and appear as a professional writing woman.

Lucy still lived in Islingon, and Charlotte kept up a few old acquaintances there. Dr Thomas Shirly was Lucy's doctor and also someone Charlotte consulted, either when she visited her aunt or by post. Charlotte Mary had been having some skin problems, and Charlotte herself was unwell. Dr Shirly sent prescriptions for both of them to Brighton. She obviously trusted him completely, and her letter of thanks is Charlotte at her most self-revealing. The Miss Berney and 'dear Boehms' in this letter are Mary Eleanor Berney, soon to be Mrs Thomas Henchman, and Mr and Mrs Edmund Boehm, the latter previously Dorothy Berney. They are the cousins who used to visit at Lys Farm and theoretical legatees of Richard's estate. Dorothy had married one of the Trustees appointed after Benjamin's imprisonment. Despite the family disagreements, the cousins were still good friends with Charlotte Mary. The letter is dated 22 August 1789.

> Dear Sir
> When first Charlotte [Mary] came hither, her Grand Mother [Lucy, Charlotte Mary's grandmother by marriage] talk'd much of coming down to Brighton under the idea that the sea air would be of great use to her & that she might be able to use the hot baths.
> Of this I now hear no more, tho the marriage of Miss Berney and their intentions of passing some time here would, I suppose, be a very strong additional motive to my Aunt. Now I am going to tell you why I wish she may again think of & execute this project. I have a

friend in Ireland whom I love extremely who is very desirous of my going over to her for a few weeks and returning with her to England in December. She is in a rank of life which enables her to be of great use to my family, & policy as well as pleasure urge me to oblige her if I could. If my Aunt would come down and inhabit my house, I should leave my Girls without being uneasy; she would have a comfortable house without any expense, and I should be able to get off the thorns for a little while & begin a New Novel at Shanes Castle.

I need not say to you that duty rather than inclination has for many years compelled me to live in a way for which I am very ill calculated. It has often been so bitter to me that nothing but my tenderness for the children could have carried me thro it. When I can escape from it without injury to them, it is a duty which I think I owe myself; I owe it indeed to them also, for on my health & power of writing depends their support, and I need not tell you that neither are promoted by incessant anxiety & sameness of scene. The two little ones will be at day school, & the old Lady will have no trouble with them; the elder Girls will be I suppose rather pleasant to her, & she will have a spacious dining room and a bedchamber adjoining within two hundred yards of the Sea. An easy staircase & a Sedan chair may always be had to carry her down to ye sea so that, consulting her own health only, perhaps she could not do better. And when her dear Boehms & dear Miss Berney, now made dearer by being on the point of marrying a Man who keeps three carriages, are here also, what can be wanting to her felicity? Unless one could transport Mrs Scrivener and the Sieur Davison also. Will you, if you think that change of air and company may really be useful to her, promote her coming if she names it to you? I shall write to her on Monday about it, & you will doubtless be consulted when you will of course say what you think right without adverting to *secret* influence.

Mrs Scrivener and the Sieur Davison may be comic names for Lucy's friends in Islington whom she talked about too much, in Charlotte's view. She still resents Lucy, and despises what she sees as her naïve pride in the cousins' marriages, but she is not the less eager to co-opt her as chaperone and unpaid babysitter. She does not pause to consider that the summer was almost over, and that an easy staircase and a sedan chair down to the sea might not look so attractive to a woman in her sixties in the months of November and December.

As ever, contemplating Lucy takes her mind back to her own marriage, but the letter is more allusive than it first seems. She is strongly tempted by something unspecified, tired of work, and so has a double reason for going to Ireland:

I am so strongly tempted on one hand & so weary of the labour of Sysyphus on the other that I am afraid I shall not hold out unless some little change renews my powers of perseverence. Virtue of all sorts is a mighty perishable commodity. Mine has held out miraculously for the space of four & twenty years, & tis not worth while to let it fail in my fortieth year. But really it is almost too much for me, having the power to live so much otherwise, to be compelled to live only to write & write only to live. While every body seems to think (I mean of the family) that I am bound to do it, forgetting that I was a mere child when *they* talk'd me into bonds, which I have found most unsupportably heavy, & that to provide for them I promis'd what it is wonderful that I have perform'd in any part. But there is a time when the soul rebels against fetters so unjustly imposed and when, if they are not a little lighten'd, they must be wholly thrown off. I say all this to you knowing that, with great liberality of mind, you are perfectly aware of my situation. Charlottes face is much better, & I have receiv'd much benefit from the remedy you prescribed for me. Nobody knows of my writing to you; you will of course let it remain a secret & believe me, with great regard, your oblig'd & obt Sert.

It is a deposition, lightly and humorously made, that she has never had a lover in the years of her marriage or following the separation, though she has had plenty of opportunities. Sophisticated women referred to their virtue with irony, or as 'vartue'; nevertheless it was crucial to their position in society and usually to their self-respect. Separation was just socially acceptable, affairs were not, at least for middle class women.

It is clear she feels she must break off her writing, and undoubtedly she had been working hard on one or more plays, as well as on the two novels. Living only to write and writing only to live must have been especially hard if work was being rejected or ignored in this year. It is less clear what she means by having the power to live so much otherwise, and by the threat of wholly throwing off her fetters. What so strongly tempts her is not the visit to Ireland, but something else. She adverts to a possibility she has already discussed with Dr Shirly, and need not elaborate. Could Hayley have offered her protection, as much protection as a mistress might expect, at Eartham? Her sentimental, inflammable friend might have responded to her complaints of poverty and defencelessness with such a proposition.

His marriage to Eliza had ended four months before the date of this letter, when he escorted her to Derby and left her in the care of a widow whom he paid to look after her. They never met again, though they corresponded. Only Hayley's narrative of their marriage survives, and it is wholly unreliable. He maintains that she was frigid from the start, or, as he puts it, he 'had married a person to whom Nature not only refused . . . the privilege of producing a child, but even those natural desires which she has wisely and tenderly given to Modesty herself for the preservation of the human Race'.[75] She was therefore responsible for his liaison with Thomas' mother and others.

He attributes Eliza's madness to her mother, who had lost her mind after the deaths of two earlier children. Eliza was begotten on the unconscious body of this unfortunate woman on the advice to her father of one Dr. Batty, whose well-meant medical opinion did not achieve its aim of restoring sanity. Thus Eliza was hereditarily both mad and – because of her mother's insensibility at her conception – frigid, and Hayley could not live with her. Sir Walter Scott was the surprised recipient of these confidences, though many years later. Hayley usually referred to his wife as 'the pitiable Eliza'. Long before the separation his letters to and about her might have driven anyone mad; hers sound relatively reasonable, however.

On the way back from Derby he made a detour to Lichfield to see Anna Seward, previously his most fulsome admirer. But since they last met, he had published his *Philosophical, Historical and Moral Essay on Old Maids by a Friend to the Sisterhood*, a curious account of what he termed Ancient Virginity. The proportion of women without the choice of marriage and therefore lifelong celibates was high, especially in the middle class. Hayley took it upon himself to be their historian and analyst in the manner of his friend Gibbon in *The Decline and Fall of the Roman Empire*. The result could be called at best inane and at worst obsessively spiteful. Perhaps resentment of Eliza inspired this work as well as *The Triumphs of Temper*; it is just possible she remained a virgin through nineteen years of marriage. He dedicated the three volumes of the *Essay* without permission to Elizabeth Carter, poet and translator of Epictetus, who was understandably furious. The Swan was not amused either, and made no pretence of being so. Hayley went on to Eartham.

It is sad Charlotte felt flattered by his friendship, though after Benjamin it is not surprising. It is sadder still that she took him so seriously as poet and essayist. But he was popular, impressive in appearance, eager to a fault to patronise his literary friends, and had a beautiful house in the part of Sussex she loved most. He turned down the Laureateship in the following year when Thomas Warton died, apparently on political grounds. The tone of her letters to him suggests how interested she was. But to become a mistress would wreck her daughters' chances of marriage into respectable families and damage her sons' prospects. Worse, it would alienate some and disappoint them all.

Hayley's first novel, *The Young Widow, or the History of Cornelia Sedley* published this year, was probably a response to Charlotte's success with *Emmeline*. The hero Henry Seymour and Cornelia are passionately in love from the start. The obstacle to their union is religion; her dying husband has urged her not to marry a sceptic. All the surrounding circumstances are different from Hayley's and Charlotte's: nobody has to work, Cornelia is rich, her children are only two in number and hero and heroine are in their twenties. But Cornelia's spinster friend, referring to the cage of marriage, says after hearing her sing, 'but this I know, if she is not put in the cage I allude to, she will certainly sing, if she sings at all, with a thorn in her breast'[76] which may be an allusion to Charlotte's Sonnet 1. Cornelia finally obeys her late husband, refusing to give her boys, the elder of whom is named William, a sceptic for a stepfather: 'she preferred their distant security to all the immediate allurements of fervent and reciprocal love.'[77] The heroine's initials can hardly be coincidental. A biographical reading of the novel's turgidly erotic sentiment may throw some light on Hayley's feelings for Charlotte, on a decision of hers to consider only her children's interests, or on a joint decision to construct their relationship in this way for some readers. But if she was strongly tempted by Hayley, or another man, she was the more desperate to get out of England for a few months, and put St George's Channel between herself and the tempter. She is holding a gun to Dr Shirly's head here: send Lucy as domestic help, or I will do something outrageous.

But she did not, at least not in the way she seems to threaten, though the Shane's Castle scheme came to nothing. Brighton was rapidly becoming more exciting, too exciting for her to wish to leave it long. For it was 'chiefly at Brighthelmstone', Catherine says in her memoir, 'where she formed acquaintances with some of the most violent advocates of the French Revolution, and unfortunately caught the contagion, though in direct opposition to the principles she had formerly professed, and to those of her family'.

3

Girondism

On 1 May 1789, three days before Charlotte's fortieth birthday, the long-delayed meeting of the Estates-General convened at Versailles. Its principal purpose was to consider more equitable methods of taxation to meet an enormous fiscal deficit. It was also tentatively pledged to consider the lists of grievances Louis XVI himself had invited from every region of rural and urban France. The three 'Estates' that formed the Estates-General were the clergy, the nobility and – broadly – the professional and business classes. These were not, however, three very distinct or necessarily opposed groups. The nobility was constantly replenished by the bourgeoisie and had interests in common with the commercial class. Opposition might be sharper within a group, between a poor *curé* and his freeloading Bishop, for instance. And some nobles, including Mirabeau, chose to identify from demagogic or genuinely altruistic motives with the Third Estate, the base most clearly associated with constitutional reform. The representatives of each group were elected, not court-appointed.

Electoral representation itself, peculiar to the Estates-General, gave a heady sense that majority participation in the ruling process had at last come to France. In February or March 1789, a taxable peasant or urban worker could walk to his parish church, see his community's grievances recorded and vote for the local man he thought would speak best for his interests at Versailles. This was still beyond the dreams of most of his English counterparts, and it raised high hopes. The three Estates might even consider constitutional issues together and vote as individuals in a single national assembly, rather than deliberating as three discrete categories. It was such a rare event that much more was expected from it than from an English Parliament. In France, the King was still absolute monarch, though Louis was as aware as anyone at court of the need for reform, and doing his dogged best to assure his people of his interest in their welfare.

Since the seventies at least, France's financial position had wors-
ened. This was mainly due to French aid in troops and naval support
for the American War of Independence. Through the seventies and
eighties a series of Directors General, Ministers of Finance, came to
office with royal and bureaucratic support and left amidst burnings-
in-effigy. Privilege meant, originally, exemption from taxes. The
nobility and clergy were privileged, though again the lines were
more blurred than this might suggest. Property was heavily taxed,
and a noble married to a bourgeoise would be liable to tax on
property so acquired; some of the lower clergy were almost destitute
and could have afforded nothing in any case. But in the First and
Second Estates there were public-spirited and reforming members
who were willing to give up their tax exemption. Tax for the very
poor might take the form of compulsory manual labour, on road
works or building sites for instance.

All household items were taxed: wood, salt, food of any kind;
clothes and journeys were indirectly taxed. Internal customs posts
prevented the transport of untaxed provisions from region to region.
Smuggling was a way of life. In *Citizens* Simon Schama records that
in just one region, Anger on the border with Brittany, 2,342 men,
896 women and 201 children were convicted of salt-smuggling, only
one possible breach of the customs law, between 1780 and 1783. They
could expect sentences of whipping, branding or the galleys; if they
resisted the guards, adult males were executed by breaking on the
wheel. Tax collectors were licensed to enter any house by force and
search men or women; the lists of grievances addressed to Louis in
early 1789 detail the resulting brutalities.

In the series of severe winters and bad harvests of the eighties, the
price of grain rose until the four pound loaf, the staple diet, was
priced out of the reach of poorer households. Resistance to the law
was widespread among rural and urban workers though their anger
was not yet directed against the monarchy; on the contrary, they
thought Louis would be their ally. Those who were cheating them
were government agents and bureaucrats, or landowners and nobles
who used the death penalty against poachers and would not even let
their peasants kill the predators of their crops. These people, they
knew, were in a conspiracy to keep up prices and leave the poor
hungry.

Titled and peasant Frenchmen had fought alongside Americans
in the War of Independence, with the great satisfaction of beating the
British and depriving them of their finest colony. The establishment

of equality, the right to life and liberty they fought for remained a model for a better society of their own. Marie-Joseph Lafayette came back to a hero's welcome; Benjamin Franklin was lionised in Paris. Historians have tried to identify the localities to which clusters of French soldiers came home after the war with those that saw the first outbreaks of the Revolution. Though there is probably no clear connection, American-style, Rousseau-inspired equality was by the middle eighties a tantalising possibility. America allowed an emotional and discursive alliance of revolution with patriotism rather than with treason, an alignment more difficult to make in England.

For the bourgeoisie and nobility, a classical tradition in literature and painting less vernacularised than in England helped to make a Republic a familiar more than a historical concept. For many people this could co-exist comfortably with the ideal of a paternal monarchy shorn of its venal fringe. In high and popular culture intellectual dissent was tolerated, even chic, despite formal censorship and ecclesiastical sanctions. Malherbes as censor protected Rousseau's work and the editors of the *Encyclopédie*. After some initial resistance from the King, Beaumarchais' *The Marriage of Figaro* was produced in 1784, with its Act Five attack on aristocracy and assertion of the rights of the little man. Liberal and reformist aristocrats in the audience applauded. Though Beaumarchais was imprisoned he was almost as soon released, a typically vacillating reaction by Louis. And a lively trade in pornography, much of it based on the supposed erotic adventures of Marie-Antoinette, flourished even under the walls of Versailles. Unlike her husband she was not popular. Her Rousseauesque taste in clothes and pastimes was not seen as a sign of solidarity with the people.

While preparation for the Estates-General inched forward, living conditions deteriorated still further in the drought of 1788 and through the terrible winter of 1788–9. Work and food were hard to find, about a fifth of the urban population was just surviving on relief and in the country thousands more than usual died of cold and hunger. The first outbreak of popular violence came at Grenoble that summer and was repeated in spontaneous riots across France in the following autumn and winter. They culminated in the Reveillon riot, the burning of a Parisian wallpaper-manufacturer's house with heavy loss of life when the *guard français* opened fire on the rioters. This happened shortly before the Estates-General assembled at Versailles.

From then on, it would seem to some historians, a series of accidents and procedural errors pre-empted the enlightened reforms that were on their way and precipitated all that followed. To others, no luck or diplomacy could have prevented the years of hunger and avoidable bereavement from becoming Revolution. Events were reported across the political gamut of English newspapers and magazines. After the government spies despatched in extravagant numbers, Brighton society was often the next to get the news, from travellers hastily crossing back to The Ship or the other great inns that served the packets, and bringing with them newspapers and pamphlets from the patriot presses. Charlotte's pro-revolutionary writing shows how fully she absorbed contemporary French problems and their causes.

Louis' elder son had been ill, probably with tuberculosis, for several years; in April and May he was clearly dying and he died in the first week of June. A loving father and never a charismatic speaker, Louis was unable to function as a credible leader. After a series of snubs that came partly from malice but mainly from mindless court etiquette, members of the Third Estate were accidentally barred out of their conference hall one rainy morning. On the nearest indoor tennis court they took an oath which, if it could be carried out, would make them the major power in the constitution. Further rioting in July ended in the release of the Bastille's few prisoners and the Governor's murder. All this was argued over endlessly at every level of English society. Its implications at home were obvious and animating, whatever one's political point of view.

In the late summer Charlotte began *Celestina*; it cost her more effort than the other two. Writing to Cadell on 8 September 1790 when she was still struggling with it, she describes herself as 'extremely sick of *my trade* and very anxious to leave it off.' She took a full nineteen months, perhaps because she led a more sociable life in Brighton, or perhaps because she felt her courtship vein was exhausted. But though *Celestina* is more derivative than the earlier novels, its narrative irony is drier and its perspective wider. The heroine is French, adopted as a child from a Provençal convent by an Englishwoman. From the start Charlotte meant to leave herself the option of taking the setting to France and making some comment on the current crisis. She does so in the fourth and final volume.

In a letter written next year to Joseph Warton, brother of the Laureate and Lionel's headmaster at Winchester, she reckoned that only this closing episode reached the standard of her earlier novels. Her hero Willoughby goes to the South of France to trace Celestina's parentage, and by one of those lucky chances that happen in final volumes, arrives at the castle of Rochemorte. There he hears the story of the young people's rebellion against the Castle's authoritarian owner, an inset narrative microcosm of the French Revolution as Charlotte saw it. The construction of her Castle in this last volume is a comment on a book every literate man and woman in London or Brighton was talking about in November 1790, as she finished her third volume. That book was Edmund Burke's *Reflections on the Revolution in France*, published on the 1st of the month, a passionate and considered reponse to events across the Channel.

Burke's *Reflections* grew out of a letter he had been writing during that year to a young Frenchman, Charles de Pont. He attacks the Revd Richard Price, a mentor of Mary Wollstonecraft and a dissenting clergyman who welcomed the French Revolution: he is of course more concerned with English than French politics. He uses throughout *Reflections* the metaphor of an old castle to represent the state, and the careful preservation or demolition of the castle as metaphors for traditional loyalties or revolutionary violence. His book was an instant success. George III said that every gentleman should read it, which probably helped the sales: 12,000 copies within a month, 30,000 by the end of the following year. Burke was a lawyer, a politician, by this time an elder statesman. A libertarian earlier in his career, he had opposed the slave trade and defended the American colonists. But he took a romantic conservative's view of the French Revolution, outraged by the attempt to destroy laws and institutions, and especially by the confinement of the French Royal family. Though *Reflections* appeared before their attempted flight to Austria, they were in effect prisoners already. Burke writes rhetorically and passionately in the famous passage in praise of Marie-Antoinette and chivalry:

> It is now sixteen or seventeen years since I saw the Queen of France, then the dauphiness, at Versailles; and surely never alighted on this orb, which she hardly seemed to touch, a more delightful vision . . . little did I dream that I should have lived to see such disasters fallen upon her in a nation of gallant men, in a nation of men of honour and of cavaliers. I thought ten thousand swords must have leaped from their scabbards to avenge even a look that threatened her with insult. – But the age of chivalry is gone.[1]

Burke's dominant metaphors are, not surprisingly given his conservatism, those of the family and the castle or old house. In *The Language of Politics in the Age of Wilkes and Burke*, James Boulton notes that as a symbol 'the family fuses some of Burke's most passionately

held ideas . . . Around it cluster the numerous references to inheritance, forefathers, posterity, records, titles and the like.'[2] Charlotte
had already satirically undercut notions of family harmony in the
interlocking and competitive families of her first two novels. But
Burke's image of the castle was to be more important for her and for
the future of the English novel.

Reflections expresses with elegance and force the average English
opinion of the time, but there were other English writers besides
Charlotte who sympathised with the early aims of the French
Revolution – Jacobins as they came to be called. However, most of
them had more in common with the moderate Republicans, the
Girondins, so-called because some of their leaders came from the
department of the Gironde in South-west France; Jacques-Pierre
Brissot was the most important of this group. The term Jacobin has
a more complicated derivation. The Dominican monks were known
as Jacobins because their first religious house in Paris was in the Rue
St. Jacques. Hence the members of a political club that rented a
Dominican refectory for its meetings also became known jokingly as
Jacobins. When the Revolution came the Jacobins formed the extreme
revolutionary party in the National Convention, with seats on the
left, while the Girondins occupied the middle and right, giving us the
concepts of left and right that dominated political thinking for the
next 200 years. The term Jacobin, which was used derisively in
England, survived well into the next century.

Burke admits that the *ancien régime* was badly in need of renovation.
He addresses the French as people who

> possessed in some parts the walls, and, in all, the foundations, of a
> noble and venerable castle. You might have repaired those walls,
> you might have built on those old foundations. Your constitution
> was suspended before it was perfected; but you had the elements of
> a constitution very nearly as good as could be wished...[3]

Instead of demolishing their inheritance, the French might have
preserved the magnificent crumbling edifice, whose tendency to
decay should have been countered by continuous patching. He uses
the house image throughout *Reflections*, as in the warning that

> it is with infinite caution that anyone ought to venture upon pulling
> down an edifice which has answered to any tolerable degree for ages
> the common purposes of society, or on building it up again, without
> having models or patterns of approved utility before his eyes.[4]

Burke sees conflicting class interests as a source of strength, a brake
against precipitate change. Diversity produces compromise,

moderation, and liberty. He puts across this idea too by using the image of a house:

> Through that diversity of members and interests, general liberty had as many securities as there were views in the several orders, while by pressing down the whole with the weight of a real monarchy, the separate parts would have been prevented from warping, and starting from their allotted places.[5]

It is the wooden wainscot he has in mind, the panelling round a room which easily twisted with damp unless held firmly in place at top and bottom. He is arguing for stability, a strong monarchy and government, an observance of rank.

The language and ideas of Burke's book had a wide and lasting influence. As Stephen Prickett notes in *England and the French Revolution*, the architecture of the state and often the state as architectural folly became familiar images, sometimes in the form of political cartoons, in the decade that followed the Revolution, and well into the next century. One of the funniest satires on Burke was not written until nearly thirty years later, when Prince Seithenyn in Thomas Love Peacock's *The Misfortunes of Elphin* proudly displays his three-quarters-rotted sea wall: 'If it were all sound, it would break by its own obstinate stiffness: the soundness is checked by the rottenness, and the stiffness is balanced by the elasticity.'[6] Seithenyn is proved to be wrong, and much of Wales is flooded.

Charlotte's castle of Rochemorte, renewed in the time of Revolution, adapts Burke's image. Willoughby learns about the aristocratic de Bellegarde family and their castle Rochemorte, hidden in the Pyrenees close to a Benedictine monastery. This close relationship of castle to abbey or church is always found in Charlotte's Gothic. Religion and the state buttress each other, threatening or crushing individual liberty. By the time of Willoughby's visit, the Benedictines have abandoned their vows and left. Rochemorte is battered and ruinous in places, but impressive and comfortable in the inhabited rooms. As Willoughby sees the castle in the first months of the Revolution, it is burgeoning with new and active life, plants growing in its mortar and birds nesting in its turrets. The greenery between the stones and in the moat and the shrill cries of the birds contrast with threatening images of darkness, stasis and enclosure to suggest the reanimation of an antiquated institution, achieved by the Revolution:

> The whole was composed of grey stone; the towers, at each end, rose in frowning grandeur, above the rest of the building; and having

> only loops, and no windows, impressed ideas of darkness and
> imprisonment, while the moss and wall flowers filled the interstices
> of the broken stones; and an infinite number of birds made their nests
> among the shattered cornices, and half-fallen battlements, filling the
> air with their shrill cries.[7]

The broken stones and shattered cornices are an improvement, since
they provide space for flowers to grow and birds to nest. One can see
the care she is beginning to give to the symbolic presentation of her
castles: the nexus of power has become a refuge. Rochemorte is
greening over with vegetation, and no longer a gloomy prison. The
influence of Rousseau is evident here, and he was to become
increasingly important to her.

M. de Bellegarde lives in the castle with his daughter Anzoletta,
who resembles Celestina. He tells Willoughby his story and reveals
the secret of Celestina's parentage. As he does so, we see how the
story of the Rochemorte family forms a French Revolution in
miniature. M. de Bellegarde and his elder brother ran away from
Rochemorte to escape their tyrannical father the Baron, leaving their
young sister Genevieve behind. Once Genevieve grows up, she is
threatened by the sexual advances of her Benedictine confessor.
Celestina is generally anti-clerical, though the Revd Mr Thorold who
befriends Celestina and works as a doctor is one of only two decent
clergymen in all her fiction.

The younger members of the family resist the Baron's and the
monk's tyranny. M. de Bellegarde and his English friend Lord
Ormond return to Rochemorte disguised as Izard hunters to rescue
Genevieve, and meet her in the forest with her friend Jaquelina, a
young woman of lower rank than the Rochemorte family. In all
Charlotte's novels sex is opposed to authority and hierarchy. The
two couples fall in love at first sight, are married by a monk from the
monastery, and unknown to the Baron de Bellegarde live in a remote
part of the castle, where Celestina and Anzoletta are conceived. The
monk betrays the secret and the men are captured and sent to prison,
while their wives are left to the rage of the Baron. Eventually Ormond
is released and forced by his military duties to fight in America with
the British army, though he is sympathetic to the American revolutionaries, and he dies there, a victim of British colonial adventurism,
while Genevieve dies a victim of the *ancien régime*.

The narrative ends in 1790, a few months before the date of its
publication. In 1790 the Revolution had not yet become associated
with the urban underclass; the people in charge just before the

summer of 1789 were broadly the people in charge just afterwards. By this time the Baron and M. de Bellegarde's elder brother are dead too, the Revolution releases M. de Bellegarde, who returns to his estate, while Jacquelina is absolved by the new regime from the nun's vows that the Baron has forced on her. Their story ends happily, though the domestic revolution has been achieved at the cost of the lives of both Celestina's parents.

In this retrospective episode, there is a contrast between young love and radical politics on one hand, and paternalistic, state-sanctioned and religious violence on the other. Rochemorte stands for the dead weight of the feudal past which still survived in social relationships in England in 1790. Rochemorte is shown passing from the ownership of the Baron to the anti-clerical and revolutionary younger son. The novel reflects Charlotte's hopes for England in the euphoric first two years, while the inset story crystallises anti-authoritarian ideas which appear more moderately and diffusedly earlier in the novel, just as Abersley in *Ethelinde* forms an appropriate symbol for threats posed earlier. But *Celestina's* castle allows for change and hope.

Charlotte makes a brave attempt to celebrate equality and sorority. In Jessy Woodburn she manages an attractive servant girl. Jessy and Celestina meet on a coach when both are being pestered by an obnoxious grocer, and Charlotte creates a believable if sentimental friendship between the two. Jessy describes her grim life as a maid of all work in the sunless basement of a parsimonious middle class family, where Charlotte drew on miserable memories of Cheapside, trapped in the dark rooms over Richard's warehouse, and longing for the country. Jessy's nostalgia and creative imaginings look forward to Wordsworth's Poor Susan, visualising the countryside from the confinement of town:

> Often of a Sunday in the summer I have gone up into our dining room, because the street was so close and narrow that below we hardly saw daylight from one end of the year to the other; and I have opened the sash, and looked against the black walls and shut windows of the houses opposite, and I have thought how dismal it was! Ah! I remembered too well the beautiful green hills, the meadows and woods, where I so often used to ramble with my sister when we were children, in our own country, before we were old enough to know that my poor mother was unhappy, and had learned to weep with her! How often have I wished those days would come again, and how often have I shut my eyes and tried to fancy I saw once more all the dear objects that there were so charming. Alas! The dream

would not last long! For if it did, it served only to make me feel more unhappy when, instead of being able to indulge it, I was obliged to go back to hard, and what was yet worse, to dirty work in our dismal kitchen. In Devonshire I had been used to work hard enough; but I had always fresh air to breathe, and could now and then of an evening sit at our cottage window, and look at the moon, and fancy that my mother might be there with my sister, and that they saw and pitied their poor unfortunate Jessy.[8]

As in the earlier two novels, the heroine is homeless, literary and sensitive. She must find tolerable ways of surviving in the world without money. But she is also sharp and charming, with a frank self-approval which must have been a pleasure to the young contemporary reader used to more traditional Christian models of self-analysis and self-blame. She is rational enough to exert a stabilising influence on Willoughby, who becomes suicidal when he thinks she is about to marry someone else. The two secondary heroines, Jessy and Sophy are also heroines of Sensibility, Jessy victimised until Celestina befriends her, Sophy bereaved of her child then of her husband.

Sense is more attractive than usual here in the form of Lady Horatia Howard, who is affectionate and philanthropic as well as placid. Since Willoughby may turn out to be her half brother, Lady Horatia advises Celestina to find a more suitable husband. Her disappointment in marriage qualifies her to give advice. She plays Lady Russell to Celestina's Anne Elliot, but Celestina is not open to persuasion. Romantic love for her and the narrator outweighs common sense, self-interest and the experience of the older generation. Sense has a better spokeswoman here than elsewhere, but passion and grief are more violent than in the earlier fictions.

There are autobiographical and metafictional aspects to *Celestina*, though they are less pronounced than in *Emmeline* and *Ethelinde*. Sophy Elphinstone's history is based on Charlotte's. She prepares to tell her story in a long, inset narrative that reminds the reader, and also reminds her, of early French romances. She admits that

'It is something like the personages with whom we are presented in old romances, and who meet in forests and among rocks and recount their adventures; but do you know, my dear Miss de Mornay, that I feel very much disposed to enact such a personage, and though it is but a painful subject, to relate to you my past life?'

'And do you know, dear Madam,' replied Celestina, 'that no wandering lady in romance had ever more inclination to lose her own reflections in listening to the history of some friend who had by chance met her, lost in the thorny labyrinth of uneasy thoughts, than I have to listen to you.'[9]

Charlotte appears at first to be using an unsophisticated plot device in the long interpolated story of a minor characeter, its introduction lacking in naturalism and demanding some smoothing over at the joins. But by reference to an earlier form of fiction she keeps us conscious that this too is story, that women's painful lives which are the subjects of such stories change little from one generation to another, that Charlotte herself, Sophy, Celestina and the reader have a story to listen to and a story to tell. Sophie has married into a family from the West Indies, and her husband Alexander Elphinstone resembles Benjamin Smith in fecklessness, though he is a more attractive version than usual. Sophy's problems arise from her husband's extravagance and the refusal of his family to help, and she is, like Mrs Stafford, recognisably the author to many readers. Celestina is the poet within the text, her elegy for a young woman of nineteen, 'O thou who sleeps't where hazel bands entwine'[10] among Charlotte's most metrically interesting sonnets.

As one would expect in a novel of more firmly focused political ideas, *Celestina* goes further than the earlier work in its challenge to established sexual morality. Emily, Sophy Elphinstone's sister, who is seduced at fifteen and becomes a prostitute, is brave, self-sacrificing, the most admirable character in the novel including Celestina, and perhaps an intertextual reponse to Hayley's courtesan Emily in *The Young Widow*. She gives the money she has made as Vavasour's mistress to pay a doctor in an attempt to save the life of her nephew, and tries to make Vavasour happy by persuading Celestina to marry him when she herself is dying. When Celestina visits her in Bristol, Emily is flooded in seraphic light:

> Emaciated, and of a delicate fairness, her hands and her face had a transparency that gave an idea of an unembodied spirit, and her dress was such as favoured the deception. The blood might almost be seen to circulate in her veins, so plainly did they appear; and her eyes had the dazzling radiance of ethereal fire, to which the hectic heat of her glowing though wasted countenance, still added – A few locks of her fine light hair had escaped from her head-dress, and played like broken rays from a receding planet, round a face, which only those who had hearts unhappily rigid, could behold, without feeling the sense of her errors suspended or overwhelmed by strong emotions of the tenderest pity.[11]

The death late in the novel offsets Celestina's happy ending. The narrator uses familiar iconography from pictures of saints, perhaps transmitted through Richardson's depiction of the dying Clarissa. By her use of cosmic imagery, Charlotte represents Emily's victimisation by the double standard as a disaster on a universal scale.

But for many readers now, she will seem here too more successful as a satirist than as an exponent of Sensibility. Her wit is laconic, as in her description of Molyneux, 'the calm coldness of [whose] manner gave an idea of latent powers, which he was supposed to be too indolent to exert'[12] or of Miss McLaurin's 'multiform attractions'[13] and claim to the name of Hamilton that make her into Lady Castlenorth. Her husband is moribund from the beginning of the novel, a representative of his class. A genealogist as soon as he can speak, Castlenorth with his wyverns and blazons becomes increasingly deluded and redundant. Titles were abolished in France on 19 June 1790 and it is clear what Charlotte's hopes were for England.

There is a network of mutually hostile family interests and a good selection of 'cats and Tiffany misses',[14] boorish squires, corrupt lawyers and irresponsible aristocrats. As a courtship novelist she was running out of exciting plots: the duel and Celestina's alarms at Ranelagh come straight out of Burney's *Cecilia*. But *Celestina* embodies a wider range of partisan and interesting political ideas. If *Emmeline* is about courtship and marriage, *Ethelinde* about marriage and poverty, *Celestina* focuses on rank and the authoritarian state, in its microcosm, the family, and in the wider world. The novel ends in France, the Revolution has begun, Rochemorte will be renovated and happily inhabited, and various domestic and hereditary tyrannies are over.

Reflections was read and discussed by people who would not have looked for political ideas in a novel, which must have encouraged her to sophisticate the image of the castle in *Desmond* published in June 1792. Then she expanded it brilliantly to fill her whole narrative in *The Old Manor House* published in March 1793. In 1789 current political passions had at last caught up with her own corrosive resentment of law and custom, which meant for her only overwork, poverty, insecurity and the scars of her marriage to Benjamin. But this 'paroxysm of political fever', as Catherine called it, is already latent in her second novel, written before she moved to Brighton. By 1791, a natural oppositionist had found her moment – and it was to be a brief one. But she could, rather brashly, celebrate the new order in *Desmond*, which even apart from its merits as fiction is an interesting piece of journalism, recording the ideas of various social groups about the Revolution. And she wrote *The Old Manor House* confident that her more politically intelligent reader would see the importance of her setting and plot, and recognise her castle as an emblem of England.

Celestina was well reviewed and widely read. She made over £200 for the four volumes and a further £40 from the second edition. *The Critical's* reviewer wrote:

> In the modern school of novel writers, Mrs Smith holds a very distinguished rank; and, if not the first, she is so near as scarcely to be styled an inferior. Perhaps with Miss Burney she may be allowed to hold 'a divided sway': and, though on some occasions below her sister-queen, yet from the greater number of her works [Burney had only written two novels so far] she seems to possess a more luxuriant imagination, and a more fertile invention.[15]

Wollstonecraft particularly admired the Pyreneean description, where Willoughby is trapped among the mountains by clouds, the scenic correlative to his confusion, just before he learns Celestina's parentage. Ann Radcliffe helped herself to this episode for the eerie passage where Emily crosses the Alps among the clouds in *The Mysteries of Udolpho*. The two most successful Gothic novelists of their time borrowed freely from each other: Radcliffe interspersed her story with pieces of poetry in *The Romance of the Forest* (1791), and in Charlotte's *Montalbert* (1795), Rosalie is carried off by banditti like Emily in the *The Mysteries of Udolpho* of the previous year.

At fifteen Jenny understood that *Celestina* was partly an answer to Burke's attack on the Revolutionaries and that it adapted his castle symbol to satirise his point of view. George Willoughby resembles Delamere, but he is the hero in this novel, not a secondary figure, and marries the heroine. By this time she was less impressed by a hero with fine feelings but no consistent ethics, let alone work ethics. Charlotte's solution to the problem of financing her sensitive heroes is completely inept in *Celestina*. Willoughby hates his uncle and aunt, Lord and Lady Castlenorth, but his uncle settles a large sum of money on him when he gets engaged on the rebound to the Castlenorths' daughter. Castlenorth then dies without finding out that the engagement is broken off. Neither Willoughby nor the narrator feel any embarrassment about his keeping the money.

The ending amused Jenny, though she envied the more dramatic episodes, like Willoughby's last-minute dash down to the West Country. But she thought how soft the novels were on politics as well as illicit sex, and probably had Willoughby in mind when she wrote a passage parodying a 'radical' young man:

> He exclaimed with virulence against Uncles and Aunts, Accused the Laws of England for allowing them to possess their Estates when wanted by their Nephews and Nieces, and wished he were in the House of Commons, that he might reform the Legislature, and rectify all its abuses. 'Oh! The sweet Man! What a spirit he has!' said I.

This is a dismissive comment on Charlotte's political ethic and on the Revolution itself which, it seemed to some, would offer little to replace the old regime. In the portrait of Jessy, and of the Lelaurier family who are restored to a Rousseauesque idyll after the Revolution, Charlotte asserts that government must take account of working-class needs and aspirations. It would be a long time before the more traditionalist writers could afford to concede that.

At some time in the second half of 1791 while she was working on *Desmond* , Charlotte went to Paris to get the feel of events for herself. She was one of many. Helen Maria Williams was there already; her *Letters* were to remain determinedly pro-Revolutionary even after 1794. Charlotte may have first met her in Paris. Wordsworth went over for the *Fête de la Féderation*, the great celebration for the first anniversary of the fall of the Bastille; he was to return in the autumn of 1791 to spend his revolutionary year there. Dr John Moore's *Journal* is especially circumstantial on court proceedings in Paris in 1791 and 1792, his account culminating in Louis' trial and sentence. Paine just escaped arrest when he left for Paris after the second part of his *Rights of Man* came out in 1792. Wollstonecraft also went in that year and published her *View of the French Revolution* two years later.

Charlotte's visit must have been brief, but it was productive. She wrote this novel remarkably fast, and her sense of engagement in its ideas is obvious, despite the formal distancing of the epistolary genre. *Desmond* was the first of her novels with a Preface, though the sixth edition of her *Elegiac Sonnets*, appearing the month before *Desmond*, contains the first open and public attack on the Trustees of Richard's will, on the

> 'Honourable Men' who, *nine years ago*, undertook to see that my family obtained the provision their grandfather designed for them

> . . . But still I am condemned to feel the 'hope delayed that maketh the
> heart sick'. Still to receive – not a repetition of promises indeed – but
> of *scorn and insult* when I apply to those gentlemen . . .[16]

The Biblical 'hope deferred that maketh the heart sick' is a frequent
quotation of hers. The authorial voice of *Desmond* too, missing in the
epistolary narrative, had to have an outlet, and for the modern reader
the Preface may be the most interesting part of the work. She seems
to have been uneasy about the adoption of the epistolary form, which
she thought might alienate a readership accustomed to the omniscient
narration of her earlier novels. In the Preface she makes claims for the
Revolution that needed even in 1792 a resolute refusal to confront its
critics:

> As to the political passages dispersed through the work, they are for
> the most part, drawn from conversations to which I have been a
> witness, in England, and France, during the last twelve months: in
> carrying on my story in those countries and at a period when their
> political situation (but particularly that of the latter) is the general
> topic of discourse in both; I have given to my imaginary characters
> the arguments I have heard on both sides; and if those in favour of
> one party have evidently the advantage, it is not owing to my partial
> representation, but to the predominant power of truth and reason,
> which can neither be altered nor concealed.[17]

The faith in enlightenment was not to last for long, but while it did,
it produced exciting work. The four main letter-writers, Desmond
himself, Bethel, Geraldine Verney and Fanny Waverly are all liberal
to varying degrees on national and sexual politics. As she admits, the
other side has no serious spokesperson.

Discussing Burke's *Reflections*, Desmond comments to Bethel:

> Abusive declamation can influence only superficial or prepossessed
> under-standings; those who cannot, or who will not see, that fine-
> sounding periods are not arguments – that *a thousand pens will leap
> from their standishes* (to parody a sublime sentence of his own) to
> answer such a book. I foresee that it will call forth all the talents that
> are yet unbought . . . in England.[18]

Though not a thousand, there were at least a hundred replies to
Burke. Wollstonecraft's *A Vindication of the Rights of Men* came out
before the end of the month, Paine's *The Rights of Man* before the end
of the year. Both saw the Revolution as restoration of a natural order.
In *The Language of Politics in the Age of Wilkes and Burke* James Boulton
writes:

the response of Burke's contemporaries was not only to a body of
ideas but rather to a complete literary achievement . . . Burke was not
only a great thinker, he was also an imaginative writer who requires
a response from the reader as a whole man and not simply as a
creature of intellect.[19]

Boulton wrote this in 1963, which accounts for the 'reader as a
whole man' phrase; in fact Charlotte's response as a whole woman
brought Burke's house image into the mainstream of English fiction.
Her interest lay in politics as much as in the novel, and she would
have made a good political journalist in a later age. After November
1790, she consciously manages political realities to oppose Burke,
constructing a version of history as experienced by history's victims.
Desmond is her most radical novel, and its castle the most uninhab-
itable. In her Preface, she warns that 'there are Readers, to whom the
fictitious occurrences, and others to whom the political remarks in
these volumes may be displeasing',[20] for 'women it is said have no
business with politics',[21] though she says she became an author to
support her children. She argues that women should be as much
concerned with politics as their husbands, brothers or sons.

The action takes place between June 1790 and February 1792 (the
date of 1791 on the last letter is a printer's error), leaving little time
for reflection on current events. *Desmond* and *The Banished Man*
(1794) are the only two contemporary novels I can trace which are set
in France during the Revolution, evidence in itself of Charlotte's
daring. Most other writers, one imagines, were waiting to see how
the cat would jump, though Godwin's *Things As They Are, or Caleb
Williams* (1794) may be read as the private and intimate working out
of an essentially political conflict, and in that sense his novel is about
the Terror.

Judith Stanton believes that Charlotte's 'real strength was as a
storyteller, an omniscient narrator in control of a large field of action
. . . The letter thus restricted her scope and diminished her power.[22]
But the form is appropriate for an argumentative and dialectical
work. The novel opens in a mood of crusading enthusiasm as she
manipulates hostilities between her English and French Revolutionary sympathisers, Desmond, Bethel and Desmond's friend Montfleuri,
and the Royalist forces of reaction, General Wallingford, Colonel
Danby and Montfleuri's uncle, the ci-devant Comte d'Hauteville.
The latter are stock types, Aunt Sallies set up for the reader's easy
contempt.

The ferment of the time is captured in the characters' debates about adultery among the French clergy, the slave trade, and the inequity of political representation in England. Desmond makes the point that 'a labourer [in England] with a wife and four or five children, who has only his labour to depend upon, can taste nothing but bread, and not always a sufficiency of that',[23] and a footnote to the page adds that more English people were being executed than in all the rest of Europe, many of them boys between fifteen and twenty hanged for robbery of small sums.

The heroine Geraldine describes to her sister the peace and relative prosperity of the French after the Revolution as she travels towards Rouen to meet her husband who has joined the counter-revolutionaries. Charlotte was able to use her knowledge of Normandy landscapes. Desmond and Bethel are scathing about the conservative response in England, and debate the freedom of the press, exchanging quotations from Paine, Voltaire and Milton, including the great 'Methinks I see in my mind a noble and puissant nation, rousing herself like the strong man after sleep, and shaking her invincible locks.'[24] Both are contemptuous of Burke. But one can see her increasing reservations about the events unrolling in France as the novel progresses. Desmond is always more optimistic about the establishment of a just society than Bethel, and by the end, the latter's doubts about politicians and about the unchangeable malignity of human nature seem to prevail, or at least are given increasing space.

The events in France are not a mere background to the main plot. Background and plot are thematically linked, and the work fulfills Georg Lucacs' definition of a historical novel. He claims that in eighteenth-century English fiction

> it is only the curiosities and oddities of the *milieu* that matter, not an artistically faithful image of a concrete historical epoch. What is lacking in the so-called historical novel before Sir Walter Scott is precisely the specifically historical, that is, derivation of the individuality of characters from the historical peculiarity of their age.[25]

The contemporaneity of a novel's setting does not debar a work from being 'historical'. What Lucacs looks for is the imprinting of a historical moment on the consciousness of the characters, and he does not find it before Scott. But *Desmond* is this kind of novel, with the heroine's impulse to rebel against her husband reflecting the political rebellion.

The Brighton background of Volume One is energetically done as English partisans of reaction and reform skirmish in libraries, drawing rooms and the streets. Desmond and Margarette Fairfax quarrel over the abolition of titles: Margarette is courting the loutish Lord Newminster as a possible husband. Desmond relays his conversation with her to Bethel:

> Let me ask you [Margarette], would the really great, the truly noble among them (and that there are many such nobody is more ready to allow) be less beloved and revered if they were known only by their family names? . . . For example, the nobleman I had the honour of meeting at your house today. – He is now, I think, called Lord Newminster. Would he be less agreeable in his manners, less refined in his conversation, less learned, less worthy, less respectable, were he unhappily compelled to be called, as his father was before he bought his title, Mr. Grantham?[26]

Margarette is not allowed much in the way of a reply.

Geraldine's husband Verney and her weak brother Waverly (whose name Scott borrowed along with the historical interest and epic sweep of her novel) are sympathisers with the *ancien régime* and under the influence of the Duc de Romagnecourt, to whom Verney tries to sell Geraldine. Verney and Waverly both bear traces of Benjamin Smith. Charlotte links the liberation of the French from authoritarian rule with Geraldine's longing to be free of an unhappy marriage, making her husband a mindless supporter of the *ancien régime*, in the service of which he dies, leaving his wife to marry Desmond, who is in love with her when the novel opens; Geraldine gradually falls in love with him. Her private rebellion, her 'proper spirit of resistance against usurped and abused authority',[27] her husband's, is worked out against the rebellion of the French citizens. The private is integrated with the public narrative.

As one might expect, the Gothic castle which represents the old régime, the home of the Comte d'Hauteville, who will not accept reform and the loss of his titles, is particularly threatening. Desmond sleeps in a sombre, damp and haunted room with a projecting chimney of blood-coloured marble, and after watching a thunderstorm, dreams that Geraldine is dying:

> I believed myself at the same window as where I stood to observe the storm; and, that in the Count's garden, immediately beneath it, I saw Geraldine exposed to all its fury. – Her husband seemed at first to be with her, but he disappeared, I know not how, and she was left exposed to the fury of the contending elements, which seemed to

terrify her less on her own account, than on that of three children, whom she clasped to her bosom, in all the agonies of maternal apprehension, and endeavoured to shelter from the increasing fury of the tempest. – I hastened, I flew, with that velocity we possess only in dreams, to her assistance: I pressed her eagerly in my arms – I wrapt them round her children – I thought she faintly thanked me; told me, that for herself, my care was useless, but that it might protect them. – She was as cold as marble, and I recollect having remarked, that she resembled a beautiful statue of Niobe, done by an Italian sculptor, which I had admired at Lyons.

While I was entreating her to accept of my protection, and to go into the house, I suddenly, by one of those incongruities so usual in sleep, fancied I saw her extended, pale, and apparently dying on the bed, which I had myself objected to go into, with the least of the children, a very young infant dead in her arms.[28]

Later, Desmond walks in the garden for several hours, reluctant to return to his bed and another nightmare:

At length, I heard the clock of the church strike three – I followed the sound for two or three hundred paces, through a cut walk that led from the garden towards it, and entering the church-yard, which is the cimetière of a large village, I was again struck with a circumstance that had before appeared particularly dismal. I mean, that there are in France no marks of graves, as in England

'Where heaves the turf in many a mouldering heap.'

Here all is level – and forgetfulness seems to have laid her cold oblivious hand on all who rest within these enclosures . . .

I listened, and found these sounds came from the farmyard, which was only two or three hundred paces before me. – Hither I gladly found my way, and saw the vine-dressers, and people employed in the making wine, preparing for their work, and going to gather the grapes while the dew was yet on them.[29]

Hauteville Castle is a good candidate for total demolition, and provides a symbol for an old order where nothing is worth saving. The description is nightmare Gothic of the kind Radcliffe developed in the nineties. It is associated with death and decay, and convincing as a correlative for a morbid social and psychological state. It is dangerous to be inside, for its cold and damp cause sickness and confusion, yet for a woman, especially a woman with children, it is still more dangerous to be excluded, unprotected from the storm. In the dream Geraldine has just emerged from the house, a movement that seems linked to her husband's disappearance, and her exposure

to the fury of the storm in the Count's garden suggests the violence
of public opinion against women who go 'outside'.

The castle here is the institution of marriage as well as the state,
and Charlotte is dramatising vividly the nightmare of being single
with children to support. Her Preface stresses her need to provide for
her own children, and her vulnerability to attack. Refuting the
position that women can only engage in political issues by the
neglect of domestic duties, she writes:

> *I* however, may safely say, that it was in the *observance*, not in the
> *breach* of duty, *I* became an Author; and it has happened, that the
> circumstances which have compelled me to write, have introduced
> me to those scenes of life, and those varieties of character, which I
> should otherwise never have seen: Tho alas! it is from thence, that I
> am too well enabled to describe from *immediate* observation,
>
> > The proud man's contumely, th'oppressor's wrong;
> > The laws delay, the insolence of office.[30]

The affairs of her family, she says, are in the power of men who
exercise all these with impunity. But she acknowledges that to
adversity she owes the kindness of the friends she has. She puts
herself with repressed pre-Revolutionary citizens in *Desmond*, and
like them fights back. And she means the reader to see the author in
the fictional Geraldine.

The sign system of her Gothic setting as an emblem of marriage
is developed in an extreme and melodramatic way, though the
turgid scene is saved from absurdity by Desmond's consciousness of
his own weakness and by the intrusion of the everyday social world,
in his embarrassment about waking up Montfleuri and his recollection
of his servant and his letters. The usurped and abused authorities of
the nobility within the state and of husbands within marriage are
linked by the location of Desmond's dream, the gloomiest of all her
castles. The *ancien régime* survives in the hierarchy and customs of
England, the marriage tie is still unbreakable, and Geraldine may be
destroyed by it. We are reminded of the dream again when Geraldine
writes to Fanny 'The prospect every way around me is darkening;
and in the storms that are on all sides gathering, I shall probably
perish.'[31] She does not, but only Verney's death prevents the nightmare
from coming true.

Desmond comes back to sanity after his dream as he moves away
from the castle. As before, the Gothic castle is linked to a medieval
religious building, emphasising the joint power of institutionalised

religion and the state. The quotation from Gray's 'Elegy in a Country Churchyard' with its imaginative regard for the potential greatness in unrecorded village lives constrasts with the smooth graveyard covering generations of villagers who have died in the service of the Comtes d'Hauteville, whose names their masters never knew, and who leave no trace behind. Hope comes only from the vinedressers in the farmyard. Desmond's optimism about the Revolution is confirmed by the rational and informed peasants who work in the open air among the vines.

Growing grapes or grain, fishing or culling game, distributing, sharing, cooking or wasting food is a major preoccupation of *Desmond*. Charlotte has thought about the causes of the Revolution in a visceral and imaginative way. Her economy is felt, as is the inequitable distribution of resources: she includes 'The Breton's Story', taken from a contemporary French pamphlet, about a small farmer whose life is gradually ruined because his overlord will not let him kill the predators of his crops. The novel is not the melodramatic confrontation of rich and poor in a cultural and economic vacuum that a lesser writer would have made it. As Diana Bowstead points out, the book is about consumerism in several ways: Geraldine and the other women are objects for barter, consumption and conspicuous display.

The passage about the peasants working among the vines was probably also intended to be proleptic when Charlotte wrote it, but by the time she had reached her ending, she may have been too aware of the growing power of the French Jacobin party and the larger changes expected to permit a tranquil and peaceful citizenry to end her work. The last pages of the novel are about Geraldine's and Desmond's marriage; the last assessments of the political situation are Bethel's, and fairly sceptical.

A contrasting political house in the novel belongs to Montfleuri, the nephew of de Hauteville and a friend of Desmond's. This is a thriving estate where the owner is attentive to the needs of his servants and farm workers. Unlike his uncle, Montfleuri has had his own old family house pulled down, for

> having no predilection for the Gothic gloom in which his ancestors concealed their greatness he has pulled down every part of the original structure, but what was actually useful to himself; and brought the house, as nearly as he could, into the form of one of those houses, which men of a thousand or twelve hundred a year inhabit in England.[32]

In her early novels Charlotte makes the improvement of the estate a real improvement. S. R. Martin suggests that 'there is in *Desmond* an interesting conflict between the sentimentalist's liking for Gothic architecture and ancient picturesqueness and the brave, forward-looking attitude required of revolutionists',[33] arguing that the hero leans towards the former style. But in fact it is a Gothic landscape not Gothic architecture that Desmond remembers with regret as part of his childhood experience, 'the cathedral-like solemnity of long lines of tall trees, whose topmost boughs are interlaced.'[34]

Montfleuri retains a few of the earlier features of the park, but replants new groups of young trees to break up the formal arrangement into avenues of the chestnuts and arbeals. Consonant with this informalisation of his landscape is his acceptance of the loss of his title, and his concern with his tenants' well-being. Charlotte has traced to Rousseau and America some of the origins of the Revolution. Montfleuri has travelled and fought in America during the War of Independence and the spirit of 1776 guides him in his pursuit of his dependents' happiness. Desmond comments:

> Montfleuri, whose morality borders, perhaps, a little on epicurism, imagines that in this world of ours where physical and unavoidable evil is very thickly sown, there is nothing so good in itself, or so pleasing to the Creator of the world, as to enjoy and diffuse happiness. He has therefore, whether he has resided here or no, made it the business of his life to make his vassals and dependents content, by giving them all the advantages their condition will allow.[35]

Sensibility is defined as sympathy with the poor and oppressed, and with women; the authority of Church and State and the authority of husbands are more closely connected than before. Unlike the first three novels, where romantic love is set in opposition to the power of money and birth, and where hero and heroine are free to marry, love is opposed to marriage, and the heroine is an unhappily married woman. The cruelty of the marriage tie is felt by Bethel as well as Geraldine, and is argued with conviction. This is Charlotte's most overtly feminist novel.

But she can make Geraldine only a partial and theoretical rebel. When Verney orders her to join him in France, she will not ignore marital duty, though she suspects Verney plans to sell her to pay his debts. Geraldine forces herself to remain the exemplary wife. Montfleuri's sister Josephine, however, equally unhappily married, makes clear her attraction to Desmond and has an affair with him that results in her pregnancy. The cloning of Josephine de Boisbelle from Geraldine Verney, creating two heroines with similar names, cruel husbands and Desmond as lover, is a witty structural device. It allows Charlotte to be tolerant of free love without alienating her average reader. Bowstead writes of Josephine that

> her audacity and ardour cast a none-too-flattering shadow over Geraldine's diffidence and chastity . . . The disposition of subject matter – the contiguity of two such similar stories – raises questions about the relationship between resignation and integrity in a morally responsible individual, even when that individual is a woman.[36]

Subversive material is handled with caution, however. Free love is still not within the compass of an English heroine's possible actions, though her French 'twin', as Bowstead says, is less restricted. Verney's death alone allows Geraldine her liberty.

But by eighteenth-century standards it is an amazing ending. Desmond and Geraldine begin their married life with Geraldine's three children and Desmond's and Josephine's illegitimate baby. Only the attentive reader will have suspected the affair and the baby until the last few pages. Josephine is a sympathetic figure, who suffers no more than Desmond from their affair, and a happy ending is found for her in a marriage to a previous lover, after her husband has died in counter-revolutionary fighting. Geraldine has helped her have her baby in secret, we eventually learn. Charlotte is still intent on extending the scope of the novel, in this case to accommodate the actual marital experience of many of her contemporaries. Though the hero's sensibility is humanitarian, he takes little part in the political action. In France he is an observer only, reserving his energies for the final dramatic rescue of Geraldine.

Geraldine and Fanny take on something of the satirical tone found in the omniscient narrator of the first three novels. Geraldine writes a parody of a very bad novel for Fanny's amusement, and Fanny is a witty satirist, a lively but subordinate heroine whose freedoms of speech are a little marginalised. Later Charlotte was to create rather battered and experienced middle-aged heroines to take the roles of commentators.

In spite of the epistolary form, then, the author's point of view is never in doubt, and the novel benefits from its journalistic method. Desmond and Bethel discuss tax exemption, Desmond reports from Paris, the working man and woman are given voices and a long History of France interpolated to orient the amateur politician every reader now emerged. English pro-revolutionary sympathisers have not had a good press, dismissed as naïve or attributed a degree of ferocity many did not possess. Certainly Charlotte is genteel. She is more eager to attack recent rather than old and romantic titles, for instance, as in the case of Lord Newminster. But she was willing to take a chance in a way we can still admire two hundred years later. *Desmond* writes:

> Mr. Burke does not directly assert, whatever disposition he shows to do so, that nothing can be changed or amended in the constitution of England, because the family who now are on the throne derive their sacred right (through a bloody and broken succession) from William the bastard of Normandy; but he maintains, that every future alteration, however necessary, is become impossible, since the compact made for all future generations between the Prince of Orange and the self-elected Parliament who gave him the crown in 1688 – So that, if at any remote period, it should happen, what cannot indeed be immediately apprehended, that the crown should descend to a prince more profligate than Charles the Second, without his wit and more careless of the welfare and prosperity of his people than James the Second, without his piety; the English must submit to whatever burthens his vices shall impose . . .[37]

As everyone knew, that period was already at hand, as was the prince in the ample form of George, Prince of Wales, living a few streets away from her. In another two years anti-monarchic polemics however coated in irony would be dangerous; even now they were controversial.

Desmond was too radical for Cadell. He was close to retirement and the firm was passing to the control of his son, Thomas Cadell junior, and William Davies. All three found it distasteful, both in its Republicanism and its love interest, and refused to take it. But George Robinson with whom she had negotiated over *Ethelinde* was glad to add her to his list. He was a Whig, and entertained at his Streatham villa more distinguished Opposition writers than anyone except Joseph Johnson. Sadly, for this most revolutionary of her novels, the *Desmond* contract was made between Robinson and Benjamin.

Reviews in the four liberal magazines, *The Critical, The European, The Monthly* and *The Analytical* were generally favourable, *The Critical* reviewer conceding that 'history may confirm her sentiments and confute ours.'[38] But Wollstonecraft's reponse is disappointing, consisting mainly of quotation and almost without comment on the subject-matter; she was getting blasée about reviewing. She makes her former qualification, that Charlotte has more knowledge of the world than of the human heart, though she praises her wit as caricaturist. The minor characters, she says, 'are sketched with that happy dexterity that shoots folly as it flies.'[39]

Charlotte made only 150 guineas, as this was a three volume novel, for the first edition. *Desmond* would be out of bounds to some young women, previously through the seventies and eighties a novelist's best constituency. In the nineties, though, this was beginning to change. The novel was becoming, as Gary Kelly notes, the most important forum for political debate outside Parliament, attracting readers of both sexes and all ages. Moving away from the traditional young-girl's-courtship plot was not in itself a bad business venture. But she felt very hard up in the winter of 1791–2. On 28 December she wrote to John Nichols, editor of *The Gentleman's Magazine* and eventual author of *Literary Anecdotes of the Eighteenth Century*:

> My situation is extremely terrible, for I have no means whatever of supporting my children during the Holidays, nor of paying their Bills when they return to School: & I am so harrassed with Duns that I cannot write with any hope of getting anything done by that time. I know not where I find resolution to go on from day to day Especially under the idea of Mr. Smith's being in London, liable every hour to imprisonment. Were it not for Mrs O'Neill & two or three other friends who soften to me the horrors of my destiny, I cannot answer for what I should do. Thus it was last Christmas, & thus for aught I can see it may be next if I so long live. Even when the present Accounts with the Grocers are settled, you heard Mr. Herman say that the Accounts could not be closed as Berney has omitted to send from Barbadoes an Account of what he had received & that there would still be something due to the Trustees. Reasons enough to be sure to keep my unhappy children starving and destitute. But would the Chancellor think so? Charlotte [Mary] talks of appealing to him, which I shall not oppose.

This is the first reference to a possible intervention from the Court of Chancery in the business of the Trust. Evidently one of Richard's family, a relative of his daughter Mary's first husband, was still engaged in running the Barbados plantations. All debts had to be called in and all credits paid before the value of the will could be calculated, and in the nature of things this perfect point of equilibrium was impossible to achieve. Duns were not supposed to force their way into a private house, but they must have made her life very unpleasant if they gathered round her front door or peered through

the windows. At times she was probably unable to go out and the
children too would have been harrassed with enquiries as to when
their mother meant to pay her debts.

There is no hint of what Jenny thought about *Desmond*. Perhaps
she did not choose to read it or was discouraged from doing so. She
was sixteen now and called by her baptismal name, which was of
course Jane. It is hard to defamiliarise and see her as an adolescent,
with 'Jane Austen' still in the future. Authority is there from the start.
None of the Austens shared Charlotte's enthusiasm for the reforms
in France. Their cousin Eliza de Feuillide, formerly Eliza Hancock,
had a French aristocrat husband who was living with his mistress in
Paris. Though not overly concerned about him, Eliza was following
events as closely as she could as she would soon have to rejoin him.
Austen did not necessarily believe everything her cousin said, but
her father too was alarmed at what was happening. Counter-
revolutionary sentiment was growing as more emigrés joined
Charles Calonne, the former Deputy-General, in London. But Pitt's
administration was cautious about committing troops to support
Louis.

Charlotte did not lack literary friends now. Her profession brought
pleasures as well as hard work. Hayley praised her wherever he
went, put her in touch with other writers and maintained a gossipy
sympathising correspondence. Henrietta entertained her in London
and could not have enough of her company. She kept a fire in the
breakfast room while Charlotte was there so she could treat the
house as her own, read and write in peace or see publishers or the
Trust lawyers. Henrietta was of much the higher rank of the two,
through her father who was one of the Boyle family as well as
through her husband, and rich, as Hoare's granddaughter. But she
was nine years younger, and though she had published in a few
magazines, not a recognised poet. These inequalities balanced themselves out in ways that satisfied both. Charlotte put Henrietta's 'Ode
to the Poppy' into *Desmond* and referred to her friendship in the
Preface as the pride and pleasure of her life. Henrietta knew how to
invite without patronising, and Charlotte would have enjoyed playing the lioness at her parties. Leigh Hunt in *Men, Women and Books*
implies that Henrietta and Charlotte regularly took opium together,
although it is not clear whether he simply infers this from the Ode
and their friendship or whether he had inside information, though it
was probably merely the former: he was only ten when Henrietta
died. But he defends the 'fair novelist' for 'trying to amend the evils

which tempted them to its use.'[40] Hayley and Henrietta were perhaps equally important to Charlotte.

If Desmond as the heroine's rescuer has a prototype in her life, she does not mean to make the identification plain. Some of the violence of the work stems from her anger at her own fetters; though separated, she was still married, and she had lost the best part of her life. But the children, and finding money to educate and establish them, were her immediate problems in the year she was writing her revolutionary novel.

After more than a year at home, Charles made up his mind to join the army. He had no money to go to Oxford, or to buy the St Mary's incumbency if he did. Charlotte Mary would perhaps have waived the money, but these could be only imaginary transactions while the will remained unsettled. It was a more painful goodbye for Charlotte even than when William and Nicholas left, though Charles was not going abroad but only to join the 14th Regiment of Foot, the Bedfordshires. Still, a year or two might bring war with France. Some alarmists even spoke of civil war. In either eventuality she would wish her son anywhere rather than in the army. But Charles would not remain at home, and claimed he was not cut out for a clergyman; Charlotte conceded how demoralising idleness at home might be. In a few years, Charles said, Lionel could have the incumbency.

But Lionel, now fourteen, was probably even less cut out for a clergyman than Charles. Joseph Warton, his headmaster at Winchester, wrote to Charlotte in the summer of 1791 complaining about his slow progress and inattention. In her reply on 31 August, Charlotte fielded this like most parents, anxiously defensive, describing a conversation of her own with Lionel when he complained he was set exercises too difficult for him but promised to do better. Warton evidently sweetened his complaint with compliments on *Celestina*, though he did not pretend to have read much of it. As mentioned earlier, in this letter she identifies the close as the strongest part, and goes on:

> I wrote it indeed under much oppression of Spirit from the long and frequently hopeless difficulties in which my children's affairs continue to be involved – Difficulties that my time & perseverance as well as the generous interposition of many friends of superior abilities in the Law have been vainly applied to conquer. For two three or four years, the burthen of so large a family whose support depends entirely upon me (while I have not even the interest of my own fortune to do it with) might be undertaken in the hope that at the

end of that period their property might be restored to them. But when above seven years have pass'd in such circumstances, that sickness of the Soul which arises from Hope long delay'd will inevitably be felt. The worn out pen falls from the tired hand, and the real calamities of life press too heavily to allow of the power of evading them by fictitious detail. Another year however is coming when I must by the same motives be compelled to a renewal of the same sort of task.

But the postscript is the point of the letter. She mentions that her friend Mrs O'Neill of Shane's Castle is coming to England to place her two sons in school. She would prefer Eton, but with her partial opinion of Charlotte's judgement will refer the matter to her. Charlotte's comments on the older O'Neill boy's inherited abilities and princely fortune are not very ideologically consistent with the fiction she was then writing. If Warton can assure her the boys can board privately, and bring their tutor, she will deliver them. She adds:

> I could wish to be able to answer these questions from the best Authority. Yet do not mean to give you the trouble of writing about them. Only, as I have not at this moment the draft for Lionel's bills ready for Mr. Goddard [his housemaster] nor time to write, I take the liberty of mentioning it here . . .

She cannot pay Lionel's bill, and offers Henrietta's children instead. The duns were bad enough, but she was used to them, and the tradespeople they represented were seldom quite real to her. Warton was different, and she must have found these shifts humiliating, especially as the O'Neill boys did in fact go to Eton. But two years later Lionel left in a blaze of glory still remembered in the annals of Winchester.

Warton's headship lurched between complete indulgence and the occasional desperate attempt to restore order. In 1793 he threatened to flog the boys *en masse*, and there was a major riot, with Lionel as one of the instigators. They stole provisions in the town, barricaded themselves in for a siege with pistols and knives, and hurled marbles at the tutors sent to negotiate. Hilbish records the story as it was handed down to Lionel's great-grandson. He

> headed a schoolboy rebellion so successfully at Winchester the troops had to be called out, to whom he surrendered with full military honours and on being sent home he told his mother not to worry as the only difference it made was he would have to become a general instead of a bishop.[41]

He became, at least, a lieutenant-general. Charlotte entirely supported him in his declining to be flogged. She was an indulgent mother, Catherine records, and however worrying expulsion might seem, she would never have to settle his bill.

Despite the plaintive tone about the worn out pen and the tired hand, a tone adopted for a practical purpose, and despite her continuing shortage of money, the *Desmond* year was not all cheerless. She heard that Nicholas had arrived safely in Bombay. She could afford to go to Paris, went often to London, and as a literary celebrity was visited by travellers to and from France. She had a house full of lively children, some of them of an age to be companionable, and a busy social life. A note on 27 November 1791 to a London friend, Mrs Thomas Lowes, who evidently visited Brighton often, catches some impression of this:

> Madam,
> I intended to have done myself the honour of waiting on you yesterday, but Augusta told me at one period of the morning you were out, and I was afterwards detain'd by Mr. Wordsworth (whom I could not take leave of, till he embark'd) till it was too late to have the pleasure I intended. This morning I am summoned to London & thus deprived of an opportunity of paying my respects to you here, but if you will allow me to wait on you in Town where I am likely to be a fortnight, I will avail myself of that permission with great pleasure. My abode during that time is at 'The Hon'ble Mrs O'Neills, Henrietta Street, Cavendish Square' where, if you favor me with intelligence of your being at your London residence, I will take the earliest opportunity of assuring you personally that I am, Madam Your most obedt & oblig Sert, Charlotte Smith

Wordsworth, though distantly related through John Robinson, visited her not as a duty but as an admired Nature poet, novelist with a passion for sublime scenery and fellow radical. He had read her first edition of *Elegiac Sonnets* as a fourteen-year-old schoolboy at Hawkshead. He was twenty-one, had published nothing and was quite unknown. She gave him letters of introduction to Helen Maria Williams and to Brissot; evidently she had used her time in Paris to talk to interesting people. His development was to follow the trajectory of hers: sympathy for the Revolution followed by disillusion and retreat into a green world. Paul Kelly argues that her 'To the South Downs', Sonnet 5, directly influenced his first publication, *An Evening Walk*. He quotes from the sonnet near the beginning of his own poem, which is however more visual and wider-ranging in subject than hers, contrasting Nature's beauty with the injustice of the social contract in his description of the evicted widow and her two babies who die on the road. Charlotte was attempting this sort of social comment in her poetry too, in 'The Dead Beggar', for instance, but she does not incorporate it into a natural setting. She showed him unpublished poems on this visit.

She saw a lot of the Lowes and of Brighton friends generally. Even casual acquaintances must have known her current novel was to be about the French Revolution. That summer a celebration of the Fall of the Bastille at Dadley's Hotel in Birmingham incited a Church and King mob to burn down the houses of the Unitarian minister Joseph Priestley and seven other sympathisers with the Revolution. The Priestleys lost everything, including his books and papers representing years of work; he took Forgiveness as his sermon topic on the following Sunday, though he failed to convince his wife. Pro-revolutionary sympathies were still just respectable in English society in the summer of 1791.

Louis and Marie-Antoinette with their two children were confined in the Tuileries. They had attempted to escape to the border of the Austrian Netherlands where her brother's troops were waiting for them. With their children and Louis' sister, Madame Elisabeth, all in disguise, they got away in the night of 20 June and covered most of the 200 miles to the border. But they were delayed at Varennes when a wheel came off their *berline*. They were brought back to Paris where an ominously silent crowd came out to watch their return. Louis was still nominally and to some extent actually King, his agreement needed to pass any new law. The plans of Charles Talleyrand, Bishop of Autun – who wore his episcopal office lightly – to annex the church's wealth for the new régime appalled him, and he used his veto to protect the traditional, unaligned priesthood as far as possible. But the little power he had was eroding month by month. The attempt to escape had associated him more firmly with Austria and Prussia, enemies now planning to invade in a bid to secure the monarchy or at least the safety of the royal family. In the following spring Prussian troops moved towards Verdun. By this time Louis and Marie-Antoinette were entirely identified as traitors by the patriots. On 10 August after tentative earlier attacks, a mixture of *gards français*, new conscripts and civilians entered the Tuileries and killed 600 of Louis' personal bodyguard, his Swiss, as they were called, though only about a third were Swiss nationals. He survived with his family, but it was the last day of his monarchy.

The news reached Brighton on the following day; it was the most alarming event yet. Previously, defenders of the Revolution had been able to point to tremendous changes made with little bloodshed, most of it on the revolutionary side. To the English pro-revolutionaries as to the *sans-culottes*, Louis and his wife were indeed in league with foreign powers and should not expect the French to forget it. Charlotte went so far, or so she is reported, as saying the Swiss Guard deserved to die. She was not a cruel woman, and this was probably said in heated argument with someone like the General Wallingford who appears in *Desmond*, a garden roller fitted with feet and determined to flatten all opposition. But Thomas Lowes never forgave her, and years later wrote an addendum of his own on her note to his wife, just quoted:

> I saw a great deal of Charlotte Smith one Autumn [i.e. 1791] at Brighthelmstone & bating a democratic twist (which I think detestable in a woman), I liked her well enough for some time, but she disgusted me completely, on the acct arriving of the Massacre of the Swiss Guards at the Tuileries by saying that they richly deserved it: I observed that they did merely their duty, & if they had not done what they did they w'd have been guilty of Treason & that I thought they deserved the pity of every person who reasoned & felt properly. After this I never wd see Charlotte, but she and Mrs L[owes] sometimes met.

Other friends and acquaintances reacted in the same way. Catherine says that *Desmond*

> lost her some friends, and furnished others with an excuse for withholding their interest in favour of her family, and brought a host of *literary ladies* in array against her, armed with all the malignity which envy could inspire!

Mary Hays in *British Public Characters* writes more generally about the exposure and vulnerability of the eighteenth-century woman writer, and the power of the press:

> The penalties and discouragements attending the profession of an author fall upon women with a double weight; to the curiosity of the idle and the envy of the malicious their sex affords a peculiar incitement; arraigned, not merely as writers, but as *women*, their characters, their conduct and even their personal endowments, become the subjects of severe inquisition: from the common allowances claimed by the species in general, literary women appear only to be exempted: in detecting their errors and exposing their foibles, malignant ingenuity is active and unwearied – vain would be the

hope to shield themselves from detraction, by the severest prudence
or the most entire seclusion: wanton malice, in the failure of facts,
amply supplies materials for defamation, while, from the anguish of
wounded delicacy, the gratification of demons seems to be extracted.
Besides her sharing as a literary woman this general and most unjust
persecution, Mrs Smith individually created enemies by the zeal and
perseverance with which she endeavoured to obtain justice for her
children, of men who hated her in proportion as they had injured her.

Hays was writing in 1801 after William Godwin published his
Memoirs of Wollstonecraft, his late wife and Hays' close friend. For
his contemporary readers he was much too frank about her suicide
attempts, illegitimate daughter by Gilbert Imlay, and relationship
with himself. The book excited a strong reaction and effectively
ended the feminist movement that began in the 1780s and nineties.
Hays was also writing out of her own experience, stigmatised as an
ugly and petticoated 'thing' by Coleridge, the butt of literary London
as 'Bridgetina Botherim'[42] for her novel *Emma Courtney* in which the
heroine pursues a married man.

If Charlotte felt similarly threatened, it does not appear in her
letters or novels at this date. Two subjects only arouse rage and
paranoia; one is her continuing tie to Benjamin, the other the non-
settlement of the will. Benjamin was living with his housekeeper in
Hamilton, Scotland in the unimaginative alias of Brian Symmonds to
avoid duns and arrest, but he would sometimes venture to London
in disguise to see old friends and try to extract money from Charlotte's publishers. It must have been on one such occasion he insisted
on signing the *Desmond* contract with George Robinson. And the
business of the Trust dragged on. By this point, both Charlotte and
Robinson agreed there were no further debts outstanding to Richard's
estate, though apparently other legatees or Trustees did not. It had
taken fifteen years to get so far. For over a year she had been seeking
a general meeting of all the Trustees, but though this meeting
eventually took place on 28 January 1792, it resolved nothing.

Yet if she complains often about her marriage and the Trust, she
seems to have been easy in her relations with friends and with that
larger acquaintance who knew her mainly through her books and
saw her only occasionally. She would become more vulnerable to
critical attack later, but in the eighties and early nineties her literary
persona was her strength, irrespective of whether her opinions were
popular, not a cause of anxiety. And though there was gossip about
her, she ignored it. Wollstonecraft and Hays never had quite that

gentry confidence, while she lacked Wollstonecraft's intellectual consistency and personal recklessness. What Stanton finely describes as the 'mannered graciousness'[43] of her literary idiom was probably observable in her social behaviour too, and swept impertinence before it. If she had a touch of the Sloane about her, it was a useful armour.

It could have been only a day or two after the fight Lowes witnessed, or engaged in, that she set out for Eartham. The visit was to last two weeks and allow her to meet Hayley's new friend Cowper, whose *The Task* she had re-read often since it first appeared. *Desmond* had only been out a month, but she was already planning a new novel. Again it would be political, about the constitution, about the way a country's wealth should be divided. But this time it would be mainly about England, not France. Whatever she maintained to Tory acquaintances in Brighton, provoked by the triumphalism of the anti-democrats after 10 August, who always knew it would end in horrors, she was herself less sure now that revolution would establish a better constitution there. On her way to Eartham she was thinking about this, wondering about Cowper and remembering his 'old castle of the state'. She thought again about Burke's use of that metaphor, and saw how she could construct a house that symbolised England, show how much it needed repair and a fairer assignment of its rooms. That would more subtly affect the reader than the arguments of Desmond and Bethel.

The road was the one she had travelled to and from The Ship eight years ago. It took her into Arundel, where the right fork went to Bignor a few miles away, the left to Eartham. The helplessness in which she had lived most of her life had to be confronted again when she made that journey; but it returned her to the place of her childhood self too.

The other guests had arrived before her. George Romney spent the late summer and early autumn with Hayley every year, painting in a studio especially made out of the old stables for him. He knew his host intimately and treated Eartham like home. Though he was never well, he had recovered from his infatuation with Emma Hart, who had married Sir William Hamilton the summer before leaving him miserable on his last Eartham visit. On earlier occasions he had painted Hayley, Seward and a lovely portrait of Thomas Alphonso, aged eleven, as Robin Goodfellow. He looked over the new arrivals with a professional eye.

Charlotte left no record of this gathering, but Romney wrote quite a detailed one in a letter to his son when his visit was over:

> I was near a month at Mr. Hayley's, where I met Mr. Cowper and Mrs Smith; and yet, in spite of such good company, and bathing, my health continues very poorly. – Mr. Cowper is a most excellent man; he has translated Milton's Latin Poems, and I suppose very well. Hayley is writing the life of Milton, so you may imagine we were deep in that poet; every thing belonging to him was collected together and some part of his works read every day. Mrs Smith is writing another Novel, which, as far as it is advanced, is, I think, very good. She began it while I was there, and finished one volume. She wrote a chapter every day, which was read at night, without requiring any correcting. I think her a woman of astonishing powers . . .
>
> She and the two poets were employed every morning from eight o'clock until twelve in writing, when they had a luncheon, and walked an hour; they then wrote again till they dressed for dinner. After dinner they were employed in translating an Italian play on the subject of Satan; about twenty lines was the number every day. After that they walked, or played at Coits; then tea, and after that they read till supper time.[44]

Cowper and his companion Mary Unwin had been three days on the road from Weston Underwood; he was amazed at finding himself and Mary so far from home, delighted by the setting and Roman simplicity of Eartham. Hayley had made his acquaintance very recently; he was sixty-one and generally lived in complete seclusion. Travel was a major undertaking, too disturbing to his equilibrium. Twenty-nine years previously he had tried to establish himself in a legal career in London. This resulted in breakdown and attempted suicide. After a brief period in an asylum he boarded with the Reverend Morley Unwin and his wife Mary, and after Morley's death, with Mary. Hayley had always admired him but with unusual reticence forborn to address him by post. But when he discovered they were both working on Milton, he wrote a very good letter in praise of Cowper's poetry and asked to meet him. Cowper's reply on the expectation of a meeting, his 'consciousness, that I shall not answer on a nearer view'[45] typifies the urbanity and sweetness of his correspondence.

So Hayley went to Weston in the spring of 1792, and the two Williams got on very well. But Mary, who was seventy, had a stroke during the visit. Hayley's care for both of them bound Cowper to him more closely than months of acquaintance could otherwise have done. He kept Cowper sane through the first few days and when she began to recover searched the neighbourhood for one of the new electrical machines he used himself at home for inflammation of the eyes. At least it did her no harm, as she recovered enough to make the visit to Eartham. In his relationship with Cowper, in his company, Hayley was at his best, and very conscious of mere literary facility in the presence of genius. He went to great trouble to get a pension for Cowper, and though not a rich man gave what help and hospitality he could. Mary's electrical treatments continued at Eartham, and Thomas pushed her out in a wheeled chair to look at the grounds and the distant view of the sea.

So Hayley's plans for making his house a Temple of the Muses were realised that summer in a lucky mixture of talents. They quickly set up a balance of work and leisure. All morning Charlotte established her old manor house somewhere between Bignor and Eartham, a few miles from the sea; Hayley and Cowper went on with their work on Milton and jointly translated Andreini's *Adamo*; Romney drew. The Cowper portrait he began as soon as the poet arrived is finer than his Emmas. The 'stricken' quality is there, but also the fortitude with which the subject faces madness. Charlotte in her pastel drawing turns her gaze a little aside. At forty-three she has a comely, gentle face; Romney gives her a guarded look, as of a person not easily known. She would be less matronly without her cap; even with it she retains something of the piquancy of her teens, though her expression is sad. She thought it 'a very good likeness, neither flattered nor otherwise'.[46]

Cowper observed her closely and did not forget her later, when he commented on her professional life, chained to her desk like a slave to his oar. That metaphor had sunk very deep into English consciousness by the last decade of the century. He added that he only regretted his own poverty when he saw someone who so deserved help. She was a new species to him. But she did not need his sympathy at Eartham. Here she could forget for the first time in ten years her financial burdens and old resentments; or at least, she transformed them into a fictional world without any trailing autobiographical ends. Now for once she did not feel as though she wrote only to live; for two weeks she lived to write, and to read her work aloud every evening.

The Old Manor House is sombre and slow-moving; the emblematic significance of Rayland Hall emerges gradually, without any of the short cuts of allegory. Unless the reader is particularly politically-minded, she may be half way through the novel before she sees that the house, its history, and indeterminate future are codes for England, or that the hierarchy of characters is representative of English society. There is no one moment when the house becomes unequivocally England. Rather, the symbolic presentation crystallises through the reader's constant awareness of the Hall, through the completeness of the social spectrum observed and through a knowledge of the absorbing political preoccupations of the time. Contemporary events in France would have made the simplest sentence reverberate. Describing Snelcraft the coachman's plans, Charlotte writes:

> Of deeper sagacity than the other two [upper servants], he foresaw that the time could not be far distant when Rayland Hall, and all the wealth that belonged to it, must change its possessor.[47]

Like some other political novels, *Animal Farm* for instance, *The Old Manor House* is not a closed system, and must be seen in its historical context to bring out its fullest meaning. But there are sometimes more direct hints to help our reading, as when the servant Jacob repeats the reflections of Mrs Lennard the housekeeper, in a clear echo of Burke:

> 'But she said to me, says she – "When you have done that job, Jacob, I wish you would just look at the wainscot under the window, and under them there drawers of mine; for it's as rotten as touchwood, and the rats are forever coming in," says she; and says she, "I never saw the like of this old house – it will tumble about our ears, I reckon, one day or 'nother, and yet my lady is always repairing it," says she; "but the wainscotting of this here end of the wing," says she, "has been up above an hundred years; and we may patch it, and patch it, and yet be never the nearer: but, for my part, I suppose it will last my time," says she.'[48]

The recall of Burke's warping wainscot is mischievous. Though all Charlotte's Gothic castles and their Estates after the *Reflections* are emblems of England, in none of her other novels – or perhaps of any writer's – is the concept worked out in such detail. Of Rayland Hall's descendants – Mansfield Park, Chesney Wold, Howard's End, Wragby Hall and all the others – only Mansfield Park fills out its novel so completely. The Manor, seen in many moods and subject to many and various uses, is the subject.

To treat a great house as an appropriate setting in a novel was not original. Mr Allworthy's Paradise Hall in *Tom Jones* is a romantic conservative's repository of squirearchical values. Harlowe Place has the rawness of new money. But these are not microcosms of England. Rayland Hall is owned by the autocratic Grace Rayland,

'Mrs' by courtesy and immensely proud of her pedigree, who keeps its customs unchanged from 1688. Its ownership is disputed by corrupt clergy and tricky lawyers, its security threatened by scheming servants and by a criminal class hiding in the cellars. The diversity of interests produces not liberty, as Burke claimed, but suspicion and hatred.

The Hall is large and rambling, incorporating several architectural styles back to the Gothic of the turret where the heroine Monimia has her isolated bedroom. It is kept vivid to our imagination by reminders of its appearance on tranquil afternoons, at daybreak or at night. Even in America, Orlando thinks about it frequently, which emphasises its conceptual centrality. The unused staterooms are preserved intact with their late-seventeenth-century furniture:

> The furniture was rich, but old fashioned: – the beds were of cut velvet or damask, with high testers, some of them with gilt cornices: – the chairs were worked, or of coloured velvets, fringed with silk and gold, and had gilt feet: – fine japanned cabinets, beautiful pieces of china, large glasses, and some valuable pictures, were to be seen in every room, which, though now so rarely inhabited, were kept in great order; and the oak floors were so nicely waxed, that to move upon them was more like skating than walking.[49]

The gilding, the oak, the order, make the well-preserved central section a shrine of traditional values. The luxury in this part of the house is suggested in the shining surfaces, but so is its fragility, and someone entering without due caution could knock everything over in venturing onto the 'nicely waxed' floor.

Mrs Rayland is the survivor of three spinster daughters of Sir Hildebrand Rayland. Like Sir Leicester Dedlock sixty years later, she comes to represent for the reader one of the owners of England, whom Charlotte sees as politically conservative, sexually repressive upholders of the established social hierarchy. Her sentiments are typical of her time and class, and she attempts to intimidate her dependents. The newly rich are her particular abhorrence, though she can be indulgent to erring servants if they are servile enough. Stasis and claustrophobia make the atmosphere of the rooms she inhabits: her sitting room with its fire and window where Monimia sits spinning, longing for one of the occasional visitors to call so she can make her escape, and the Long Gallery with its family portraits where Mrs Rayland walks. In her family pride as she contemplates the portraits of her ancestors, Charlotte satirises Burke's veneration of inherited rank. In the following passage from the *Reflections*, Burke means by a 'liberal descent' the ability to trace an unbroken line of ladies and gentlemen among one's forebears:

> This idea of a liberal descent inspires us with a sense of habitual native dignity, which prevents that upstart insolence almost inevitably adhering to and disgracing those who are the first acquirers of any distinction . . . It carries an imposing and majestic aspect. It has a pedigree and illustrating ancestors. It has its bearings and ensigns armorial. *It has its gallery of portraits* [my italics]; its monumental inscriptions; its records, evidences and titles. We procure reverence to our civil institutions on the principle upon which nature teaches us to revere individual men: on account of their age; and on account of those from whom they are descended.[50]

She mocks Burke's solemnity with her picture of Sir Hildebrand, 'who in armour, and on a white horse whose flanks were overshadowed by his stupendous wig, pranced over the great gilt chimney-piece, just as he appeared at the head of a county association in 1707.'[51] Mrs Rayland and the elderly, authoritarian General Tracy are both examples of unvenerable age.

The silence of the Hall's staterooms is broken only by occasional dinner days or by the Michaelmas feast for the tenants. Mrs Rayland 'was never known to have done a voluntary kindness to any human being: and though she sometimes gave away money, it was never without making the wretched petitioner pay most dearly for it, by many a bitter humiliation.'[52] She is especially antagonistic to the Somerive family, the descendants of her aunt by a socially unacceptable marriage to a gentleman farmer. The Raylands, the Somerives and their cousins the Woodfords form a network of hostile family relationships; Charlotte images through them the competitiveness and cruelty of eighteenth-century society, and undercuts Burke's image of the family as sacred.

She is deft in showing how the older characters' thoughts and feelings are coloured by the past, by events that fester in the memory fifty years later. In this way she suggests England's resistance to change. The son of Mrs Rayland's aunt married, disgracefully in the Raylands' eyes, the poor companion to the Miss Raylands, though he might have married one of them, and Mrs Rayland has never forgotten the insult. The son of this marriage, Philip Somerive, has two sons, Philip, wasteful and arrogant, a typical elder son, considering himself the heir to Mrs Rayland, and Orlando, the hero of the novel, and four daughters, of whom Isabella the secondary heroine is the most vivid. Mrs Rayland cherishes a violent dislike for all of them except Orlando. This is psychologically convincing, and also contributes to that sense of the past which has an important place in the novel. The problems the young face in breaking free from their families and living their own lives show Charlotte's increasing recognition of the great difficulties that stood in the way of change and a fresh start.

Early in September, news of the prison massacres at Paris began to arrive in England. It may have reached the party at Eartham before Charlotte left, or she may have heard it when she returned to Brighton where she started on the next volume without a break. The Prussian army was thought in Paris to be advancing against the revolutionaries. There was a hasty enrolment of volunteers, while rumours circulated that the new régime's prisoners would break out as soon as the troops had gone, murder patriots and hand over the city to the counter-revolutionary forces. The city's prisoners were mainly non-conforming priests, those few Swiss Guards who had survived 10 August, prostitutes, and suspect members of the old court including Princesse Marie-Thérèse de Lamballe, a friend of Marie-Antoinette. On the night of 1–2 September and during the next day about 1,400 prisoners were brutally murdered, including de Lamballe, whose head was waved on a pike under Marie-Antoinette's window. As Charlotte's narrative goes on, she becomes less hostile to authority, more pessimistic about liberty and the rearrangement of the constitution.

A sense of stasis is created by weighty and complex sentences, always a quality of her style but especially effective in *The Old Manor House*. Antithesis and parallels pull in a past well-established in the narrator's imagination:

> And indeed it was on these occasions that Mrs Rayland seemed to take peculiar pleasure in mortifying Mrs Somerive and her daughters; who dreaded these dinner days as those of the greatest penance; and who at Christmas, one of the periods of these formal dinners, have blest more than once the propitious snow; through which that important and magisterial personage, the body coachman of Mrs Rayland, did not choose to venture himself, or the six sleek animals of which he was sole governor; for on these occasions it was the established rule to send for the family, with the same solemnity and the same parade that had been used ever since the first sullen and reluctant reconciliation between Sir Hildebrand and his sister; when she dared to deviate from the fastidious arrogance of her family, and to marry a man who farmed his own estate – and who, though long

settled as a very respectable land owner, had not yet written Armiger after his name.[53]

One extended meditative sentence envelopes the times the Somerive women came to dinner and the times they escaped. Charlotte's guarded and hesitant style is most pronounced in *The Old Manor House*, which is poised between the revolutionism of *Desmond* and the conservative stance of *The Banished Man*. The lexis and dominant metaphors are grave and weighty like the sentence structure, and are those of government, in 'important and magisterial', 'sole governor', 'established rule', and 'parade'; and of religion, in 'mortifying', 'greatest penance', 'blest', 'solemnities' and 'reconciliation'. The dominance of these clusters in the language enacts the dominance of the political and religious hegemony over the lives of the Somerive women, the intimate encroachment of the state upon the daily life. She shows two generations of Somerive women humiliated into submission through fear. In the ironic tone of 'that important and magisterial personage, the body coachman of Mrs Rayland' she establises a competing and assertive hierarchy amongst the servants, ready to fill the gentry's places. Within the antithesis of the sentence structure she presents the poles of nominal social celebration and actual social unpleasantness. Her narrators like her heroes and heroines and her poetic personae are always looking back to the distant past, as in the last sentence. Her heroines, especially, live in a tangle of conditional and concessive clauses. Compared to this cautious advance, Austen narrative leaps forward clear and certain.

Apart from the American section, this is a static book, with many of the main characters pulled in two directions and unable to act. Orlando and Monimia are especially indecisive, not sure whether to obey parents and authority figures, or whether to rebel and try to create a new life independent of their families and pasts. So their love story becomes a political fable for its time, when Charlotte's contemporaries could not decide either what to feel about the confrontation of tradition and democracy.

But *The Old Manor House* resists simplification into allegory. Charlotte brought her whole personal history, political insights and imagination to this dramatisation of a historic moment, when England suddenly seemed accessible to change and new ownership. Major Danby and the Comte d'Hauteville in *Desmond* are caricatures held up for the reader's easy contempt. But Mrs Rayland is her most subtle characterisation. Initially two-dimensional, a figure of fun, she goes on to provoke the reader's anger at her cruelty, but in the end we feel some respect for her determination and courage, and at the Tenants' Feast she is superior to the toadies who preponderate among her guests.

Charlotte implicitly admits that the class Mrs Rayland represents will not be easily set aside, and we would not want her replaced by Snelcraft, or Pattenson the butler. She creates a domestic Elizabeth Tudor, authoritarian and capricious, but lonely and disappointed, and almost an object of sympathy. She is easily duped by flattery: Lennard, the housekeeper, who hopes to inherit some of her money, successfully pretends to be older than her, and deflects her attention from anything she does not want her to see by turning the conversation to family honours, family ghosts, or the murder of Charles I by the demagogues. Mrs Rayland has a cutting turn of speech and a duplicitous epistolary style which enlist the reader's sympathy. The growth of her affection for Orlando, and even for Monimia, also humanises her somewhat. Initially the three Miss Raylands are as formidable as Megara, Alecto and Tisiphone. But by the time Orlando leaves Rayland Hall for America,

> it seemed as if towards the close of her life Mrs Rayland had acquired, instead of losing, her sensibility; for she, who had hardly ever loved anybody, now found that she could not without pain part from Orlando.[54]

But her family affection is inseparable from a sense of pride and prestige acquired through a relation she can boast about, and her brutal lack of imagination is evident when she encourages Orlando in his military career and welcomes his opportunity to fight the American rebels for the reflected lustre it will shed on her. Mrs Rayland has an antediluvian admiration for the trappings of chivalry, although unlike Burke she is hypocritically puritanical.

The depiction of England is also worked out in the characterisation of upper and lower servants, who represent aspiring commercial, lower-middle and lower-class interests. Never until Mrs Henry Wood's *East Lynne* (1861) is there such a cross-sectioning of a house, showing the working and idling of the servants as often as the life of the owner. Orlando has to exercise caution to avoid meeting a groom at work late in the stables, or a gardener out before daybreak, when he escorts Monimia between her room and the library. The upper servants, Lennard, Snelcraft, and Pattenson, all hope to inherit part of the Manor or some of Mrs Rayland's money. They wait patiently for her death, while other hopeful inheritors among the clergy, the lawyers and her own family wait less patiently.

In this most subtle of her novels, Charlotte analyses the fluid nature of class. None of the simple signs of *Desmond* are used here. The crude imposition of class labels on other characters by Mrs Rayland draws attention to the futility of such labelling in a mixed and mobile society. Monimia is classless. A harsh critic might argue that this is why she is a failure, a sympathetic one might see in it the measure of Charlotte's originality. Her idiolect never admits the elaborate 'do me the honour'[55] phrasing which Emmeline somehow acquires in her Welsh ruin. A classless heroine has seldom been attempted, before or since. Monimia is partly self-educated, partly taught to read and write better by Orlando, and her speech patterns are neutral as to class. Other characters are the offspring of mixed marriages, and many see themselves as mobile socially, or capable of using their sexuality to marry above their birth. Such patterns of aspiration are set against the petrifaction and sterility of the Raylands.

Plots enact, of course, what authors assert, and her characterisation and plotting are beautifully congruent with her dominant social and political themes. Mrs Lennard has been unclassed by the South Sea Bubble of 1720, in which her father lost his money, forcing her into service. But she has a well-developed property instinct and a talent for flattery. She is using Monimia to entrap Orlando, but it is not clear whether she means to disgrace Orlando by revealing his liaison with her niece or gain her own security by marrying her niece to the probable heir. It is implied that she will adapt her plans as circumstances suggest, though her infatuation for Roker makes her careless. She is one parodic version of Monimia and Isabella, as Betty Richards the chambermaid is another; all are divided between prudence and passion, a conflict which in each case passion wins.

Snelcraft intends to marry his elder daughter Patty to Orlando who, he believes, will inherit. Pattenson's greed for future gain is somewhat deflected by his conquests among the maids. Promiscuous sex and a capacity to live in the present have their place in the depiction of some of the servants. Lennard, Pattenson and Snelcraft are fully realised characters, though Pattenson and Snelcraft are minor ones, and all three are wily politicians who recognise the fortune to be made by controlling Mrs Rayland. Charlotte frequently uses the word 'politics' to mean schemes or trickery, but also in its emergent modern meaning. She ends Volume Two Chapter Twelve, about Lennard's plans, with 'such were, at this juncture, the politics at Rayland Hall.'[56] Stanton notes this use of political language both in her stylistic study and in her introduction to *The Old Manor House*.

Such language sharpens the focus on national politics, on a ruling class committed to resisting change, and public servants intent only on enriching themselves, while the clergy and lawyers are more greedy for money and power than the mercantile class. Not that Charlotte emerges as democratic, for the lower servants are not represented in a sympathetic light. Betty is more in need of control than emancipation. Charlotte's own class bias as a daughter of the landed gentry never deserted her. But Betty's portrayal is less offensive than we might expect – much less so, for instance, than Fielding's contemptuous portrait of Molly Seagrim in *Tom Jones*. Like Mrs Rayland at the other end of the social hierarchy, she is at first treated in a comically distancing way. A workhouse orphan chosen by Mrs Lennard for her sober appearance, she is described as a

> ruddy, shewy girl with a large but rather a good figure; and her face was no sooner washed, and her hair combed over a roll, than she became an object which attracted the attention of the great Mr. Pattenson himself.[57]

She has much more vitality than the heroine. Orlando's dismissive attitude to her is in part the narrator's, and minor characters see her as only fit to beat hemp in Bridewell. But the narrator does some justice to Betty, who rejects Pattenson to elope with Philip Somerive, is unfailingly good-humoured, and ends up rather well in London in her carriage. Charlotte constantly uses techniques of marked parallelism, as in the subplot of Isabella Somerive, whose parents are worried about what will happen to her if her father should die. They persuade her to accept the sixty-year-old General Tracy's proposal. Her story enacts in a more lighthearted way the author's preoccupation with the entrapment and waste of the young. Isabella is flighty and vain, but while her marriage articles are being prepared she has the courage to run away to America with the General's nephew. Isabella escapes fairly easily, but her later experiences are harsher, and formed a sequel, *The Wanderings of Warwick*. Isabella, Monimia and Betty all escape ancient authority to find some kind of love and freedom, with one story qualifying our response to the others. Betty's sense of fun, stylish language and generosity make her a less embarrassing working-class character than we often find in the eighteenth-century novel – or the nineteenth.

A complex image of England itself is thus formed by Rayland Hall, its inhabitants and visitors. But the image would not be complete without some representation of England's large criminal underclass,

in the early nineties a more formidable threat than ever to the
propertied and literate. The Gothic chapel, the vaults, and particularly
the cellars are associated with the smugglers who store tea, rum and
sugar there, with Pattenson's assistance. Appropriately, their place
is at the bottom of the building. Rayland Hall is six miles from the sea
and contraband is brought in on stormy nights when noise is muffled.
The story of a ghost in the vaults, circulated among the servants and
half believed by Monimia, helps to prevent their discovery. But Jonas
Wilkins, the leader of the gang, is surprised by Orlando one night as
he returns to his study. Orlando regards him with horror, but also
with understanding for his outcast situation. Jonas'

> dark countenance, shaded by two immense black eyebrows, his
> shaggy hair, and the fierce and wild expression of his eyes, gave a
> complete idea of one of Shakespeare's well painted assassins, while,
> in contemplating his athletic form, Orlando wondered how he had
> been able a moment to detain him. He wore a dirty round frock
> stained with ochre which looked like blood, and over it one of those
> thick greatcoats which the vulgar call rascal-wrappers . . . He found
> him one of those daring and desperate men, who, knowing they are
> to expect no mercy, disclaim all hope, and resolutely prey upon the
> society which has shaken them off.[58]

Orlando passes here from some fear of the violence of the criminal
to the acknowledgement that Jonas is a victim of society. Though a
liberal, Orlando's first response to Jonas is the one a gentleman's
education has imposed on him, a response of suspicion and alarm,
associating Jonas with Shakespearean villains. But though the ochre
from Sussex earth looks like blood, it is not. Orlando learns about
Jonas' way of life and point of view, and the smuggler is as glad to
find somebody willing to listen to his grievances as the French
peasantry were in 1789. He has a hold over Orlando, having seen him
with Monimia, but this alone does not account for Orlando's failure
to hand him over to the magistrates. Charlotte gives her hero a
certain fellow feeling for the criminal, who is more sympathetically
represented than the lawyers, clerics and lower-middle-class
characters.

Rayland Hall then embodies her radical views with a greater
effectiveness than the polemics and tangential political discussions
which she had always permitted herself within the elastic confines of
her novels. The surroundings of the house, its lake, its two pathways
to West Wolverton where the Somerive family lives, and the woods
and Downs are clearly mapped. On the periphery is Stockton's

house, whose new money is encroaching on the old. The lower path is travelled by Orlando in different moods and at different seasons. It is territory intensely familiar to the narrator, as to the characters in the novel; and it becomes as familiarised to the reader as if she too had lived there. This is an important aspect of the novel's persuasiveness: the reader gradually becomes sufficiently used to the place to hope the right owner is found. The whole has solidity and particularity as a metaphor.

Once this is recognised as a condition-of-England novel, the American section no longer appears as a digression but as part of the political focus. Although the story opens in 1776, the section extends the consideration of English attitudes to custom, authority and rebellion in the early 1790s. Charlotte was well aware that America functioned as a model. The conservatives, especially General Tracy, expect the American rebellion to be over almost at once, as contemporary English military and political opinion predicted that it would be, and nobody is well informed enough to point out the problems of victualling and supplying an army so remote, though Orlando learns from experience. His parents and Mrs Rayland also expect the revolution will be crushed at once. They are ignorant of what is happening in America, but even Lieutenant Fleming, Orlando's friend, decides that he must not judge the rights and wrongs of the American cause; he has taken his pay and must act as his superiors direct.

But Charlotte makes Orlando too sensitive to be a good soldier, though of course he has to be personally brave. She allows us to see through his eyes the sacking of the colonists' settlements and the destruction by war of the pastoral and civilized life the rebels had created. In a footnote, she directs her reader to the *Annual Register* for 1779, which gives a circumstantial account of Wyoming, a village community on the Susquehanna split by the war. A largely Oppositionist publication, it tells how pro-British colonists went off to the forest, joined with Indians and 'Tory' militia and returned disguised – though they were recognised – in paint and feathers to cut down or burn inside their houses their relatives and former neighbours. She asks the reader to compare these atrocities to

> anything that happened on the 10th of August, the 2nd of September, or at any one period of the execrated Revolution in France – and own, that there are savages of all countries – even of our own![59]

She evidently thought the story too hideous for anything other than a footnote reference.

She was in a sense playing safe by setting her novel sixteen years back and focusing on a Revolution whose successful outcome was by the time of writing fully established. She had written to the moment in *Desmond*, and was beginning to see that her optimism had been premature. But the dating of *The Old Manor House* works well, as she can show the results of a backward-looking authoritarianism abroad as well as in the domestic English world. As in all her mature work, her plot situations give rise to arguments about an estate's actual owners, its would-be owners and its best owners which are artfully manipulated reformist arguments about the ownership of England, about the politically and socially over-privileged, the politically and socially dispossessed. The difficulties she has with her sometimes amorphous heroes are those of a radical satirist who is no leveller, and finds it hard to envisage the leaders of a future society.

We recognise early on that Monimia and Orlando are the best heirs of Rayland Hall, though they seem to have no legal or inherited right to it, which is of course the point. Burke shows in his *Reflections* that the problem of money is inseparable from consideration of how the state should be run, and the problem as we have seen troubles many of her heroes and heroines. The legal, ecclesiastical and military professions are closed as satisfactory ways of life to her heroes, though Godolphin, in her first and most conservative novel, is a successful naval officer. The employments for unsupported heroines are even more unthinkable. It is painful to imagine, for instance, 'the lovely, delicate and graceful Ethelinde employed in the occupations of a laundress or a domestic.'[60] Such qualms verge on self-parody for us, especially as Charlotte does not spend much time wondering whether domestic service might be unpleasant for women neither lovely, delicate nor graceful. But her contemporaries were equally blinkered; she knew her daughters might have to go into service if she could no longer support them, and she cannot spare her sympathy for young women who were born to it.

She never clears up the mystery of Monimia's birth, which may or may not be legitimate. Orlando though born into the landed gentry is a younger brother, a scholar and intellectual. He does not share the usual tastes of the landed gentry and though an affectionate son, his outlook socially is quite different from his parents'. We first see him as a child brought by a clergyman's widow to the Hall in her hand (whom she had met by chance fishing in a stream that ran through their domain), without being chidden for encouraging an idle child to catch minnows, or for leading him all dirty and wet into their parlour, at a time when the best embroidered chairs, done by the hand of Dame Gertrude Rayland, were actually unpapered, and uncovered for the reception of company.[61]

Orlando takes his name from an earlier Roland in his family but also from the hero of *As You Like It*. His elder brother Philip, the heir, dissipates the family inheritance leaving no money to support Orlando at university, but he educates himself in Mrs Rayland's library. The setting of Rayland Hall is forest interspersed with downland where sheep graze. But Orlando, though a poet too, carves only his own name on a forest bench for Monimia to read: in this more anxious and threatened pastoral, it would not be safe to carve hers. In *As You Like It* a virtuous younger brother, Orlando, and a virtuous elder brother, Duke Senior, are reassuringly restored to prosperity and happiness, though in an ending which is patently fictional. Like Shakespeare, Charlotte explores the injustices and dangers of primogeniture. Her ending too is self-conscious, though she refuses the solution of repentance for her elder brother, and Philip dies.

The Old Manor House is immensely ambitious in scope. She is prepared not only to rewrite Burkean-conservative perceptions of current politics but to adapt Shakespeare's preoccupation with land-ownership to her own times. That she read *As You Like It* economically and politically is in itself proof of unusual imagination and powers of mind. A play about escape from social constraints to a freer life in the forest, it was often performed in the seventies and eighties, with Tom King as a famous Touchstone. Though pastoral traditionally encompasses satire of social abuses, I can find no contemporary criticism which even comes close to addressing the play as she does, by implication, within her novel.

Orlando and Monimia retain something of the child's helplessness and the child's secrecy. Charlotte endows them with intelligence and generosity, but their love for each other is preserved through deception. She creates a world governed by greed and bullying, and they are its victims. In the end, Orlando inherits the Hall solely by an acknowledgement that this is, after all, only a novel. Her frequent recourse to the well-established novelistic tradition of closure and the happy ending is never so brilliantly deployed as here. As Orlando searches through the hidden passages of Rayland Hall for the will in his favour, he

> could not, amid the anxiety of such a moment, help fancying, that the
> scene resembled one of those so often met with in old romances and
> fairy tales, where the hero is by some supernatural means directed to
> a golden key, which opens an invisible drawer, where a hand or an
> head is found swimming in blood, which it is his business to restore
> to the inchanted owner.[62]

Without magic, and outside a fairy tale like this, Orlando and
Monimia will never inherit England and set the house in order. The
records, evidences and titles hymned throughout Burke's *Reflections*
will never belong to them. And the reference to hand or head
swimming in blood points to the brutality accompanying the swift
change of power outside the novel in the world of real politics. By the
beginning of December 1792 it was well known that Louis would be
put on trial for conspiring with France's enemies, Austria and
Prussia. Nobody could doubt the outcome although he was not
executed until 21 January, after Charlotte had completed her novel.
France declared war on England on 1 February; the Terror was about
to begin.There were no political resolutions in sight, and Charlotte
gracefully acknowledges that satisfactory solutions to England's
problems too will probably be fictional.

Richard Gill is one of only two critics I have traced who link
Smith's political satire with her representation of houses. In *Happy
Rural Seat*, he writes:

> Moreover, like the poets, she anticipates the much used nineteenth-
> century technique of contrasting houses – balancing Ragland [sic]
> Hall and the loyalty of its inhabitants to immemorial custom against
> the once-splendid neighbouring castle purchased, remodelled and
> abused by rich merchants. Therefore despite lapses into melodrama
> *The Old Manor House* not only prefigures the social themes of later
> novelists like Wells, Galsworthy and Waugh but their literary
> strategies as well.[63]

As Gill points out, there are symbolic houses in English poetry long
before the 1790s: Jonson's Penshurst, for instance (a subject on which
Smith also wrote a sonnet) or Pope's Timon's Villa. But he is I think
mistaken in his polarisation of the two houses. The only person loyal
to immemorial custom at Rayland Hall is Mrs Rayland. Everyone
else longs for change.

Diana Bowstead recognises that 'characters in the novel represent
old and new social forces',[64] and finds that the questions the novel

raises

are about what kind of a significance old manorial buildings will
have in the future; it is impossible not to recognise that postulates
about the future of Rayland Hall are also postulates about the future
of the economic resources, political power, and social significance
formerly lodged in the hereditary landed gentry.[65]

She sees the novel's subject as the perpetuation of manorial values,
claiming that 'when at the end of the novel Orlando comes into
possession of Rayland Hall, it is because he is the one person who can
best preserve old values, regenerating the estate instead of destroying it.'[66] She does not however take far enough her perception that
this is a political novel; Orlando is more than a conserver of traditional values. And she is mistaken in saying the novel's 'design is too
blatant.'[67] Nobody except Austen has left a record, *Mansfield Park*,
that she saw Rayland Hall as a Burkean house whose need for change
is disputed.

As Anne Ehrenpreis says in her introduction to the OUP edition,
Charlotte's characterisation and technical skill are best displayed in
the groupings at the tenants feast in the second volume. Behind this
lively episode appears the template of the *Reflections* but the contrasted
ideologies are condensed into two chapters. As already noted, Burke
argues in *Reflections* that diverse and conflicting interests in the state
are sources of strength, acting against precipitate change. When a
real monarchy applies pressure from above, the separate parts of the
state will be prevented from warping, and starting from their allotted
places. Firm government and the observance of hierarchy are desirable
for all, he implies, not just for the rich, since they prevent anarchy and
promote harmony. The tenants' feast epitomises authoritarian rule,
but instead of harmony Charlotte presents a kaleidoscope of malignity
and deviousness. Mrs Rayland has all the weight of a real monarchy,
and she presses down hard on everyone beneath her. But the ideal
Burkean order is disrupted by all the dependants and aspiring
legatees who start from their allotted places throughout the evening
and the following night.

The slow pace and wealth of detail add weight to the sense of
stifling and archaic custom. Charlotte lavishes almost as much space
and detail on the preparations for the dinner and its aftermath as on
the event itself, which is both effective and symbolically appropriate,
conveying the ponderous elaboration of England's government. She
presents Mrs Rayland as a woman ruled by memories and prec-

edents. She makes her credible, odd and in this scene slightly more sympathetic:

> The Misses Rayland notwithstanding the state in which they had been educated, had been always, during their youth, led to the company by their father, and accompanied by Lady Rayland, had each gone down one dance with some neighbouring gentleman who was invited on purpose, or with the chaplain of the family. Those days, though long since past, with almost all the witnesses of their festivity, were still recollected by Mrs Rayland with some degree of pleasure . . .[68]

The elegiac and distancing tone is characteristic of the treatment of the Hall. We are always kept aware of the Manor's antiquity and ambiguous value as preserver of custom. Mrs Rayland decides to hold the feast as usual in spite of illness and pain, and displays considerable stoicism in presiding over her dinner party and appearing downstairs for her tenants. General Tracy and Doctor Hollybourn fail to impose on her, and she commands more respect than earlier in the novel. The change reflects a deepening of Charlotte's pessimism, now she was back in Brighton, about the possibility of successful revolution.

She brings together the different members of a party who all arrive with or soon acquire conflicting aims, farcically conflicting aims in some cases: General Tracy, who is determined to seduce Isabella, hopes to see her alone in a mixed party at a large house; Mrs Somerive, whose suspicions of the General have already been aroused though she conceals them from her husband, prevents this. A dance is itself an emblem of social harmony and of marital choice. Though some of the dancers enjoy themselves, the pairings achieved are schematically unsuitable, inappropriate to their personalities: Monimia is excluded as usual, and Orlando is forced to take the top of the set with Miss Hollybourn, his social equal and a good match. But this novel celebrates exogamy. Monimia finds her way from her locked turret room to his study only to be locked in again. Gary Kelly notes:

> society was often imagined as a prison . . . the imprisonment motif had a sharper edge in English Jacobin fiction of the 1790s than hitherto, and a greater ambiguity, owing to the image of the Bastille, but also to the image of the Terror.[69]

Charlotte makes in Monimia's entrapment that night a sardonic comment on Burke's assumption that autocracy guarantees security and freedom. The reverse is true: Mrs Rayland's harshness spreads an atmosphere of terror. Much of the tension of these chapters stems from uncertainty whether Orlando can leave his place at the top of the set and join Monimia in the distant study before she is discovered.

Charlotte always shows eroticism disrupting order, but this is particularly true of *The Old Manor House,* where the concept of Sensibility is most fully and oddly developed. At the tenants' feast the attractions and desires of Monimia, Isabella and Betty disturb Mrs Rayland's plans. Monimia is terrified as she sits waiting, hearing the music faintly, afraid that Jonas Wilkins is behind the outer door. The night outside threatens her as she sits in the dark, and her social isolation is sharply conveyed, but her meeting with Orlando at last takes place successfully. Isabella is a disruptive presence too, and of all the young people, she enjoys the dance most, though her attractiveness and vitality annoy Mrs Rayland. Tracy, her 'ancient lover' does not dance, but follows her as she moves down the set. The allusion here is to Rochester's 'A Young Lady to her Ancient Lover', suggesting a worn-out libertinism: Isabella eludes him to elope later with his nephew. Philip gets drunk early in the evening and joins Betty, who is a constant, comic advocate of rule-breaking and minor rebellions. Philip's relationship with Betty parodies Orlando's with Monimia. Their assignation leads to Betty's dismissal next morning, but Betty leaves the Hall cheerfully, and goes to London as Philip's mistress. In each case a version of Sensibility successfully challenges power.

In this episode Charlotte provides a spokesman for Burke's Toryism, Dr Hollybourn, whose enthusiasm for the reinstatement of lapsed titles cannot conceal a dynastic ambition of his own. His portrayal embodies her opinion, advanced earlier by Desmond, that the advocates of reaction have sold themselves to the government cause. Like Burke, Dr Hollybourn comes from no very distinguished family himself, as Mrs Rayland remembers with satisfaction. He intends to discover which of the Somerive young men she prefers, and to bring about his engagement with his daughter Ann-Jane-Eliza, who is now twenty-six, though admitting to twenty-two. Mrs Rayland easily sees through him and, though she approves of his reactionary politics, has no wish to make Orlando independent of her, and snubs him repeatedly, without effect. The satirical portrayal of Miss Hollybourn is bitter rather from Charlotte's attitude to inherited wealth than from any anti-feminist prejudice about learning in a young woman. Like Anne de Bourgh in *Pride and Prejudice,* Miss Hollybourn represents the suitable, commonplace match the hero might make if love and the heroine did not intervene. It is a portrait so venomous as to be out of control. She falls in love at first sight with Orlando, and is angry at his lack of response to her. As with Clarinthia, Charlotte cannot resist a malign Smollettian satire of personal appearance in this more generous novel:

> The worthy archdeacon's short legs detracted less from the height of his amiable daughter, as she had the long waist of her mother, fine sugar-loaf shoulders that were pronounced to be *extremely genteel,* and a head which looked as if the back of it had by some accident been flattened, since it formed a perpendicular line with her back. To dignify with mental acquirements this epitome of human loveliness, all that education could do had been lavished.[70]

Miss Hollybourn knows Italian, Spanish, French, Latin and some Greek, is learned in astronomy and mathematics, takes 'most inveterate likenesses'[71] of her acquaintances, and paints very green and blue landscapes; but what Charlotte dislikes (as distinct from Dickens for instance) is not accomplishments in a young woman but the ease with which they have been acquired, through inheritance and a protective family. As Orlando thinks over the evening later, 'the image of the arrogant heiress arose with redoubled disgust to his mind, when he compared her situation with that of his desolate, orphaned Monimia.'[72] The unjust power of money is Charlotte's constant theme, and she can hardly bear to contemplate the young and wealthy. The unexpected addition of the Hollybourns to the tenants' feast chapters enlivens and enriches them.

Order and formality then are fragile constructs, for many characters leave the lighted Hall where Mrs Rayland sits in state, and meet in the dark peripheries of the sprawling Manor, though the subversive activity that would affront her takes place at a distance or in whispers, and love and sisterly affections that ignore the boundaries of rank are marginalised to a remote room. This is as close as Charlotte ever comes to showing us a successful traditional ceremony, for Mrs Rayland displays her hospitality, and appearances are on the whole preserved. Though this is the time when rents are paid, the feast and dance provide some pleasure for the tenants, but for most of the named characters, openness and enjoyment are impossible. Orlando and Monimia are the greatest deceivers, as they must be or risk destitution, and they are the most distressed and uncomfortable under the 'real monarchy'. Philip breaks up the party when he and a young farmer strip to box: despite Mrs Rayland's authority, violence erupts between the representatives of hostile classes, ends the celebration, and ends her precarious order.

Plate 2 'On some rude fragment of the rocky shore'
by Thomas Stothard, from *Elegiac Sonnets*, 1789.

Plate 1 'The Infant Otway' by Thomas Stothard,
from *Elegiac Sonnets*, 1789.

Plate 3 Henrietta O'Neill by William Hoare.

Plate 4 William Hayley by Romney.

Plate 5　William Cowper by Romney.

Plate 6 Tom Hayley as Robin Goodfellow by Romney.

Plate 7 'The Female Exile' by Harriet, Countess of
Bessborough from *Elegiac Sonnets* Vol. 2, 1800.

Engraved by I. Neagle from a Drawing by the Right Hon. the Countess of Bessborough –

The gentlest fairy Ships with its welcome and spreading.
They passed on the soft Port the side left behind.
Ah! victims for whom their seat, Mother's dreading,

Plate 8 'The Forest Boy' by Richard Corbould,
from *Elegiac Sonnets*, Vol. 2, 1800.

R. Corbould del.   J. Heath R.I sculp.

By the Brook where it winds thro' the wood of Arbeal.
Or amid the deep Forest, to mourn;
The poor one mutering, there well silently steal.

Plate 10 Anna Seward by Romney.

Plate 9 Frances Burney by Edward Burney.

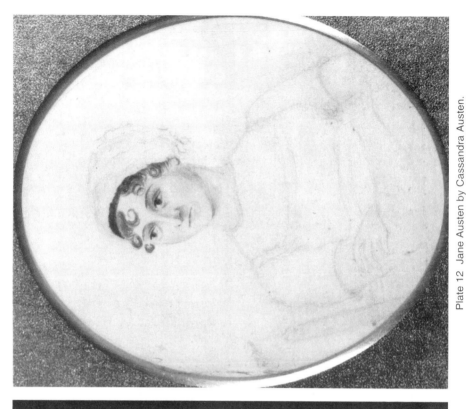

Plate 12 Jane Austen by Cassandra Austen.

Plate 11 Mary Wollstonecraft by John Opie.

The tenants' feast looks back and forward. The mural of Cupid and Psyche reminds us of Orlando's midnight visits to Monimia, and shows Charlotte creating her own legend about the power of romantic love in a materialistic world. The mural contrasts effectively with the stiff family portraits in the gallery which the guests also visit during the feast. The paintings visualise contrasted concepts of erotic love and sterile hierarchy. The scene is also proleptic: Mrs Rayland's jealousy over Orlando and Lennard's love of dress and flattery anticipate later developments. Charlotte is concerned with the most intimate workings of politics. She explores morbidity, the anxieties and emotional pressures that come from class mobility, and the painful concern parents have for children wasted by the social order: this scene marks the beginning of Mr Somerive's illness when he thinks Philip has drowned in the lake on his way home. Always the body reflects the mind, and mental anguish results in sickness and death; she links the body politic and the individual's health.

Areas of Rayland Hall, especially the staircase to Monimia's turret bedroom, function also as codes for the heroine's body, like the door and the turret room in *Emmeline*. But in *The Old Manor House* this symbolic use of the Gothic is much more extensive; the ambiguous nature of Monimia's and Orlando's relationship, which both is and is not innocent, emerges slowly through emblematic presentation of the building.

Apart from her much-praised beauty, Monimia is in some ways an unsatisfactory heroine. She is passive, frightened and persistently lachrymose. She has the limitations that a woman brought up as a dependent on charity might well have. The monotony of her days at Rayland Hall, whose grounds she never leaves until she goes four miles to the nearest village, makes every alarm insupportable. And Charlotte refuses the convention that makes of many poor heroines, including her previous ones, unrecognised heiresses. But there are moments when Monimia almost acquires confidence

> The reading [Orlando] had directed her to pursue, had assisted in teaching her some degree of self-value. She found that to be poor was not disgraceful in the eye of Heaven, or in the eyes of the good upon earth; and that the great teacher of that religion which she had been bid to profess, though very little instructed in it, was himself poor, and the advocate and friend of poverty. In addition to all this knowledge, so suddenly acquired, she had lately made another discovery. Her aunt had always told her that she was a very plain girl, had a bad person, and was barely fit to be seen; but since the

> marriage of the servant who had lived at the Hall during the infancy
> of Monimia, Betty Richards, the under housemaid, had been ordered
> to do the little that Monimia was allowed to have done in her room
> . . . as she could not forbear repeating all these extravagant expres-
> sions of [Mr. Pattenson's] admiration, Monimia could as little help
> reflecting, though she was somehow humbled as she made the
> comparison, that if Betty was so handsome, she could not herself be
> so ugly as her aunt had always represented her.[73]

Her determination not to be parted from Orlando grows. She is
torn between love for him and terror of Mrs Rayland, and her
vulnerability is shown with some psychological insight. Charlotte
makes this heroine what is now known as a cutter. When she is called
to wait on Mrs Rayland, her nervousness is extreme and as Orlando
comes in, she cuts her wrist with scissors to give herself an excuse to
leave, fearing to show her love in front of her aunt and Mrs Rayland.

This will strike some modern readers as late eighteenth-century
novelistic Sensibility pushed beyond belief, but cutting is a well
documented phenomenon, though less common than anorexia or
bulimia. K.A. Menninger's pioneering study in the *Psychoanalytic
Quarterly* in 1935 has been followed by some dozen articles in the
American Journal of Psychiatry and the *British Journal of Medical
Psychology*. Self-mutilators are generally women, and the average
age of the first intentional injury is fourteen, as in Monimia's case. In
an article in *The Guardian* in 1988, Michele Harrison writes that
according to the specialists the typical wristcutter is 'young, attractive,
female, intelligent, talented and, on the surface, socially adept.'[74]
These are the qualities of most heroines and Monimia has them all
except perhaps the last, though she could be described as socially
adept since she manages to propitiate Mrs Rayland and Lennard
while she continues to meet Orlando. Women with this compulsion
cut their arms, sometimes their bodies or faces, with a sharp
instrument. It is an involuntary act, generally followed by temporary
relief from anxiety, though they usually believe they are unique in
yielding to the impulse, and feel more isolated.

In *The Old Manor House*, the act only occurs once, and does not
seem gratuitous. Mrs Rayland and Lennard are so repressive and
Monimia's position so precarious that her self-injury appears
reasonable. She is ashamed of her birth and her secret relationship
with Orlando, and afraid of being cast out of Rayland Hall into a
world she has hardly seen. The representation of her helplessness is
so powerful that we too feel the wrist-cutting as a trivial matter, a

good excuse to leave the room. But Charlotte also suggests Monimia's slowly growing self-assertion, and Harrison's proposal that cutting is the result of anger that cannot be directed outward is interesting. Monimia is a character who becomes more disturbing the longer we look at her. In *Les Liaisons Dangereuses*, Choderlos de Laclos also introduces cutting, when the young Madame de Mertreuil runs a fork into her hand beneath the table while keeping a smiling face.

Monimia's looks are emphasised from her first description as a child whose appearance cannot be obscured by poverty, for her 'dark stuff gown gave new lustre to her lovely complexion; and her thick muslin cap could not confine her luxuriant dark hair.'[75] She is difficult to confine in other ways. Her beauty is a motivating force for the other characters. Lennard soon introduces her to Mrs Rayland, realising that 'a beauty of four or five years old would be much less obnoxious than one of fifteen, or even of nine or ten.'[76] She fears Monimia will arouse Mrs Rayland's jealousy, and the association of sexuality with a four year old girl is disturbing. Once grown up, she can shake the determination of Orlando's father:

> Mr Somerive again looked at Monimia as she left the room, and he saw that Orlando was lost, if his being so depended upon his attachment; for the extreme beauty, sweetness and grace of Monimia, so unlike the coarse, cherry-cheeked rustic which his fancy had represented her, amazed and grieved him. He felt at once, that a young man whose heart was devoted to her, could never think of Miss Hollybourn, and that he himself could not blame an attachment to an object so lovely, however imprudent, or however ruinous.[77]

Charlotte's standards for her young heroines are male standards, and firmly rooted in a class system. Delicacy and thinness are essential. Plain women, particularly plain women with intellectual ambitions like Miss Hollybourn, are treated as crudely as Dickens treated Julia Mills.

Monimia is little more than a child when her friendship with Orlando becomes lovemaking. Charlotte establishes their adolescent relationship in scenes emblematic in themselves and integrated into the novel's symbolic Gothic. Bowstead comments on the scene where Orlando throws his cricket ball through the window of the picture gallery to surprise Monimia. It ricochets off the sacred portrait of Sir Hildebrand Rayland and rolls across the room to disappear under Monimia's skirt. Noting the gallery is a symbolic place, Bowstead argues:

> It is as symbol of an excessively high value placed on family that this
> room – and within it, as emblematic focal point, Sir Hildebrand's
> portrait – is threatened by the relationship between Orlando and the
> plebeian Monimia. When Orlando's ball comes through the window,
> the room is, as it were, invaded .[78]

This is an invasion with sexual undertones too, and the scene is
described with intensity. Charlotte's treatment of the Gothic turret
and the enclosed room makes her heroine a symbol of sexuality,
clandestine but powerful, opposing conventions by which the old
can control marriage choices, or prohibit marriage altogether. On the
level of narrative, Orlando's visits to Monimia's room are innocent,
like the hours of the night they spend in the library, which is where
he sleeps. As the tears roll down her cheeks

> Orlando was tempted to kiss them away before they reached her
> bosom; but he remembered that she was wholly in his power, and he
> owed her more respect than it would have been necessary to have
> shewn, even in public.[79]

The innocence of the lovers is maintained by the narrator against
the slander of Orlando's brother Philip and the young men at
Stockton's house. Anne Henry Ehrenpreis notes that according to
The Critical Review, 'the clandestine meetings in Monimia's turret
were immoral', but she maintains that 'they are patently innocent.'[80]
Though Ehrenpreis is right according to the narrative, the anonymous
reviewer is right according to the symbolic implication. Orlando's
visits to Monimia dramatise an irrepressible sexual impulse in a
rank-obsessed and commercialised society.

He first finds his way to her room when he is training his young
colt, and decides 'to give it among other accomplishments that of
leaping.'[81] While he is looking for timber to make a jump, he finds the
concealed entrance to the stairway up the turret to Monimia's room.
To a twentieth century reader the symbolism is almost too obvious,
and it would have been equally clear to many contemporary readers.
The fourteen steps up the Gothic turret's stairway correspond to
Monimia's age, often the age of puberty. He breaks the rusty lock on
the hidden door, and she cuts the old fashioned fragile glazed linen
that lines the walls of her room. The emblematic loss of virginity is
evident. The secret way leads up to the head of her bed. There is
ambiguity in Charlotte's treatment; the marked absence of links
between narrative and emblematic direction ensures that decoding
becomes a matter of choice. The meetings both are and are not

'innocent', depending on whether we follow the surface narrative or the implications of the Gothic symbolism. By such means, innocence is questioned and redefined. Charlotte is not necessarily advocating free love and the end of marriage. To balance the unconventional symbolic associations of their courtship, she makes Orlando and Monimia a particularly prudent and chaste couple. Monimia is modest, while Orlando, though anxious to marry and take her to America with him, will not distress his father by following his own wishes. But the clandestine meetings and the secret stairway dramatise sexuality's resistance to custom and authority. This function of the plot has been unnoticed before. Bette Roberts concludes that the hero and heroine are conventional; Carroll Fry claims that Monimia like all Smith's heroines is never guilty of any real breaches of morality, even of the moral precepts of her day.

Lennard has given Monimia her name from the heroine of Otway's *The Orphan*, a play that Mrs Rayland remembers as shocking, so she insists on calling Lennard's niece by the virginal name of Mary. 'Monimia' has other associations. The heroine of *The Orphan* is loved by twin brothers, Castalio and Polydore; she loves Castalio, and secretly marries him. Polydore overhears their agreement that Castalio should go to her room at night, and hears them arrange a signal for her maid to open a door at the bottom of stairs that lead to her room. Polydore, not knowing they are married, assuming she is a 'whore', takes his brother's place and spends the night with her while Castalio is locked out. Monimia, learning the truth, takes poison, Polydore incites Castalio to kill him, then Castalio stabs himself. It was still a well-known play in the late eighteenth century. In *Celestina* Belle Thorold refers to Castalio and Polydore in a spiteful joke about her brothers going to Celestina's room, and Celestina understands her implication at once, as Charlotte assumed her readers would.

In *The Old Manor House* Sir John Belgrave learns the secret of Orlando's access to Monimia's room, and determines to go the same way himself, to Monimia's horror; she prepares to confess the secret meetings to her aunt rather than risk this. By a reference back to Otway's play, Charlotte can convey, as subtext rather than as polemic, her response to the assumption that an unmarried woman who has lost her virginity is fair game, and that where one man has secretly gone, anyone may follow. Like Monimia and Castalio, Monimia and Orlando are essentially married, though not in the view of the Church. Charlotte redefines innocence in *The Old Manor House* as fidelity in love, inside or outside marriage, and does it without frightening her more conventional readers. Blake was working on *America: A Prophecy* and on *The Visions of the Daughters of Albion* in this year. His biographer Mona Wilson describes the *Visions* as being in part about 'the tragedy of enforced chastity.' As David Erdman says in *Prophet Against Empire*, Blake distinguishes between pure and impure unmarried sex in this poem. Within her own very different Gothic coding, Charlotte does so too.

Her urbanity in handling the subject is so accomplished, as when Orlando has to break off his reading to Mrs Rayland, that paraphrase can only coarsen her tone. Monimia is adjusting the flannels and cushions around Mrs Rayland's feet, and

> as she knelt to perform this operation, Orlando, who was reading a practical discourse on faith in opposition to good works [to Mrs Rayland], was surprised by her beautiful figure in her simple stuff gown, which had such an effect on his imagination that he no longer knew what he was reading; but, after half a dozen blunders in less than half a dozen lines, he became so conscious of his confusion that he could not proceed at all, but, affecting to be seized with a violent cough, got up and went out.[82]

The word 'imagination' in this passage is closely associated with sex as it was increasingly in the eighties and nineties; but the correlation is particularly clear in Charlotte's writing, where 'imagination' is used almost as a synonym for sex, as when Philip went after his own imagination, in other words, Betty. It is indicative of her originality in the links she forms between a range of concepts – feeling, sympathy, imagination, sexual responsiveness – which for her inform the term Sensibility. Whether we accept the reading of Orlando and Monimia as lovers almost from the start, or see the emblematic ambiguities as indicating the sexuality in an unconsummated relationship, the implication is the same: erotic love is not controllable by the regulations of the state. It is the one thing capable of undermining hierarchy. *The Old Manor House* has merely a sense of novelistic closure in its hero's and heroine's final prosperity, but the Orlando-Monimia story has its appropriate happy ending when the two meet in Hampshire beside the ruins of an old house, its foundations just visible under snow and ivy. Love is anarchic, capable of overturning the authority represented in the houses. In *The Old Manor House* Charlotte attributes to sex much the same power as D.H. Lawrence does in *Lady Chatterley's Lover*, a novel which also has a Gothic quality, though the conventions of her time insisted on indirection.

As in the earlier novels, the landscape descriptions are detailed and sympathetic to the solitary character's mood. In his *Enquiry Into the Origin of our Ideas of the Sublime and Beautiful* (1757), Burke makes a distinction between objective and subjective description when he says

> it will be difficult to conceive how words can move the passions which belong to real objects, without representing these objects clearly. This is difficult to us, because we do not sufficiently distinguish, in our observations upon language, between a clear expression and a strong expression . . . The former regards the understanding; the latter belongs to the passions. The one describes a thing as it is; the other describes it as it is felt.[83]

Burke's views were influential, and Charlotte would certainly have been familiar with his aesthetic, which disparages the specific and clearly defined in favour of the grandly impressionistic, since , he says, we yield to emotion what we refuse to description. From the manner she adopted in her own landscapes it seems Burke on the sublime as on the French Revolution incited her to prove him wrong. Her landscapes are characterised by their detail and clarity, though suffused also with the feelings of the solitary observer.

A good example is her account of the lower way to West Wolverton. The narrator designates each new noun by a subordinate adjectival clause or appositional phrase. The trees are specified, though the wild fowl, which cannot be seen, are not. The narrator's omniscient vision blends with Orlando's view, showing nothing that he cannot see, and so making the woods and lake distinctively his. Measurements are given, and the contours of the scene defined:

> The other path, which in winter or wet seasons was inconvenient, wound down a declivity, where the furze and fern were shaded by a few old hawthorns and self-sown firs: out of the hill several streams were filtered, which uniting at its foot, formed a large and clear pond of near twenty acres, fed by several imperceptible currents from other eminences which sheltered that side of the park; and the bason between the hills and the higher parts of it being thus filled, the water found its way over a strong boundary, where it was passable by a foot bridge unless in time of floods; and from thence fell into a lower part of the ground, where it formed a considerable river; and, winding among willows and poplars for near a mile, again spread into a still larger lake, on the edge of which was a mill, and opposite, without the park paling, wild heaths, where the ground was sandy, broken, and irregular, still however marked by the plantations made on it by the Rayland family . . . Just as [Orlando] arrived at the water,

> from the deep gloom of the tall firs through which he passed, the
> moon appeared behind the opposite coppices, and threw her long
> line of trembling radiance on the water. It was a cold but clear
> evening and, though early in November, the trees were not yet
> entirely stripped of their discoloured leaves: a low wind sounded
> hollow through the firs and stone pines over his head, and then
> faintly sighed among the reeds that crowded into the water: no other
> sound was heard, but, at distant intervals, the cry of the wild fowl
> concealed among them, or the dull murmur of the current, which
> was now low.[84]

She has broken with eighteenth-century poetic pastoral more
successfully than in the sonnets. The verbs, active or passive, suggest
purposiveness in nature: trees shade and self-sow, streams are
filtered and unite, feed and find their way. Effects of dissonance that
make a calculated awkwardness – 'opposite coppices', 'stone-pines',
'now low' – prevent the language relaxing into prettiness. It is a
peopled landscape, as she shows in the path, footbridge and mill, and
the word 'bason' with its suggestion of artefact emphasises a nature
marked by human cultivation. But on the heath outside the park
paling, the impression is of wildness and irregularity which the
Raylands have only partially tamed. The ground is 'marked' or
scarred by plantations made for the sale of the timber, but the uneven
and unsafe ground, the diversity of nature, oppose the Raylands'
dominance and their attempts to exploit their possessions for financial advantage. Her landscapes remind us of the destructive socio-
political setting she has created in the more evidently satiric passages
of the novel. She creates a political context: nature's power shows
itself in the water's capacity to find its way over a strong boundary
and throw off man's contrivances, close the footbridge or even a
well-marked path. Human society is fragile and 'in time of floods' –
the metaphor for revolution was well-established – may be violently
changed. Her descriptions are never merely decorative,and here the
ideas of Rousseau lie behind them. Even in the description of the
moon rising, the most lyrical moment in the passage, Smith avoids
Burkean sublimity and keeps her language spare.

But the moon and her trembling radiance are personified, and her
long line shines out sympathetically as Orlando appears by the water
to find temporary peace and express his dread of the world of cruelty
and injustice outside. He is just about to embark for America with the
army. In *Natural Supernaturalism*, M.H. Abrams says that for Coleridge
'a cardinal value of the arts was that they humanised nature and so

helped to repossess it for the mind from which it had been alienated.'[85] Charlotte suggests such a possession of, and by, nature in her alienated hero. We are familiarised with the setting, which is presented in close-up, and so gain a proprietorial stake in it, which makes us feel the importance of what happens to this tract of land, and beyond it, to England as a whole. She reworks in prose the poetic tradition of moral, historical and political landscapes exemplified by Sir John Denham's *Cooper's Hill* and Pope's *Windsor Forest*.

The first three heroine-centred novels were the most popular, and contemporary reviews of *The Old Manor House* were slightly less favourable. Wollstonecraft was in France by now; only *The Critical* reviewer was hostile. While relieved to find as he thought that politics intruded only occasionally, he considered it to be about 'the most ordinary and trivial occurrences in life . . . the eternal theme of love and sentiment',[86] as if to compensate for the magazine's overindulgence to *Desmond*. This critic was also concerned about the novel's possible influence in encouraging young gentlemen to marry servants. Charlotte made about 200 guineas from it, and a further sixty from the second and Dublin editions next year.

The novel had a profound and lasting effect on Austen's imagination; she adopted the house metaphor and aspects of the plot for *Mansfield Park* twenty years later. From just after the first publication it has received the greatest critical attention and esteem, chosen by Anna Barbauld for her *British Novelists* in 1810, and in print more often than the others. Sir Walter Scott, Julia Kavanagh and Edward Wagenknecht especially praised the characterisation of Mrs Rayland.

Unlike the earlier novels *The Old Manor House* makes no appeal to public sympathy in the form of author-representative characters though there are the usual corrupt lawyers. Stanton sees Philip Somerive as a version of Benjamin in his charm and depredations on his family, but Philip has no wife and the character is fully embedded in the plot. Charlotte ridicules in the figure of the pretentious Mrs Manby an old irritant the playwright Hannah Cowley, a recognised plagiarist and salon hostess; but this is a cameo. More interesting to the biographer are the nocturnal meetings of Orlando and Monimia in Volume One and all they represent of sex in rebellion against society. Given Charlotte's way of harnessing her life to power her writing, one might be forgiven for wondering about this. Eartham was not a big house, and according to Romney, with four guests Hayley slept in the library like Orlando, the heroine's literary mentor whom she meets at night. But biographical criticism can never properly pry open the life without the author's consent. And it would have needed only the slightest velleity of fancy on Charlotte's part to turn this situation into intriguing and passionate but wholly fictional episodes.

Relations with Cadell were strained, and she had as little as possible to do with his son and William Davies. She was still angry at their refusal to take *Desmond*. Robinson's firm had made a complete hash of it; whole chapters were sewn into the wrong volume of the first edition and there were many typographical errors. Henrietta thought he treated Charlotte cavalierly. Unlike Cadell Senior, he or his printers could not deal with her manner of working, her last-minute amendments and odd pages sent by the coach and needing retrieval. Cadell had put up with this quite good-humouredly. For *The Old Manor House* she contracted with Joseph Bell, who was more efficient, and she agreed to write a two-volume sequel about Warwick and Isabella's adventures. But he too only gave her 50 guineas a volume for what she knew was her best novel so far.

She was able to negotiate a little profit on a Dublin edition. Hayley put her in touch with Joseph Cooper Walker, a Dublin clergyman and antiquarian, who arranged this for her. He was interested in Irish history and Ireland's traditional music, poetry and dress. Like John O'Neill who, though a Protestant, supported Catholic emancipation and voted against the Riot Bill of 1787, he was involved in an early phase of Irish Revivalism and nationalism. He became a good friend of Charlotte's, though only by correspondence. She sent the manuscript to him so that it should come out as soon as possible after the English edition and before a pirated version was feasible. There was no law of copyright, a serious financial injustice to her and other eighteenth- and nineteenth-century authors. Walker's letters must have been agreeable; they gained her confidence and she wrote to him in an easy intimate way from the start. After the business part of her letter of 16 December 1792 she goes on:

> I know Mr. Hayley received your *Adamo* [the work he was translating with Cowper at Eartham] and he expressed himself extremely in-debted to you for sending it, as it is a very scarce book. He told me when I last saw him that he should write to you & in the mean time if I had that pleasure, desird me to mention it.
>
> I am so extremely harass'd today – for 'Sunday shines no Sabbath day to me' – that I have no other time to write this than what I snatch while my maid is dressing my hair, an operation that I very seldom undergo. Will you forgive my writing to you so very vilely & thus

abruptly assuring you that
I am, Dear Sir, your most oblig'd Ser't Charlotte Smith.

In fact her writing is always clear and her syntax usually graceful. Her casual use of a line from Pope's 'An Epistle to Dr Arbuthnot' – on the aggravations and pleasures of literary fame – suggests how well at ease she was with her success, though never allowing anyone to forget how much effort it cost her. Henrietta and John were now at Lisbon for Henrietta's health, and Charlotte passes on the address Walker evidently wanted. The Dublin edition only made £20, and she reluctantly decided to return to Cadell and Davies, who were still the publishers for her *Sonnets* editions. While she had been working on *The Old Manor House* she was also writing her first blank verse poem, a sustained meditation on the Revolution called *The Emigrants*.

After 1790 large numbers of the aristocratic and middle class and of the clergy who refused to conform to the new régime's edicts left France as refugees. Many arrived on the South Coast at night by rowing boat; smugglers and fishermen found a new source of income, but often the emigrants paid everything they had to get a passage and arrived with no more than the clothes they wore. In the Vendée, counter-revolution had sparked widespread atrocities. Some had seen family or friends killed and were still in shock. The women, children and clergy who had permission to leave arrived by the packets. Charlotte and her family made room for groups of emigrants in her lodgings, an extraordinary act of kindness given her anxiety then about duns and debts. She seems to have first offered shelter in November and December 1792 and enlisted Hayley's help in finding longer term accommodation for them. On 20 February 1793 some of them were still there, as she wrote to Walker:

> Will you forgive this short and incoherent Letter? My Son Charles goes to London tomorrow to see if he can prevail on the Trustees to let him have three hundred pounds to purchase an Ensigncy in some of the new raisd companies as nothing can be more distressing to him & to me than his being at home witht any plan of Life. I send up by him several letters on business – which I must write in company as the Emigrants who are yet here, some of whom are very agreeable Men, find some consolation in the society my small book room affords them of an evening. The confusion of tongue therefore that I have around me prevents my adding more at this instant than a repetition of that gratitude & regard with which I must ever be, Dear Sir,
> your much oblig'd and most obed Ser't, Charlotte Smith

Not surprisingly then, once she had listened to the emigrants' stories, her poem presented if not a complete *volte face* from her previous attitudes, at least an acknowledgement that many of the Revolution's victims were innocent of anything more than an accident of birth.

While she was writing it she made a carefully considered attempt to influence the course of events in France through a letter of 3 November 1792 to Joel Barlow, who knew, or knew of, most of the English republicans as well as the Girondin leaders. He was an American poet, one of the Connecticut Wits, who came to Europe in 1788, saw the beginnings of the Revolution, and wrote pamphlets in its defence. He was made an honorary French citizen and as an American was always free to travel between London and Paris. Charlotte's letter compliments him on his *Advice to the Privileged Orders* and *Letter to the National Convention*, and reaffirms her loyalty to the ideals of the Revolution. But she goes on to urge the cause of the emigrants and Louis, whose trial was now close:

> The magnitude of the Revolution is such as ought to make it embrace every great principle of Morals, & even in a Political light (with which I am afraid Morals have but little to do), it seems to me wrong for the Nation entirely to exile and abandon these Unhappy Men. How really great would it be, could the Convention bring about a reconciliation. They should suffer the loss of a very great part of their property & all their power. But they should still be considerd as Men & Frenchmen, and tho I would not kill the fatted Calf, They should still have a plate of *Bouille* at Home if they will take it & not be turnd out indiscriminately to perish in foreign Countries and to carry every where the impression of the injustice and ferocity of the French republic. That glorious Government will soon be so firmly establish'd that five and twenty thousand emigrants or three times the number cannot affect its stability. The people will soon feel the value of what they have gain'd and will not be shaken by their efforts in arms from without, or their intrigues within (even if they were to intrigue), & many of them have probably sufferd enough to be glad of returning on almost any terms. Their exile includes too that of a very great number of Women and Children who must be eventually not only a national loss but on whom, if the Sins of the Father are visited, it will be more consonant to the doctrine of scripture than of reason.

> I not only wish that an amnesty was pass'd for these ill advisd Man, but that their wretched victim Louis Capet was to be dismiss'd with his family and an ample settlement made upon him & his posterity so long as they do not disturb the peace of the Republic. I do not understand of what use it can be to bring to trial an Officer for whom the whole nation determines it has no further occasion. To punish

him for the past seems as needless as to make him an example for the future, for, if no more Kings are suffer'd, it will avail nothing to shew the ill consequence of being a bad one by personal punishment inflicted on the unfortunate Man who could not help being born the Grandson of Louis 15th. Surely it would be great to shew the world that, when a people are determind to dismiss their King he becomes indeed a phantom & cannot be an object of fear, & I am persuaded there are on all sides much stronger reasons for dismissing than for destroying him. On this occasion, the Republic should perhaps imitate the magnanimity of Uncle Toby, 'Go poor devil! why should we hurt thee? There is surely room enough in the World for Us and thee!' It is making this unhappy individual of too much consequence to suppose that his life Can be demanded for the good of the people. And when he was reduced to the condition of an affluent private Gentleman, & even that affluence depending on the Nation, I cannot conceive that he would do any harm but w'd sink into total insignificance & live a memento of the dependence of Kings, not on hereditary and divine right, but on the will of the people.

Like her earlier and later novels, *Desmond* was quickly available in translation in France. She evidently hoped Barlow would be persuaded and would show her letter to Brissot and the other Girondins as an example of what even pro-Revolutionary writers thought in England. It is a generous effort, with its appeal to Shandean Sensibility. Her preliminary praise of democracy – and in the follow-up letter, her *Citoyen* adieu – is as tactful as her appeal to reason is touching.

Brissot was in fact eventually accused with the other Girondins for his lack of anti-monarchist zeal at Louis' trial. The son of a restaurateur and editor of the *Patriote Français*, he was temperate and humane, and did not want the death sentence for Louis. He would not, of course, have been influenced by an English letter, but with a much more intimate knowledge of the possibilities he was trying to act moderately as a Republican. The term Jacobin is now firmly associated with a spectrum of English nineties writers, and difficult to dislodge. Initially a term of insult, it has been perpetuated by academics to attach to them spuriously the spurious glamour of violence. Charlotte was a Girondin, not a Jacobin, as her letter makes clear.

The Emigrants begins with the speaker's personal griefs. At first these seem obtrusive, but like *The Prelude* her poem is partly about the growth of a poet's mind and about the angle of vision, where the subject is inseparable from the sensibility that contemplates it. Only those who have suffered will consider figures as remote as refugees from another country. In the Dedication to Cowper she speaks of herself as having a 'heart that has learned, perhaps from its own sufferings, to feel with acute, though unavailing compassion the calamity of others.'[87] Her prefaces seldom do justice to the work that follows them, however, and *The Emigrants'* concern with its narrator's sorrows is more sophisticated than this suggests. As in *The Prelude* and in 'Tintern Abbey', the seeing eye of the poem half creates what it perceives.

Volume One opens in the setting of Brighton beach on a November 1792 morning, with the speaker describing the new crescents,

> buildings new and trim
> With windows circling towards the restless sea[88]

and the disembarking parties of refugees, mainly aristocratic women and children, and clergy. The speaker is sometimes accusing, when she remembers the past practices of the priesthood in France who

> held forth
> To kneeling crowds the imaginary bones
> Of saints supposed.[89]

But the narrative tone is generally sympathetic to those who

> Hopeless houseless friendless travel wide
> O'er these bleak russet downs.[90]

In the second volume, the time is April 1793 and the tone is more dramatic and violent. Individual scenes of terror are described: a mother hiding in the woods with her baby after the rest of the family has been murdered, a man returning home in disguise to discover the dead bodies of his children. The narrator goes on:

> Woes such as these does Man inflict on Man
> And by the closet Murderers, whom we style
> Wise Politicians, are the schemes prepared
> Which, to keep Europe's wavering balance even
> Depopulate her Kingdom and consign
> To tears and anguish half a bleeding world.[91]

These lines would make an appropriate epigraph for *The Old Manor House*, written in tandem with the poem, where the scheming of the powerful forces the dispossessed to suffer in silence or to leave. In *The Emigrants* however it is the revolutionaries who are autocratic, not the aristocrats.

She traces the growth of her mind to the intense pleasures of childhood, and to the suffering that began in her mid-teens. She implies that she could not have written *The Emigrants* without the experience of childhood joy and later pain. Memory is traditionally the mother of the Muses, and she invokes memory as she ascribes the growth of her individuality and selfhood to the remembered happiness of her freedom at Bignor Park, a passage quoted in Chapter One. She goes on:

> How little dream'd I that the time would come
> When the bright sun of that delicious month
> Should from disturbed and artificial sleep
> Awaken me to never-ending toil
> To terror and to tears! – attempting still,
> With feeble hands and cold desponding heart
> To save my children from the o'erwhelming wrongs
> That have for ten long years been heap'd on me!
> – The fearful spectres of chicane and fraud
> Have, Proteus like, still chang'd their hideous forms
> (As the law lent its plausible disguise)
> Pursuing my faint steps, and I have seen
> Friendship's sweet bonds (which were so early formed
> And once, I fondly thought, of amaranth
> Inwove with silver seven times tried) give way
> And fail.[92]

She takes her personal history, motherhood, family quarrels, debts and law suits as part of her subject. Like *The Prelude*, *The Emigrants* shows a mind coming to terms with the sufferings of adulthood and hearing the still sad music of humanity in the recognition of universal sorrow. It is a theme that runs through much nineteenth-century poetry, as in George Eliot's 'Brother and Sister', for instance, where recollections of childhood with Isaac become her 'present past', the 'root of piety'[93] which feeds the writing. Charlotte stops short of such a claim. Writing is a never-ending toil here rather than a release or manifestation of power. But happiness and its loss have combined to make her capable of sympathy: 'I too have known Involuntary exile',[94] she writes in Book One. The phrase implies an Eden from which she has been exiled. The experience of childhood happiness and its loss has enabled her to write the poem.

She finished it in April 1793, three months after *The Old Manor House*. Cowper corrected an early version for her. Eagerly opening a swingeing packet one morning – the recipient paid the postage, not the sender – expecting notification that his pension was approved, he found instead the manuscript of *The Emigrants*; but he gave advice with his usual amiability. Charlotte's dedication, dated 10 May, acknowledges that

> the composition . . . would never perhaps have existed, had I not, amid the heavy pressure of many sorrows, derived infinite consolation from your Poetry, and some degree of animation and of confidence from your esteem.

England and France were now formally at war, but Fox opposed counter-revolutionary measures in the House of Commons, quoting Cowper's *On Liberty* against the conservatives, when 'the eloquence of Fox did justice to the genius of Cowper', as Charlotte says in her Dedication. Pitt did however commit some British troops to the counter-revolutionary coalition, among them the Bedfordshires and the ensign Charles Smith. Charlotte refers to 'the dreadful scenes which have been acted in France during the last summer', referring to the Tuileries invasion and the September massacres, though maintaining that 'the original cause' has become confused 'with the wretched catastrophes that have followed its ill management.'[95]

Among the emigrants was Alexandre Marc-Constant de Foville, an aristocrat who had served that year as an officer in one of the Royalist levies that were routed by the patriots. His estate in Normandy was seized, but he escaped to Brighton some time in November or December. He and Augusta fell in love and determined to marry as soon as the complicated legal requirements could be decided. The same scenes were acting all over Southern England in coastal towns and as far inland as the emigrants could find hospitality. Strangers, George Eliot observed, whether wrecked and clinging to a raft, or duly escorted and accompanied by portmanteaus, have always had a circumstantial fascination for the virgin mind, against which native merit has urged itself in vain.

Shortly before this, Frances Burney met General Alexandre d'Arblay among the witty and disreputable company – including Talleyrand and Germaine de Staël, no less – whom revolutionary tides had washed into the neighbourhood of Dorking. Though a devout Anglican and an equally devout (in her novels) supporter of paternal authority, she lost no time in marrying him against her father's heated objections. For some emigrants, marrying an Englishwoman must have seemed their best or only hope, but the d'Arblays had a long and mutually devoted marriage. Alexandre de Foville certainly convinced Charlotte he loved Augusta; he appealed immensely to her as well as to her daughter. She was delighted Augusta would make the love-marriage denied to her.

Augusta's other relatives on both sides of the family, including Lucy and Catherine, were against it. They had reason on their side in her age – she was just nineteen when she married – and in his destitution. But Charlotte ignored them. It is another proof of her generosity and of a certain unworldliness, despite her general lack of scruples about money. In Augusta she had a potential asset, as nobody would have known better than herself. She might have tried to manage her daughter, even without a dowry, into a choice more judicious than had been made for her, secured at least a lodging for herself, and been considered an exemplary mother in doing so. It says much for her that she never seems to have glanced in that direction. Alexandre was charming, accomplished, and had probably never done a day's work in his life; his chances of getting a job seemed slight. Charlotte was particularly desperate for money at this time, with rent overdue on her lodgings. In April, Hayley persuaded Cadell to give her an advance of £50 on sales of her poetry, yet she wrote two further drafts, the equivalent of dud cheques, on her overdrawn account with the firm. Both men were extremely annoyed with her. But she took Alexandre on, with any children he and Augusta might have, as further dependants on her own earning ability.

Her letter to Barlow shows how much she hoped the emigrants would be permitted to return and take up something of their former lives again; but she must always have known this was not very likely. The letter was not necessarily dictated by family interest: on 30 July 1793, she wrote of Augusta's having known Alexandre for eight months. He may not have come to England until after the date of the letter to Barlow, written early in the previous November. Whenever he arrived, it seems unlikely he got engaged to Augusta at once. The dates are worth considering because so many people assumed Charlotte's changed political attitudes were due only to Augusta's marriage. Mr. Thomas Lowes finishes his addendum on Charlotte's note to his wife, quoted earlier:

> Not long after this Augusta (mentioned in the note) married an emigrant French nobleman, & I understand that her style both in her conversation and novels altered considerably.

He is glad to see the silly woman prove her mind is only fit for family matters. But her ambiguity is evident in *The Old Manor House* and even in *Desmond*.

No doubt she hoped Augusta's and Alexandre's story might include the return to the family estates so dear to novelists; perhaps no eighteenth-century woman writer or reader was quite free from the pull of the novelistic narrative. But her letter about the emigrants and Louis was probably not written to forward the happy ending; the date is too early. The reverse chronology is quite as likely: Charlotte's growing sympathy for the emigrants prompted her to ask some of them to her lodgings, which was how Augusta and Alexandre met. Augusta's future must have seemed very uncertain; but if Charlotte ever wanted proof she was doing the right thing, Lucy's opposition would have provided it.

The family moved to Storrington in the summer, partly because she thought it would be cheaper and partly because George was going to school in Midhurst. It was closer to Bignor and Eartham too. Charlotte was anxious to ensure that Augusta and Alexandre should be legally married, though nobody quite knew how to achieve this. She asked advice from a Catholic bishop and several Catholic priests, but her greatest help was Dr Charles Burney, historian of music and father of the novelist. He and Charlotte had never met, but they knew each other's writing. Frances Burney was married in both Protestant and Catholic ceremonies, and Charlotte wanted to find out how the latter could be arranged, as an episcopal dispensation was needed. Alexandre's marriage in a Protestant ceremony alone would not be valid in France in either the new or the old régime. Though she expressed confidence in his honesty, she had no intention of leaving room for his mother or other relatives to declare later that he was not married.

The Protestant ceremony was arranged in the parish church, and Augusta's relations on both sides arrived. This was long before the days of big weddings, but a fair number of Smiths, Berneys, Turners and Dorsets may have assembled. Charlotte had as she thought engaged a priest, William Pierpoint, to come very early and perform the Catholic ceremony first. Though Pierpoint turned up, he made a series of objections, questioned when Alexandre had last been to confession and whether he was over thirty. Under that age, though his father was dead, he would still need proof of his mother's consent. The priest did not think he was thirty, and he was right: Alexandre was twenty-eight, and lying. He refused to marry them, but gave the name of another priest who might do so. The Protestant ceremony went ahead, then they travelled to Burton chapel. In a letter of 21 August, Charlotte describes to Charles Burney a more than usually trying wedding day. Pierpoint

> ownd that Mr. Douglas [the Bishop] had given him a sort of dispensation to enable Mr. Fortier, an Emigrant Priest, at Petworth to perform the Ceremony who we were then directed to meet in the Chapel at Burton. Instead however of meeting Mr. Fortier, we received a note from him with an *Excuse* that he was *busy*!

> The parties being met from a considerable distance in the morning, it was quite impossible to put off the ceremony in the Parish Church here even if it had not been perform'd previous to this unexpected refusal. But that it was perform'd & the marriage completed is now one of the reasons given for the Catholic Priests declining to perform the Ceremony according to the rites of the Gallican Church. I am under peculiar circumstances with regard to the disapprobation of all my child's family for no other reason but because she has chosen a *French Man*, for individually his character is irreproachable, and they chuse (tho my poor Girl is not under the least obligation to any of them) to tieze me with prognostics and reproaches. They tell me that if my daughter should have Children, they will not inherit the Estate Mr. De Foville has at present lost or that which remains in possession of his Mother unless the Marriage is performed according to the Laws of France. What the Laws of France now are I believe nobody knows. Nor can it be guessed, I fear, what they will be. What they were however can be ascertain'd & to these Mr. De Foville and his Wife are willing and desirous to appeal in repeating the Ceremony of their marriage as those laws direct with regard to those persons who consider them still in force.

> Not having the honor to be acquainted with you Sir, or with your daughter, tho I have the highest esteem for the private, & admiration of the literary, characters of both, I know not what I have to plead in excuse for thus intruding upon you unless it be my conviction that you will both feel for my situation from the general goodness of your hearts. If then you, Sir, can give me any information how I may now proceed to put an end to the cavils of persons who seem to have a malignant pleasure in encreasing the number of thorns which infest my pillow, I am persuaded you will.

Nothing brought Charlotte to the boil faster than interference from her family; Lucy and Catherine were probably the chief prophets of disaster here. Charlotte's brother Nicholas seems to have been the only relation who backed Augusta, perhaps surprisingly for an Anglican clergyman; she and Alexandre stayed with him after their marriage.

Dr Burney put Charlotte in touch with a Mr Jamart, who was able
to get a dispensation for a priest then teaching French at George's
school in Midhurst to perform the second ceremony. When Charlotte
wrote her letter of thanks to Dr Burney on 31 August, it still had not
taken place, but by this time she was more philosophical:

> As it was impossible for [Alexandre] to ask his Mother's consent, he
> trusts that the circumstances he was in and the character of my
> daughter will reconcile her to the step he has taken. I am myself
> perfectly easy about it, as I am sure the simplicity of Augusta's mind
> & her affection for him (with the advantage of a person reckon'd very
> beautiful) will not only plead with Madame de Foville the pardon of
> her Son, but interest her in favor of his choice.

She goes on to ask whether Dr Burney knows any means of
getting a letter to Madame de Foville in Normandy, not only to ask
consent for the marriage but to reassure her that her son is well, and
to receive reassurance in turn that she is safe. Charlotte Bolingbroke
and her husband were going to Italy via Germany but her courier
would not risk taking any letters directed to France in the carriage.
Charlotte goes on:

> I have since been trying what could be done with certain Country-
> men of mine who deal (I am afraid not according to Law) on the other
> side of the Water, & whose traffic, if I may judge of it by their nightly
> convoys, is not at all impeded by the War or by the Anathemas of the
> Conventionists against Englishmen (I conclude honest Englishmen
> only are proscribed), but these Men, besides that they are not much
> to be trusted, say that they now go to Ostend instead of Fescamp tho
> there is one of them who for ten Guineas seems dispos'd to tempt
> putting in a Letter at Fescamp into the Post. I hardly dare trust him,
> and the Sum is very great, unless paid on better assurance than one
> can have on the conduct of such a person. So that upon the whole, we
> have determin'd not to confide in him till we are more assur'd that
> we may do so in safety and, in the mean time, to enquire among those
> equally interested, if any way has yet been found to get over the cruel
> impediments which exist between the Emigrants & their friends.

Her smugglers were not all fictional. She ends with another blast
against 'my relations & the sneers and sarcasms of *soi-disant* friends'
with their illiberal and absurd prejudices, but also with warm
expressions of gratitude to Charles Burney for the help he had given.

But anxieties about the wedding and family squabbles were
forgotten a week later. From September 1793 onward she began to
live out Geraldine's phrase: 'the prospect every way around me is

darkening.' Charles had gone with the Bedfordshires to the borders of the Dutch Republic and France, where the Duke of York's army was making incursions into French territory in coalition with Austrian and Prussian forces. There were rebel counter-revolutionary bases inside France too, in the Vendée and the South and West. Early in September the British besieged Dunkirk. Charlotte sent Walker the news a month later on 9 October:

> I have perhaps appear'd negligent in that I have left your last very obliging Letter so long unanswerd. Alas! Dear Sir, if you have not overlook'd in the papers two paragraphs that have lately appear'd there, my apology is already made. Every year of my unhappy life seems destin'd to a new course of suffering. The year 1793 and the month of September has been productive of unusual sorrow. My gallant Boy lost his leg on the 6th before Dunkirk, & the retreat, which was immediately and rapidly made, compell'd them to remove the wounded at the utmost risk of their lives. My poor Charles was remov'd only two hours after his leg had been amputated and not only sufferd extremely in consequence of it but has had the cure much retarded. I received this cruel intelligence on the 11th, and it was a shock almost too severe for me. A few days afterwards I heard from Lisbon of the death of my amiable and invaluable friend Mrs O'Neill. Yet I must bear these and probably many other evils –
>
> We must endure
Our going hence, even as our coming hither . . .[96]
>
> . . . My poor invalid, to whom I have sent his next brother, is at Ostend; he has now left his bed and thinks he shall be at home in about three weeks. Nothing can be more dreadful to my imagination than to figure to myself his appearance; a fine active young Man, twenty years old, thus mutilated for life, must appear an afflicting object to a stranger . . . but to me! I really know not, ardently as I wish to have him at home, how I shall support the sight.
>
> You who have heard much of the perfections of my belov'd friend, tho I think you were not personally acquainted with her, will easily imagine how irreparable her loss must be to all her friends. To me, who have been too long suffering the bitter blasts of adversity and have of course not many friends to spare, it is one of the most cruel blows I could sustain. But let me not dwell too long, dear Sir, on subjects so mournful.

She had not seen Henrietta for more than a year, and her death is not quite real at this point. It is the loss to herself of Henrietta's friendship she feels more than Henrietta's loss of her life at thirty-five. Or perhaps she knows or guesses already what gossip was saying, that Henrietta died of an opium overdose, and even to

Walker she cannot touch on that. But she suffers intensely for Charles:

> The only consolation I can now feel will be in rendering his life as comfortable as I can; and this consideration has set me to work again on a Novel, which as fast as I write I get my daughters to copy.

Lucy as well as Charlotte Mary was an amanuensis now; the rheumatic pain in Charlotte's hands must have made writing difficult, and they saved her days of copying. She blames the Trustees more than she blames the French: Charles had only gone into the army because the money from the will was still withheld. She confides to Walker the details of the will, reverting as always when deeply depressed to her marriage:

> You are very good to interest yrself so much in my unfortunate situation in regard to Mr. Smith. Tho infidelity, and with the most despicable objects, had renderd my continuing to live with him extremely wretched long before his debts compelld him to leave England, I could have been contented to have resided in the same house with him, had not his temper been so capricious and often so cruel that my life was not safe. Not withstanding all I sufferd, which is much too sad a story to relate (for I was seven months with him in The Kings Bench Prison where he was confin'd by his own relations) I still continued to do all that was in my power for him; I paid out of my book money many debts that distress'd him & supplied him from time to time with small sums.

In the same letter to Walker she also refers to a Miss Bartar, who wanted to publish a novel under Charlotte's name, to support an invalid father. As she tells Walker, Charlotte gently explained that she could not do that, but offered to read the novel and make suggestions. While she waited with a mixture of longing and dread for Charles' return, she used her letter, which is remarkably controlled, to inventory shock, routine literary business and hope. She tells him, and reminds herself, that 'The Chevalier de Foville is still in my opinion worthy of [Augusta], which is saying every thing.' This letter functions like her novels, allowing her to impose some shape on grief, to set it out, look at it, distance it. Her writing life however exhausting or disappointing was still her main resource, sometimes all that could negate the pull towards death and keep her planning forward. To call writing therapeutic is commonplace; for her it was more like a bandage held to a massive injury.

Lionel, recently expelled and a few weeks short of sixteen, travelled to Ostend, looked after Charles in the field hospital and brought him home a month later. This was even more painful in fact than in anticipation, but she applied herself to making what practical arrangements she could. She hired a manservant for him, and bought a low chaise which he could get into easily and drive himself.

Cowper's and Hayley's correspondence refers to her several times this summer and autumn. Cowper wrote to Hayley on 23 July about her dedication of *The Emigrants*:

> I doubt not her having said everything that is proper and everything that will make me proud and happy, and if she has taught the world to think more highly of me than I have hitherto deserved, as I dare say she has, I must endeavour to justify her by proving myself more worthy of her commendations hereafter.[97]

Charlotte wrote to them both about Charles and Henrietta, though both letters are lost. On 6 October Cowper wrote to Hayley commending the benevolent attempt he was making on her behalf. Hayley was probably urging the Earl of Egremont, to whom Charlotte had written an early sonnet, to intervene with the Trustees. Cowper mentions without naming another unfortunate wife with a vicious husband, but 'she does what poor somebody else [Charlotte] does not, she believes the gospel and enjoys the comfort of it.'[98] On 26 October he replied to Charlotte's apparent complaint that Hayley no longer cared for her as he once did: 'Had you no other title to his esteem, his respect for your talents and his feelings for your misfortunes must insure to you the friendship of such a man forever.'[99] Cowper had little sense that Hayley could be ruthless, in his sentimental way, with women who somehow or other failed to come up to expectations, though he may have been right about his friend here and Charlotte wrong. He goes on:

> I was much struck by an expression in your letter to Hayley where you say that 'you will endeavour to take an interest in green leaves again'. This seems the sound of my own voice reflected to me from a distance, I have so often had the same thought and desire. A day scarcely passes at this season of the year when I do not contemplate the trees so soon to be stript, and say, perhaps I shall never see you cloath'd again. Every year as it passes makes this expectation more reasonable, and the year, with me, cannot be very distant when the event will verify it. Well – may God grant us a good hope of arriving in due time where the leaves never fall, and all will be right.[100]

But that hope was never very present to Charlotte. He sent her Mary Unwin's compliments, whose illness, he said, was like a Damocles sword hanging over him.

On 20 January Charlotte wrote to Walker again. He had mentioned a novel called *D'Arcy*, published in Dublin under her name. Charlotte recalls Miss Bartar, and the impossible novel she had sent for approval just as the news of Charles and Henrietta came, and that she had managed to look through, though she could not recommend it to a publisher. She goes on:

> Still however, perhaps from 'seeing feelingly' the fondness of an Author (and a Young Author) for A work of fancy, I did not like to shock Miss Bartar's *amour propre* with saying in plain terms that her work was worth nothing, but I desir'd My daughter de Foville to write to her to inform her that the anxiety and concern I had sufferd about My Son Charles and the recent death of my ever lamented Harriet had so much affected my health that there was little probability that I should be able to attend to the correction or disposal of the work in question – & that as it was uncertain how long it might be before I could be of any use to her, I thought it best not to attempt it, as it would be perhaps to her prejudice from the delay. Wherefore I entreated of her to Lane's [The Minerva Press]. Thither I sent it & have heard nothing more of it since, but that he receivd it. How far this attempt of mine to be of what little use I could to a Stranger has expos'd me to the inconvenience of having my name us'd, I know not, but I own it is very disagreeable to me on more accounts than I will now enumerate, and should it be in your power, dear Sir, either by an advertisement or in any other way that you may judge advisable, to signify publickly that it is not mine, I shall be very much oblig'd to you.
>
> It is quite enough Heaven knows, to answer for the nonsense one writes oneself, & there are a thousand reasons why to answer for more (tho among it was prose like Gibbon's and Poetry like Gray's) would be particularly disagreeable to me. Perhaps it may not be improper to insert in the Dublin Paper most read an Advertisement to this Effect: 'We are authoris'd to say that the Novel calld D'Arcy said to be by Charlotte Smith, is not written by Mrs Charlotte Smith, Authoress of the Elegiac Sonnets, Emmeline, Ethelinde, Celestina, Desmond, the Old Manor House, and the Wanderings of Warwick'. Perhaps this D'Arcy may have been written by a Charlotte Smith, for one of that name was divorced not long since, and another hang'd. If I were to indulge a *jeu de mots*, I should say that I am neither so *fortunate* or so *unfortunate* as to be either of those Ladies.

She complains of increasing ill health and the cost of food in a country village, admitting a dislike of England: 'there is no country in the World where one pays so much for accommodations so inferior.' She had all her father's instinct to put many miles between herself and her sorrows, but she had a conflicting and stronger impulse to act responsibly. The longing to escape abroad, to see the Alps before she died, found expression in the closes of several of her next novels. The one she mentions in her letter of 9 October to Walker had the working title of The Exile, but she found a better in *The Banished Man*. The setting is partly contemporary France, and the hero and heroine are based on Alexandre and Augusta, with a narrative point of view which is firmly counter-revolutionary. It was not simply that Augusta's marriage and Charles' mutilation changed her. The Revolution changed more than she did.

Brissot and the other Girondin leaders went to the guillotine on 31 October, accused of royalist sympathies and plotting to put the Duke of York on the French throne. Rational defence was impossible: the prosecutor Fouquier-Tinville operated on a near-vertical playing-field. Brissot had been among the Third at the Estates–General, and commented fairly on the Revolution's first years in his *Patriote Français*. He was in Paris in August 1792 when the Marseille contingent arrived singing Rouget de Lisle's new song, the month the monarchy ended. He must have felt a strong sense of the surreal as the Girondins climbed onto the carts outside the Conciergerie prison and set off singing the Marseillaise. '*Contre nous, de la tyrannie*' meant something different now. The Jacobins – Danton, Robespierre, Hébert and Fouquier-Tinville himself – were soon to follow as the Revolution sloughed its skin with each new metamorphosis.

In Schama's epic *Citizens* there are three or four heroines including the Princesse de Lamballe, and two heroes, Malherbes and Louis XVI. Brissot might also be identified as a hero, since Schama is scrupulous in recording events, but he is a revolutionary, so the reader has to make an effort to pick this out. Louis is the true protagonist of Schama's Revolution. He is brave and conscientious; in prison awaiting trial he leads family prayers and continues his son's education. 'At the moment of their most complete ostracism from the body politic', Schama writes, 'the royal family had finally become plain citizens.'[101] This is touching, and fair. It would be fairer still if Schama gave us any sense of those citizens who were not royal, nor clever aristocrat-politicians, nor witty bishops, nor particularly prominent in any way. We learn everything about Louis' murder. But we learn little about the thousands of judicial murders in the 1780s. If we want to know more about one of the salt smugglers who was broken on the wheel for resisting arrest, we are left with a statistic, though Schama refers to Olwen Hufton's book on the poor of eighteenth-century France in his bibliography. We do not know whether the condemned man's daughter fainted when she heard the sentence, or whether he sent his wedding ring – if he had one – back to his wife. Elisabeth Vigée-Lebrun did not paint him, and we do not see with what fortitude he met his death. Probably not with much. Judicial murder in the 1780s was designed to eliminate the victim's last shreds of courage. *Citizens* controls its detail with brilliant sweeps of perspective, but it is about only the important citizens, and a deeply conservative record.

Whatever her limitations, Charlotte imagined her Girondin histories so as to take in a wider range. She gave a presence and a voice to her smuggler in *The Old Manor House*, and let her reader feel the despair and potential destructiveness of someone who has nothing to lose. She let a small farmer tell his story in *Desmond* and took a female servant for a sub-heroine in *Celestina*. The dispossessed are part of her narrative of France's provisioning problems and of England's hierarchy. With the failure of the Girondin theme and with still-darkening prospects in her own life, she had to find other subjects and muster her remaining energy to feed her family and keep herself out of prison.

4

An Interest in Green Leaves

There can be no series of letters in English that charts the relations of author and publishers with the immediacy and detail of Charlotte's. The letters that survive obviously represent just a small fraction of her correspondence over a lifetime. Mostly we have only her side in the publishing wars, though occasionally Thomas Cadell Senior, his son or William Davies would add a terse note to the bottom of a letter, and Joseph Bell responded in print.

Her career of course began in a dispute with Dodsley over advance payment. She switched to Cadell and Davies on Hayley's advice, then to the liberal G.G. & J. Robinson firm for *Desmond*. Everyone who has thought about Charlotte's life has regretted she did not approach the most distinguished publisher of his time, Joseph Johnson, when she was seeking another publisher for *Desmond*. His experience and encouragement would have been valuable in the promotion of her career. It is possible she tried, and that the reluctance was on his side. He had probably heard rather often that she never hesitated to ask for advance payment from Cadell, or to use his firm as a delivery service and corporate agony aunt. He may have thought her too innately county for his list and his Tuesday evening dinner parties. Whatever the reason, it is sad she missed him and the circle that eddied around that imperturbable centre.

Bell's contract with her for *The Old Manor House* included a two-volume sequel; Charlotte was writing this in tandem with *The Banished Man* in the summer and autumn of 1793 when Augusta married and Charles came home from France. Not surprisingly, *The Banished Man* with its self-portrait of the author as Charlotte Denzil, its fictionalisation of Augusta's and Alexandre's courtship and revisioning of the Revolution engaged her completely. *The Wanderings of Warwick* is her most cursory piece of writing and she could not take it beyond one volume. Though she wanted to believe, and indeed claimed, she had fulfilled her contract with Bell, he thought otherwise. While writing *The Banished Man* she hoped to go back to Cadell's

firm, which was still the publisher for continuing editions of her
Sonnets, but she was embarrassed about making the overtures. She
was very close to Cadell Senior in some ways, and treated him like
an elder brother, confiding her anxieties and attacking him when he
slighted her. On 16 December 1793 she writes that she has a first
volume that will be completed soon; her tone is quite conciliatory,
conceding that he cannot be expected to pay anything in advance:

> The truth is that my expences are very considerably encreas'd by the
> return of my poor Charles, for whom I am under the necessity of
> keeping a ManServant; & Government has yet done nothing for him,
> nor has he any prospect at present, but of an Ensign's pay, on which
> he could not exist unless he lived with me. I am inform'd by the
> Medical Men that the contraction of the poor remains of his leg –
> which is now drawn up close to the ham (& prevents his having an
> artificial Leg either of wood or cork) – might be removed & his
> misfortune greatly alleviated if he could have the benefit of the Bath
> Waters. I have been desired to go thither myself for my own health
> but cannot afford it, as all I receive from my own labour is not
> sufficient for the common purposes of my family, & from Mr [John]
> Robinson and the other Men who have so long detain'd my unfortu-
> nate children's property, I now receive nothing, nor can I obtain any
> remedy against their injustice and oppression. If I could sell the Book
> I am writing for a certain Sum to be paid for on the delivery of each
> volume, I might possibly continue to pay for a lodging there for a
> month or six weeks, which is all the difference between living there
> & at home. I have no right to expect however that you will break thro
> any resolution you may have formed to oblige me. But merely
> propose it to satisfy myself that I have endeavour'd to do for the best.

> The work in question is to be call'd 'The Exile' and is a story partly
> founded in Truth, & as I beleive myself will be particularly interest-
> ing & somewhat on a new plan, for it will be partly narrative and
> partly Letters. It is some satisfaction to me to possess twenty volumes
> of my own writing (without reckoning the Sonnets) all of which are
> in the second and one in the third Edition. As to the work I sold to
> Messrs G G & J Robinson, it has been in a second Edition a long time
> tho they never advertis'd it, & of 'The Old Manor House' a new
> edition was call'd for in two months, tho Mr Bell for some reasons or
> strange management of his own never got it ready till lately. I do not
> like for many reasons to continue my dealing with Mr Bell with
> whom I have now compleated my whole engagement. And should
> you adhere to your resolution of withdrawing your property from
> the purchase of Copy right, and either for that or any other cause
> decline this proposal, I shall either endeavour to print the work at my
> own expence or seek some purchaser or publisher who is in a more
> respectable line of business than it seems to me Mr Bell adheres to

(who has lately I see publishd trials & other very discreditable works) and one too who may know a little more how to treat me, for by Mr Bell I seem to be considerd as a miserable Author under the necessity of writing so many sheets a day. This is but too true, but I have not yet learned to endure contempt & very naturally wish to return where I have always received the treatment of a Gentle-woman. If however your mind is made up, I have only to beg you would not name what I have herein mention'd to any person in the trade, as it might prevent my success elsewhere, & I beg for the reason I have given to be favour'd with your early answer.

Cadell was touched by her circumstances and her unassuming tone; and he had no objections to this novel's politics as he had to *Desmond*'s; he accepted The Exile, afterwards *The Banished Man*, on the terms Charlotte proposed.

Her demands on her publishers were not unreasonable in that they never lost money on a project of hers. Cadell Senior retired at this time though Charlotte continued to deal with him. She took a long time to accustom herself to young Mr Cadell, who was less inclined to let her overdraw her account, or to allow her complimentary sets of her books, send them to her friends, and find the works she wanted to supply the place of a library when she was away from Brighton or Storrington. She often needed a book, like the physician Erasmus Darwin's *The Loves of Plants* for her poetry or Diane de Polignac's ghosted Memoirs for French atmosphere, and works of reference or a Shakespeare to check her quotations. She expected the firm to provide these.

Cadell and Davies functioned as her bank. When hard-pressed she ran up bills in shops and referred tradespeople to the firm for repayment sometimes, as in April 1793, when there was nothing in the account. William and Nicholas, twenty-five and twenty-two in that year, now began to send drafts, the equivalent of cheques, back to their mother, between £100 and £300 annually. This was a great help to the whole family, but when India ships were expected and arrived without money, the disappointment was correspondingly bitter. Communications were of course chancy. Two Persian shawls worth 40 guineas each vanished on route to her and Charlotte Mary, and probably other presents too. Cadell and Davies took charge of the receipts and kept separate accounts for her and Charlotte Mary. Though the money was so welcome, she could not receive it without regretting that it was not, rather, going in the other direction, from the Trust Fund to the elder boys. They could have made good use of it in ways she does not specify, but perhaps by becoming importers of Indian artefacts, for which there was already an eager market in England. The Trust remained unsettled. Woven through her complaints to her publishers is that complaint also.

She probably missed Henrietta's friendship more acutely now the first misery of Charles' injury was wearing off. In fact he made an unexpectedly good recovery. The knee gradually straightened, allowing an artificial leg to be fitted; he went back into the army though to a non-combatant post, travelled abroad with his regiment and was stationed in Gibraltar by September 1795. Henrietta's death took longer to sink in, but there was no consolation in its circumstance as there was, to some slight extent, in the regiment's praise of Charles' courage at Dunkirk, and in his partial recovery. She missed the O'Neills' town house on visits to London, and the society Henrietta gathered to meet her, but that was trivial compared to the loss of her friendship. She now refers frequently to Hayley's negligence in her letters. She seldom saw him after 1794, although he was among the friends who recruited the Earl of Egremont to help in the Chancery suit that was under discussion for the settlement of the Trust. Hayley had for several years undertaken the education of Egremont's elder illegitimate son along with his own Thomas, and the boys were friends as well as their fathers.

Perhaps his neglect of Charlotte was imagined, or perhaps, as he had just met Blake, he was absorbed in this new friendship. More likely, though, Thomas' developing illness made intimacy with the mother of a large and – at the time he knew them – healthy family hard to bear. As Thomas went into the growth spurt of his teens, he developed scoliosis, a curvature of the spine. If he was intended to be tall like his father, the curvature would be the more severe. Eventually it crushed his lungs. The promising apprentice sculptor died, to Hayley's great grief, in 1800 aged nineteen. Charlotte does not mention this illness in the middle nineties, and perhaps Hayley was unable to talk to her about it. His son's scoliosis would have absorbed him after 1796, but it was probably apparent to father and son two years earlier, when Thomas was fourteen.

For whatever reason, their old friendship lapsed, and her letters to him in the next eighteen months have a formality meant to be felt, even when she expresses gratitude for some good turn. Though they were not entirely estranged, he no longer kept her in touch with other friends. When gossip said that Cowper had relapsed into depression, then madness, she had to ask elsewhere for news. It was true. As Mary Unwin slipped into senility, his voices came back. They were in his head or in the house at night. An especially frightening one called, 'Bring Him out, bring Him out'; it sounds like a flashback to the terror and humiliation of school.

To Charlotte also, the weeks at Eartham must have seemed a long way off. Her rheumatism was worsening; at times she could not get out of bed. Stanton suggests that her sadness about the loss of her looks may be referrable to her illness, which can effect facial changes. As early as 1791 she described herself as looking sleek and smug enough by candlelight but much altered by day; she attributed this to overwork. By the time she had the Romney portrait engraved for a new subscription edition of her poetry, *Elegiac Sonnets II*, she felt the need for the *Comedy of Errors* quotation placed beneath it:

> Oh! Time has Changed me since you saw me last
> And heavy Hours with Time's deforming Hand
> Have written strange Defeatures in my Face.[1]

She thought readers who knew her might consider the addition of her portrait vanity, as she no longer in the least resembled it.

But through all this she continued, with help from her two elder sons, to support a family consisting of nine people in 1793 and 1794, one an invalid, one pregnant, then confined and ill. They were supplied with all the comforts she could buy them. The letters of the middle years of the nineties grow steadily more painful to read. But she wrote on. Creative imagining, that independent source of enjoyment as Hays calls it, remained a pleasure sometimes as well as a necessity. *The Wanderings of Warwick* is more travelogue than novel, and written to order; *The Banished Man*, one can believe, she partly enjoyed as she wrote.

When he received only one volume for the sequel, Bell had her arrested in the street. A failed contract was a form of debt. It seems that the publisher Sampson Low and another acquaintance stood bail, so she probably did not spend any time in prison. But she was extremely shocked; going to prison, dying in prison, were present possibilities after that. Bell printed an insulting note on the flyleaf of *The Wanderings of Warwick*: 'the delay, and the promising it in two volumes, are imputable solely to the Author, to whom I leave the task of justifying her own conduct'; her reputation must have been at a low ebb for him to do this. English public opinion had almost entirely turned against the Revolution, and *The Banished Man* had not yet appeared.

The Wanderings of Warwick is politically neutral, with a mainly foreign setting, describing the adventures of Isabella and Warwick after they leave West Wolverton for America. Warwick is the chief narrator, and Charlotte manages a laconic 'male' style at crises in the action, as when the ship is captured by American pirates. He is not always a reliable narrator, but she shows him gradually growing up, learning to appreciate Isabella's loyalty, to be a disinterested friend and to accept financial responsibility for his children. It is unusual for a novel of education by a woman to take a young man as learner, but she had her boys as models. She had an example in *Tom Jones* too, but Tom never learns to be domestic as Warwick does, and one might wish like Bell that she had spent more time on this story.

Much of the interest of the book lies in its depiction of foreign scenery and manners; she draws on several sources, notably William Beckford's *A Descriptive Account of the Island of Jamaica* (1790). She makes Warwick an observer of the customs of Barbados and Jamaica, and a lively essayist who addresses contemporary topics of debate. He describes the conditions of the slaves from a fairly liberal point of view, condemning slavery, though claiming that in many cases blacks born in the West Indies enjoyed better living conditions than English agricultural workers. When the hero and heroine recross the Atlantic the setting shifts to Portugal, and much of the volume's second half tells the story of the Portuguese nobleman Don Julian's unhappy love affair, narrated in part by himself. The episode is mediated without irony or social satire, though the authoritarianism of parents is condemned. This novel's castle is non-political, a decaying Moorish palace, exotic, sombre and overgrown, where Don Julian, whose melancholy temperament prefigures Childe Harold's, shoots himself.

Isabella and Warwick return to London where Warwick, just about convincingly given the control of different literary styles and tones he has demonstrated in his narrative, becomes a hack writer for the magazines and a cynical commentator on London salons; the work ends on his reconciliation with General Tracy, who dies in a duel, leaving the hero and heroine in comfort. Though her ideas about the slave trade and marriage remained liberal, *The Wanderings of Warwick* is silent on French politics.

This sequel came out in January 1794. Charlotte's rheumatism was by then severe enough for her to try Bath. She had *The Banished Man* to finish and writing was increasingly difficult. There was not enough money for them all to go, but at the end of March she took

Harriet, now twelve, and her maid to lodgings in Pulteney Street. George was in school and Lucy a young woman, but Charlotte continued to teach Harriet. She was considering whether she could turn her long experience of teaching to some advantage. Anna Barbauld and her brother had published *Evenings at Home; or, The Juvenile Budget Opened* with Joseph Johnson's firm two years earlier. There was a good profit to be made on educational books, and she began to sound Cadell and Davies about a similar work of her own. The spa waters, she thought, did her a great deal of good.

But she had new anxieties. Lionel had been at Oxford with a view to taking orders, a view which was entirely his mother's. It was impossible to find the money to keep him there, and he took instead the ensign's commission vacated by Charles, with the permission of the regiment's commanding officer. Charlotte wrote to Walker on 30 April, after a passage where she regrets the loss of Hayley's friendship:

> I have a new subject of heartache; my poor wounded boy has been persuaded . . . to give his Commission of Ensign in the 14th Infantry to his Brother Lionel. It is entirely against my inclination, & I have said so. But as it is very true that a young Man of six feet high & upwards ought to do something for his support, and as I am denied the means of keeping him at Oxford to be qualified for orders for which he was always intended, I do not know that I ought to oppose his inclinations, tho certain that in suffering him to follow them, I must be condemned to such misery & anxiety as I endured for Charles, perhaps to be follow'd by a Catastrophe as shocking. It is very difficult for a Mother to know how to act with Boys when there is no Father or near relation who has authority over them, & it would be unreasonable were I to expect that all my Sons should be what the eldest is. He is indeed '*jeune homme comme il y en a peu*' [an exceptional young man]. But I shall probably never see him again.

Augusta's pregnancy was presenting alarming symptoms, though the letters do not reveal what these were. She and Alexandre made the journey by coach to join her mother in Bath. Charlotte had ridden to Eartham when five months pregnant, but she was physically very tough when she was young. Augusta made the journey with some trepidation in June. Something about her looks or symptoms terrified Charlotte as she continued proofing *The Banished Man*, which took this – by now dearest – child for its heroine. On 11 June she wrote to Cadell :

> Tho my daughter de Foville bore her journey extremely well, she was taken dangerously ill 3 days afterward, & from the reasoning of the

Medical Men who attended her, I have been under the most terrible
apprehensions which alone had occasion'd me to neglect sending up
the proofs Mr Stafford sent me, which I meant to have done days ago,
for there are several such mistakes as I fear can hardly pass.

But she failed to notice many other mistakes in the proofs.

The obstetrician Thomas Denman was prominent in his field and
attended Augusta with his former resident, Caleb Parry. The cost
alone must have been worrying, though Parry later attended Augusta
without fee. On 22 June Charlotte again wrote to Cadell :

> Within these few days, thank God, my dear Augusta has suffer'd less
> & I think gains strength So that I have more hope than I had that the
> event will be favourable. I have at intervals continued my work &
> have now finish'd it all but the last two Chapters, which I wish, like
> the last line of a Sonnet, to have forcible and correct. They will I hope
> be concluded in the course of this week.

She did not know how either story, Augusta's or the heroine's,
would end. It must have been a strange sensation, perhaps unique.
Probably she and the doctors feared the baby was already dead
which, if Augusta's contractions did not come on soon, would be
fatal to her. But Charlotte pressed on with the only story she could
control. She wrote to Cadell on 22 July:

> My mind is at present in such a state that I really know not what I say
> or do. Mrs De Foville continues still in so dangerous a way, and the
> event is so very uncertain in the opinion of Mr Parry who attends her,
> as well as in that of Dr Denman, that nothing but the necessity of my
> keeping up an appearance of courage on her account could induce
> me to struggle with the terror that overwhelms me. I have no
> consolation but that of having procured for her every assistance &
> every comfort possible, for ill as I can afford it, considerd in a general
> light, Every thing I can do will be cheap if I can *but* save her – for
> should I lose her – It is presumptuous to say I could *not* bear it, for
> perhaps I must, but I do not know whether it would not put a final
> end to all my troubles. I am always so unfortunate that I think I have
> not, for some reason or other, any thing but misery to expect. This
> would indeed compleat the bitterness of my destiny, for tho I have
> so many other Children, this dear child is the most precious. Nor do
> I reproach myself with this partiality as a crime, for the others have
> never found it make any difference to them, & I think it is not caprice
> as *they* all equally love her – & her Uncle, his Wife, & even many
> unconnected persons idolize her, which must be the effect of her
> disposition. As to her husband, he worships the ground she treads
> upon & is in a state of suffering equald only by mine. God Almighty

knows how long we shall be in this suspense. It cannot be very long as she is at her full time.

If I get an hour's respite this afternoon, I will copy the preface &c which I have finish'd & will send them up by the post tomorrow. In the mean time, I send you a receipt for the money for the copy right of 'The Banished Man', which I suppose will be necessary, tho there is no longer any thing to fear from poor Mr Smith who contents himself with taking my fortune, or considerably more than half of it, & desires me to do with the children as well as I can. There are but three things that can releive me – Chancery, where I have at length a suit in some forwardness; the death of my own Father's Widow, which will be some encrease to my fortune; & remittances from India. But these last are not only uncertain, but I receive them with pain as the price of my dearest William's banishment & as kindness which will lengthen that banishment, for so high is the interest he cd make of money in India that *we* ought to have sent him his Grand-father's Legacy long since instead of receiving Money from him.

She is optimistic in describing the Chancery suit as 'in some forwardness'; it was only under discussion as a possibility. She was never to pretend any concern about the former Miss Meriton. The letter ends with a list of new Bath subscribers to her forthcoming *Elegiac Sonnets II*.

But however worried she was about Augusta, and busy with her forthcoming books, she did not forget Cowper. On 23 July she wrote to Samuel Greathead, a dissenting minister and Cowper's friend, after thanking him for undertaking some business transaction for her:

My poor Girl is not yet in her bed, & tho the symptoms which have for some days terrified me almost to frenzy are abated, I fear her sufferings will be long and severe.

I cannot but express, hurried as I am, my concern to hear that the admirable mind of so invaluable a Man as Mr Cowper is still in a state so very distressing to his friends & so injurious to the moral interest of mankind. From Mr Hayley, I hardly ever hear as I used to do, & he never said more to me than naming, at first, the unhappy circum-stance and his own solicitude &, since, that our excellent friend continued still in a state of mental indisposition, but that there were hopes of his speedy restoration as his bodily health was restored.

A few days later Augusta got through the birth alive. Charlotte wrote to Thomas Cadell on 3 August:

I beg you will accept my sincere thanks for yr Letter which I received yesterday. My belov'd Augusta is pronounced out of danger unless any thing happens very unexpectedly. She was inform'd last night of the death of her Child which expired a few moments after I seal'd my Letter to you. She bore the intelligence with more fortitude than we expected & is this morning calm & reasonable.

This would have been the first grandchild she saw – though possibly Nicholas and William may have acknowledged paternity of illegitimate children by now – and she must have felt some sadness herself, but the loss of the baby was trivial compared with the danger to Augusta. There is no indication of how long the baby lived.

The Banished Man was published in August with an epigraph from Montaigne:

> Et de vrai la nouvelleté couste si cher jusqu'à cette heure à ce pauvre Estat (et je ne scay si nous en sommes à la dernière enchère) qu'en tout et partout j'en quitté le party.[2]

The setting of the opening chapters, the castle of Rosenheim on the borders of France and Germany develops the concept of Rochemorte in *Celestina;* it is a refuge for exemplary characters, not their prison. Rosenheim provides the most dramatic opening of all her novels, which usually start with an accumulation of background detail. Here suspense begins to build up from the first lines. She is attempting action on an epic scale with northern Europe as her setting, drawing in the political situations of Germany, Austria, Poland and England as well as France. For once she begins *in medias res:*

> It was a gloomy evening in October 1792, the storm which had never ceased the whole day continued to howl round the castle of Rosenheim; and the night approached with ten fold dreariness. The Baroness de Rosenheim and Madame D'Alberg her daughter and their attendants and servants, tho' wearied by anxiety, dared not think yet of repose. All day they had been listening to the sound of cannon, which a strong wind brought from the French frontier, whence they were seventeen miles distant. In the course of the last twenty-four hours they had received undoubted information that the French army were following the Austrian and Prussian troops in their retreat, and would soon be in the dominions of the Emperor.[3]

By dating her opening scene just after the September massacres, she makes clear the reason for her seeming change of heart since *Desmond.* The Baron de Rosenheim and his son-in-law M. d'Alberg are with the counter-revolutionary forces, leaving the middle-aged Baroness, her daughter Adriana and Adriana's children alone in the castle with their servants and the almoner, one of Charlotte's sly and malignant priests, the Abbé Heurthofen. Charlotte was increasingly to take the mother and daughter bond as her subject: she does so also in *Montalbert, Rural Walks* and *The Young Philosopher*. The Abbé is revolutionary in his sentiments, becoming more so as the *sans culottes* approach closer to the castle. Egalitarianism is now 'that fallacious, that pernicious philosophy that has undone us all',[4] as one of the royalists calls it. The Baroness and Adriana prepare to defend their house, though the servants are becoming disaffected. When a young man shouting for help is heard outside, the Baroness goes out to find him. Charlotte creates a romantic entrance for her most decisive and energetic hero, Armand D'Alonville, who carries his dying father, perhaps in allusion to the story of Aeneas and Anchises, into the castle.

Before the *sans culottes* arrive, the Baroness and Adriana set out for Prague with D'Alonville as escort. As soon as they have gone, the castle is entered and largely destroyed by fire, to the distress of the villagers, for 'one such good house as our castle above was, is a thousand times better for the poor man than all these new notions that have brought us no good yet.'[5] Since the Baron has left the title deeds to his estate in a safe at Rosenheim, D'Alonville returns to rescue them. As elsewhere in her fiction, narrative excitement and consistency of characterisation are sacrificed for an idea. She encourages us to expect a siege at the beginning but it never materialises, and the Baroness unconvincingly allows her home to be destroyed. The change in narrative direction allows Charlotte to incorporate, through the usual medium of an emblematic castle, the notion that the *ancien régime* contained much worth saving in its rights of property and forms of law. She was more concerned here with ideology than narrative interest.

In these opening chapters, she emphasises the massive and solid quality of Rosenheim, rather than its decay, though it is weaker and less defensible than it used to be. In her attitude to France (though not to England) she has come round to Burke's way of thinking. The powerful castle-state of the old régime with a stable hierarchical order is a refuge against anarchy rather than a base for oppression, and its weakening in modern times is regrettable. Though she sympathises with the counter-revolutionaries, she is still satirical about the unreformed state of England.

The position of radicals and reformers in England was now frightening. John Horne Tooke, Thomas Holcroft, Thomas Hardy and other members of the London Corresponding Society had been arrested for assembling to discuss Parliamentary reform. Their

Convention took place in the spring, during the worst months of the Terror, and they were tried in the autumn, when the government's hostility to English liberals was at its height. Godwin's *Cursory Strictures on the Charge Delivered by Lord Chief Justice Eyre to the Grand Jury, October 2nd, 1794* gives an insight into the repressive temper of that year. The Lord Chief Justice's remarks to the jury were made before the date of the actual trial, which gave Godwin time to publish in the *Morning Chronicle* of 21 October a defence of the accused and a rebuttal of Eyre's argument.

Eyre had extended the name of treason to any speech, writing or act that tended towards the subversion of the monarchy. Acting as judge and prosecutor together, he claimed that an association for Parliamentary Reform may desert its object, and be guilty of High Treason. Godwin argued:

> True: so may a card club, a bench of justices, or even a cabinet council. Does Chief Justice Eyre mean to insinuate, that there is something in the purpose of Parliamentary Reform, so unhallowed, ambiguous and unjust, as to render its well wishers objects of suspicion, rather than their brethren and fellow subjects?[6]

He makes it clear that Eyre addressed the issue of treason in a sweetly reasonable way:

> Chief Justice Eyre says today 'all men may, nay all men must, if they possess the faculty of thinking, reason upon everything that sufficiently interests them to become an object of their attention; and . . . the constitution of the government under which they live, will naturally engage attention and provoke speculation.'[7]

But this was only a gesture towards free speech, and Eyre was pressing for a death sentence. Godwin wisely toned down his own radicalism for once, and appealed to traditional authority and the carefully circumscribed definition of High Treason formed in the twenty-fifth year of Edward III's reign, sanctioned by Hume, whose *History of England* praised that law as a discouragement to tyranny and governmental caprice. Godwin ended with the words of the sentence for High Treason, which was still, in the 1790s, to be hanged, drawn and quartered. It is impossible to guess how much influence he had, but the jury brought in a verdict of not guilty.

Some of Charlotte's comments in *Desmond* tend towards the subversion of the monarchy. But though she understood the concept of institutionalised violence, even that was preferable to the Terror, and in the preface to *The Banished Man* she compares the contemporary situation in France to the times of Nero and Caligula. In the character of Charlotte Denzil, a novelist engaged in a law suit and writing to support her children, she places herself within the novel and gives an account of her struggles to meet her publisher's deadline while pigs get into the garden and scarlet fever rages in a neighbouring cottage. She comically suggests the nervous response of the book trade to the government's repressive policy in the letter from Mrs Denzil's publisher, Josepth Clapper – clearly a retort to Joseph Bell – who

> must insist on having an hondred pagges at least by Satturday night. Also the Odd to Liberty mentioned by you as a close to the same, but I shall change the tittle of that, having promised the trade that there shall be no liberty at all in the present work, without which asshurance they would not have delt for the same.[8]

There is some liberty in the present work, however, in the subplot of the patriotic Polish revolutionary Carlowitz and his daughter Alexina, who are idealised figures, and *The Banished Man* contains some of Charlotte's sharpest satire on corrupt politicians, dishonest lawyers and meretricious Englishwomen. Despite the prevailing mood of national self-congratulation, her response to the Terror is never chauvinistic. As Stanton perceptively points out, in *The Banished Man* Charlotte 'delineates the characteristics of individuals in terms of their attitudes to language.'[9] D'Alonville and Ned Ellesmere are friends, and marry an English and a Polish woman. As Stanton says, Charlotte's 'admittedly generalised hope for a universal brotherhood of man is symbolised by the success of the international – and multilingual – relationships.'[10] The novel ends with a cosmopolitan grouping of the sympathetic characters in Italy.

Her satire on the corrupt social and political life of England finds its focus in the second great house of the novel, Rock-March in Merionethshire, the home of Lord and Lady Aberdore, where D'Alonville gets a job as tutor. This house and its surroundings is like Rayland Hall a microcosm of the English hierarchy. Lord and Lady Aberdore are indifferent to their tenants and autocratic to their servants. Rock-March is modern, not Gothic. Charlotte had subverted Burke's image of the venerable castle in *The Old Manor House* and capitulated to his political attitudes in the presentation of Rosenheim. In her later writing she increasingly deviates from the Burkean paradigm. In describing Rock-March, her tone is flippant, as if moral earnestness is irrelevant or wasted in the English climate of 1794:

Its outward walls shall not be roughened by former sieges, or its entrance guarded by portcullis; the wallflower and the fern shall not nod over the broken battlements, nor shall the eastern tower, nor any tower, be enwreath'd with the mantling ivy. On the contrary, the entrance hall is stuccoed ... and in the vestibule beyond it ... is a very large billiard table ... should the imagination refuse to fill up the lofty and spacious rooms, the little printed book, sold by the housekeeper, Mrs Empson, will give a perfect idea of it all.[11]

The dismissive tone suggests the hopelessness of reform in such an efficiently controlled estate as Rock-March. The castle is almost burned down in a fire started through the exhaustion of two laundry maids, who fall asleep while trying to carry out Lady Aberdore's capricious orders. This fire too is emblematic, a threat of possible insurrection through the exploitation of the lowest class. But the more conservative tendency of this novel is enacted when D'Alonville organises the servants to put out the fire and so prevents Rock-March from suffering the same fate as Rosenheim. And she creates an atypical eldest son for Lord Aberdore: the clever and energetic sixteen year old Lord Aurevalle, who admires his tutor, will one day fulfil his responsibilities better than his father.

In poetry and prose she had always been admired most for her landscapes and her 'interest in green leaves', in the phrase that so struck Cowper. Quitting the party of faith in innovation and a new society, she made the green world more central to her characters' thoughts and hopes. In contrast to Rock-March is the Cottage on the Cliffs, as D'Alonville calls it, where the heroine comes to stay with her mother, her brothers and sisters. It is closely assimilated into the surrounding wooded landscape:

Angelina now had nothing else to wish – for she was near her husband – and when a few days should leave him at liberty to dispose of some portion of his time by the departure of the family from Rock-March she hoped to have the inexpressible delight of wandering with him among the rocky wilds and deep woods of a country altogether new to her.[12]

The 'sullen magnificence'[13] of Rock-March can be seen from the Cottage. Angelina

found a spot from whence one end of the house of Rock-March was visible; the broad sash windows glittered in the setting sun, and Angelina loved to believe that they were the windows of D'Alonville's apartment.[14]

There is a careful working out of the ideas of Rousseau in the opposition between the Cottage on the Cliffs and Rock-March. The cottage is associated with youth and spring:

> Already in the tall woods beneath the mountain, the rooks were busied in feeding and attending their almost fledged young; the ground was covered with the early flowers of spring; and the paths Angelina trod were literally 'primrose paths'. In their little garden below, her brother, a child of eight years old, was already making his arrangements with the infantine delight natural to that age, on coming to a new abode; and her youngest sister was producing her collection of flower seeds, which she proposed to divide with him on condition of his digging the border for her. Every simple object around her spoke to Angelina of hope and pleasures.[15]

Nature and love are set against the boredom and cruelty of life at the Castle, where Lady Aberdore precariously maintains her self-esteem by refusing to meet the neighbours, and her male guests go out looking for women in the surrounding villages. The influence of Rousseau's *Emile* is evident in the pastimes of the children, who spend much of their time working on their gardens.

The setting sun is associated with the castle, while the little house, its garden and woods are taking on new life in the spring. Charlotte took her title from the medieval ballad of the Nut-Brown Maid, which she knew in Prior's and perhaps in the original version, where the heroine runs away to join her outlaw lover in the forest. The refrain runs:

> So shall I to the greenwood go
> Alone, a Banished Man.

Her disillusion with the Revolution leads her increasingly to celebrate a Rousseauesque green world outside the politics of left and right, and in this she anticipates Wordsworth. Charlotte Denzil regrets the loss of her garden more than anything else about her past affluence.

Charlotte satirises England's social and colonial corruption in her analysis of consumerism, which includes women as consumer objects, a more prominent subject here even than in *Desmond*. Sir Maynard and Lady Ellesmere dislike their neighbour, a prosperous manufacturer of buttons who 'had Ludlow among his books, quoted Milton to his companions and drank to the rights of man.'[16] Mr Nodes dies and his property is bought by the ex-Indian Mr Darnly, who sweeps away Franklin and his Roundheads and substitutes painted satin, fosses amd mandarins of gold and ivory. This makes the Ellesmeres more aware of their own shabby gentility, but they plan to settle their elder daughter as Darnly Park's best ornament; Mr Darnly however chooses Theodora, the much younger daughter. While Charlotte writes out again her own childish compliance, she succinctly indicates moral styles and the direction of change in county families through three styles of furnished interiors.

The Banished Man contains a higher proportion of action and event than the other novels, from the exciting opening of the storm, and approach of the *sans culottes*, to the duel at the end. Though deprived of his estate and country by the Revolution, the hero D'Alonville always acts decisively. The element of passive suffering in hero and heroine is absent. S.R. Martin says that 'a welcome characteristic . . . is the warmth of its principal male characters.'[17] In this more patriarchal novel male friendship and the courage of the two heroes, one French, one English, are more central. But the contrast between sensitive heart and cruel world is worked out in the minor characters and their relationships, especially in the women: the Baroness de Rosenheim and Adriana are sympathetic, but prevented by their husbands from helping D'Alonville, and accept that a wife's duty precludes individual initiative; Theodora is sacrificed by her parents before she has time to develop preferences of her own; Charlotte Denzil the novelist overworks to support her family and is ignored by her rich relations.

Like Orlando and Monimia, D'Alonville and Angelina marry before the close of their novel, but in *The Banished Man* Charlotte is more hopeful that marriage can be happy despite poverty. Orlando and Monimia are still anxious and depressed after their marriage, while D'Alonville and Angelina are not, reflecting the more tolerant attitude of the narrator now towards the strange inequalities of fortune. Strong feeling is evinced in marital or maternal relations or in royalist sympathies outraged by Louis' execution. Sensibility is differently defined here. Charlotte conveys the shock of the news even to the English, and the emigrant women can speak of it only in whispers.

Charlotte Denzil is overtly Charlotte herself with children to support, and rude publishers and tricky lawyers to deal with. Readers could see the poverty, isolation, love for her children and angry dependence on titled relatives which are in keeping with the 'I' of the poems or the more argumentative writer of the Prefaces. Charles' injury is written into the plot in the secondary hero Ned Ellesmere's injury in nearly identical circumstances – but Ned does not need to have his leg amputated. In a long letter from Charlotte Denzil to Ned, Charlotte indulges her own regrets about Hayley and Henrietta. For three years, Charlotte Denzil writes, a good friend championed her, and

> set about in earnest cleansing the Augean stable, where the evil-doers had been acting their works of darkness; and papers were dragged from their holes in dusty compting-houses, which were said to be *mislaid*, or even *lost*; when suddenly something or other happened – I know not what, nor can I in gratitude even try to guess, which most abruptly ended his knight-errantry ... he left me to continue the perilous warfare as I could, aided by no fitter weapon than that unfortunate wit, that he often assured me would do me *no good*.[18]

Charlotte's own wit is seldom less in evidence than in this published reproach to Hayley.

In the same letter Charlotte Denzil writes that she had

> till within these last nine or ten months, one dear, dear friend, whose heart was as excellent as her talents were brilliant ... But that friendly light is set for ever. She was lost in the meridian of life ... I dare hardly Trust myself to think of the irreparable loss I have sustained ... and exclaim, with the wretched Lear:
>
> > Why should a rat, a dog, a horse have life,
> > And thou no breath at all?[19]

She refers to the friend's illness, severe enough to affect her looks. Through Charlotte Denzil, Charlotte is evidently trying to make the point that Henrietta died of an illness, not by suicide, though the opium she took as a painkiller may have hastened the end. The relation between autobiographical fiction and the real is often opaque and coded. But Charlotte lived so completely in her fictional character she lost at times all sense of the boundary between text and life. The result is painfully immediate, as if she is breaking through the type to emerge scratched and dishevelled on the page. At the end of this letter the name Henrietta Denzil appears instead of Charlotte Denzil, and the mistake – if such it was – passed the copier and printer.

A poem Charlotte wrote a year after Henrietta O'Neill's death while she was working on *The Banished Man* appears as Charlotte Denzil's memorial to her friend. It is a love poem:

> Twelve times the moon, that rises red
> O'er yon tall wood of shadowy pine

Has fill'd her orb, since low was laid
My Harriet! that sweet form of thine!

While each sad month, as slow it past,
Brought some new sorrow to deplore;
Some grief more poignant than the last,
But thou canst calm those griefs no more . . . . . .

Bright visions of ideal grace
That the young poet's dreams inflame,
Were not more lovely than thy face;
Were not more perfect than thy frame . . . . . .

But ere that wood of shadowy pine
Twelve times shall yon full orb behold,
This sickening heart, that bleeds for thine,
My Harriet! – may like thine be cold![20]

It would be crass to assume that this is the record of an overtly homoerotic friendship. Charlotte was passionate in all her feelings, of love or hate, and possessive and physical in all love relationships; beauty seems to have engaged her emotions intimately, perhaps even in her children. The language of Sensibility of course always connected with the physical, with the sense of a body and how it looks or how it moves. But it would be still more crass to assume that the feeling here is merely a matter of literary convention. She lost in Henrietta someone who had taken to some indefinable extent the place of a loving and encouraging partner.

D'Alonville, despite the formal disclaimer in the Preface, is based on Alexandre de Foville, and his courtship of Charlotte Denzil's daughter Angelina evidently involves the author deeply. From this and the letters, it is clear that Augusta's marriage was the one great pleasure of Charlotte's adult life. It was the chance she had wasted, unexpectedly given back to her.

In the Preface she describes in more detail than ever before some of the consequences of Richard's will, and accuses the Trustees of allowing their agent to put the money into his own pocket from year to year. This may mean an agent in the West Indies in their pay, as there are references in Charlotte's letters to embezzlement of money at its source in the plantations. In the narrative of Charlotte Denzil's business affairs, Anthony Lambskin, a fictionalised Anthony Parkin, defends his agent Mr Prettythief, a fictionalised Mr Prettejohn who was a legal advisor to the Trust in the West Indies. The Preface continues:

> A Novelist . . . makes his drawing to resemble the characters he has had occasion to meet with . . . I have 'fallen among thieves' and . . . I have only made sketches of them, because it is very probable that I may yet be under the necessity of giving the portraits at full length, and of writing under those portraits the names of the *weazles, wolves* and *vultures* they are meant to describe.[21]

Cadell and Davies seems to have been less effectively managed under the younger Cadell as well as less accommodating, and the first edition of *The Banished Man* was riddled with embarrassing errors. She wrote him a typical Charlotte broadside on 29 August 1794:

> I receiv'd the 6 copies of the Banish'd Man in due course. I observe with extreme vexation such numerous errors of the press as I never observed before in any work. It is very certain that Mr Stafford's compositor cannot read my hand, Almost universally mistaking a's for o's, or o's for a's, but it is astonishing that the corrector of the press did not detect this & that he has suffer'd many words to pass which are not English or any other language under Heaven – Now tho I may have written very ill (& indeed I inform'd Mr Stafford that from having the Rhumatism in my hand I could not write as I usd to do), yet as I never could have meant to have written words that do not exist, the corrector should most certainly have changed these. The Stopping is in many places so sadly managed as totally to alter the meaning and sense of many sentences. And as to the French, Italian, and Latin sentences, they are made sadly incorrect, & of that perhaps the discredit will fall on me.

It must have been sickening to see her work treated so cavalierly. She returned to the attack on 9 September, begging the printer, if he saw any word he could not read, to apply to her for an explanation as she would

> rather pay any postage than have *Calamites* printed for Calamities, dinging for dingy & etc, etc, etc, etc, etc, and *other* words that exist in *no* language & that a very small portion of attention or intelligence w'd convince a compositor c'd never have been meant by an author not qualified for Bedlam.

But this was not all the fault of the unfortunate Mr Stafford. She was too shaken with worry to write clearly or check the proofs. Her fury made the younger partners less willing to take new work and incur more reprimands.

But she made more than £200 in spite of its being a printer's disaster. Some potential buyers found the type so faint they decided to wait for the second edition, though this was in a smaller print run. It had a mixed reception from the reviewers, sometimes with amused reference to her supposed change of heart. *The Critical* considered it 'unjustifiable to make a novel the vehicle of accusations that ought only to be made in a court of justice.'[22] Wollstonecraft was still in France; her substitute considered it improper to shade a novel with

> the gloom of political controversy . . . We must add, that we cannot think it any recommendation of this novel, that the authoress has so frequently introduced allusions to her own affairs.[23]

But her symbolism here was better understood than in *The Old Manor House*. The *European* reviewer for instance praised the description of Rosenheim, adding that the novel would encourage an Englishman to

> hold faster than ever to his own political constitution, whose fabric, though not faultless, is built on a broad and solid base, which will afford him a firm footing, when the airy castles of democracy are no more.[24]

Burke's and Charlotte's metaphor was fast becoming a political cliché, though it had a lot of life left in it as a fictional device, from Wemmick's private castle to Wragby Hall's grime. After Rosenheim, Charlotte became more varied and unexpected in her fictional architecture; it became more insistently ideological in the late nineties.

The bills for Augusta's medical attendance up to the confinement came to twenty guineas; luckily, a £100 draft from William arrived in time to pay them, but even with the remainder and her own earnings, her family's needs still kept Charlotte in debt. This was however one of her highest-earning and most productive years. There were second editions of *Desmond* and *The Old Manor House*, and a Dublin edition of the latter, though that paid very little. *The Wanderings of Warwick* made £50. She detested Bell for the rest of her life, and stayed with Cadell and Davies for her first children's book, *Rural Walks*. She started this just after Augusta's confinement, and Alexandre offered to make a French translation as she worked. He may have done so, as an anonymous French translation came out in Geneva in 1799.

At the same time she began 'Rosalie', eventually called *Montalbert*, and sent the first chapters to Cadell and Davies, who returned them without comment. She despised the changes in the firm since the days of Mr Cadell Senior. 'By the mail yesterday, I sent up a considerable Quantity of your recent purchase', she writes to Cadell Junior on 10 September, with heavy irony directed at his tradesman's manners as compared to his father's. He and Davies claimed that the second volume of *Rural Walks* had not been revised properly; her letter to them of 2 October gives some idea of the humiliation she felt at their treatment:

> I am . . . beyond measure vex'd at the contents of your letter, but indeed I am so enured to mortification I expect nothing else. . . . However, Gentlemen, if such is really your opinion, I recommend it to you to stop the press, and to have the work revised, which I will do to the best of my power. More I believe it is useless to say. I really did flatter myself that – As I have not in any one instance fail'd of fulfilling my engagement And as You are so well acquainted with my situation – that I should have received more kindness from you . . .

But her letters were often more aggressive, though she was under the necessity of asking the publishers for advances on her *Sonnets* editions, now in their sixth edition and issued in different collections by two American presses. She did not of course earn anything from American editions. Sampson Low was to deal with her next two novels, though the Soho location of his shop embarrassed her.

Advances against the publication of *Rural Walks* managed to pay some of the costs of the four in Somerset, Charlotte, Augusta, Alexandre and Harriet, and the two left in Storrington, Charlotte Mary and Lucy. George was still at school in Midhurst, Lionel was waiting to join his regiment, and Charles rejoined his, which was stationed in Gibraltar for the next two years.

Once Augusta got used to her baby's death, once she could walk again, Charlotte thought, her health would come back. But Augusta had never been strong, and though at times in the autumn she improved, relapses quickly followed. Charlotte persuaded her to leave Bath, as she never felt well in a big town, and go to the nearby spa, Bristol Hotwells, with Alexandre. Charlotte could not give up the Bath lodgings because she could not pay the bill, and would not make more difficulties for the young couple who sublet to her. So she would travel to Bristol Hotwells to see Augusta then, feeling more sick with apprehension each time, return to Bath to continue *Rural Walks*. Stanton believes that like Benjamin Berney Augusta had tuberculosis, and pregnancy was too great a strain on her. Dr Parry called every other day and began to refuse his fee, he was so touched by the anxiety of the family. Charlotte was convinced, and the doctors agreed, that Augusta should go to the sea or preferably south to a warmer climate that winter, but it was impossible to find the money.

The best she could do was to install her with Alexandre in a little village outside Bath. She was now trying to support parts of her family in three separate places as well as George in school, and failed to pay the Storrington rent. On 16 October she wrote to Cadell and Davies that there was an execution, a bailiff's sale, in the Storrington lodgings for £25 back rent, and the bailiffs had seized and would sell her books, the collection she had been making since she was twenty when she first moved to Southgate. But Charlotte Mary or Lucy must have acted quickly when the bailiffs got in, perhaps sending to Nicholas Turner or a friend nearby for help, as these books do not appear to have been sold. Charlotte was referring to her library at Storringon a year later.

It is surprising *Rural Walks* shows so few signs of these stresses. Educational walks were commonplace in children's literature, but this is an unusually child-centred book for its time. She drew on her long experience of teaching her daughters, itself based on recent educational theory. Harriet was twelve now, and appears in a fictional form as Henrietta.

The Sensibility Charlotte projects in her poems, and which alone distinguishes good and bad characters in her novels, could be cultivated, she thought, by education. All her children's books are strongly influenced by *Emile*. This seminal work emphasises outdoor pursuits and the avoidance of rigorous formal education in the early years. She follows Rousseau's plan for Emile himself, not for the appalling Sophie, though her children's works were intended mainly for girls and their mothers. She eventually produced six: *Rural Walks: in dialogues intended for the use of young persons* (1795); *Rambles Farther: A continuation of Rural Walks* (1796); *Minor Morals, interspersed with sketches of natural history, historical anecdotes, and original stories* (1798); *Conversations, Introducing Poetry: chiefly on subjects of natural history* (1804); *A History of England, from the earliest records to the peace of Amiens; in a series of letters to a young lady at school* (1806); and *The Natural History of Birds* published posthumously. Her writing for children soon began to pay well, although the *History of England* was particularly difficult to write without access to a library, and the third volume is by Mary Hays.

Apart from the *History*, all her writing for children encourages the development of Sensibility by living in the country, the study of nature, caring for birds and animals and helping to relieve the sufferings of the poor. The popularity of this kind of children's writing established the routine of country walks and cottage visiting that played an important part in middle- and upper-class women's lives in the nineteenth and early twentieth centuries, though evangelicalism and an increasing social awareness amongst the gentry would also account for the cottage visiting. Charlotte thought an education which encouraged outdoor pursuits made a healthy antidote to the taste for luxuries and sexual precocity of girls growing up in towns. A program of social awareness and contact with poverty, however paternalistic and condescending it may seem now, must have had some effect on several generations of villagers who had no access to other help.

Rural Walks, Rambles Farther, Minor Morals and *Conversations, Introducing Poetry* consist of a series of dialogues interspersed with poems and short stories. The first of these, *Rural Walks*, is the most interesting. *Rambles Farther* like many sequels does not quite sustain the impetus of the first work. In *Minor Morals* the observation of natural landscape and the discussion of poetry are lost among the exemplary stories, while *Conversations, Introducing Poetry* is more academic than any of the earlier books. By the time she wrote *Rural Walks* her faith in revolution has become the mild reformism of teaching middle-class children about social inequality. Her love of poetry and botany remains, and forms the basis of her curriculum.

In the Preface she says that she 'wished to unite the interest of the novel with the instruction of the school book, by throwing the latter into the form of dialogue, mingled with narrative, and by giving some degree of character to the group.'[25] The familiar polarity between 'interest' and 'instruction' is not confined to the discussion of children's books but lies at the heart of novel-writing and novel-reading in the eighteenth century. Her need to include both interest and instruction in her children's writing is closely allied to her uneasiness about the rival claims of Sensibility and sense in her novels. The children's works reveal in simplified form some of the preoccupations of the novels; and, in turn, *The Young Philosopher* is centrally concerned with the relationship between mother and daughter and with young women's education. Mrs Woodfield, the teacher of *Rural Walks*, has two daughters, Elizabeth and Henrietta, and has undertaken to look after her brother's child Caroline Cecil, whose mother has recently died and who has been living in London. Caroline provides a slight interesting waywardness which could not appear in the Woodfield girls without compromising Mrs Woodfield's competence. But even Caroline soon settles down to enjoy the country walks, botanising, flower drawing, reading and memorising

poetry and the contacts with villagers and neighbours in the surrounding countryside which make up their education.

The book begins with what will seem to a modern reader the
dismayingly moralistic tone Mrs Woodfield takes to Caroline. The
child arrives late at night, frightened and ill at ease in the country,
with her mother just dead and her father abroad. Nevertheless she
shows signs of dissatisfaction with the spartan life of the Woodfields,
and as in a typical Enid Blyton school story, her taste for luxuries has
to be replaced by a more wholesome outlook. Mrs Woodfield clearly
did not care for her sister-in-law, and there are dark warnings against
'dissipation', though Caroline is only fourteen. Charlotte stands
behind Mrs Woodfield in every point, and the latter's absent husband and constant need to write business letters would make the
identification clear to any reader familiar with her other work.
Woodfield in *Emmeline*, for instance, is the house of Mrs Stafford,
who was understood to represent Charlotte Smith. Mrs Woodfield's
strictness reveals the rigours that even privileged children endured
in the eighteenth century, though *Rural Walks* is less moralistic and
coercive than most books for children of its time. It is entirely free
from threats of punishment in an after life, and even in this one Mrs
Woodfield displays nothing worse than dictatorial kindness.

Margaret Shaw in her M.Ed. thesis on women writers who
interested themselves in girls' education in the late eighteenth and
early nineteenth centuries estimates that 'religion is the subject
generally regarded as the most important.'[26] In *Strictures on the
Modern Method of Female Education* Hannah More argues that it is
better to cultivate even religious prejudice than to allow much
latitude. But there is no sign of scriptural study in Charlotte's
children's books.

Rural Walks came out in January 1795; the Preface is dated
19 November 1794. It had an immediate success. In the Reading
University copy the flyleaf reads 'Harriet N. Metcalfe, her book, and
I think it is a very entertaining one,' which from the form of the
genitive is probably a contemporary comment. As Charlotte becomes
more absorbed in the writing, the excessively didactic note gradually
fades, though it never disappears altogether. Caroline and Elizabeth
are allowed to criticise the adults they meet to Mrs Woodfield, while
Henrietta emerges as that rarity, a likeable fictional child, absorbed
in small animals like her 'sleeper' or dormouse, rescuing fledgelings
from boys who rob nests, examining plants and flowers close up on
her knees in the garden.

The inculcation of sense has its place in the work, and the girls are urged to the cheerful acceptance of a life which may be limited. But good manners spring rather from Sensibility than from sense: Elizabeth is at fault for not remaining in the set after having gone down the dance herself, a slight to Miss Harley, who has fallen from an enviable social position and lost her fiancé to her cousin. Mrs Woodfield tells Miss Harley's story to excite the children's sympathy. The book is centrally concerned with fostering Sensibility, and the inset stories of encounters with distressed characters all have this aim, as if Charlotte were rewriting Henry Mackenzie's *The Man of Feeling* for the next generation.

These stories of pathos vary greatly in quality. The first, 'The Sick Cottager', is brief and inconclusive while the later ones are more elaborate. The most interesting is 'The Fishermen', a chapter which mixes a beautiful detailed setting – many child readers would never have seen the sea, like Emma Woodhouse – with a vivid narrative where a storm threatens the fishing boats and the wives and children wait for the men to come back. This episode is full of poetic allusion and entirely free of condescension for the fishermen, who risk their lives 'pursuing the occupation on which their subsistence depends.'[27] The description of the wives and children waiting on the beach in the storm forms an introduction for the eighteenth-century child reader into the nature of the social contract and the economic basis of society. In this chapter too come excellent examples of her descriptive writing. As the storm approaches,

> the sun sunk, fiery and half-obscured by brown and purple spots and wandering clouds, beneath the horizon, tingeing the air with that red and lurid appearance which always foretells violent winds. [28]

She aims at a tragic tone in the ominous quality of her storm scene

> Tremendous Thunder now seemed to rival the fury of the winds; and floods of fire mingled with the rain that drove in torrents so violent that it seemed as if the sea itself were rushing upon the land. Could the danger of the poor men who were out, and the agonies of the women who belonged to them, have been a moment dismissed from her mind, there would have been something of sublime horror in this war of elements. But her solicitude for these unhappy people suffered her not to feel any other sensations than terror and pity.[29]

Mrs Woodfield and Elizabeth discuss these sensations after the suspense is over, each of them quoting from the storm scene in *Lear*. *Rural Walks* helped to establish the genre which produced *Little*

Women, with the March girls taking their Christmas dinner to a sick family. Though *Little Women* is more sophisticated in character and plot, *Rural Walks* assumes a readership with a more mature taste in verse and descriptive prose. Her readers evidently admired the chapter about the fishermen, for in *Rambles Farther* she includes a similar episode called 'The Excursion to the Sea' when the children revisit the sea shore, which allows for speculation about shells and seals, and discussion of Ariel's song and Clarence's dream. But not all the inset stories even of the early children's works are so imaginative. In *Rural Walks* the last story is the absurdly novelistic tale of Eupheme and Mr Charles Widdrington, presented as an example of the way fiction develops the judgement, but anti-climactic, and incongruous in its context. She evidently finished the volume in a hurry.

Throughout her children's books, she suggests that Sensibility is developed not only through sympathy with suffering but by reading and memorising poetry. She took the same attitude to teaching poetry that Arnold and Leavis were to take: the appreciation of poetry is the index and nourishment of Sensibility, and takes the central place within a culture. She never introduces overtly didactic poetry, as might be expected in an eighteenth-century children's book. Mrs Woodfield's and the children's favourites are Shakespeare, Thomson, Gray, Collins, Cowper, Prior, Darwin, Bowles and, rather surprisingly, Burns. Burns' *Poems Chiefly in the Scottish Dialect* was published in 1786, nine years before *Rural Walks*. Nine years can be a long time in literary history, but considering Charlotte's isolation and poverty, her recognition of Burns' genius and her ingenuity in getting hold of new volumes is impressive. Through the nineties and into the last years of her life she continued to besiege her publishers with requests for the loan of books. Burns was an alarming figure to some of his contemporaries; in Austen's 'Sanditon' the heroine is disapproving. Mrs Woodfield quotes 'To a Mountain Daisy' and 'Man was Made to Mourn'.

The lines Charlotte introduces from her favourite eighteenth-century writers are often ones chosen by David Nichol Smith for his *Oxford Book of Eighteenth Century Verse* in 1926. For instance she quotes like the later Smith from 'Spring' in Thomson's *The Seasons*:

> The yellow Wall-Flower, stain'd with iron brown
> And lavish stock that scents the garden round:
> From the soft Wing of vernal Breezes shed,
> Anemonies, Auriculas, enrich'd

With shining Meal o'er all their velvet Leaves ....
Then comes the Tulip-Race, where Beauty plays
Her idle Freaks: from Family diffus'd
To Family, as flees the Father-Dust,
The varied Colours run; and while they break
On the charm'd Eye, th'exulting Florist marks
With secret Pride, the wonders of his Hand.[30]

This is the pictorial poetry she tried to write herself, closely observant of texture and colour, though Thomson is playful in a way she seldom attempts. Such a passage is not in any way didactic but it conveys the intricacies of Tulip-breeding in the puns of 'Freaks' and 'break'. 'Freaks' refers both to the variegation of colour and to the bizarre quality of this new species' beauty, while 'break' suggests their sudden flashing on the sight but is also a technical term for the propagation of an original type in size or marking.

Botany is presented both as pleasure and science, with a concealed lesson about reproduction as part both of nature and civility. These ideas had been developed in Erasmus Darwin's *The Loves of Plants* (1789), one of her favourite poems. Beliefs about the importance of botany in education had a long after-life in schools, surviving in the twentieth century in the form of Nature Study, of excursions into the country or neighbouring bomb site to find wild flowers and frog spawn, both now rapidly diminishing.

S.R. Martin quotes from Richard Polwhele's *The Unsex'd Females* a passage where the clerical poet adverts to the great dangers of teaching plant reproduction to children. The Rousseauesque educationalists like Charlotte, in his view,

With bliss botanic as their bosoms heave
Still pluck forbidden fruit with mother Eve

while their charges

For puberty in sighing florets pant
And point the prostitution of a plant.[31]

Martin finds the passage interesting 'because it shows that even her books for children must have been scandalous in some quarters . . . Perhaps Polwhele genuinely thought that a child's knowledge of reproductive processes might lead to precocious sexuality',[32] an idea he regards as absurd. Polwhele was the spiteful clergyman who referred to Wollstonecraft's death in childbirth as a useful reminder of the difference between the sexes, and a regular contributor to the *Anti-Jacobin*. But of course he was correct in seeing Erasmus Darwin's botany and a freer type of education for girls with an emphasis on health, nature and their feelings as a threat to what he considered morality.

In an early talk about poets, Mrs Woodfield says:

> The same keeness of perception that makes them poets, that awakens in them the warmest relish for the enjoyments of life, [gives] of course the most poignant feelings of its disappointment . . . It is from hence that we fancy that poets have a greater share of calamity than other people; whereas in fact it is only that they possess superior power of description. Certain however it is that in reading the lives of the poets, it appears as if they were an assemblage of the most unhappy men that could be collected.[33]

Mrs Woodfield mentions Savage, Otway and Chatterton as typical examples; she articulates a romantic myth about poets, before the Romantics. But as in the novels, there is a conflict between Sensibility and sense. Her attitude is ambiguous, the ambiguity dictated by the fact that she is presented within the text as a poet, as a recognisable persona for Charlotte herself, but also as a necessarily sane and cheerful teacher of young girls. She is entangled, as she often is, between genteel conventions and the impulse to tell the truth as she sees it.

She cannot ascribe to Mrs Woodfield, a mother and teacher, the depression, excessive Sensibility and self-destructive impulses experienced, as she saw it, by her typical poets, and experienced also by herself. This tension between Mrs Woodfield's poetic and social selves is one further sign of Charlotte's problems in trying to reconcile Sensibility and sense. But if we consider Mrs Woodfield as the heroine of a novel rather than as the instructor in an educational work, we can see how close she is in situation to a later heroine, Laura Glenmorris, and how *The Young Philosopher* grew out of the earlier book.

In *Women in Romanticism* Meena Alexander writes,

> To instruct others, particularly other women, presupposes a bond of experience, a veracity of knowledge that can be passed on, a sense that the intimate self however betrayed by the state of the social world is part and parcel of a finer order, a world that must be brought into being through mental labour. To be a mother, however fraught with anguish, is to be part of the future.[34]

Alexander is writing about the impulse of Wollstonecraft's Maria to transmit her experience to her lost daughter, linking this with Wollstonecraft's own impulse to write for women. Alexander's words seem more appropriate to Charlotte even than to

Wollstonecraft. It is characteristic of critics of the 1790s, and I have also noticed this in Todd and Steeves, that what they say about other authors often seems more true of Charlotte than of the writer they are discussing, so immersed was she in the currents and undercurrents of her time.

The mother and daughter relationship is close and protective in *The Banished Man* and in *The Young Philosopher*. Both mothers are storytellers, both educate ideal daughters through the veracity of their knowledge. Charlotte began writing *Rural Walks* when she was more than usually desperate for money while Augusta's health deteriorated. Her first children's book begins in a fairly uninspired way. But as she began to write in this genre she became increasingly confident that she did indeed have a 'veracity of knowledge that can be passed on.' In the sequel, *Rambles Farther*, Mrs Woodfield tells Elizabeth that 'the end of all instruction is good sense and good temper'[35] but this is too bland an objective to mean much. What she and Mrs Woodfield try to teach is poetic Sensibility, 'seeing feelingly.' There is little appeal to sense or to established religion. There is still less emphasis on household management or the expectations of husbands, as is usual in the conduct books.

The most popular, and one of the most sexist of these, John Gregory's *A Father's Legacy to his Daughters* (1774) was attacked by Wollstonecraft in her *A Vindication of the Rights of Woman*. Charlotte follows the general lines of the *Vindication* in its remarks on the education of girls, though she shows in much more detail how a sample day should be spent, with a long walk for exercise and for the observation of plants, flowers and animals, leading to an encounter with someone from the neighbourhood to enlarge the children's understanding of other people's ways of life. In the afternoons the characters discuss what they have seen, and write about it or read poetry which has some bearing on their morning's experience. Poems are reproduced at length, so that *Rural Walks*, *Rambles* and *Conversations* can be used as textbooks, unlike *Emile*.

Her writing on girls' education forms part of an already well-established genre. Shaw found that Hester Chapone's *Letters on the Improvement of the Mind, Addressed to a Favourite Niece* (1773) was only the first of a flood of treatises written by women for the middle-class parent in the last quarter of the eighteenth century. Books on women's education and conduct proliferated, though Charlotte's are particularly vivid and specific. The subject was a political one, as it always is, and particularly so in the decade when she began, with traditionalists and progressives at odds here as on more overtly political topics. The great popularity of authoritarian male conduct books for girls, *A Father's Legacy* or James Fordyce's *Sermons to Young Women* (1765), is attested by their numerous reprintings, though they were probably more popular with relatives than with the recipients. Austen and Susan Ferrier mention Fordyce as boring Lydia Bennet in *Pride and Prejudice* and Mary Douglas in *Marriage*. He intended to inculcate piety, but the *Father's Legacy* was about social conduct and the stratagems for getting a good husband. This work was seldom out of print in the hundred years after its publication, superseding the Marquis of Halifax's *Lady's New Year's Gift* (1688) which ran through twenty-five editions and held the field for almost a century before Gregory.

There were many women in the paternalist camp, of course. The *Legacy* was often reprinted with Mrs Chapone's *Letters on the Improvement of the Mind* (1773), and Mr Tyrold's advice to his daughter from Burney's *Camilla* to make up a volume. A reading of these educational works reveals the intense pressures applied even to very young girls. Such pressures were psychological, such as threats of unmarriageability or family disgrace, and actual, such as backboards and collars. They throw into relief Charlotte's stress on knowledge as a pleasure, undertaken for its own sake and without regard to the girl's marriageability.

At the beginning of *Rambles Farther*, Ella Sedley, a little West Indian girl is introduced, who might represent in fiction a child of one of Charlotte's sons. The dialogues consider such subjects as slavery and the rights of servants. Towards the end, Mrs Woodfield and the girls go to London, and the problems of the social world and the ultimate destiny, marriage, come to the fore. In London, the narrative becomes duller and the poetry almost nonexistent though the book finishes with a long quotation from Cowper's *The Task*, still Charlotte's favourite poem. The original faults of Caroline's earlier education reappear, and the suitor who presents himself is nearly scared off by her flirtatiousness. The instructive dialogues blend gradually into the genre of the courtship novel, with Mrs Woodfield as mentor. *Rambles Farther* ends with Caroline's marriage, which is shown as in some ways the end of freedom and the beginning of such domestic business as engaging suitable servants. The tone of the ending is hard to guage. Caroline's fiancé suddenly produces a baby which has been left on his hands, he says, and Caroline sweetly agrees to bring it up. At times it would seem Charlotte got so sick of inculcating virtuous wifehood she almost openly guyed the whole thing. Caroline will have to accept whatever lies her husband tells her.

As always, the point of view is divided. Girls must be brought up to be good-tempered, sensible and well-mannered, and to marry. They are also capable of literary and scientific interest, of developing sensibilities which are individual rather than specifically 'womanly', and of discovering like Mrs Woodfield-Smith that marriage creates new problems. The contradictions about girls' education and preparation for marital subordination are never resolved, but the study of Sensibility and sense, individualism and conformity in girls' education would develop a few years later into the more profound and painful analysis of *The Young Philosopher*.

While she was working on *Rural Walks* and 'Rosalie', she was still attempting to persuade the Trustees to release money so that Augusta could go to the sea. The Trust was making between £700 and £900 with each year's cargo of sugar from Barbados, money which was at least in part her children's, but Robinson and Anthony Parkin insisted that this could only be dispensed according to the letter of Richard's will, which nobody could yet agree on. The Trust seems to have been in a transitional stage now. Egremont, probably at Hayley's request, had agreed to take over part of its administration, but Chancery had not yet finalised the arrangements, so it may have been even harder to gain access to any interest than before he began to be involved.

But Charlotte had acquired some powerful allies. Thomas Erskine, later Lord Chancellor, a liberal who defended Tom Paine at his trial for treason in the second part of *The Rights of Man* and some of the accused in the Holcroft trial, the Duchess of Devonshire and Sheridan had all become interested in the problems of Richard's will. They were Charlotte's contemporaries, fellow writers, and Foxite Oppositionists who had shared her political feelings. Sheridan detested John Robinson. Erskine particularly admired Charlotte's novels. When he had an important speech to make, he used to read her works to catch her grace of composition. He may have wanted to catch her crusading aggression too. She alludes in a letter to George Fordyce, a friend of Sheridan and Fox, to the deed of 1784, made by her when Benjamin was in prison, as one cause of her calamities. Charlotte Mary and Lionel were also now involved in correspondence over the will.

Charlotte went to London in January 1795 on Trust business. Augusta stayed with her uncle at Fittleworth, while Alexandre and

Lionel were apparently in London together. Infuriated by the Trustees' refusal to help Augusta they both sent challenges to Thomas Dyer. Duelling was illegal, and he responded by taking out warrants for their arrest. They were bailed in the sum of £100 each, the money put up by Colonel North, an old friend of the family, and Augusta's Dr Parry. Probably neither of the young men took this very seriously. Lionel went off on a recruiting party to Northampton and Alexandre returned to Fittleworth. Dyer managed to bring the date of the magistrate's hearing forward by two months, to the following week, knowing they would fail to turn up, in which case the bail would be forfeit and both imprisoned until they could pay £200 each.

By the time she heard this, Charlotte was back in Bath. She wrote to the Duchess of Devonshire on 8 February 1795:

> I think I never was so miserable as the dread of this makes me, & yet I thought I had experienced every degree almost of sufferings, from every kind of anxiety. I still feel myself however confident in Mr Erskine's protection, & think it impossible that the chicane of an infamous Grub Attorney can baffle his upright and enlightened mind.

She writes also of her second volume of Sonnets, for which the Duchess as well as Cadell and Davies was collecting subscriptions, and of a play that the Duchess had encouraged her to write. This was of course an old dream of hers. She claims here to have destroyed a play she wrote in the late eighties, but she may have reconstructed it. Her health was now so bad that at times, she says, she cannot walk across the room or even get out of a chair without help, but 'fortunately my hands, which were affected a few days ago, are now restored to me, & as necessity is imperious & irresistible, I must continue to work.' She adds that she has just finished the second volume of *Montalbert*; there is no explanation for the change of title. She ends her letter more cheerfully with the hope that Erskine may settle the matter of the will by compromise. Perhaps he or the Duchess intervened with Dyer, for neither Lionel nor Alexandre were imprisoned for their challenge.

Augusta had apparently been feeling better, as she and Alexandre were still with her uncle Nicholas, but her improvement was brief. Two successive letters from Charlotte to Cadell and Davies tell the rest. One was in mid-March:

> Gentlemen,
> My daughter de Foville is dangerously ill at Fittleworth near Petworth

& order'd immediately to Bristol as her only chance of life. I have not the means of having her sent, for the Bills to a considerable amount announced by my Sons Letters are not come to hand. If you have any money of mine in your hands, I beg you to send her an order for it by the first post that her journey may not be delay'd an hour for want of money. If you have not any, I have no right to ask any favr of you.

The direction is Mrs De Foville (Fittleworth) at the Revd N Turners. Fittleworth near Petworth, Sussex. Even 5£ wd be of use should you have no more. I am half distracted & know not what I write. I am, Gentn, yr obedt Sert, Charlotte Smith March 15th 1795.

I am persuaded that Mr Cadell Senr would have the humanity to assist me with this trifle which shall be deducted out of the first money I can by any means procure.

The next one is dated 2 May:

Gentlemen,
On the other side you will find an advertisement which I beg you will insert in such Papers as you usually engage. That I might not commit you, I have not even named your house as that where application should be made for the restoration of the subscription money, for which my Sons will give me the means of providing. I Trust you will approve of this precaution and oblige me with the immediate insertion of these lines, so as to diffuse the notice as generally as possible. The Trustees have refus'd me not only assistance for my daughter while she lived, but wherewithal to bury her. However as I do not name any names, there is no libell in this I Trust, & what I may do else will not affect any person but myself. Your speedy answer will oblige, Sir,
your most humble Sert, Charlotte Smith

The advertisement, which Cadell and Davies did not print, describes her as too overwhelmed with sorrow to complete the engagement she has made with the public. She alludes to her second subscription volume of *Elegiac Sonnets* which was due out but which she was too acutely depressed to complete. It did not in fact appear until 1797. By that time the Duchess, notoriously scatty about money and living a complex life in a *ménage à trois*, had lost her subscription list and part of the receipts; some subscribers began to suspect they were being embezzled.

Augusta died on 23 April 1795, aged twenty; her grave is in a burial ground of the former St Andrews, Clifton. Charlotte's better life died with her, and she never fully recovered. In her *British Public Characters* account Mary Hays included part of a letter written by Charlotte to a friend at some unspecified later date:

How lovely and how beloved she was only those who knew her can tell. In the midst of perplexity and distress, till the loss of my child, which fell like the hand of death upon me, I could yet exert my faculties; and, in the consciousness of resource which they afforded to me, experience a sentiment not dissimilar to that of the Medea of Corneille, who replied to the enquiry of her confidant – 'Where are now your resources?' – 'In myself.'

But she still had these resources, though they were depleted, and she would use them as before to feed her other children, some of whom had been neglected for a long time. Charlotte Mary, now twenty-six, sometimes stayed with her cousin Richard Smith and his wife in Islington or with Mary Gibbs Smith, now Mary Allen, in Lymington. Lucy, who was nineteen, never quite recovered from Augusta's death either. From that Charlotte dates her severe bouts of depression. Growing up in the Smith household can never have been easy, and Charlotte Mary may have been the worst affected as the eldest daughter. But nothing is known for certain as to why she spent so much time away, or how the children left in Storrington dealt with Charlotte's long absence in Somerset, or how the less favoured daughters felt about their mother.

Charlotte had sent Harriet and George to Exmouth, to a friend, Miss Peckham, once she knew Augusta could not live long. When she was buried, the obituary inserted in the *Bristol Journal* and the headstone chosen, Charlotte joined them, probably with Alexandre who remained in close touch with her until he eventually returned to France.

Several of her sonnets are about Augusta. One, written the previous summer, records ebbing hope at Clifton, whose romantic rocks and green woods inspired the poets Chatterton and Ann Yearsley but have no effect on an invalid's torpor. This sonnet is ascribed to Charlotte Denzil, in Charlotte's established manner of using poems to extend a character's consciousness before they went into the next *Elegiac Sonnets* edition. She also addressed one to Caleb Parry, evidently written before Augusta died. She wrote another at midsummer 1795 while she was at Exmouth:

> Fall, dews of Heaven, upon my burning breast,
> Bathe with cool drops these ever-streaming eyes;
> Ye gentle winds, that fan the balmy West,
> With the soft rippling tide of morning rise,
> And calm my bursting heart, as here I keep
> The vigil of the wretched! – Now away

Fade the pale stars, as wavering o'er the deep
Soft rosy tints announce another day,
The day of Middle Summer – Ah! in vain
To those who mourn like me, does radiant June
Lead on her fragrant hours; for hopeless pain
Darkens with sullen clouds the Sun of Noon,
And veil'd in shadows Nature's face appears
To hearts o'erwhelm'd with grief, to eyes suffused with tears.[36]

In the last volume of *Montalbert*, which Charlotte must have been writing just before and after Augusta died, Rosalie thinks she will lose her baby, and we are 'in' madness rather than observing it from the outside, with a young female Lear. Shakespeare is present to Charlotte's imagination in all her writing, especially the sonnets and letters: 'we must endure' she says, or speaks of herself 'seeing feelingly', while she tries to force language to extremity and break the mundane. As a Shakespearean, at least, she might fairly be called a Romantic. The passion for Shakespeare is what they all have in common, and hers was as strong as and her knowledge probably more extensive than any except Lamb's. In the opening of this sonnet the desire of the soul in hell for cooling water and the bursting heart are reminiscences of *Lear*, the play she quoted most often.

Montalbert appeared in June while she was still at Exmouth; it has no Preface. She could yet not address her readers on the subject of Augusta's death. It is a novel without the polemics of *Desmond* or *The Banished Man*, in fact without national political content altogether. As in *Desmond* she is concerned with the subjection of women's rights and feelings to patriarchal violence, but her ideas are worked out without reference to a national background. Her retreat from national politics results in a more insistent politicisation of the hero's and heroine's relationship. The two Gothic castles are more specifically emblems of paternalism than emblems of the state, the church and the law. The two kinds of authority are intimately connected of course, but in *Montalbert*, the whole focus is on sexual politics, the confinement of the heroines and nervous illness.

The novel is preoccupied with childbirth and the anxieties of raising children but there is also a compensatory emphasis on maternal love, women's strongest passion, she claims. The elder Rosalie endures her unhappy life for the sake of having her daughter near her, the younger Rosalie goes mad when her baby is taken from her. Both are rash heroines though the elder is hurt more by her unconventionality. One of the narrative strands, the treatment meted out to an unmarried woman who gets pregnant – the loss of her baby and her punishment by church and family – has been the concealed history of many women in England even into the latter part of the twentieth century.

All but one of the male characters are destructive. The elder Rosalie is made miserable by her father, lover and husband, while the daughter discovers that her romantic hero, once married, can be as authoritarian as any father. It is a sophisticated novel in its attitudes to gender and marriage, and the most pessimistic of the fictions – which is claiming a great deal – though because of the formally happy ending, it is described by Stanton as 'the least reflective of the novels.'[37]

The influence of Burney is strong, but Charlotte radicalises her, bringing Burney's underlying feminism from subtext to surface. The heroines of *Evelina* (1778), *Cecilia* (1782) and *Camilla*, published a year after *Montalbert*, all suffer breakdown from trusting their feelings rather than obeying strict patriarchal codes for women. The authorial voice is finally on the side of obedience, though the appeal of the novels lies in Burney's division of sympathies between self-assertion and conformity. As Jane Spencer shows in *The Rise of the Woman Novelist*, Burney follows in the conservative tradition of reformed heroines initiated by Eliza Haywood's *The History of Miss Betsy Thoughtless* (1751). But Burney's conclusions are claustrophobic, especially *Camilla*'s, with a once-lively heroine boxed in psychologically by family and husband.

Rosalie is brought up in the Lessington family, believing herself to be the youngest daughter. She secretly marries Harry Montalbert, the nephew of Mrs Lessington's old friend Mrs Rosalie Vivyan, her godmother. Like Mrs Vivyan, Montalbert is a Catholic, and his Italian mother would oppose her son's marriage to a woman who is poor and Protestant. The narrator ends the first volume with Mrs Vivyan's revelation that young Rosalie is her illegitimate daughter.

Even in this first volume, Harry Montalbert's character is ambiguous. He is arrogant in his relations with the admittedly tiresome Lessingtons, and careless about Rosalie's peace of mind and reputation, persuading her into a secret Catholic marriage which was doubtfully valid in England. The second, that is, the middle volume is taken up mainly with Mrs Vivyan's story, told to her daughter Rosalie. Formerly Rosalie Montalbert, she was brought up in seclusion by her rich, autocratic father. What may seem in synopsis a confusing and pointless doubling of the names has its purpose. This inset story is sombre, and the ruin of a Gothic monastery in the grounds of her father's house links her girlhood with images of passivity, isolation and death:

> At the end of a long row of elms, of which a few single trees only remain, you recollect a high mount now planted with firs, poplars and larches, into which, as it is railed round, nobody now enters; you perhaps remember too, the very large yew tree that shadows a great space of ground near it, and which is also railed round. That mound covers the ruins of a small parish church, and that yew tree was in the churchyard. An avenue of ancient trees was terminated by this church, at the distance of something more than a quarter of a mile from the house.[38]

The elder Rosalie goes on to describe the vaults and underground passageways with their offices, the ruins covered in ivy and a half-effaced representation of the crucifixion. Charlotte emblematises the control of a debased religion (the only type of religion she ever represented) over servants, children, and women. The monastery, with its double railings, its remains of Latin sentences, claustrophobia and darkness, effectively symbolises the weight of paternal authority and superstition.

But old Montalbert is unable to prevent his daughter's love affair with her cousin Charles Ormsby. Seduction is not an unusual plot development for a secondary heroine of the mid-nineties: Inchbald creates seduced heroines for A *Simple Story* (1791) and *Nature and Art*. But as late as 1941, Charlotte's American biographer and enthusiastic advocate Florence Hilbish felt it necessary to write as if Rosalie and Ormsby were married. When Rosalie becomes pregnant, an anonymous letter alerts Montalbert, who forces Ormsby to embark for India. Rosalie meets Ormsby's brother hiding in the vaults of the monastery, and expects help from him as a male relative. But Charlotte was now using stereotypical conventions like the Rescue in unexpected ways, and his hiding place in one of the most sinister of her Gothic buildings should warn the reader: the brother is in league with Montalbert to prevent Rosalie's marriage.

After she has had her baby, and passed her off as twin to Mrs Lessington's youngest child, she is forced to marry her father's friend Mr Vivyan. Old Montalbert dies soon afterwards, and one of the most painful circumstances of her mother's story, as young Rosalie unsentimentally considers it, is the fact that he did not die sooner. Charlotte gives Rosalie a pragmatic and sensible tone: had he died, her mother and father could have married and kept her as their child, and time would have 'effaced the remembrance of their earlier indiscretion.'[39] Her thoughts diverge from the moral norms of eighteenth-century novels. Heroines from Evelina to Grace Nugent of Edgeworth's *The Absentee* (1812) faint at the suspicion of a mother's sin, though suspicion usually proves groundless. Rosalie Vivyan spends eighteen years as a repentant wife, having three more children, but often inviting young Rosalie to stay, until her son's growing affection for his half-sister forces her to send Rosalie away.

The novel is imaginatively and cleverly structured. The retrospective central volume, with its villain, old Montalbert, its thoughtless hero, Ormsby and its victimised Rosalie, prefigures the injustice and violence with which the younger Montalbert will treat the younger Rosalie. After the elder Rosalie's narrative, the contemporary story is resumed. The young couple go to Italy, where Rosalie gives birth to a son, another Harry, and is separated from her husband by the earthquake of 1782. She is helped by her husband's friend Count Alozzi, but when he makes advances to her, she appeals to Montalbert's mother, who has her kidnapped. At this very late stage, the novel's true hero appears. He is F. Walsingham (we never learn more than the initial of his first name), an English traveller and connoisseur, who rescues Rosalie from the castle in Calabria where her mother-in-law has imprisoned her, and brings her back to England.

Long before *Montalbert*, the convention had become established that the hero of a novel is the man who rescues the heroine, so the practised reader would expect love and marriage to follow a rescue. The traditional rescue introduces Sir Charles Grandison to Harriet Byron, and is a stereotype that helps to support Emma Woodhouse's delusion that Jane Fairfax is in love with Mr Dixon. Charlotte uses the convention in a sophisticated way to emphasise the mismatch of Montalbert and Rosalie. Walsingham is gentle and full of sensibility, grief-stricken over the death of his fiancée, but he comes to love Rosalie. He is more companionable and better educated than Montalbert.

The qualities that first make Montalbert attractive to Rosalie, his pride, impatience and recklessness, are a liability when he is her husband. He believes Walsingham is her lover, takes her baby away, and mistaking Walsingham's cousin Sommers Walsingham for the man reported to have brought Rosalie back to England, challenges him to a duel. By this time Rosalie's supposed brother, her brother and her father have arrived in Sussex, and Rosalie is driven mad by the hostility between her father and her husband and by her husband's abduction of her baby. The duplication of the two names, Montalbert and Rosalie, merges identity in concept: overhearing male authority, supported by religion, law and custom, is destructive to all women, wives or daughters. Ormsby articulates Charlotte's point about legally sanctioned male bullying, saying when his daughter seems to be dying, 'She too is destroyed – destroyed as her mother was, by the accursed house of Montalbert – Yes! The nephew resembles the uncle – he has murdered my daughter.'[40] But he himself has been almost as much to blame by getting the elder Rosalie pregnant in the first place, an imprudence duplicated by the younger couple's doubtful wedding ceremony. William Lessington responds to young Montalbert's brutal treatment of young Rosalie with, 'Alas! Which of us, situated as you were, might not have acted as you did?'[41] The rhetorical question implies that any man might, and this point has already been made by the nomenclature and the construction of the plot. *Montalbert* is more subtle than *Desmond* in its criticism of marriage. The younger Rosalie convinces herself that she loves her husband, and never falls in love with Walsingham, though the reader can see that he is the hero she should have married. *Montalbert* advocates divorce only by implication.

The ending is very like *Camilla's* a year later, though Charlotte's ending is subverted by all that has preceded it:

> Rosalie passed her life in studying how to contribute to [Montalbert's] felicity, and that of her father, and, by her sweetness and attention, she won them both from those asperities and differences of temper, which had once threatened to destroy their domestic comfort.[42]

There is bitter humour in the assumption that a heroine's happy ending begins a lifetime of propitiating men. F. Walsingham and the younger Montalbert exemplify different styles of Sensibility. Walsingham is the poet within the text. Montalbert is the stock hero, jealous and possessive like Montgomery and Willoughby. Charlotte's version of her own earlier ideal is darker by 1795. The presence of Walsingham, the superior hero, with whom the novel ends, remains a comment on careless, incompatible marriage. But in a clever ideological Parthian shot, Charlotte makes Walsingham's cousin, Sommers Walsingham, predatory and aggressive, doubling him to represent a side of F. Walsingham we have never seen. Within the text the latter is an impossible novelistic ideal, his credibility undermined by his missing first name and by the presence of his identically-surnamed cousin.

In the story of the elder Rosalie, the heroine's rashness leads to years of unhappiness during her patched-up marriage. Charlotte shows this as legalised prostitution, though Rosalie considers her situation not unusual. In *A Vindication of the Rights of Woman* Wollstonecraft had also considered it the common fate. The younger Rosalie's foolishness in agreeing to a secret marriage with a man she scarcely knows is punished, though by self-suppression she will keep the peace. The stoicism of both women is a kind of common sense, a necessary resignation to the inevitable, but we are shown how these lives have been wasted by overbearing or irresponsible male authority. The younger Rosalie's love of Sussex and Italian landscape gives her however a core of selfhood that promises a little better for the future than her mother's depressed piety.

Discussing the patterns of duplication in the heroines of Inchbald's *A Simple Story*, published in the following year, Patricia Meyer Spacks finds that the plot embodies a struggle 'between anger at the necessities of female compliance and awareness that no viable alternative exists.'[43] Hers is a well-established approach to women's writing. Mary Anne Schofield comments:

> Nancy K. Miller in her essay, 'Emphasis Added: Plots and Plausibilities in Women's Fiction', succinctly draws attention to the pervasive problem: there are two plots, two stories in fiction: the masculine and the feminine. As sophisticated critics of the novel and students of Sandra Gilbert and Susan Gubar (*The Madwoman in the Attic*), Carol Christ (*Diving Deep and Surfacing*), and Annis Pratt (*Archetypal Patterns in Women's Fiction*), for example, we have been taught to look for 'two stories' in nineteenth- and twentieth-century fiction. The same critical apparatus and sensibility can and must be applied to eighteenth-century fiction as well.[44]

The elder Rosalie's story echoes and parodies the precarious happiness that is won by conformity. But the bitterness is, to a close reading, out in the open, and the love and marriage plot comes ready-subsumed into the story of defeat. This is not dichotomy: there is scarcely a lingering commitment to love and marriage. In her first three courtship novels, Charlotte is more optimistic, though in *Celestina* Emily's story of seduction and death darkens the ending. The manipulation of two opposing narratives is absent in *The Old Manor House* and in *Marchmont*, but this construction returns in *The Young Philosopher*.

The autobiographical element in *Montalbert* is diffuse. There are two inquisitive literary ladies, one of whom, the 'Muse', may target

Seward. Charlotte does not attack individual lawyers but the law in relation to marriage, and marriage-customs generally. Montalbert's Catholic mother has an obvious basis in Charlotte's former worries about a Catholic ceremony. This may never have taken place, as the family was absorbed in Charles on his return from France, and soon Augusta's pregnancy would perhaps have made a wedding ceremony a matter of embarrassment.

Montalbert undermines the happy-marriage ideal in any form, and this might imply a changed attitude to Alexandre she could not afford to articulate in any other way. Through her established technique of duplication she casts doubt on even the literary and cultivated Rescuer Walsingham. Perhaps her disillusion with Hayley lies behind this. In fact he wrote to her kindly and fully on Augusta's death, though apparently with no mention of Thomas, as in her reply from Exmouth Charlotte does not refer to the boy. A friendlier relationship was re-established, though they seldom met now.

Wollstonecraft's substitute in *The Analytical* described *Montalbert* as 'a pleasing tale well told'[45] and perceptively commended its unity of design, though claiming it lacked the feeling or vivid descriptive passages of her earlier work. *The Critical* praised the sonnets ascribed to Walsingham and perceived the novel as a defense of virtue; this magazine too may have had a change of reviewer. On the whole the response was tepid. Two months later she needed to find new lodgings. Charlotte Mary and Lucy had joined her at Exmouth; but Miss Peckham, who had been ill for at least a year, probably with tuberculosis for which Exmouth's waters were thought beneficial, was now recommended to go to Portugal as her best hope of surviving the winter. Charlotte was especially grateful to her for looking after Harriet and George for so long, as she was young, ill and neither a relation nor a particularly old friend. She must have first met the Smiths in Sussex.

Charlotte could not yet bring herself to go back there; a year after Augusta's death she was writing to Cadell and Davies, on 1 May 1796, 'I shall soon make another move towards, if not to, Southampton in order to be nearer Sussex without quite returning to a scene which I do not know that I could bear.' The worst premonitions she had felt when Benjamin Berney died had come true. Sussex, where she had written late into the nights and spent the days with a houseful of lively children, the duns at the door, looked Edenic compared to the present. In late summer of 1795 she moved to Weymouth, and took lodgings at 7 The Esplanade, now no. 25.

By now she was beginning to hope, with remittances coming in from William and Nicholas, that she might soon give up the author's miserable trade. Charles was in Gibraltar and Lionel in Quebec with their regiments. She was so depressed she could hardly force herself to write, but she went on with the sequel to *Rural Walks*, though she could not think of a name for it. And she corresponded with Cadell and Davies and the Duchess about her new volume of sonnets and the illustrations to go with them. The portrait continued to bother her. Hayley would not let it be reproduced by anyone but Romney, but would not send it to him either. She had started on a new novel, *Marchmont*, but as with *Montalbert* the publisher for this was to be Sampson Low, and that series of letters does not survive, so there is no commentary on the evolution of these two books as there is on much of her work.

She was at Weymouth on 18 November during one of the worst storms in the lifetimes of even the older people on that coast, when six ships out of a fleet of 200 on their way to the West Indies were thrown onto Chesil Bank, and many more wrecked further along the South Coast. There were a few survivors. One, who was pregnant, especially appealed to Charlotte in her bereaved state. The woman lost her husband in the wreck; the celebrated poet and novelist then in Weymouth undertook to write an account to raise money for her and for the baby born in the town a few months later. It was an especially treacherous Bay. Wordsworth's brother John died there ten years later in the *Earl of Abergavenny*.

This is Charlotte's one piece of reporting, and conveys the sympathy for individual suffering and awareness of the wonderful malignity of human nature which together made her a satiric novelist. Two hundred and thirty-four lives were lost from among the passengers and crew on the six military-transport and merchant ships. Apart from *The Old Manor House* the pamphlet is her most vivid piece of writing. *A Narrative of the loss of the Catharine, Venus and Piedmont Transports, and the Thomas, Golden Grove and Aeolus Merchant Ships, near Weymouth on Wednesday the 18th of November last. Drawn up from Information taken on the Spot by Charlotte Smith, And published for the Benefit of an unfortunate Survivor from one of the Wrecks, and her Infant Child* (1796), is splendid journalism, arousing pity for the victims and horror at the villagers who robbed them. Her imaginative sympathy is as deeply engaged as in her novels.

The *Narrative* begins with a description of the troopships' departure from St. Helens. The sky is described as red and 'scumbled', and the unusual word is proleptic; it suggests the looting to come. As night fell,

> the fog now gathered more heavily around them, mingling the sea with the sky in drear confusion – they could distinguish nothing through the impenetrable gloom – they could hear nothing but the roaring of the wind; – yet, imagining they had sea-room enough, they were not aware of the extreme peril they were in, and that, instead of having cleared the Isle of Portland, they had driven to the Westward of it, and were rapidly approaching the tremendous breakers that, driven by a South West wind, thunder with resistless violence against that fatal bank of stones, which beginning at the village of Chisle, on the Presqu' Isle, connects it with the coast of Dorset.[46]

She writes as if she had been there and takes the reader with her, while her ruminant, exploratory sentences build suspense. She describes outer and inner action, the immense black waves that 'rose like tremendous ruins',[47] Gothicising the sea, and the 'speechless agony',[48] as those on deck waited for shipwreck.

Stories proliferate within the story: of Fifer Ensor who went back for his wife, Lt Jenner who had thought himself so fortunate to catch his ship, Mr Darley who was cast up on the beach injured and lay under a boat all night until a fifteen-year-old boy called Smith helped him. One unnamed woman, too terrified to jump into the sea, went back to her cabin and lay down on her bunk. Charlotte's cinematic description vividly images the woman's dressing-gown entangled with the floating furniture; eventually she plucked up courage to disengage her arms, made for the shore naked, and survived. The dead bodies of men, women and horses and the wreckage spread along two miles of Chesil Bank, and 'no celebrated field of carnage where the heroes of mankind have gathered their bloodiest laurels, ever presented, in proportion to its size, a more fearful sight . . .'[49] Coffins were sent from London for officers and women, not for other ranks.

As the first ship struck, villagers from Fleet and Wyke arrived at the beach to strip rings from the hands and clothes from the bodies of the dead and the exhausted survivors. Charlotte contrasts their looting, well known to be organised by the local clergyman, with the rescue parties led by the Revd Dr Sharp on the equally dangerous Northumbrian coast, and commemorated in his friend George Richard's poem 'Bamborough Castle' three years earlier. Charlotte writes:

In the course of collecting materials for this little narrative, I have been impelled to remark a character altogether different [from Dr Sharp]. One who seems to watch the Chisell Bank in the time of tempest, with views very unlike those of the venerable Dr Sharp; and far from teaching, like a good shepherd, humanity to his flock, he seems to encourage, by his example, their cruel rapacity, and to repeat with them in listening to the rising tempest:

> Blaw wind, rize zay
> Zhip azhore afore day.[50]

This was, presumably, a well known prayer along the South Coast; her transliteration of standard into dialect spelling effectively suggests the transformation of human to demonic. The *Narrative* is mainly a work of imagination, since she was not personally involved in the wreck, and it is unlikely she was at the beach until later in the day, if at all. It stands halfway between reporting and fiction, exemplifying her characteristic strengths. Some of the events in the *Narrative* are reused in *Marchmont* for the story of Phoebe Prior, which is about the risks necessarily taken by those who must leave the land.

The *Narrative* was published by subscription, with all profits going to the survivor and her child. It was typical of Charlotte's generosity to take this on at such a time. From Exmouth she had written to Hayley, of Cowper's madness, that imaginary evils at least block out the sense of real ones, and there are some states of mind to which madness is preferable. It is the only unsympathetic comment she is known to have made about Cowper, and understandable in her circumstances. But she used all her skill for this unnamed woman, whose shipwreck seemed an epitome of her own long struggle.

She found cheaper lodgings at 1, Belle Vue, and stayed on in Weymouth until the summer, when *Marchmont* and *Rambles Farther* came out in August 1796. The acute depression she felt is reflected in the sombre tone of the novel. Her political sympathies here fall back on a romanticised landed gentry whose power has been lost to the newly rich. Althea Dacres, the heroine, is sent to Eastwoodleigh House, just taken over by her unscrupulous and newly rich father, on her refusal to marry the dissolute Mr Mohun. She is shown over the principal rooms by Mrs Mosely, the old housekeeper to the previous owners, the bankrupt and dispossessed Marchmonts who lost their money in the Cavalier cause. The epigraph to this chapter, 'Far, far away thy children leave the land', from Goldsmith's 'The Deserted Village',[51] a line that must often have run in her head, sets the tone of regret for a lost rural community, demoralised by the disintegration of the Marchmont estate.

Althea walks through rooms of decaying furniture and tapestries, and looks at the few remaining family pictures, stacked against the wall. They no longer have a gallery for their display, as the impoverished old aristocracy has made way for absentee owners who have acquired fortunes by the war or by selling their votes. Mrs Mosely takes over the narrative to tell the story of the Marchmont heiress engaged to a young man who is on the Parliamentarian side in the Civil War. Charlotte distances herself from standard Cavalier attitudes, and Marchmont is no Tory, remarking 'if I go supperless to bed, fate will not deal worse with me than she does continually with those who have toiled all day.'[52] He does not see the Civil War in the same light as his father, much less his great-grandfather.

This house would be a candidate for restoration rather than for total demolition. The earlier Marchmont owners of Eastwoodleigh are represented kindly but not uncritically, and Mr Estcourt, the Parliamentarian, would be the best husband for the Royalist Marchmont heiress, though both die. While Charlotte takes the Civil War as starting point to examine the need for reconciliation between opposed interests, she recognises that compromise is unlikely. The former splendour of Eastwoodleigh is still visible in the architectural details, and in the furnishings and paintings the bailiffs have left behind. Althea wants the Marchmonts reinstated, so they can take back their former role in the villages and countryside.

Her hopes are thwarted by the monstrous lawyer Vampyre. The satiric subject of this novel is less the social hierarchy than the law. Vampyre represents John Robinson, and the violence of Charlotte's anger makes him into a mythic figure. Many of her lawyers are given Bunyanesque names: Mr Solicitor Cancer, Petrifie & Co; she gives Humour names to some non-legal characters too, like Mrs Aconite and the Henbanes. Vampyre hunts Marchmont through the intricate suites of rooms at Eastwoodleigh, though he manages to escape. Creditors, encouraged by lawyers, try to arrest his father's body on its way to the graveyard. The 'myrmidons of the police'[53] are everywhere, while Althea wonders whether the bailiffs are 'common robbers', or 'ruffians authorised by law to hunt some unhappy person to destruction',[54] the latter seeming more detestable.

Vampyre and his cronies prey on England like Tulkinghorn in *Bleak House*, though Vampyre is a coarser and bolder figure. He is distorted – Robinson suffered a paralytic stroke in the early eighties – and ubiquitous, moving between town and country, sometimes in disguise, his appearance always unexpected and shocking. He has a demonic quality which lifts his portrayal out of naturalistic characterisation and into allegory. He is larger than life, and until the ending capable of controlling the novel's plot. Martin comments that 'both Charlotte Smith (in *Marchmont*, 1796) and William Godwin (in *Caleb Williams*, 1794) mounted direct literary attacks on the British Constitution. Both heroes learn that their country's laws are completely subservient to the powerful.'[55] The resemblance is effected by the times, however, as Charlotte did not read *Caleb Williams* until long after *Marchmont* was finished.

The narrative opens with a description of Althea's upbringing by her aunt Mrs Trevyllian in a small house with a well-stocked library and French windows opening onto a lawn surrounded by flowers and shrubs. The house is arranged for the private pleasures of reading and gardening. It represents what was to become the great bourgeois ideal of the nineteenth century, the ideal of a private life uncontaminated by politics or trade. It is not an emblem of England's constitution, decaying or restored, but remote from political ordering of any kind. Here books offer comfort rather than controversy and the garden consoles with the interest of designing and planting. Althea regrets the garden more than the house when she leaves, and longs for the countryside while in London. This novel like the others after the Terror presents a green world as solace for lost political hopes.

Althea is the heroine most clearly created to understand the world she lives in. She has a satirist's eye. It is through her consciousness, for instance, that we see the disreputable lawyer Mohun surveying her 'with the sort of look that a sagacious jockey puts on when he is about to purchase a horse.'[56] She has the insight to see her society as the narrator sees it, though Charlotte feels the difficulty of marking strong features in a heroine of the 1790s:

> How difficult then it is for a novelist (compared to Shakespeare) to give to any one of his heroines any very marked feature which shall not disfigure her. Too much reason and self command destroy the interest we take in her distresses.[57]

She claims that heroines of Gothic novels, which are also novels of sensibility, and written in a time of reaction, must be vulnerable to be popular. Celestina is the most independent of her women, and answerable to nobody, but frankness and freedom must have appeared inappropriate for the less ebullient later works, where they are retrospective and restricted to a heroine's mother.

Althea's refusal of her father's demand that she should marry Mohun is kept in admirably low key. The situation is stereotypical, but Charlotte adopts it as a focus for her satire of London society and an excuse to banish her heroine to Eastwoodleigh, where Althea learns about the distresses of the agricultural poor. She is pleased to leave London, thinking of 'the insipid and wearisome sameness of the tables where I used to be placed, with giggling misses enjoying their own little jokes under a general eagerness for the pool.'[58] Her acidity of tone is Charlotte's, and in this novel even more than others the malignity of human nature is prominent. The narrator and Althea together recognise that there is no relief in country society from the corruption of cities. While shut up at Eastwoodleigh, Althea reads Rousseau and English history. She makes the connection, often made by the narrator, between black slaves and English labourers, asking

> if scenes like these are to be found in the cabin of the industrious labourer, who can wonder that any man should quit his paternal cottage? – or how can it be strange that our peasantry fly to America? I have heard that ideas of equality are visionary, and I believe it. But surely, though there must be hewers of wood and drawers of water, they ought to have the absolute necessaries of life.[59]

She thinks about economics, the cost of war, and how money might be better spent. Charlotte is returning to a consideration of those domestic and national problems she had written about in *Ethelinde*, but Althea brings more reading and detachment to the subject than the earlier heroine. She gives all the money she has to a starving woman and her children, and promises to find more, while later events increase her radicalism and dissatisfaction with the condition of England.

As the Preface says, she exemplifies fortitude, and has 'so much sense as well as sensibility.'[60] The narrative is plain and low-keyed except where it rises to virulence in Charlotte's depiction of lawyers. There is little liveliness of characterisation except in cameos like that of Mrs Polwarth and her *carissimo sposo* as she calls her husband. She is indeed like Mrs Elton, though more raffish and disreputable. But there is little humour in *Marchmont*, and the language is unusually austere. Sympathetic characters typically attempt to restrain feeling in the interest of good manners. When Althea visits the hero's sister, Charlotte writes:

> Having sent in this note, her anxious expectation did not last long, for Lucy Marchmont, whom she would almost anywhere have known from her resemblance to her brother, came down to receive her. In that sort of breathless agitation, which a desire to please particularly, and the fear of not pleasing, give to a young and timid mind, she led her visitor to a small sitting room on the first floor, and introduced her to her youngest sister; then, recovering a little from her confusion, Lucy began to express her gratitude to Althea for coming; but, trying to speak of her mother and of her brother, her voice failed her, and she burst into tears . . .

> As there was a great deal of good sense on both sides, without any of that affected sensibility which is hardly less unpleasant than cold indifference, they soon recovered their composure.[61]

Underlying embarrassments and anxieties, though strong, are assimilated into the conventional form of the visit, into composure. Althea and Lucy set up a haberdashery shop in a country town, claiming 'we shall be happier if we have something to employ us,' though acquaintances disapprove. They want to avoid living like 'ancient forlorn spinsters, just creeping through a vegetative sort of life in a cheap country'[62] [i.e. county] and they run their shop with a modest profit for a while. Marchmont struggles to make a living by journalism. Charlotte anticipates the themes of George Gissing's *The Odd Women* and *New Grub Street* by a century, but she cannot write an ending that excludes marriage entirely. Like Wollstonecraft's *Maria*, Althea goes to prison, though she willingly accompanies her husband. Charlotte's fudged ending comes in the shape of a childless and wealthy benefactor, but even he cannot restore Eastwoodleigh to the Marchmonts, and is, like F. Walsingham, obviously a novelistic device, not intended to blur the uglier outlines of Charlotte's England. Of all the heroines, Althea sees most consistently with the narrator's eyes, and it is often difficult to distinguish the point of view. Sense and Sensibility are examined in a more minute and mundane context than usual, and the novel is more sympathetic to self-control and rationality than to disruptive feeling: of all Charlotte's fictions this is the one which eludes classification as Novel of Sensibility.

In the Preface she blames the corruption of Richard Smith's executors for the death of Augusta, claiming that she met 'refusal of the most necessary assistance, taunts and insults' from them. But

> to a physician [Caleb Parry] at Bath I was indebted for every friendly, every skilful exertion which I could not purchase, but which were unremmittingly applied to save me from the blow that has indeed

crushed me to earth, and rendered the residue of my days sorrow and labour . . . I have no hesitation in saying, that in the present work, the character most odious (and that only) is drawn *ad vivum* – but as it represents a reptile whose most hideous features are too offensive to be painted in all their enormity, I have softened rather than overcharged the disgusting resemblance.[63]

The novel is intended to exemplify fortitude, she says, and if the reader knew her state of mind as she wrote it he would be willing to allow she practised what she preached. On the endpaper of the last volume is a notice:

Mrs Smith takes this Occasion of informing the Subscribers to the Second Volume of Poems With a Portrait and Engravings, that her domestic Misfortunes and personal ill-Health, together with Difficulties that arose in procuring a likeness, have unavoidably delayed the publication of the Work.

From Preface to endpaper, she made her presence felt.

Wollstonecraft was back in London, and reviewing in *The Analytical* again. Her tone is somewhat patronising:

It is be lamented that talents such as hers had not a more genial sky to ripen under; and that the delightful task of invention has for her been a labour of patience rather tending to embitter than sooth a wounded mind. Her manner, indeed, of alluding to her domestic sorrows must excite sympathy and excuse the acrimoney with which she execrates, and holds up to contempt, the man to whom she attributes them.[64]

By this last comment she can only mean John Robinson; there is no portrait in *Marchmont* that corresponds to Benjamin. The manner of the review is elegiac throughout, as if she thought Charlotte was dying. If so she soon discovered her mistake, as Charlotte certainly met Godwin in that subsequent year of the Godwin–Wollstonecraft partnership. Godwin appears as quite evidently himself in her next novel, *The Young Philosopher*, which praises Wollstonecraft in its Preface and is closer to both Godwin and Wollstonecraft in ideology than any other work of Charlotte's. *Marchmont* was in general very well received and represented in volumes of extracts, a good indicator of popularity, more often than other novels of that year.

Like *Marchmont*, the letters of the late nineties usually lack the brio of her earlier writing. The years from the summer of 1795 to 1800 were not necessarily uneventful, but there are a smaller proportion of her letters to judge them by. A few months after Augusta died, one male member of her family, she wrote to Walker, wanted to make a marriage that would leave her more wretched than ever. She never names him, but it was someone in England, which eliminates all her boys except George, who was only ten. A son of Nicholas Turner might have been the right age, and yet her emotional involvement seems too great for a nephew. If Alexandre was showing in a haste to remarry that his marriage to Augusta had been partly a matter of convenience, Charlotte's regrets must indeed have been bitter, and she might have been unable to acknowledge the truth to anyone. But Alexandre continued to live with the family for another two years.

Rambles Farther was the subject of an especially long battle with Cadell and Davies. She had originally planned a four-volume *Rural Walks*, while they argued that no school book should run to more than two volumes. They cavilled about her revisions, or lack of them, and what they might pay; they rubbed in that there had been little demand for a second edition of *The Banished Man* though they had supplied one, and rejected *Montalbert* without a word – though they had some excuse for that as Charlotte had boasted she had a publisher ready to buy it. Admittedly she was difficult to deal with, and asked a lot of them. But it is pleasant to see their change of manner when she secured the Duchess of Devonshire's permission to dedicate *Rambles Farther* to her twelve year old daughter. The Duchess wrote to them asking them to come and see her; their subsequent note to Charlotte, surviving on the end of her 17 May 1795 letter to them, still bears the impress of their visit to Devonshire House:

> Madam
> The day after we were favoured with your Letter of the 17th we received a Note from the Duchess of Devonshire desiring to know when she could see us on the Subject of two more Volumes of 'Rural Walks' in answer to which we informed her Grace that we would wait upon her whenever she would be pleased to direct; the Expectation of receiving her Grace's Commands, which we have not as yet been honoured with, induced us to delay writing, or we should have immediately answered your Letter – We are surprised to find that some Misapprehension had led you to understand that we declined the Purchase of your new Volumes . . . . . . we are ready to undertake if it meets with your Approbation to pay you *fifty pounds* for the Copyright of them the Instant we receive the MSS. compleat.

They were soon to turn down a novel called 'First Impressions'.

She moved to Oxford in the autumn of 1796, first to Headington then to lodgings in the High Street opposite University College.

Perhaps duns were now aware of her address in Weymouth, or perhaps she was too restless to stop anywhere for long. Around this time she was asking Cadell and Davies to address letters and parcels to her as 'Mrs Smith' without the identifying Charlotte, or asking them to post correspondence to Charlotte Mary. They were to tell enquirers she was travelling in the West Country for her health, and could not be contacted. By now she had hopes she would soon see William again, after eleven years. He had heard of Augusta's death and his mother's impoverishment, and promised to get home leave. At Oxford she began on *The Young Philosopher*, but much of her time was taken up with arrangements for the production of *Elegiac Sonnets II*.

Egremont's and the Duchess's influence had so far made no difference to the Trustees' administration of the will. John Robinson, by Charlotte's account, persuaded her to agree to receiving £100 immediately instead of the £900 profits due to her from a cargo of sugar, but then changed his mind after paying her only ten pounds. On 26 March 1797, she wrote to Davies that Anthony Parkin

> hopes to tire me quite out . . . but he will for once reckon upon pusillanimity that he will not find. I am determined rather to perish with the rest of my family than to submit to his impudent robbery.

Three weeks later on 16 April she reluctantly wrote asking Hayley for help. She wanted him to persuade Davies to accept her next novel, and also to urge Egremont to oversee the Chancery suit for the recovery of the Smith children's legacies. Erskine had talked to her about this already, and said that nothing could be done without money. He had suggested that Egremont and the Duchess might be prepared to contribute towards the cost of the suit. Charlotte could not make such a proposition to either of them directly, but hoped Hayley would sound Egremont out for her. It was of course a large request, but she evidently felt her children's circumstances justified it. She wrote:

> Famine, which I have often seen very near, seems nearer than she has ever yet been – To add to my satisfaction. The Bankers who lent me £80 to send to my two poor Lieutenants, Charles and Lionel, who were quite destitute (& for whom the Wretches who possess their property refused me the least assistance) – The Bankers who so obligingly accommodated me have written to me to say that if it is not immediately replaced, they must proceed to recover it; that is to say I shall be arrested & sent to Prison. To that I am however quite reconciled & had rather it should happen than not, if it would bring the business to an issue . . .

If you knew the extreme misery, I am subject to & which I must yet
bear, – for what can I do with my three daughters & a boy of twelve
years old? You wd wonder how, shatter'd as my health is, I get on
from one day to another. It is rather despair than fortitude that
carries me on. I have so little to hope, I am so little sensible to the
pleasure which they say there is even in existence that I seem
habituated to suffering just as a wretch is to his dungeon, & I do not
beleive that any thing less than such misery as I am compelled to
endure would make me feel at all. I am not yet I think at the very
bottom of personal suffering, for I imagine I shall die in a prison. So
am I rewarded for my wretched & laborious life – with the loss of all
that is accounted good & with that of the one good which wd have
reconciled *me* to the deprivation of every other. Will you see if you
can be of any use to me with Davies, and let me hear from you soon?

In this letter we first hear of Lucy's fits of depression and threatened
decline since Augusta's death. On the same date, Charlotte also
wrote to Davies and casually mentioned a Mr Newhouse, who
would call on him later. Thomas Newhouse was the son of a Petworth
attorney and perhaps already courting Lucy by attempting to help
her mother with her complicated financial affairs. Charlotte ends her
long letter to Hayley affectionately: 'God bless you. Forgive my
being so great a plague.' Egremont eventually contributed a large
sum towards the settlement of part of the Trust, probably on Hayley's
persuasion. However, Egremont's intervention did Charlotte no
good at this time, and such applications, even made vicariously,
must have been humiliating. But Cadell and Davies agreed to publish
The Young Philosopher.

In the Preface to *The Banished Man* and more explicitly in later
letters she said she wished that when she separated from Benjamin
she had decided at once on rejection of gentry status for herself and
her children. Many of her problems lay in her determination to
educate and maintain the boys for professions and the girls as
middle-class young ladies helping their mother at home until they
married. She felt that Richard's money in Trust for them and her own
landed background entitled them to that. Perhaps inevitably, the
boys who survived fared better than the girls, and this might have
been the case however much money the family had. Marriage and
pregnancy killed Augusta or hastened her death. Marriage was
further to demoralise Lucy. Nothing is known of Charlotte Mary's
attitude to spinsterhood, but something might be guessed from the
fact that Harriet would soon take a tremendous gamble to avoid it.
In retrospect, Charlotte thought it might have been better if she, and

her daughters as they grew up, had decided to go into service. Certainly she could scarcely have worked so hard as a housekeeper or upper servant as she did as a novelist. Her residual pride in landed ancestry, mannered graciousness and domestic impracticality would have made her an alarming acquisition as a servant. But she might have had more security in a good household.

The letters between Augusta's death and *Elegiac Sonnets II* sometimes give a more cheerful glimpse of her. Writing to Walker on 29 May 1796 some satirical sharpness comes back as she alludes to the Prince of Wales. His marriage to Maria Fitzherbert took place when they were both single with the exchange of a ring and promises before witnesses: it constituted a valid marriage. George III however had already reacted violently to his son the Duke of Cumberland's marriage to a commoner – who was, incidentally, the chief patroness of Charlotte's first subscription *Elegiac Sonnets* and dedicatee of *Ethelinde*. George had introduced the despotic Royal Marriages Act, which gave Prinny, as he was unaffectionately known, an excuse to jettison Maria Fitzherbert when he wanted to. In 1795 he bigamously married Caroline of Brunswick on the understanding that Parliament would pay his debts, and made his current mistress Lady Jersey, a grandmother several times over, one of Caroline's Ladies of the Bedchamber. Prinny and Caroline separated almost at once. Charlotte writes:

> and then the *brouilline* of the *illustrious pair*, and the grand-meretricious influence of Lady Jersey . . . occupy every mind that has not some urgent troubles of its own.

She always wrote better to Walker than anyone else whose letters survive, though the wordplay is listless compared to some of her earlier correspondence.

Marchmont is a convalescent novel in its quietude and return to heritage, as well as in its necessary extrusion of intensified hate for Robinson. But she was working on *The Young Philosopher*, 'a composition of some novelty, and of more solidity than the usual croud [sic] of Novels',[65] which would articulate more precisely the Rousseauesque philosophy diffused through all her earlier poetry and fiction. And she was increasingly absorbed in preparing the subscription edition of *Elegiac Sonnets II*, now two years overdue. As far as she ever would, she was recovering, and though she was suicidal and close to madness at times, she already knew how to exert some control by writing herself into the plot.

5

The Goddess of Botany

The production of *Elegiac Sonnets* was intensely important to her, partly because it might be her last collection of poetry, partly because she always needed a focus for her enormous intellectual energy. For more than a year the volume engaged her as art critic as well as poet. After much discussion of various possibilities with Cadell and Davies, four drawings were included, three by Richard Corbould, who had contributed to *Elegiac Sonnets I*, and one, the illustration for 'The Female Exile', by Harriet, Countess of Bessborough, the Duchess of Devonshire's sister. The drawings were engraved by Heath and Neagle. On 20 November 1796 Charlotte wrote to Cadell and Davies that she was concerned about the high cost of producing the book, as artists and engravers were expensive, but

> all that can be said is, that if the price of Artists is rais'd in proportion to the prices of almost every thing else, there is nothing to be done but for the writer to have less profit. There are no set of Men to whom I would so willingly pay money if I had it as Artists of merit; therefore, if you think Mr Neagle more likely to do justice to the drawing, I beg you will put it into his hands . . . As the whole Subscription money does not amount to above a hundred & fifty pounds, this will be but a losing game for me. I mean if the expence of plates amount to ten Guineas each besides the drawing I am to pay for. However circumstances may arise which may make this no object to me, & if it be, I had rather gain less from a subscription I was never very anxious about than have the last book of the kind I shall ever publish appear shabbily done and in a bad taste.

In fact Lady Bessborough did not expect to be paid, and Cadell and Davies covered the whole cost of the plates.

She meant to include fewer sonnets and more pieces in other verse forms. Henrietta's 'Ode to the Poppy' was included and illustrated – rather surprisingly, perhaps – and her verses on seeing her two sons at play. With a mixture of affection and business sense she wrote to Cadell and Davies on 24 December:

I have complied as well with my own wishes as the earnest desire of my friends in inserting in the Collection the three pieces by Mrs O'Neill. Not only because they are exquisitely beautiful but because I am persuaded it will engage all her friends & connections to become purchasers & gratifies at once my taste and the tender affection I had for her.

But one of Henrietta's poems written in Portugal, Charlotte was sure, gave wrong names for some of the plants she described. Erasmus Darwin had teased Charlotte once about printing a poem that showed some gap in her knowledge of natural history. Without the right botanical reference book she felt unable to edit the poem properly and left it out.

She was now reading Godwin on progress and perfectibility, and probably met him first at this time; Gary Kelly believes he was a close friend by 1798. She was not isolated intellectually or socially, in spite of her debts; by her account she saw too many people. On 26 February 1797 she was writing to Cadell and Davies from Oxford about the Preface and subscribers to the new collection, and promising to send them back the handwritten book full of poems:

> And the printer may almost immediately proceed on the book you have returned which I will send up as soon as filled & will obtain time for it tomorrow if no way but by shutting myself up in the garret, for I am worn to death by company from morning to the night.

She returns to the question of her portrait, which had at last been copied by John Condé from Romney's picture:

> I think Mr Condé has done all that could be done save only that my family say, what I do not venture to suggest myself, that there is a want of spirit in the Eyes. I see not any great cause myself to find fault with it. I only fear that it is done so delicately that it will not bear so many impressions as will be required for your sale.

She thought the face too long, but the picture in *Elegiac Sonnets II*, with its appealing Shakespearean disclaimer of present likeness, is an interesting variation on Romney. She considered the image important as an encouragement to follow her story and buy her work. Another picture of her by Thomas Hardy, a London portraitist and engraver, she described as a likeness of Old Mother Shipton, the legendary witch. It sounds as if the children at home entered into the production of this volume. Probably they did with all her work, as well as being amanuenses. Charles, when he returned injured from France, asked for a complete set of her books as his surgeon preferred that to a fee, and the boys were known in the East India Service or in the Army, much to their advantage, as the sons of Charlotte Smith.

By 25 April 1797, two years and two days after Augusta died, when the proofs came, she was entirely absorbed in the project. Part of her energy came from her determination to record Charles' injury, Augusta's death and the Trustees' inhumanity in her Preface. In her detailed comment to Cadell and Davies she sounds more like the old Charlotte:

> I am now to speak of the proofs, & let me before I forget it say that I was disappointed at not having Lady Bessboroughs & the other two drawings sent down with the proofs. Pray let me have them with the next pacquet without fail. I cannot say (because I cannot say the thing that is not)[1] that I am satisfied with either of Mr Heaths engravings . . . It is of no use to complain now, for I know it cannot be alterd & if Mr Heath did it, as assuredly he did, to the best of his comprehension, I may perhaps be merely fastidious & fancy perfection which is not to be found in engraving on so small a scale, except with French Engravers, who certainly do execute small plates with an elegance & delicacy that we have not yet reached. I have two small plates done in France that have perhaps set my expectations too high. Do not therefore say any thing to Mr Heath for he will hate me, & it will be of no use. As to the single female figure, Mr Corbould originally faild in comprehending my idea which perhaps was for want of my expressing myself clearly. But my notion which I meant to give him was that of a River Nymph. The fat girl he first produced was any thing but such an ideal Sylphish representation. She is now a little subdued but still not a river Nymph, not the Naiad of a Stream or any thing like one, but the figure is now simple & pretty, and the Landscape, tho a little too dark, very much what it ought to be in general. But I wish that, if it can be done without much trouble, a little more of sorrowful, mournful expression may be given to her Countenance which may I beleive be done with a single stroke of the Graver about the mouth or perhaps brows. Allow me also to remark that the Water *wants effect*: it is almost mingled with the rock near the right margin, & the piece of ground on which her feet rest looks too much like a twelfth [night] cake, it *is so extremely regular*. The trees too on the left margin in the first distance are very *shelly*, not to say *wiggy*. A very little trouble only (as I suppose) is necessary to break the straitness of the fore ground & give a little more freedom to the Trees in the second distance. I do not mean those on the rock over her head. If there is any risk of spoiling the face, it is better to let it go as it is.

Corbould's picture engraved by Heath was used to illustrate 'The Forest Boy'. She included only 49 lines from *The Emigrants*, those describing a woman hiding with her child and a father returning home to find his family murdered. This was not her last publication of poetry, as she wrote new verse for *The Young Philosopher*, for the children's book *Conversations, Introducing Poetry*, and for *Beachy Head*. But *Elegiac Sonnets II* was the last collection she prepared for the press. With its companion, the eighth edition of her earlier *Sonnets*, it formed a uniform two-volume Poetical Works issued in May 1797.

Some poems in Volume II had appeared earlier, some were very recent. An earlier poem in quatrains was printed here: 'The Dead Beggar: an elegy, addressed to a lady, who was affected at seeing the funeral of a nameless pauper, buried at the expense of the parish, in the church-yard at Brighthelmstone, in November 1792.' Two stanzas run:

> Rather rejoice that here his sorrows cease,
> Whom sickness, age, and poverty oppress'd;
> Where Death, the Leveller, restores to peace
> The wretch who living knew not where to rest.
>
> Rejoice, that though an outcast spurn'd by Fate,
> Thro' penury's rugged path his race he ran;
> In earth's cold bosom, equall'd with the great,
> Death vindicates the insulted rights of Man.[2]

She pays tribute in 1797 to the survival of Wollstonecraft and Paine beyond the immediate occasion of their writing, though there are universalising and diluting reminiscences of Gray's 'Elegy' here too. Ships at Portsmouth and the Nore mutinied in May and June 1797, and some subscribers objected to this revival of early nineties political language. She also reprinted here the poem to Henrietta O'Neill first published in *The Banished Man*. The last line prophesied her own death within twelve months, and in a note Charlotte regrets that her prophesy had not come true, Augusta's death following within the year instead.

In 'Reflections on Some Drawings of Plants', the feminine and the female are violently juxtaposed. An eighteenth-century woman's approved pastime and acculturation of her sexual self is suddenly displaced by the speaker's actual experience of womanhood, which is only maternal bereavement:

> I can in groups these mimic flowers compose,
> These bells and golden eyes, embathed in dew;
> Catch the soft blush that warms the early Rose,
> Or the pale Iris cloud with veins of blue;
> Copy the scallop'd leaves, and downy stems,
> And bid the pencil's varied shades arrest
> Spring's humid buds, and Summer's musky gems:

> But, save the portrait on my bleeding breast
> I have no semblance of that form adored,
> That form, expressive of a soul divine,
> So early blighted; and while life is mine,
> With fond regret, and ceaseless grief deplored –
> That grief, my angel! with too faithful art
> Enshrines thy image in thy Mother's heart.[3]

The speaker's first easy acceptance of the old association between women and flowers is wrenched into recognition of botanical and human blight. The form itself is wrenched: the subject breaks in two after line seven, giving what must perhaps be called two septets rather than octave and sestet, while the rhyme scheme spans the break, this inconsistency making the redirection more disconcerting. She manages a long bleak stop after 'blighted'. The bleeding breast with its resonance of cancer strikes shockingly after the composure of pleasantly fertile flowers and ladies.

Flowers here and nature itself are deceptive, but this is rare in the sonnets. 'Vegetable nature' as she called it in distinction to human nature, is more usually a consolation and a retreat. It had been so for Ethelinde, Geraldine recovering after the separation from her husband, Mrs Denzil, Althea, the mother and daughters in the children's books and in other heroines to perhaps a lesser degree. But by the later nineties her verse and fiction acknowledge that the association of women with the natural world risks relegating them to passivity and mindlessness. She emphasises increasingly an intellectual and academic rather than a sensuous engagement with nature, often adding Linnaean names and explanatory footnotes like Erasmus Darwin. This academic engagement is conceptualised in 'To the Goddess of Botany', a title taken from Darwin's *The Botanical Garden*, which contains in embryo theories of evolution developed by his grandson. The goddess is the Wisdom of Nature which, though not careless of human life, tends the progress of all life forms:

> Of Folly weary, shrinking from the view
> Of Violence and Fraud, allow'd to take
> All peace from humble life, I would forsake
> *Their* haunts for ever, and, sweet Nymph! with you
> Find shelter; where my tired and tear-swollen eyes
> Among your silent shades of soothing hue,
> Your bells and florets of unnumber'd dyes
> Might rest – And learn the bright varieties
> That from your lovely hands are fed with dew . . .[4]

The eyes may rest but the mind catalogues species. In a long note on this sonnet she writes that botany 'seems to be a resource for the sick at heart – for those who from sorrow and disgust may without affectation say "society is nothing to one not sociable"[5] and whose wearied eyes and languid spirits find relief and repose amid the shades of vegetable nature. – I cannot now turn to any other pursuit that for a moment soothes my wearied mind.' She traces the literary return to nature to its textual source in Rousseau, especially to his *Rêveries du Promenade Solitaire*. But the feeling can be understood by anyone who gardens, or just buys flowers on the way home from work. For her it has been the sole comfort in contending with human cruelty. This note ends with the *Lear* quotation that comes most frequently to her mind:

> Oh! I am bound
> Upon a wheel of fire which my own tears
> Do scald like melted lead.[6]

Twice in the volume's notes she seems to hint that her work has been plagiarised by Robert Southey. And 'The Forest Boy', the story of William who is half persuaded, half forced into the navy and never returns to his sweetheart and mother would have looked at home among Wordsworth's *Lyrical Ballads* a year later. Though there is no question of direct plagiarism, its risk-taking *faux-naïf* quality and anti-war polemic would have encouraged him to publish. The last two stanzas, where Phoebe waits for her dead William, run:

> Her senses are injured; her eyes dim with tears
> By the river she ponders; and weaves
> Reed garlands, against her dear William appears,
> Then breathlessly listens, and fancies she hears
> His light step in the half-withered leaves.

> Ah! such are the miseries to which ye give birth,
> Ye cold statesmen, unknowing a scar;
> Who from pictured saloon, or the bright sculptured hearth,
> Disperse desolation and death thro' the earth,
> When ye let loose the demons of war.[7]

In her Preface Charlotte makes the most sustained attack yet on the Trustees, to whom she attributes responsibility for Charles' mutilation and Augusta's death, but

> however soon they may be disarmed of their power, any retribution in this world is impossible – they can neither give back to the maimed

the possession of health, or restore the dead. The time they have occasioned me to pass in anxiety, in sorrow, in anguish, they cannot recall to me.[8]

As Sarah Zimmerman says, in *Elegiac Sonnets* she 'assumed a role that was already available – the heroine of Sensibility – but she revitalised the story by providing her readers with details from her own life – an on-going plot. The prefaces that open most of her works became, in effect, a serialized autobiographical narrative'.[9]

The Preface was not reprinted in the next edition of 1800, perhaps on the insistence of Cadell and Davies. Problems arising from the lost subscription lists continued to worry her for more than a year with irate contributors wanting their copies or demanding that they be acknowledged in the newspapers. But despite the long delay in publication and the fewer listed subscribers – there were only 283 this time – she made £220 from the volume's first edition, by Stanton's estimate. Coleridge in the Preface to the second edition of his *Poems*, published this year with contributions from Charles Lamb and Charles Lloyd, refers respectfully to the Sonnet's revival by Charlotte and William Lisle Bowles. Much later on 23 October 1833 he suggested almost casually how Romanticism had come to be defined when he spoke of Elegy as a form that 'must treat of no subject for itself, but always and exclusively with reference to the poet himself.'[10] Despite the automatic male gendering of 'the poet', such an insight came at least in part from *Elegiac Sonnets*.

Contempt for England's legal system, desire for a green retreat from the deadlocked politics of reaction and reform, the need to write and rewrite her bereavement and the preoccupation with mothers and daughters, a matrilineal schooling at odds with patriarchy, issued next year in her patchily brilliant last novel – for *The Letters of a Solitary Wanderer* is a collection of novellas. She thought it different from the others, and it is halfway between a novel and a philosophical work, though *Desmond* too might be considered a hybrid of novel and social history.

In *The Young Philosopher* she contrasts her castles with lavish descriptions of plants and greenery. This novel contains the most programmatic and bizarre of her emblematic dwelling places; she no longer saw reform, much less revolution, as a practical possibility, and her just society is located in America. The heroine Medora has spent her childhood there, and will probably return. Earlier hopes that the castle-state might be renovated and comfortably inhabited, as in *Celestina*, are parodied.

Lady Mary, Medora's grandmother, inherits Sandthwaite Castle, a bleak medieval ruin on the Northumbrian coast, and modernises it with her newly-rich husband's money. She orders new plantations in the grounds, which obstinately refuse to grow and have to be replaced each year; the unnatural, destructive quality of the social system is suggested by the withering of the trees around Sandthwaite. Lady Mary's main efforts are reserved for the principal suite of rooms, incongruously modernised:

> The old wainscotting was removed, and its place supplied by french damask in pannels with gilt frames. The sophas and low chairs, stuffed with down, were covered with the same, and the most extensive Brussels carpet covered the floor. A chimney piece of statuary marble, enclosing a register stove, and all the lesser inventions of modern luxury, entirely obliterated in these rooms, and in those appropriated to Lady Mary, which were still more splendidly furnished, all ideas of antiquity – and in his easy chair my poor old father sat like the statue of a gothic king, brought from some other part of the house, and new clad and modernised to represent the passive master of this.[11]

Though Lady Mary modernises a few rooms, she displays in the entrance hall the tattered banners and medieval armour that attest the antiquity of her family. No amount of modernisation in her castle can effect any changes in her prejudices about blood and rank. In the conservative England of the late nineties, even an improver makes no attempt to alter the fabric of the building, though Lady Mary imports luxurious furnishing. The rich are enclosed behind thick walls with double glazing. Sandthwaite represents the triumph of reaction, a show of adapting to the modern world while remaining more rigidly authoritarian then ever.

Following the *Montalbert* pattern, *The Young Philosopher* contains the one-volume, first-person embedded narrative of Medora's mother Laura told to the hero George Delmont. Sandthwaite Castle appears in Laura's story: she is removed there by her parents from the radical Glenmorris. He follows her to Northumberland, and they elope one night, Glenmorris wearing a rusty helmet which Lady Mary believes was once the property of her putative ancestor, Geoffrey Plantagenet. Laura and Glenmorris are nearly drowned on the sands by the incoming tide, but finally make their way to his castle in Scotland, marry, and enjoy a brief time of happiness there.

Laura's incarceration in the Ladie of Kilbrodie's Gothic castle – where again no trees grow for miles around – is longer, with touches of horror. Laura's section of the novel is concerned as much with women's entrapment as with the condition of England. Once deprived of her husband who is kidnapped by privateers and taken to America, she is abducted by the servants of the aged Ladie of Kilbrodie, Glenmorris' distant relative. The Ladie wants Laura's baby to miscarry, so her son the Laird will inherit Glenmorris' land, and helped by the Howdie, or midwife, she frightens Laura into premature labour. The baby dies, and Laura buries him under a cairn of stones in the courtyard of the castle. She is forced to run away to avoid rape by the Laird of Kilbrodie, attempts suicide, but is rescued by fishermen as she sits on a rock waiting for the tide to cover her.

Charlotte's vision is too bleak, her rejection of society too complete to offer a Grasmere Abbey or a Cottage on the Cliffs as a refuge for her older heroine. The emblematic dwelling place which shelters Laura and contrasts with Sandthwaite and Kilbrodie castles is a cave, and surreal in its sudden appearance and symbolic implications. Though Laura is exhausted, bereaved of her child and still in danger of rape if not death, the plant-life of her cave refuge receives meticulous examination and cataloguing:

> I had soon collected courage enough to remark the outward appearance of my rustic house, where the little art that had been used was so connected with nature's masonry, which had laid horizontal strata of rock easily excavated, that without it could hardly be distinguished from the mass it belonged to, especially mantled as it was with such plants as wind over rocks and walls under the shelter of trees. – The holly,[1] whose shining thorny and spiny head so much shadowed the whole eminence, had found amidst the roof place for three or four young plants mingling with the larger growth above them; the common bramble[2] crept over another part of it, and hung in long festoons, half concealing the windows; the net-work of the houseleak[3] clothed another spot; and from others waved the pellitory,[4] the fescue grass, and the poa. The stonecrop[5] had in summer made one place gay with its yellow blossoms, and near it were yet a few lingering flowers of the mountain crane's bill[6] – All these I knew and recognised as once of my acquaintance under warmer suns, and for the most part associated with very different objects. – Within, my hermitage was not wholly destitute of those vegetable ornaments with which nature delights to decorate, or to hide the deformity of her most rugged surfaces. – My walls, which were only partially damp, were tapestried with the rock-lichen,[7] the tesselated lichen, and the silver-bryum.[8] Through the defects in the roof, some of the plants growing without had insinuated themselves, and dangled over my head with the spleenwort[9] and the wall[10]

hawkweed. Amidst the many sad hours I have passed, I have never failed to feel my spirits soothed by the contemplation of vegetable nature, and I have often thought that, whenever I could gaze on the clouds above, and see the earth below me clothed with grass and flowers, I could find some, though a melancholy, pleasure in existence.[12]

And in the footnotes Charlotte carefully specifies: (1) The holly (ilex-aquifolium). The beautiful plant with which Burns composed the chaplet of his Scottish muse, (2) Rubus preticasus. There is something particularly elegant in the alternate triple leaves and the long weak branches of this plant, (3) Sempervivum tectorum, (4) Parietaria officinalis, (5) Sedum acre, or wall-pepper, (6) Geranium sylvaticum, (7) Lichen scruposus, (8) Bryum argenteum, (9) Asplenium tricomanoides, common maiden hair, (10) Hieracium murorum. She drew on James Lightfoot's *Flora Scotica* for botanical information.

Although interesting as the proposal of an alternative, female epistemology, the description and tabulation feel grotesque at first, especially when the narrator supplies the Latin names in the footnotes, with marks indicating annotation which are more elaborate than can be shown in modern type. The point she wants to emphasise is clear: nature alone offers protection to Laura, and botany is worth her serious study. And the sense of the grotesque she registers through the symbolic cave is strangely effective. She disconcerts her reader by Laura's academic detachment, marking Laura's mental alienation from the familiar Gothic world, already remote in itself. There is an analogue to Laura's refuge in Geoffrey Household's *Rogue Male*, where the narrator, also a political outlaw at odds with society, finds an appropriate dwelling place in a tunnel in the earth, described in detail that forces belief. *Rogue Male* is unified by the tension and wariness of the narrator, but *The Young Philosopher* shifts from social satire to romantic idyll to the often paranoiac narrative of the hunted Laura, and the reader must constantly adjust to the tone.

In the last volume, 'vegetable nature' comes to the rescue again when Medora is imprisoned on the top floor of an isolated house, but slips through a window and climbs down the vine. Her descent is precarious, but the vine holds firmly to the wall and makes her escape possible. Plants and flowers play an astonishing part in *The Young Philosopher*. Following Darwin, Charlotte gives them a life of their own, like benevolent Triffids, and shows them assisting in the action, friendly to the heroines and hostile to the confining castles. They are the proper study of women, their recreation and symbols of their ideal selves, the antithesis of all that custom, law and religion have deformed.

Medora's education is largely in botany and astronomy. Taught by Laura, she spends much of her time making botanical drawings and painting flowers, as Charlotte loved to do as a child when she took lessons at Chichester from George Smith. Medora habitually sits to work at Upwood, Delmont's house, in a bow window filled with shrubs and greenery, and carries cuttings around with her affectionately in her pockets. Upwood, small and unpretentious with a conservatory Delmont's mother has stocked with flowers, is the ideal dwelling of the novel, a fuller version of Mrs Trevyllian's house in *Marchmont*. But Delmont is unable to live there peacefully for long. He is drawn out to oppose legal injustice. All this prepares for the novel's ending: the exemplary characters, disgusted by European and especially by English society, see their best hope of freedom and happiness in the wilderness and primitive settlements of North America.

In her Preface, Charlotte says that she intends 'to show the triumph of fortitude in the daughter [Medora], while a too acute sensibility, too hastily indulged, is the source of much unhappiness to the mother [Laura].'[13] But she had written prefaces claiming impeccable moral messages for *Manon* and *The Romance of Real Life*. Whatever her intention, the effects she achieves are always more complicated than her programme promises. Mother and daughter are treated equally sympathetically.

Robert Kiely points out the difficulty, once an author has established a tone of rationality, of allowing for 'the extremes of experience, for once a too sensible, solid, prosaic tone has been successfully established, it is difficult to raise it passionately without sounding inconsistent, unconvincing or silly.'[14] Charlotte solves the problem by Laura's long narration. As Gary Kelly says:

> The nature of first-person confessional narration itself could have political and revolutionary implications: to the protagonist first of all, but then to listeners within and readers outside the novel, it may possess the force of a revelation or demystification of the system, normally concealed, of 'things as they are'.[15]

Laura's point of view is endorsed by the narrator. Charlotte varies the significant naming of *Montalbert*, rhyming Laura and Medora to suggest that they are permutations of the same qualities, hybrids of Sensibility and sense. Medora tells the story of her abduction, and the gap between her narrative irony and the author's is narrow: she is naive but intelligent. The gap between Laura's style and the narrator's is wider, but her experience too is validated by the narrative of the novel as a whole.

Medora is the most likeable of Charlotte's heroines, growing from a child absorbed in botanical studies to a self-possessed woman. She is abducted from a London hotel by Darnell, a lawyer who has read her grandfather's will and knows she is entitled to half his fortune, and who tricks her into a coach intending to marry her in Scotland. This episode, narrated by Medora to her fiancé Delmont, reveals the self-reliance promised in the Preface; though innocent she is not ignorant. In the coach she 'assured Darnell in plain terms that the first attempt at personal rudeness or impertinence he attempted should be the last he would have in his power to make.'[16]

But her difficulties increase when she escapes.She is hunted and frightened, mainly by men, but with the collusion of women, and tricked by a servant into taking refuge at Arnly Park, the country house of Sir Harry Richmond, who has arranged a setting like that of a pornographic novel. This manor and its landscaped garden is a showplace, admired by visitors, perhaps the most ingeniously ideological of all Charlotte's houses. Sir Harry has constructed a number of 'chalets' to house abducted young women, a harem for himself and his friends. These are described to Delmont by a woman lodgekeeper who like most of the other servants is one of Sir Henry's cast-off mistresses and the mother of his illegitimate child; they sound like a Sadeian fantasy. Sir Harry has run

> a stream of water through them from the lower cascade; and there's rooms fitted up very grand indeed, with sattin and silk and chinch's for curtains and settees, and such like, and sweet smelling flowers in pots, and oranges and gereeniums – fine large looking – glasses, shells, china and a heap of beautiful things that there's no telling . . . The cold bath is the most beautifullest thing; all lined with moss and shells, and clear streams of water that comes as 'twere out of a rock, where there's a white image of a lady, that they say is a roman catholic goddess, brought from the pope of Rome.[17]

Delmont later recognises the 'luxuries collected by a determined voluptuary.'[18] It is possible that Charlotte had access to de Sade's work through Joseph Johnson. Many of his friends had been in Paris during the early nineties, though it is hard to imagine him offering her copies of de Sade. Perhaps her source was curious English literature. But as has been pointed out, most perceptively by Angela

Carter, de Sade merely takes to an extreme the concepts of gender found in reputable fiction. Female passivity and male aggression were the staple assumptions of most contemporary writers. In *Justine, or The Misfortunes of Virtue* (1791), de Sade like Burney writes about a young lady's entrance into the world, and the worlds are not so very dissimilar. Charlotte wants to include the Sadeian ethos and the danger of rape for Medora within her own novel. As Carter points out, 'Justine's pilgrimage consists of the road, the forest, and the place of confinement.'[19] This is also true of Medora's. Arnly Park is an English version of St Mary-in-the-Woods in *Justine*, where a group of men terrorise a harem of kidnapped women.

In her construction of the layout of the estate, Charlotte shows the respectable side of Arnly Park, a restored Gothic manor which Miss Richmond, Sir Harry's daughter, exhibits with pride, in close contiguity with the Sadeian world of pain and abuse. Arnly Park suggests in its frightened hierarchy and male domination the final triumph of political and sexual reaction in England in 1798, the year after Wollstonecraft's death. In *Justine*, one of the imprisoned women is 'retired', that is murdered, each time a new recruit is brought to St Mary-in-the-Woods, but Sir Harry's women once their first youth is gone become domestic servants. Charlotte's vision is less nightmarish and apocalyptic than de Sade's, but she makes her own comment on her society's uses for women.

She is cautious in her presentation of disturbing subjects. By the time Delmont arrives, Miss Richmond has saved Medora from the threat of rape. But we see through Delmont's account a young woman in one of the chalets who resembles Medora and for whom he mistakes her. She is elegant, middle-class, a woman of Sensibility who sings verses from Metastasio (Charlotte's favourite Italian poet) to her own accompaniment, and is kind enough to assure Delmont that Medora has managed to escape.

This is another doubling and the woman 'is' Medora after a rape: but Charlotte will neither have Medora raped nor make the raped girl wholly sympathetic: her kindness may spring from her wish to be rid of Medora as a rival, we learn. Here Charlotte partially endorses the contemptuous male ethos she is attacking. She had read *The Wrongs of Woman* by this time and was interested in its ideas, but draws back into a certain novelistic conformity. It is too late to help Medora's double, who perhaps does not 'deserve' help, and it never occurs to Delmont to go back and rescue *her*. Wollstonecraft makes her raped Jemima an unsentimentalised and degraded yet entirely sympathetic figure,[20] but she never accommodates the prejudice of her readers; her fiction reads like a cry forced out into the void. Charlotte accommodates the readers' needs: to identify with the heroine, to deny there can be a post-rape story, to be shocked but not too shocked. She can never quite lose sight of her reputation and the sales. It is the difference between her great talent and Wollstonecraft's uncomfortable genius.

Medora's sense and fortitude with the help of another woman carry her unscathed back to London, though the alternative possibility is contained by the doubled narrative. Her story is witty and detached, even when she relates her worst dangers. Her anxieties are mainly on her mother's account. Laura's story though with touches of sardonic humour is more intense and emotional, set in the past and the wilder parts of Britain. She runs away from home with Glenmorris, but her parents have taken so little interest in her that this is not surprising, and her marriage is entirely happy. Her troubles begin because Glenmorris is abducted and because the Ladie of Kilbrodie wants her child to miscarry. Charlotte's assertion in the Preface that she is critical of the Sensibility constructed in Laura's story is misleading.

As I have suggested, the cave on the hillside is a green hiding place contrasted with the absurdly restored Sandthwaite Castle. Diana Bowstead comments on the restorative properties of the cave:

> each of the places [Laura] lives in is conceived of and presented as a significant station in a symbolic journey. There is, for example, a cave at the shore which she perceives as a tomb and, in contrast, a grotto-like cave in a forest which is for her Arcadian and hence restorative ... An imagination like hers will, under duress, take control as hers finally does; the consequence is madness.[21]

But Bowstead's assessment makes Charlotte too objective, too detached from Laura. Though Laura is telling her story, she is not responsible for the footnotes adding the Latin names of the plants that grow around her shelter. These are supplied by the author, and give Laura's perceptions the stamp of authority for the reader. If Laura is going mad, so is the author. It is part of the book's intention that we should see Charlotte in Laura, but before considering the autobiographical content, it is true to say that all the houses in *The Young Philosopher* are symbolic, not merely the dwellings in Laura's story. They are created with a zany sophistication that discards naturalism.

Upwood's landscapes and surrounding varieties of soil resemble those around Bignor. A footnote referring to the author's youth helps to make the identification clearer. Its most conspicuous feature is the conservatory. This tempts Laura and her daughter to spend much of their time there, and Delmont and Medora fall in love. The narrator, not just Laura, creates emblematic houses and associates greenery and nature with love, learning and health, buildings lacking vegetation with confinement and death. Far from distancing, exaggerating and reproving Laura's feeling and imagination, the author identifies with her very closely. As self-projections Mrs Stafford, Mrs Woodfield, Charlotte Denzil and Laura Glenmorris are sometimes embarrassing in their glowing attractions and moral superiority.

The loss of Laura's first baby is a good example of Charlotte's stark representation of bereavement. As with the grave of Alexander Elphinstone in *Celestina*, she uses the cold stone of the Gothic setting to suggest the chill of death. Laura displays fortitude in giving birth without calling the midwife, whose intentions she fears. The child dies at birth, and the Ladie of Kilbrodie refuses to let him be buried in consecrated ground. As I suggested earlier, Charlotte drew here on her own experience when at seventeen she lost her own first baby while giving birth to the second. Her Gothic is unsentimental, authentic in its bleakness.

Laura's life is endangered further by isolation, lack of money, male lust and female envy, but she survives and remains sane, ending her narrative with a résumé of sixteen years in Switzerland and America with her husband and second child, Medora. But her determination to inherit what is due to her and Medora from her father's will brings her back to England and a lawsuit. As Charlotte manipulates the narrative, financial prudence or what some would call sense initiates Laura's second series of disasters and her madness. Although Bowstead refers to her 'temporary insanity',[22] Laura never fully recovers, and anxiety about her health still disturbs Medora's happiness at the end. The greed of cunning lawyers and hypocritical Christians, as well as suspense about what will happen to her daughter, drives Laura mad; hers is the natural reaction of a sensitive mind to the evil of such a society. Charlotte takes the Laingian view of societally induced madness in her last novel, and it is implicit in *Montalbert* too.

In *Sentiment and Sociability*, John Mullan compares novelists' and doctors' attitudes to melancholia and madness in the second half of the eighteenth century. Both professions drew from a specialised discourse to describe the conditions that afflict the sensitive mind. Both see nervous disorder as the disease of the educated. Mullan writes:

> In the novels of the mid-eighteenth century, it is the body which acts out the powers of sentiment. These powers, in a prevailing model of sensibility, are represented as greater than those of words. Tears, blushes, and sighs – and a range of postures and gestures – reveal conditions of feeling which can connote exceptional virtue or allow for intensified forms of communication. Feeling is above all observable, and the body through which it throbs is peculiarly excitable and responsive. The construction of a body attuned to the influences of sensibility is not, however, uniquely a project of the novelists. We find the same kind of body, and the same concentration on the gestural force of feeling, in the writings of many eighteenth century physicians. These writings do not merely share a vocabulary with novels of sentiment, they also represent a capacity for feeling as ambiguous in similar ways. In the novels, sensibility can become excessive and self-destructive, it can declare itself reclusive and retreat into the, sometimes histrionic, postures of melancholy. Comparably, the [medical] texts discussed in this chapter ponder a susceptibility which can be either a privilege or a weakness.[23]

George Cheyne, author of *The English Malady; or a Treatise of Nervous Diseases of all kinds* (1733), was doctor to Richardson and David Hume, and he is typical of his time and profession in associating melancholia with imaginative or scholarly minds. Depression was considered a disease to which both writers and women, especially celibate or menopausal women, were prone. It was not only doctors who took this view, and according to Mullan, Mackenzie attributed the genius of Collins and Cowper to their being 'both nervous in constitution, and both having fits of low spirits approaching to derangement.'[24]

Most of Charlotte's sensitive heroines suffer nervous illness. She does not make the common eighteenth-century distinction between 'white', creative and 'black', self-destructive melancholy. Emmeline and Celestina are the healthiest, Ethelinde and Geraldine are often depressed. Monimia's cutting is the strangest reaction to the threatening world. The younger Rosalie becomes temporarily mad. Laura's response is one of permanent mental confusion. She is not the typical female hysteric of contemporary medical textbooks, not celibate but married, though living apart from her husband, a mother, and not menopausal but only thirty-seven. Charlotte creates a woman whose mental illness is not to be explained away as lack of self-control or failure to find a husband. It can only be explained by societal abuse of women.

There is a disconcerting parallel when Laura's husband and Medora's fiancé become jealous without cause; after long absence, both men are suspicious. Some of the anti-male bias of *Montalbert* reappears in *The Young Philosopher*. Authorial sympathy inclines as much towards Sensibility as sense, whatever claim Charlotte makes in the Preface. She dares to write sympathetically on subjects which are seldom handled vividly, if at all, in the courtship novels of her time: insanity, sex, culturally induced paranoia. The sharp reaction of Austen to such subjects in 'Love and Freindship' and *Sense and Sensibility* is some measure of how well she succeeded.

So although the contrast of sense and Sensibility constitutes a programme, the qualities are not clearly differentiated. Sex is not associated exclusively with Sensibility, with Laura's story. Her daughter is first introduced to the reader in a pastoral setting that places her as a principle of innocent sexuality in a hypocritically puritanical world. We see Medora through the eyes of the bigoted Mrs Crewkherne who goes with her friend Mrs Nixon, a gossiping widow, to spy on the young woman Delmont is said to meet at a remote farm:

> The path they followed was high and dry for some time. It then led them into a copse, where, as autumn was now very far advanced, the fallen leaves, loaded with moisture, augured but ill to the shoes of Mrs Crewkherne . . .
>
> Busied, therefore, in guarding against the inconveniences of this rude walk, the eloquence of Mrs Crewkherne for a while was suspended, and her companion, equally silent from the same careful attention to her garments, followed her, when suddenly the path stopped short into a somewhat wider way; and Mrs Crewkherne hearing voices, looked up to enquire if she was right, when she saw before her a young woman certainly not a peasant; her straw hat, filled with nuts, lay on the ground beside her, and her gown was held out to receive more, which were showering from the hazle trees above her, among the boughs of which appeared George Delmont, who, little guessing who was the spectator of his activity, was now shaking their fruit from them, and now crushing down some of the most flexible, that his fair companion might herself gather the nuts.[25]

The natural growth of the wood is hostile to the invaders from the censorious social world, and the intruders make their way into it from their 'high and dry' path only with difficulty. Mrs Crewkherne sees the young people as lovers, or rather reacts violently without scrutinising her interpretation. Though she brings her own prejudices to the scene, latent symbolism associates Delmont's and Medora's relationship with fruitfulness and the natural world. Medora has a mother who encourages rather than suppresses her emergent sexuality and helps her to make a satisfactory if not ideal marriage. Charlotte was aware of the implications of her double plot, of the tensions between patriarchal convention and feminist ex-centricity, in Eleanor Ty's term. But we are allowed to accept that marriage is still viable, and this is because of, rather than in spite of, Charlotte's refusal to give Medora the usual unclouded happy ending.

Gillian Beer writes in 'Our Unnatural No-Voice' that the Gothic novel's problem is to find a language for what cannot be said about sexual experience. This seems to be the consensus among critics of this period. Jean Hagstrum writes in *The Romantic Body: Love and Sexuality in Keats, Wordsworth and Blake*:

> Even the Jacobin novel of purpose, which often tried to liberate love from parental tyranny and introduce the idea of simple candour between the sexes, did not often dare to absorb the energies released by its own freedoms; and sexuality tended to remain tepid when it was not evaded altogether.[26]

But this is not true of Wollstonecraft, or of Charlotte who in the first description of Medora creates a pictorial evocation of an attitude which is sexual and natural. Hagstrum argues that the Jacobins lacked the Romantics' power to depict the energy of sex. Yet Wordsworth's 'Nutting' was probably written in the late autumn of 1798, a few months after the publication of *The Young Philosopher*, and may have been suggested by this scene. Charlotte's woodland is idyllic, if threatened. Wordsworth's symbolic landscape is altogether darker; on it is inscribed rape or masturbation from which the speaker, who finds his way in easily in beggar's clothing, experiences a mixture of guilt, savage pleasure and denial; both writers were using landscape to mediate complex sexual emotions impossible to express directly.

The novel's title is ambiguous, suspended between Sensibility and sense. A 'young philosopher' is oxymoronic. Delmont is unable to maintain his stoicism, his self-contained retirement at Upwood.

He is, like Laura, a seeing eye and suffering heart in the novel. While at Eton he evades academic education to wander into the country-side and witness scenes of hunger among the farm workers, a mutilated soldier and 'a woman pale and emaciated' with 'one infant hung on her breast, two others following her';[27] her husband is dead in the West Indies. Unlike his cynical elder brother Adolphus he is close to his mother, who nurses him through smallpox then dies; he is acculturated by her rather than by father and school.

His initial reaction is to run his small estate on fair principles, retreating from the world. But the world breaks in on him, at first comically, when the predatory Winslows take up residence at Upwood, then more seriously, as family pressures and new affections draw him back into the society he despises and each new revelation confirms his sense of society's oppression. He loses his 'philosophy', in its sense of detachment, and *The Young Philosopher* resembles *Candide* in its disillusionment. But Rousseau is the presiding genius. Todd says of the Age of Sensibility, 'Rousseau took as the centre of interest the subjectivity which Locke and Shaftesbury had probed, and sensibility as special and refined susceptibility became a source of authority to which traditional morality had to bow.'[28]

Traditional morality is embodied in Dr Winslow, Mrs Crewkherne and Mrs Grinstead, who all feel a sense of inferiority in the presence of the characters of sensibility, though pride forbids their acknowledging it. As a philosopher Delmont is associated with the *philosophes* who were seen as inaugurating the French Revolution. Charlotte depicts an England hardened into reaction against events in France, glad to use the failure of the Revolution as an excuse to block reform in England. *The Young Philosopher* is as much as *Desmond* or *The Banished Man* a political novel, but it is more reflective than either. The author has the advantage of hindsight, while the earlier political novels were written to the moment.

In her Preface Charlotte places herself among the radicals once more. She defends herself from a possible charge of plagiarism of *The Wrongs of Woman* by saying that the asylum scenes were planned before she read Wollstonecraft's novel. This is undoubtedly true; she had been confining her heroines emblematically since *Celestina*. The two writers learned from each other. In *The Contested Castle*, Ellis points out that *A Vindication of the Rights of Woman* reacts against the sentimentalism of *Emmeline*, where Adelina's seducer is anxious to marry her, a dangerous reassurance for the reader. *A Vindication* praises reason and control, and one would hardly recognise the same hand in *The Wrongs of Woman*, which is violent and personal. Experience might account for the change, but Wollstonecraft's reviews attest to her appreciation of Charlotte, whose subjective confessional manner may have influenced her. Charlotte's Preface praises Wollstonecraft as a writer 'whose talents I greatly honoured, and whose untimely death I deeply regret.'[29] She wrote this in June 1798, following the January when Godwin published his wife's novel and the *Memoirs* which helped to silence radical feminist protest for two generations. Godwin's honesty about Wollstonecraft's life provoked anger rather than sympathy. It is a mark of Charlotte's courage that she was eager to pay her own tribute to the younger woman and place herself in the radical feminist camp, by then in disarray.

After Delmont visits Arnly Park, and hears about Sir Harry Challoner, 'These are indeed,' thought Delmont, as he walked towards the great house – 'these are indeed among the wrongs of woman.'[30] Charlotte provides a brief summary of Wollstonecraft's *Vindication* in Laura's definition to Medora of the well-educated woman:

> She who has learned to despise the trifling objects that make women who pursue them appear so contemptible to men; she who without neglecting her person has ornamented her mind, and not merely ornamented, but has discovered that nothing is good for any human being whether man or woman, but a conscientious discharge of their duty; a humble trust that such a conduct will in any future state of existence secure more felicity than is obtainable here; and an adherence to that pure morality that says, Do what good you can to all; never wilfully injure any.[31]

The last injunction echoes Mrs Mason's first precept in Wollstonecraft's children's work, *Original Stories*, 'first, to avoid hurting anything; and then, to contrive to give as much pleasure as you can.'[32] This is not plagiarism but the recognition of a close literary relationship, and a last tribute to Wollstonecraft.

Armitage and Glenmorris are famous radicals who arouse the indignation of conventional characters. Armitage is clearly based on Godwin, who argued in *An Enquiry Concerning Political Justice* that 'man is perfectible. By perfectible, it is not meant that he is capable of being brought to perfection . . . But . . . of being continually made better and receiving perpetual improvement.'[33] Armitage is the novel's proponent of progress and perfectibility. But he is execrated by almost everyone in the novel who has heard of him, and the narrator is pessimistic about the direction European society is taking.

The malignant nature of most of the characters refutes the doctrine of perfectibility. There is a strong resemblance between Armitage and Mary Hays' Mr Francis in *The Memoirs of Emma Courtney*, whose tendency to archness and teasing is still more noticeable in Armitage. Both characters are feminists, both satiric in their conversation, constantly on the move and hard to find.

Glenmorris resembles Paine in revolutionary commitment and in his long stay in America, though no work of fiction could equal the legends attaching to Paine's life: his enlisting with Captain Death on the *Terrible*, the warning from Blake at Joseph Johnson's house and the departure from Dover just before the warrant for his arrest arrived, his narrow escape from the guillotine. Glenmorris' kidnapping and service in the War of Independence are tame by comparison. But it is Armitage who has been in Paris at the beginning of the Revolution, not Glenmorris, while in fact Paine was there, not Godwin. Charlotte creates her characters from a recognisable intellectual context, allowing recall of the Revolution and the disappointments that followed it. She makes two of her characters famous radicals who can look back with some detachment on the historic events they lived through.

The Young Philosopher contains no hope for England. By the end, Medora is anxious to return to America with her parents, and Delmont willing to leave his estate at Upwood and try a new life in the wilderness, away from the corruption of Europe. Glenmorris argues the case for emigration, since the injustices of the English social contract far outweigh the possible benefits. He describes the ugliness and humiliation of life in London where he hears hawkers announcing the number of men and women dragged to the gallows every few weeks. Yet he intends to take both ideas and agricultural tools to America with him, without considering that 'progress' will eventually corrupt the American Eden too.

The clever, mundane couple Adolphus and Martha settle down together to a life of bickering in the great house as Lord and Lady Castledanes, after the two puny sons of the previous Lady Castledanes obligingly die off. *The Young Philosopher* parodies the stock novelistic ending where remote deaths are lucky for a young couple, and values even excessive Sensibility. Elizabeth Lisburne, who is seduced and abandoned, and drowns herself, leaves one of the best of Charlotte's poems. But the satiric side of Charlotte's talent is also well represented, the genuine bursts of comic vitality, the irony, and the sophisticated reflexive handling of autobiographical material and literary stereotypes.

Charlotte claims that as lawyers are

> such mén as in the present state of society stand in place of the giants, and necromancers, and ogers [sic] of ancient romance, men whose profession empowers them to perpetrate, and whose inclination generally prompts them to the perpetration of wickedness, I have made these drawings a little like people of that sort whom I have seen, certain that nothing I could imagine would be so correct, when legal collusion and professional oppression were to be represented.[34]

Sir Appulby Gorges and his colleagues amply fulfil her promise of ogres. Sir Appulby's name makes the identification with John Robinson, who came from Appleby in Cumberland; Mr Solicitor Cancer may have represented Anthony Parkin.

Charlotte of course becomes a presence in the novel through the account of Laura's lawsuit, the loss of her daughter and her approach to insanity. Laura's attempts to have her father's will settled, her disgust with lawyers and preoccupation with business matters would make her recognisable to anyone who had read the earlier prefaces or the children's books. She is at first presented as mother and teacher, demonstrating the educational precepts of Charlotte's schoolbook personae. She soon becomes identifiable with the author in other ways. Charlotte had made her bereavement public in the prefaces to *Marchmont* and to *Elegiac Sonnets*, and in many of the sonnets themselves. In the novel Laura's daughter eventually returns to her for the happy ending, but Laura does not fully recover. We are meant to understand that one daughter will never come back.

Twice in the narrative Laura sits on a rocky shore, watching the tide come in, as the speaker sits in one of the earliest *Elegiac Sonnets*, 'On some rude fragment of the rocky shore',[35] with its Stothard illustration in Charlotte's first subscription edition. The continued reprinting of the sonnets through the nineties allowed Charlotte to superimpose her own image on the image of the despairing Laura. Early in Laura's story her baby has died, Kilbrodie is hunting her, and she sits on a rock waiting for the tide to drown her. As if directing the reader's attention back to Charlotte's sonnet, Laura says,

> I saw myself destitute of everything, and cast like a shipwrecked wretch on the shore, from whence, if I attempted to return, greater horrors awaited me than those I was sure, by staying, to encounter from famine.[36]

Near the close of the novel she has lost Medora, and has gone mad. We see her sitting on the Sussex seashore, and Sussex is the background for much of Charlotte's poetry. Although Laura holds no book in her hand, the scene is again reminiscent of 'On some rude fragment of the rocky shore':

> It was on an heap of the fallen cliff, and where other fragments beetled fearfully overhead, that the poor mourner sat; her eyes were concealed by her hands, her arms resting on her knees. She seemed listening to the burst of waters on the shore, and to be quite regardless of our approach.[37]

It is no accident that Laura is twice placed in a pose so characteristic of the 'I' of the sonnets. As cruelty and corruption took Medora from Laura, the author implies, so Augusta was taken from me, and as Laura has been driven mad, so have I. Sometimes Charlotte's intertextual games remind one of Philip Roth, but they are not funny. With admirable tenacity she projected her grief and mental disturbance into her novel, and remained in control of her material. She made herself in both senses heroic.

Of many reworkings of literary stereotype in *The Young Philosopher*, the most remarkable is the multiplication of heroines. The novel begins with the hero's rescue of Martha Goldthorp from a carriage accident when the horses run away, a familiar novelistic situation which introduces hero to heroine in *Hermsprong, Emma Courtney*, and probably many lost novels. So far Martha, though pert, has done nothing to disqualify herself from the heroine's role, and it takes several chapters to see that she is too knowing and urban for the heroine of a novel which privileges the natural and pastoral, and finally rejects European society altogether. We have to use our discrimination and recognise that despite the stock situation of the rescue we have not yet met the heroine. The subsidiary heroines proliferate through the novel.

The more cerebral quality of *The Young Philosopher* evident in Charlotte's presentation of its unusually programmatic dwellings, Sandthwaite Castle, Laura's cave, and Arnly Park, extends to her manipulation of plot structures, stereotypes and allusions to earlier fiction. Arnly Park, from which heroines escape, has its evident source in a Sadeian text in which they do not. Like Laura's illness, these structures disturb the complacency of the happy ending. There is a non-stereotypical rescuer, Miss Richmond, who helps Medora to escape. The heroes are poor rescuers. Glenmorris nearly drowns himself and Laura when he miscalculates the time it will take to cross the estuary at Sandthwaite as the tide is coming in.

S.R. Martin considers this episode 'perfunctory and bloodless',[38] comparing Scott's similar rescue when Sir Arthur Wardour and his daughter Isabella are cut off by the tide and rescued by the Antiquary, Jonathan Oldbuck. But Charlotte's rescues undercut received notions of gender and hierarchy. Delmont is the rescuer of a parodic heroine who billets herself on him for weeks, and he never catches up with Medora until she is safely back in London. Given the sophistication with which Charlotte and Wollstonecraft had by this time treated the Rescue, the men's incompetence seems part of the feminist, anti-sexist bias of the novel. Mary Cardonnel, Medora's generous cousin, sufficiently like her to be mistaken for her, appears as a spare heroine at the end. She is in love with Delmont, but gives Medora the money due to her from their grandfather so that Medora and Delmont can marry. Her courtship story, we infer, is about to begin as the novel closes. That closure depends for its happiness on the prospect of emigration to America. Like Gaskell in *Mary Barton*, Charlotte presents America as an alternative for characters who cannot endure the England she depicts.

The novel's praise of Wollstonecraft and its version of Godwin as the progressive Armitage might alone have ensured a good review from *The Analytical*, where Joseph Johnson chose the reviewer. It could have been Hays, from the style and judgement, who commended Charlotte's ability to keep up suspense through four volumes and acknowledged she had justification for mixing gall with her ink. *The Monthly Review*, a more conservative magazine than Johnson's, took the opposite point of view. He defended lawyers and the law, accusing Charlotte of attempting to instill prejudice into young minds. *The Critical*, however, admired the novel's 'truth to nature', and more reasonably, the 'romantically strange'[39] passages. *The Young Philosopher* is perhaps too contrived, too busily ideological ever to be very popular. Like all Charlotte's fiction, it demands the close attention of the reader, but more than most it takes for granted a reader with previous experience of eighteenth-century novel reading. Sensibility and sense, though more blurred and shifting than in *Sense and Sensibility*, forge a firmer structure in her last than in some of her earlier novels, which probably first strike the reader of Austen as formless, with tones that shift from satiric to sublime to confessional with disconcerting speed.

She moved to Frant near Tunbridge Wells but lived much of the time in London during the winter of 1797–8, first in Duke Street, then Upper Baker Street, then in lodgings with Mary Barker, a friend of the Southeys, returning frequently over the next three years to deal with Trust business. She was looking for a house in Clapham, which would be cheaper and on a route family and friends used when they went out of town, but never succeeded in finding what she wanted. Though the children were often away on visits, and some abroad, she still needed a large house and servants for when they were at home. Given the wear of family life in the easiest circumstances and the fact that she had grown up without a mother, her relations with the children, especially her sons, were generally close. At times she was inclined to doubt this, once commenting bitterly that of her four daughters only Augusta had really loved her. This was probably said in a fit of depression, though her undisguised preference of their dead sister must often have hurt the others. Her only surviving letter to a child is to Charlotte Mary. It confides her more recent worries about the Trust and adds a humorous note about a friend of Harriet's who was pursuing a Sussex curate:

> Miss H. S. [Harriet] is desir'd by Miss Ann Eydes to desire you to buy for her a pair of patent net gloves, *very nice and fine*, for which she will pay Harriet. She is supposed to have a son of Melchisidec in view who is to be *netted* at Ashburnham.[40]

Charlotte Mary was inclined to bouts of the sore throat which before pennicillin always threatened to turn malignant. For about eighteen months she acted as housekeeper to her brother Charles, who was posted from Gibraltar to a Lieutenancy of Invalids at Berwick-on-Tweed in August 1797.

Lucy married Thomas Newhouse with prospects Charlotte considered not very flattering and against her advice. Newhouse was in his mid-thirties and without money or a profession, though he now began to train as a surgeon. There were three children in the next four years whom Charlotte considered spoilt and noisy as they grew up, but she continued to help Lucy, who lived near Frant, with food, furnishings, and her rent.

Alexandre's mother was an invalid by this time; his sister had married a Republican and gained possession of his Normandy estate. During the mid-nineties he was on a bounty list for pursuit and arrest, which did not discourage Charlotte from offering him a home. He then found work in a boys' school near Wansted. Charlotte was contemplating a letter to Napoleon on his behalf; she continued to treat her son-in-law like a son, determined that Augusta's share in Richard's money – itself a matter of debate – should go to him. It was a point of principle and of respect for Augusta's memory she was prepared to do battle for, but it annoyed several members of her family and the Trust lawyers.

After thirteen years abroad, William returned on leave in July 1798, just after *The Young Philosopher* came out. It was a disappointing reunion. He found a mother he had left still a young woman now ageing and querulous, and brothers and sisters he hardly recognised. Culture shock for the Empire's administrators was overwhelming at both ends. He discovered a genetic fascination for the London gambling houses, and lost large sums he had saved in India, to Charlotte's disgust. She could see Benjamin in him now he was older.

But he and Harriet bonded at once. Between them they decided she should return with him to Bengal and find, like many dowerless young women with relations in India, a husband in the army or Civil Service. It must have sounded a wonderful adventure to a seventeen year old, and whatever the risks, better than growing old in an English village with no fun or money. Officers and senior Civil Servants could not marry Indian women of whatever caste. Some formed long-term relationships with Indian or Arab women. When he was posted as Resident to Bushire in Persia, Nicholas Smith and a Persian woman had at least three children whom he loved and provided for. But young Englishwomen were at a premium, and those who went out on the fishing fleet, as it was called, could usually marry within months or even weeks.

It was a piquant subject for fiction, reducing courtship to the baseline of supply and demand. Kitty Percival in 'Catharine, or The Bower' considers the despatch of a childhood friend to India with indignation for the relatives who enforced it.[41] Austen's Aunt Philadelphia went out to Madras in 1752 and married a middle-aged surgeon. Her daughter Eliza who married the Comte de Feuillide then, when he was guillotined and she escaped to England, Austen's brother Henry, was almost certainly Warren Hastings' child. In *Vanity Fair*, a thirteen year old is snapped up on arrival in Madras by old Mr Chutney of the Civil Service. Charlotte confided her feelings to Joseph Cooper Walker about William's extorting her consent:

> She was the only one of his family that appeared to interest or attach him. Some of the others nearer his own age and with whom he has

been brought up seem'd to be a poor substitute for the sister he had
lost, who was indeed the darling of all her family even from her
earliest infancy. Beauty has probably its influence even in the person
of a Sister, & Harriet having an uncommon share of it (tho not in my
mind by any means equal to what my adored & lamented Augusta
possess'd) her Brother, who fitted her out with even a profusion of
accommodations imagines she will marry to advantage in Bengal
which is certainly very probable. They sail'd from England on the
2nd April [1799], & we have since had intelligence they were all well
off Madeira twenty days afterwards. There are very respectable
Ladies on board, two of them married Women going to their husbands; Harriet was accommodated with a very useful female servant
and indeed every thing that could make such a voyage tolerable. Still
my heart reproaches me for having sent this young creature or rather
suffer'd her to go, for it was quite her own inclination, & tho I could
hardly do otherwise circumstanced as I was, yet I shall be most
miserably anxious till I know my child is safe, & then perhaps,
sacrificed as I was to a chimera of fortune, she may live only to be
miserable.[42]

Once in Bengal, though, Harriet could not go through with it.
Perhaps the ideal military figures described by William and glimpsed
through a golden haze from Frant looked different close up and
sweating, with an implicit licence to bid for her. Her mother's
influence may have been greater at a distance than when they lived
in the same house. For whatever reason, there is no hint in Charlotte's
letters that Harriet met anyone she could accept. Instead, she came
down with a bout of malaria that nearly killed her. William spent
enormous sums in medical fees and as a last resort, since she failed
to recover, put her on the *Lord Hawkesbury* in a fleet returning to
England.

The news came to Charlotte overland and before the ships were
due; she went down to Bignor intending to go on to Portsmouth, but
a storm drove the fleet off course. It eventually docked at Deal on
23 September 1800. By now Charlotte was sure Harriet had died at
sea, and could not face the confirmation. Charles and Charlotte Mary
happened to be visiting their mother on Trust business; Charles went
to Deal and found his sister somewhat better for the voyage. She
gradually recovered, though she had several dangerous and expensive relapses with high fever. She had never been matinal, her mother
observed tolerantly, never much of an early riser, but her lassitude
increased after her return.

Charlotte's Turner relations were a lesser but an ongoing anxiety,
though perhaps a source of some reluctant amusement too. A quarrel

flared over Nicholas Turner's inability to pay Catherine, now a widow, the annuity their father left her out of the Bignor Park estate. Nicholas like Charlotte seems to have been hopeless with money. He was trying unsuccessfully to raise some by suing his parishioners at Fittleworth, presumably for non-payment of tithes, when Catherine brought a lawsuit against him that lasted for two years. Charlotte was sorry for her brother and even lent him money, hard up as she was. He and Egremont were now preparing by an act of the Court of Chancery to take over from Robinson and Parkin as Trustees. Nicholas held power of attorney for his nephew Nicholas Smith and was already trying to abuse that position, Charlotte thought. But she was appalled when the Turner lawsuit ended with the transfer of Bignor Park to Catherine in default of his payment. She wrote to Egremont, 'I was really unwilling to believe all that narrowness of heart existed in my Mother's daughter which now forces itself upon me too strongly.'[43] Catherine, it seems, now fluent in an Evangelical discourse that infuriated her sister,was willing to send her brother to prison rather than write off the debt. Charlotte however did not break with her completely and still visited Bignor from time to time. Catherine's son had died young and her daughter Lucy would inherit the estate.

The original Lucy, Lucy Towers Smith, probably died in June or July 1799. On 19 July Charlotte wrote to Cadell and Davies, 'the death of a near & beloved relation has prevented my noticing yr Letter sooner', and from Charlotte's later letters it is clear that Lucy is dead. She seems to have stayed on good terms with all the branches of her late husband's family and her own, an astonishing feat, and especially with Charlotte Mary and the Berney sisters. It sounds as though even Charlotte's resentment fell away at the end of her aunt's life and she could forgive the woman who had acted with nothing but affection for her, however foolishly.

Charlotte's rheumatism was worsening and she complained of dropsy, for which she tried foxglove as a remedy to avoid medical bills. But she considered her extended visits to London and correspondence over her 'everlastingly tormenting business'[44] of the Trust were worthwhile. The date of the handover from Robinson and Parkin to Egremont and Nicholas Turner was 27 August 1799, and she expected a favourable judgement soon afterward. She felt her life was valueless to herself but necessary for her children and for her knowledge of the intricacies of the Trust's history that could bring about a settlement. A large part of the property, Gay's plantation in

Barbados, was now to be sold to a planter, William Prescod, who offered £10,000 down and £3,331 a year over the next six years; the negotiations over this and other transactions took months of calculation and letter-writing and were never satisfactorily resolved.

She was jubilant when Egremont paid Thomas Dyer £6,000 of his own money to end the Dyer claim. 'By Lord Egremont's having lent me a sum of money I have paid off and got rid of the Dyer family forever',[45] she wrote to Cadell and Davies, inaccurately as there was never the slightest likelihood of repayment. From the first Dyer had been a major obstacle to settlement: he wanted more money for his three children than Charlotte was prepared to concede. As he was in no hurry, he insisted nothing could be done until his youngest child was twenty-one. She was extremely grateful to Egremont for buying him out.

But hope was still deferred. Sometimes she had not a shilling in the house, sometimes she could not afford coal; her intermittent immobility would have made that dangerous. Her tradesmen were still often unpaid and supplied her reluctantly and because they were sorry for her, which was humiliating. What money she could spare went to support George and Lucy Newhouse. She was still hoping for an undertaking from Benjamin to settle annuities, when she died, on the three youngest children out of her own fortune, now in his control after Robinson's withdrawal from the Trust. When it increased by £2,000 on Mrs Chafys' death, she pointed out bitterly to one of the Trust lawyers, Benjamin allowed her less than in the days of Robinson, not even £70 a year, but kept the interest for himself. Her £7,000 capital would be his to do as he liked with when she died. She began, very reluctantly, to consider selling her books to pay immediate debts. Certain 'internal notices'[46] were telling her, she wrote to Mary Hays, that she might not have much time left.

Her circle of friends increased now she was often in London. Among many new acquaintances she got to know Godwin better and wrote the Prologue for his disastrous tragedy, *Antonio*. She compared publishing deals with Elizabeth Inchbald and had Andrew Caldwell round to dinner to talk about botany. She liked Eliza Fenwick, a novelist and children's writer in similar circumstances to her own and who like Hays had been with Wollstonecraft while she was dying, and cared for the baby afterwards. Hayley edited the first volume of *The Young Philosopher* but his son needed all his attention and he could not go on. Charlotte described his grief to Walker with fierce imaginative sympathy combined with egotistical displeasure that he had not turned to her for help. The other volumes were edited by someone she describes as a literary man of considerable reputation, perhaps Godwin. She discussed with Mary Hays Richard Phillips' proposed biography of herself in *British Public Characters*. Once, she said, she and Hayley had agreed half as a joke that the survivor would write the other's obituary; he had forgotten those times now and his visits were short and formal. Hays offered to write the *Public Characters* entry herself. Despite poverty and occasional self pity, she still impressed. Robert Southey, with the lifelong prejudice Charlotte Brontë was fortunately to ignore, wrote:

> Miss [Mary] Barker is at last settled in town with Charlotte Smith, whom I like very much; though it gave me an uncomfortable surprise to see her looking so old and broken down. I like her manners. By having a large family she is more humanised, more akin to common feelings, than most literary women. Though she has done more and done better than other women writers it has not been her whole employment – she is not looking out for admiration and liking to show off. I see in her none of the nasty little envies and jealousies common enough among the cattle. What she likes, she likes with judgment and feeling, and praises warmly.[47]

During the late nineties she was planning with Catherine a book of botanical drawings for students, illustrating each of Linnaeus' orders, and another volume of fourteen sonnets in Quarto like her first edition of 1784. Cadell and Davies were affronted by the latter idea, as they had just published her two-volume subscription edition and suspected she meant to sell the new poems elsewhere, endangering their profits. Relations with the firm were worse than ever. They turned down *The Letters of a Solitary Wanderer*. Her new children's book, *Minor Morals*, appeared along with *The Young Philosopher* in the summer of 1798, inferior to the earlier ones, less green in its sensibilities, less vivid on birds and gardens, more moralistic. It seems to have had little effect on its dedicatee, Harriet Bessborough's daughter Caroline, later Lady Caroline Lamb. The last year of the old century found her transferring *The Young Philosopher*'s pieces of poetry to another edition of *Elegiac Sonnets*, which continued to run and run.

A comedy, *What Is She?*, was performed at the Theatre Royal, Covent Garden from 27 April to 2 May 1799; the Prologue declares it to be the work of a woman. According to Hilbish, Elizabeth Inchbald's edition of 1811 gives the name of Mrs Charlotte (Turner) Smith in brackets, though I have not seen an example of this. Perhaps Hilbish meant it was pencilled in on an individual copy. The heroine Mrs Derville's dissipated husband and the satiric comment on Chancery suits and literary ladies also help to mark the play as Charlotte's. This may be a reworking of something she wrote in 1789, when she discussed her Sir Arbitrary – a name she felt unsatisfactory – with an unnamed correspondent connected with the theatre, perhaps the elder Colman. The dogmatic Sir Caustic may have replaced this character.

Light comedy was not her vein. The repartée is seldom even mildly funny. The narrative voice of the novels is at its best in a glinting world-weary irony of multi-claused, ruminant sentences impossible to translate to the stage. *What Is She?* is sometimes smart, as in its satire of that ever-popular duo from Restoration Comedy, the poetess with delusions of genius and her longsuffering Cit husband. But the dialogue is usually forced, and Mrs Derville excruciating. The five-day run must have been a great disappointment after such long anticipation, and it is unlikely she made any money out of it.

The Letters of a Solitary Wanderer was planned as six volumes; Sampson Low published the first three in 1800, but died that year; the contract was sold at the auction of his property to Longman and Rees. Charlotte produced only two further volumes. The sixth was to be the story of the frame narrator, the Wanderer. Though there is some sharp observation in these novellas they are too disparate and the last volume too autobiographical easily to admit a satisfactory conclusion. And as she hints in the Preface, dated February 1802, to volumes four and five, she had been writing under more than usually painful circumstances.

The Wanderer is young and grief-stricken – though the cause of his grief is withheld – a mixture of cynicism and benevolence: he makes a good speaker for Charlotte's satire and sensibility. He listens to the five stories and uses his wealth, prestige and sympathetic heart to alleviate distress. As an urbane commentator in flight from fashionable society he lends credence to narratives of adventure in distant regions. 'The Story of Edouarda' is set in remote Yorkshire and mediated (apparently) through an elderly woman servant. The resemblance to *Wuthering Heights'* narrative strategy is striking though probably coincidental. Lockwood is an uncomprehending version of the Wanderer.

Charlotte's long hatred of Catholicism emerges in this first volume; Alexandre may have shared it, as he did not hesitate to deceive

Father Pierpoint. Edouarda's father Sir Mordaunt Falconberg is a fanatical Catholic controlled by the greedy libertine priests Golgota and Galezza, who want him to die without heirs. The Gothic castle symbolises Catholic oppression – perhaps religious oppression generally – of women and the young, and comes complete with owls, ivy and baying bloodhounds. The focus is too narrow to include social satire or any alternative house with greenery.

Edouarda returns from her convent to find her elder brother dead and her mother imprisoned in Palsgrave Abbey for eighteen years because of her supposed infidelity, a calumny invented by the priests which makes Sir Mordaunt doubt his children's paternity. He stabs Edouarda's younger brother Henry then dies by suicide. Lady Falconberg dies of grief leaving Edouarda, because of the strain of madness all too evident in her family, to a single life, though she renounces her religion and escapes to Rousseauesque territory in Switzerland. Charlotte creates an exceptionally claustrophobic castle. As in Inchbald's *A Simple Story* the daughter lives unrecognised in the father's house. The detective element of Gothic where the heroine discovers secrets – here about the violence of the family – is well paced.

The atmospherics are equally good in 'The Story of Henrietta', set mostly in Jamaica. Since she wrote *The Wanderings of Warwick* Charlotte had read fuller accounts of the scenery and customs of the West Indies. This tale must have felt authentic and truly 'novel' to the contemporary reader, especially in the voyage out with its dolphins and flying fish and the tropical sun rising, and in the deeply forested gorges with their networks of pathways where maroons, the descendants of escaped slaves, had lived for generations. The hero, Denbigh, owns a plantation as does Henrietta's father, Mr Maynard, but Denbigh is anxious to sell, though it

> 'has belonged to my family ever since the first settlement of the island; but though I know, from the utmost amount of the sale, I shall not make anything like the income it brings me; yet I so extremely dislike the nature of the property, that I should, I think, determine to part with it, even if my wife's great aversion to residing there did not weigh so heavily with me.'[48]

Charlotte's surviving letters never express regret about the source of the money she claimed for her children. She was of course dealing with people who would regard such regret as a sign of insanity. And since she had been sold like a Southdown sheep, as she felt now, it must have seemed unbearable not to have even a little money in return for her life. In her last decade she was too obsessed by minutiae of the will to consider its larger context much. But her own wish to sell Gay's may have sprung from unease like Denbigh's.

She constructs race relations from a fairly liberal perspective: the insurrection of maroons and negro runaways is the inevitable result of old Maynard's treatment of his slaves. But the main narrative interest is the white heroine's threatened rape by a black servant and then by a band of maroons. She is rescued by Denbigh and an elderly man who proves to be her uncle. Such plot 'surprises' are the pleasure of romance, and her story's intercutting with other narratives that withhold the dénouement is sophisticated as to form. But the racial take on rape is opportunist, and Henrietta's standard response that rape would unfit her to marry or even to live returns to conventional pre-1790s treatments.

The black threat to the white woman at the edge of Empire anticipates Victorian genetic anxieties that issued eventually in *Nostromo* and many minor texts in English. The slave Amponah's proposal of marriage to Henrietta, Charlotte writes in a footnote, 'is taken from a real event, though not happening under similar circumstances.'[49] Such stories must have been popular. But though the thought of maroons terrified her at that time, she makes them victims rather than demons, and old Maynard with his harem and his sadistic discipline is the only entirely evil male in the novella.

'The Story of Corisande' is set in sixteenth-century France against the conflict of Catholics and Calvinists during the Wars of the League that followed the St Bartholomew's Day massacre. Corisande runs away from a forced Catholic marriage disguised as a boy in clothes provided by an old family servant. As in many Gothic romances there are elements of Shakespearean comedy. Walpole's *Otranto* itself was a response to the denigration of Shakespeare by Voltaire, and the emotional reassertion of strangeness. Corisande however cannot pass for a boy or dominate her forest world like Rosalind. The story moves into the realms of chivalry and intrigue, royal favourites and spiteful maids of honour, like an Alexandre Dumas novel. Corisande and her lover rescue her father from Mont St Michel. Charlotte is attentive to historical accuracy: the progress through France of Margaret of Navarre and her baggage train is the result of research.

These romances are passionately anti-war, and 'Corisande' especially so. The heroine treads on 'pavements slippery with blood'[50] and takes refuge in a church where the victims of war are vividly described. The rival French and Navarre courts

> not infrequently met: and, amidst scenes of luxurious magnificence and refined debauchery, the misery of the insulted people was forgotten. But this was an age *when vice lost half its depravity by losing its grossness.*[51]

Though Burke had died three years earlier, he has remained an irresistible target for reformists' darts ever after.

The Critical's reviewer of May 1801 unsheathed his claws at once. The review opens:

> Genius has its dawn, its maturity, and decline. While we admit that Mrs Smith has possessed this quality in a considerable degree, we must also confess that it sparkles now only in occasional corruscations, and that she often borrows from 'meaner spirits of the Muse's train' and not infrequently from herself. Yet while she has in no part of these volumes risen to her former excellence, she has not debased them by her former errors. We have no examples of rash and unequal attachments [Note: The Old Manor House]; of a giddy girl captivated with the imprudent or unfortunate victim to the laws of his country [Note: Marchmont]; we are not compelled to attend to declamations on the injustice of attorneys and trustees, or the cruelties of bailiffs; we find no respectable old women, the world's brightest ornaments [Note: Ethelinda; and it was uncertain whether the world yet contained one of its brightest ornaments (Mrs Montgomery)]; or peculiarly prudent ladies of a middle age [Note: Emmeline (Mrs Stafford)], whose prototypes are not hard to find. A little of the political tendency remains; and the attachment to the cause of the French Revolution, so conspicuous in *Desmond* but almost lost in *The Banished Man* appears in one or two solitary passages.[52]

The reviewer went on to quote at length, and added some patronising commendations at the end, but this was sharp enough to hurt.

Charlotte replied evenly in her Preface to the next two volumes, regretting the decline in standards of the 'monthly oracles'.[53] The critics, she says, have in the last seven or eight years resorted to 'a style of animadverion . . . subversive of all the purposes for which these pamphlets are professedly published',[54] falling back on personal invective to disguise their paucity of taste and information. She refutes the critic's assumption that only novels about young girls can be of interest, and points out that the characters he considers self-portraits differ greatly from each other.

The last two volumes, published by Longman and Rees, find the Wanderer in the remote forests of Germany, negotiating precipices and banditti; he meets a Hungarian Hussar called Sommerfeldt who takes over the narration. The condition of central Europe following the siege of Dresden in 1750 is the context of the first part of Volume Four, and Rousseau's philosophy still underpins the plot and descriptive passages. But Charlotte soon moves into reconstruction of her marriage when an Englishwoman, Gertrude Leicester, implausibly appears. She is robbed while walking in a wood by Zingari or gypsies, who 'seemed to have terrified her so much she had no power to move from there',[55] but Sommerfeldt rescues her. Gertrude returns to London to look for her sister Leonora, a celebrated poet, who is married to a vicious though frequently absent husband.

Further grief and anxiety, failing invention and Benjamin's withholding even the interest from her marriage settlement precipitated Charlotte's bitter retrospection. She was evidently determined to ignore *The Critical* reviewer's attack on her auto-biographical material. She is fuller and more circumstantial here than in *Emmeline*. Leonora's father Mr Leicester's courtship of the grim Miss Mabben, Mr Wardenell's courtship of Leonora, present again her apology for her life and misfortunes. Leonora takes over the narrative, which has the analytical inwardness encouraged by the epistolary form. Looking back on her marriage she thinks:

> . . . while in England I have felt no other sensation in seeing the loveliest landscapes, than that of envying the female peasants, who, assisting in the fields, or unemployed at the doors of their cottages, have gazed with admiration on my coach and my servants, while they, perhaps, repined at their laborious poverty, and compared it with the luxury and pleasure which they imagined attached to my position.[56]

While one could dismiss this as precious or insensitive, perhaps Charlotte's energy might indeed have made her life more endurable as a peasant than it was as Benjamin's wife.

There is a nightmare trip to Italy to buy paintings for resale in England, with Wardenell as the main satiric target:

> Though he could speak no French, and Madame D'Orimarre had very little knowledge of the English, they continued to hold dia-logues, which were as deficient in sense as they were in decency.[57]

Leonora decides that as soon as she returns to England she will try to arrange an amicable separation and support her children herself. Wardenell goes to prison for debt, and expects her to set about extricating him 'with as much zeal as if he had been the best and tenderest of husbands, whom misfortune only had brought into distress and confinement.'[58]

Inspired with platonic devotion and determined to help her, the Wanderer follows her to Kellashaugh in Ireland. Her husband is stationed there when he joins the army at the time of the 1798 rebellion, which was initiated by Lord Edward Fitzgerald, Henrietta O'Neill's fellow actor in *Cymbeline* years before. Lord Edward died like John, now Viscount O'Neill, Governor of Antrim and on the other side, with many others in the rising. All that delirium of the brave is notably absent from *The Solitary Wanderer*, reasonably enough given Charlotte's views on fighting. Leonora, exuding devoted maternity and elegant literary taste, takes the centre stage:

> 'she has been the idol of the country ever since she has been here, and done more good in one week to the poor wretches round the place than all the priests together will do in a hundred years.'[59]

The Wanderer, surveying the condition of the Irish peasantry, can only wonder 'Was it here I was to seek for the polished Leonora?'[60] One would like to think Charlotte was laughing as she wrote some of this, but her family circumstances, as we shall see, were so wretched she was reduced merely to covering enough paper to fulfill her contract. Precisely because her invention is failing, Volume Five is horribly interesting as psychohistory, the writing sometimes uncharacteristically plain. Leonora records her husband's weak attacks on herself when things go wrong, her contemptuous amusement at his affairs, his making her sleep on the floor when the bed is not big enough for both when they are travelling. She records too the death of her little girl at Naples and the bond she forms with Guilelmine, who is not yet married and whose problems therefore allow some happy resolution. The Wanderer falls in love with Leonora only by reading her story, and they never meet. The volume is left hanging, and the short-changing close of this collection makes a disappointing end to Charlotte's career as a novelist.

The Critical reviewer's response was sillier this time, mimicking the language of her Preface, which was clearly addressed to him, and resorting to Latin paraphrase to put a woman in her place:

> We are sorry to have incurred Mrs Smith's displeasure, and beg leave to observe, in our own defence, that the remarks were not, *designedly*, invidious. Certain it is, that we have drawn on ourselves her direst vengeance . . . 'we are inadequate to the task of correcting the advertisements in a county newspaper' – Can a woman rail thus? –

tantaene animis muliebribus irae? We trust that 'after speaking her mind' in common language, or what may be styled a little scolding, she is more comfortable, and in as good humour as ourselves.[61]

But there were no enthusiastic reviews to counter this. Though she began another novel almost at once, she did not dash into it with her usual energy, and it has not survived.

The romances are sprawling and de-centred, but interesting politically and historically. The same could be said of some of the novels. Perhaps only *The Old Manor House* is what used to be called an 'organic' structure. Walter Allen uses the term, paying the critical compliment of his time, when he says that the novel 'lacks few of the preoccupations that distinguish the fiction of the last few years of the century, but they are all fused into an organic whole . . . she incorporated into her work a sense of history.'[62] He does not identify Rayland Hall itself as the dominant symbol, nor does he see this work as the first condition-of-England novel. He claims that Charlotte was 'scarcely a satirist,' though 'her work and the characters in it spring from a considered point of view . . . she was using it to embody her criticism of society.'[63] This brief mention has never been improved by later criticism, for Allen sees a unifying social and political concern, and perhaps a unity of tone.

Novels were differently evaluated in the eighteenth century. We admire *The Wrongs of Woman* and *The Monk* for their unified vision, towards which each episode, each detail contributes. Henry Home, Lord Kames in *The Elements of Criticism* (1762) is typical of eighteenth-century critics in considering that fiction should imitate the richness and variety of life. It should be diversified in character and incident in proportion to its length. That Charlotte was capable of spare and focused writing is evident from her pamphlet, the *Narrative of the Loss of the Catharine*, but for many critics such focus in a novel was evidence not of artistry but of narrowness of mind. And of course she needed the money longer novels brought. *Tom Jones* was still greatly admired, for Fielding was, or appeared to be, giving a picture of English life, seeing it steadily and whole, on different social levels, in town and country, among the just and the wicked, writing a tragi-comic epic in prose which announces its right to change its mood and its mind.

She may have been drawn to Fielding because of his satirical portraits of lawyers and clergymen. His hold on her was perhaps unfortunate; his own tone, in spite of his declared eclecticism at the beginning of *Tom Jones*, is far more consistent than hers, but she

probably took from him an encouragement to be discursive. Both
Fielding and Sterne gave her the confidence to step forward into her
novels, to discuss her private affairs and relate her fiction to the
circumstances in which it was created. But her adjustment to the
comic Fielding template became increasingly difficult as her sense of
isolation increased. As David Punter says:

> Gothic works, it is often objected, are not fully achieved works: they
> are fragmentary, inconsistent, jagged. This is frequently true, but it
> is also frequently a source of their value and a guarantee of the nature
> of the task which they set themselves. If Gothic works 'do not come
> out right' this is because they deal in psychological areas which
> themselves do not come out right.[64]

In the 1790s novels were not marketed specifically for women, but
for women they were universities, the best access to ideas they had,
frequently offering more thought-provoking courses of study than
their brothers found at Oxford or Cambridge. Charlotte's are unusually stimulating in the many controversial subjects they raise, and
like a good seminar leader she takes no responsibility for settling
disputes. Except in *Desmond* she hedges on most contemporary
issues. In *Primitivism and the Idea of Progress in English Popular
Literature in the 18th Century*, Lois Whitney explains that she became
interested in the idea through reading Charlotte's novels. She found

> theories of the superiority of primitive man and of man's natural
> goodness all huddled together with theories of perfectibility, some-
> times two antagonistic points of view in the same sentence. The
> primitivistic ideology bade men look for their model of excellence to
> the first stages of society before man had been corrupted by civiliza-
> tion; the ideas of progress represented a point of view that looked
> forward to a possible perfection in the future.[65]

Whitney disentangles and traces the history of these two incompatible clusters of ideas, beginning with Joseph Glanvill, Benjamin
Whichcote and Henry More in the middle of the previous century
and ending with Edward Fitzgerald and Tom Paine in the last years
of the eighteenth century. But though these clusters of ideas are
traceable in Charlotte's novels, especially in *The Young Philosopher*,
she accepts neither. She could not imagine either a primitive or a
future society radically different from her own; instead she increasingly imagines a female hegemony with its own body of knowledge
about the natural world.

Discussing the good society in *Virtue in Distress: Studies in the
Novel of Sentiment from Richardson to Sade*, R.F. Brissenden notes that

'one of the deepest and most pervasive fantasies of the age was the assumption that man is innately benevolent, or, at least, that he is not innately malevolent.'[66] Brissenden shows that for the eighteenth century the good society was one capable of evolving, which enabled the maximum number of its members to be happy, or to pursue happiness. The phrase 'the greatest happiness of the greatest number'[67] is an eighteenth-century invention, and is attributed by John Rae to Francis Hutcheson in Rae's *Life of Adam Smith*. The Revd William Leechman, Professor of Divinity at Glasgow University, in a preface to Hutcheson's *System of Moral Philosophy* published in 1755, after Hutcheson's death, commends him for placing

> the highest virtue and excellence of a human character where all sound Philosophy and Divine Revelation has placed it, viz, . . . in that sort of behaviour which will promote the happiness of mankind in the most extensive manner to which our power can reach.[68]

Leechman habitually urged an active social benevolence in his sermons, insisting that 'the duty of a Christian, according to the principles of his religion, lies in doing good, in promoting the happiness of others to the utmost of his power.'[69] Schemes of social and political reform could therefore receive the blessing of the clergy, certainly of the dissenting clergy like Leechman, Hutcheson and Richard Price.

But Hutcheson and Leechman were working and preaching in Scotland, where the church was disestablished and to a lesser degree an arm of the state. Anglican clergy often taught that one should wait for the next world to redress the injustices of this. Sterne, a clergyman unorthodox in his life and pursuits, though not in his theology, gives to his 'Sermons of Mr Yorick' the title 'Enquiry after Happiness' and begins, 'the greatest pursuit of man is after happiness. It is the first and strongest desire of his nature.'[70] But Sterne then describes the disappointments of every stage of life, reverting to the wisdom of Solomon who 'advises every man who would be happy, to fear God and keep his commandments.'[71] And Samuel Johnson warns in *Rasselas* that 'human life is everywhere a state in which much is to be endured and little to be enjoyed.'[72] *Candide* too is trenchantly anti-optimistic, though all the characters have so much bounce the effect is exhilarating.

Rousseau, whose influence in England was strongest in the 1770s and 1780s, links private sensibility and singularity with a quest for freedom. Brissenden quotes from the opening passage of the

Confessions (1782): 'Myself, alone. I feel my heart, and I know men. I am not made like anyone I have seen; I dare to believe that I am not made like anyone who exists. If I am not worthy at least I am different.' Brissenden goes on:

> If you have feelings, and those feelings tell you that you are different from other people, the obvious implication is that you have the right to enjoy your sense of otherness, you have the right to be free. And in 1782 such an assertion would have the clearest of political implications.[73]

Louis Bredvold claims that 'it was no mere accident that Locke's three basic rights of life, liberty and property were changed to the rights of life, liberty and the pursuit of happiness in Declaration of Independence',[74] replacing the traditional Christian belief that all men had an obligation to be good with the idea that all men had a right to be happy.

Montfleuri in *Desmond* is Charlotte's character most strongly influenced by the American Revolution and the Declaration of Independence. He tries to run his estate for greatest good of the greatest number, and achieves a small enclave of prosperity and social justice. But *Desmond* loses its political confidence towards the end, as the situation in France deteriorated, and we are not allowed to assume that Montfleuri's ideas will prevail. By the preface to *The Banished Man* Charlotte is comparing the time of Robespierre to the times of the most degenerate Roman Emperors, implying that history is circular, not progressive. She had a much stronger sense of the amazing malignity of human nature than of the benevolent heart.

For the time her letters are remarkably free of religious reference, though contemplating Augusta's possible death she writes, 'it is presumptuous to say I could *not* bear it, for perhaps I must',[75] where she comes close to a discourse of Christian stoicism. Her novels are full of male and female religious hypocrites; this does not of course prove the author's scepticism; indeed it could make a case for her orthodoxy. But her only two good clergymen, Mr Thorold in *Celestina* and St Remi in *The Banished Man*, are humanitarian rather than religious. *Emmeline*, the brightest but most conformist of the novels, ends with the heroine's thankfulness to Providence. Yet even the early heroines rarely look for guidance through prayer and the later novels are more positively satirical about the church and the debasement of religion into the service of the state. But if she was sceptical herself, like Thackeray and Dickens she always assumes a Christian readership. The authorial voice is never antagonistic to Christian teaching, which is enlisted in the reformist cause.

Throughout her novels her writing about class is contradictory, revealing attitudes she might not have assented to if they were stated theoretically rather than arising in her rapid flow of composition. Her sympathies are generally on the side of genteel rather than ungenteel poverty. But sometimes she can empathise with her working class characters, and there are many small, tentatively democratic cameos scattered through the novels. She changed in her attitude to French republicanism, but she does not change back to a more conservative position on class after *Desmond*.

Many of her most successful satiric portraits – Lord Castlenorth, General Tracy, Mrs Rayland – are aristocrats, and she is informed in her account of aristocratic style and conversation. But she hedges, as usual. Even as late as *The Young Philosopher* her heroes have to be of 'good' family, the impoverished descendants or younger sons of nobility. Almost all her contemporaries needed, it seems, to put their stories into an aristocratic setting, if only to denounce aristocracy. The exceptions are Wollstonecraft and Hays. Edgeworth's regional novel, *Rackrent Castle*, focuses more on the peasantry, but most novelists seem to have assumed that to sustain interest in a courtship novel, aristocrats must appear, if only to be virtuously rejected by the heroine. Even Austen's 'The Watsons' which begins in an impressively original mundane setting, soon moves into higher society. But Charlotte's novels, at least after *Emmeline*, are not Cinderella stories. Unlike Burney, she brings the notion of class out into the open and castigates the mindless rich like Maria Newenden or Sir Audley Dacres, attributing their failings to their assumptions of class superiority. And in her best novel she attempts to create in Monimia a heroine who is 'nobody' but who unlike Evelina makes herself somebody by education and endurance rather than by marriage or the discovery of high birth.

Her attitude to gender is more within the mainstream of her time. The three early heroines are consistently graceful and ladylike, though spirited and determined. As the nineties went on and she became more embittered, her women find themselves in extreme situations where the expected sweetness cannot be maintained. But she preserves the conventions by making the elder Rosalie and Laura middle-aged when they relate their adventures, though creating young heroine-daughters for those readers whose tastes run more to the novel of courtship than the novel of ideas. The younger heroines though clever are never allowed to display much singularity, which is reserved for the anti-heroines. The learned and accomplished Miss Hollybourn is set up as a foil to Monimia's sincerity. Ellen Newenden is an interesting case of Charlotte's treatment of a woman who, though not learned, claims masculine freedom and enjoys masculine pastimes. The portrait is purely satiric, even more so than Burney's treatment of Mrs Selwyn in *Evelina*. Ellen has a passion for horses and hunting, and she dresses and talks like a jockey. She is at first quite free from envy or malice, but the authorial attitude to her is contemptuous. Sir Edward says:

> My sister, though without the slightest disposition to do wrong, is not only singular and absurd in her pursuits but thinks in a manner peculiar to herself; while other women at her time of life, for she is not yet thirty, solicit the sanction of some older woman, or take the utmost care to preserve a punctilious decorum in their company and manners, Miss Newenden has determined to live her own way, and to associate with men, as well as rival them in field sports. Tis an unfortunate turn, in my mind.[76]

And the narrator entirely validates Sir Edward's opinion: Ellen's character deteriorates rapidly, and she joins with men in endangering Ethelinde's safety. To be singular, to live one's own way, to be 'masculine', is to be morally wrong as well as socially disadvantaged in Charlotte's world. But she is aware of the limitations of gender stereotyping. Her heroines all need fortitude badly, to support their trials and adventures. The society she imagines is destructive and does indeed destroy the health and sanity of some of her women. Attention to an expected reader-response is at work through these compromises as well as her own division of sympathies between loyalty to the values of the gentry and the need she saw for change.

Butler writes in *Romantics, Rebels and Reactionaries* that the writer of the 1790s is

> much more inclined than the Romantic to express sympathy for certain well-defined social groups. Humanitarian feeling for the real-life underdog is a strong vein from the 1760s to the 1790s, often echoing real-life campaigns for reform.[77]

She argues that the writer of the 1790s seldom achieves such emotional force as his nineteenth-century successor, because unlike the Romantic it is uncommon for him to complain directly on his own behalf. But Charlotte is an exception, identifying herself as oppressed, making common cause with characters and readers. To tell her story, she saw, was to exert some control, even when the story contained crushing defeats.

There are no clear divisions between life and fiction in her writing. Both true and false heroines see themselves as central to a story which partly resembles and partly diverges from the stories they have read. Some make their grief into poetry. The author projects her painful experience into her novel in an overt bid for the reader's recognition and sympathy, but her experience also gives her the power to rewrite her world, and she manipulates novelistic conventions to surprise her reader and differentiate her own political and feminist views from those of earlier novelists. These sophisticated constructions of text, author and reader were there and ready for use when Austen began to publish.

6

Jane Austen

The Letters of a Solitary Wanderer was Charlotte Smith's last published fiction, so this is a good place to leave for a time the circumstances in which she wrote it and consider her influence on Austen's novels. Until now the focus has been on her life and historical context, and here 'Charlotte' seemed the most suitable name. In comparing her with Austen, problems of naming recur. To continue calling her Charlotte while Austen remains Austen is to put them on the playing-field of a Fouquier-Tinville: it emphasises Austen's fame and professionalism at the expense of the obscure, domestically-encumbered and self-referential novelist. In fact Charlotte Smith was the professional and Austen the amateur, judged solely on their motives for publishing and their profits. Since I will be considering here only the effect of her work on a writer of the next generation, I will switch to the surname in which she published. Austen never wrote under her own name; in her lifetime her novels were issued as 'By a Lady'.

As a child Austen was a parodist, and a parodic element survives in her mature style. Smith seems to me her strongest single inspiration and antagonist. Both novelists were interested in the balance of Sensibility and sense. It was once assumed Austen's literary mentors were male, from Henry Austen's comments on her evaluation of Richardson and Fielding, reported in James Austen-Leigh's memoir. But Henry was not interested in the well-established tradition of woman authors – Lennox, Burney, Radcliffe, Wollstonecraft, Hays, Inchbald, Edgeworth, Smith and many others – who (like Richardson) wrote about the chances for women in a male-dominated society. He would have preferred to distinguish his sister from all this company except Burney. But Austen grew up with that tradition, and knew it very well.

Mary Lascelles, whose book contains much that later twentieth–century Austen criticism was to develop, notes her debt to Smith. Frank Bradbrook points out that Catherine Morland, who 'never could learn or understand anything before she was taught, and sometimes not even then, for she was often inattentive, and occasionally stupid',[1] is a parodic version of Emmeline, who learns without the help of a teacher from old volumes in the library at Mowbray Castle. Bradbrook traces some of the echoes of Smith in Austen's work, and sees the influence as one of occasional verbal reminiscence.

William Magee's 'The Happy Marriage: the Influence of Charlotte Smith on Jane Austen', is exhaustive in its tabulation of verbal echoes. He finds parallels in character, incident and theme, showing that Smith influenced Austen 'the most frequently and profoundly of any of her predecessors.'[2] Some of the parallels he mentions are convincing, some less so, and they appear from *Northanger Abbey* to 'Sanditon' as well as in the Juvenilia. Like Ehrenpreis, he sees a strong resemblance between *Northanger Abbey*'s Isabella Thorpe and *The Young Philosopher*'s Martha Goldthorp: Martha reads romances and pursues men, though she is more intelligent and satiric than Isabella, and an heiress, not motivated by greed. Magee also traces significant resemblances such as the accidental meeting of Celestina and Willoughby at a party in London and Celestina's distress when he ignores her, like Marianne's when Willoughby ignores her in *Sense and Sensibility*. This is a resemblance J.M.S. Tompkins had noticed earlier in *The Popular Novel in England*. Magee sees many other parallels between *Celestina* and *Sense and Sensibility* in language and plot, and concludes that 'all these parallels early and late in *Sense and Sensibility* suggest that Jane Austen had Charlotte Smith in mind.'[3] He believes that Smith suggested to Austen marriages which are both financially secure, and affectionate. But happy marriages portrayed with varying degrees of plausibility have ended English fictions since Chaucer. Magee apparently believes that arranged marriages were the norm in life and fiction until the late eighteenth century. When he discusses verbal reminiscence or parallel situation, his concept of influence is one of simple absorption: Austen merely had Smith 'in mind', consciously or unconsciously, as she wrote.

The relationship is more grating than that. While Austen enjoyed Smith's novels, she was hostile to some of the ideas she found in them. She cut her teeth on Smith in early parody, and in her mature work continued to attack the easy emotionalism and soft morals she saw in the older novelist. Austen wants us to be aware of Smith in her writing, giving sharper definition to her own attitudes and placing herself more firmly within an anti-Jacobin political tradition. Like most of her contemporaries, she would have defined Smith as a Jacobin, and she saw what Smith was doing with her Gothic castles.

Fielding had used the great house as appropriate setting, but Smith taught Austen the use of a great house as a precise emblem of England; from Smith's political castles Austen took the idea of a building's maintenance, improvement, neglect or loss as an organising emblem for her own opposing political and religious ideas.

Alistair Duckworth's *The Improvement of the Estate* shows how central the house symbol is for Austen, and relates her intellectual standpoint to Burke's, though without reference to the castle emblem of Burke's *Reflections*. But Austen's adoption of the emblem came through Smith, a link missing in Duckworth's account. In Convention and Innovation in Charlotte Smith's Novels, Bowstead claims that 'a careful study of the literary relationship between Austen and Smith might indeed be a significant contribution to Austen studies',[4] and suggests that 'Charlotte Smith is the most important among Austen's literary mentors',[5] remarking in a footnote the resemblance of *Mansfield Park* to *The Old Manor House*. Austen takes a great estate as setting, rather than a castle, and uses it like Smith as a metaphor for family and state. Without Smith and *The Old Manor House*, she would have written less clearly focused novels.

In *Northanger Abbey* Radcliffe's *The Mysteries of Udolpho* is the obvious satiric target, with the Radcliffian Gothic world in general. But what Catherine Morland thinks she has found at Northanger, a wife and mother of two sons and a daughter locked away in a disused wing of the Abbey, is closer to Smith's 'The Story of Edouarda' than to Radcliffe's *A Sicilian Romance*, otherwise the closest analogue. *Northanger Abbey* was written between 1799 and 1803, Austen recorded; Catherine's imaginings may have been suggested by *The Letters of a Solitary Wanderer*. But though *Northanger Abbey* makes fun of Gothic atmospherics, it validates the Gothic insistence on evil: General Tilney is not like Montoni but in his own mundane way he is vicious, and Catherine Morland is certainly not wrong about him.

Austen collected her Pythonesque Juvenilia to form three manuscript volumes; except in 'Lesley Castle' she parodies the sentimental novel or play. The pieces are not arranged chronologically, and only a few are dated. The dating however is problematic, as R.W. Chapman has pointed out. Austen continued to make alterations after she was grown up, and it is impossible to tell how extensive they were. In 'Catharine' she substituted Hannah More's *Coelebs in Search of a Wife* (1809) for Bishop Secker's *On the Catechism* (1769) as a book Kitty's aunt recommends her to read, so updating a story that was clearly begun in the nineties. And a letter in 'Evelyn' is dated 19 August

1809, as if this story too were in process of preparation for the press, or at least for wider readership.

The earliest date given is 13 June 1790, for 'Love and Freindship', when Austen was not yet fifteen, which rules out *The Young Philosopher* (1798) as a satiric subject. The parallels are strong: the name Laura, the retelling of the story to one of the next generation, the absurd cosmopolitanism of the heroine's background, the loves and friendships – and the antipathies – at first sight. Laura Glenmorris says of Mrs Mackirk that

> the common habits of civility, and the necessity she was under to please her brother, were sufficient to induce her to conceal her coldness under such forms of hospitality as the occasion seemed to call for.
>
> Far different, however, are these from the genuine and interesting expressions of real sympathy and generous affection. I felt, even in the first interview, that Mrs Mackirk would never be my friend, that I could never communicate to her the emotions which swelled or depressed my heart.[6]

Austen's Laura says of the young woman who takes her and Sophia into her house: 'She was nothing more than a mere good-tempered, civil and obliging Young Woman; as such we could scarcely dislike her – she was only an Object of Contempt.'[7] There are further resemblances, but given the date of 1790, *The Young Philosopher* cannot be a source, and one could not propose any single book or author as the subject of the satire. But the ethos attacked is a Smithian sensibility and a Smithian political outlook. The romantic passions and financial problems of *Emmeline* and *Ethelinde* reappear in 'Love and Freindship'. Austen's young heroines take a revolutionary attitude to other people's property, and steal without scruple. But no doubt other revolutionary writers and writers of novels of Sensibility, and of course epistolary novelists also, contributed to the final effect. As Austen was still adding to the Juvenilia as late as 1809, it is possible 'Love and Freindship' may have undergone some alteration after *The Young Philosopher*.

The stories often parody novels of the benevolent heart like Mackenzie's *The Man of Feeling* or Frances Sheridan's *The Memoirs of Miss Sidney Bidulph*, as well as novels of Sensibility like Smith's. In 'Evelyn', where everybody is benevolent, the Webbs give away their house, their daughter and a large sum of money to a complete stranger. Austen duplicates the 'do me the honour' language that irritated Seward. Mrs Webb introduces the hero to her daughter:

> 'Our dear freind Mr Gower my love – He has been so good as to accept of this house, small as it is, and to promise to keep it for ever.' 'Give me leave to assure you sir', said Miss Webb, 'that I am highly sensible of your kindness in this respect, which from the shortness of my Father's and Mother's acquaintance with you, is more than usually flattering.'[8]

The intensifiers Stanton notes in her study of Smith's style are here and in the right proportion to mimic her mannered graciousness, though that 'accept of' marks the genius. This parody seems aimed directly at Smith, who introduces philanthropic hearts only to close her novels, an absurdity Austen emphasises by putting the closure at the beginning.

R.W. Chapman says of 'Lesley Castle' that 'parts . . . are relatively so dull that one may suspect that a serious intention was creeping in.'[9] The story is not dull; the author already knows how ludicrous sense sounds to the bereaved. But it is true that while 'Love and Freindship', a piece of similar length, remains parodic throughout, 'Lesley Castle' begins to evolve into a straight novel. The domestic, cooking, officious Charlotte Lutterell, who has been organising her sister Eloisa's wedding breakfast, has to break the news to her sister that her fiancé has been injured in a riding accident and is unlikely to live. The name Eloisa comes from Rousseau's *La Nouvelle Eloïse*, a novel immensely popular and often translated in the eighties and nineties and well into the nineteenth century, and a touchstone of Sensibility. But Eloisa is treated not parodically as one might expect from the name, but sympathetically, and Charlotte is the comic. After briefly condoling with her sister, she goes on:

> though perhaps I may suffer most from it after all; for I shall not only be obliged to eat up all the Victuals I have dressed already, but must if Henry should recover (which however is not very likely) dress as much for you again; or should he Die (as I suppose he will) I shall still have to prepare a Dinner for you whenever you marry anybody else.[10]

Unusually for the Juvenilia, sense rather than sensibility, heartless-ness rather than the good heart, is the target of Austen's satire here. 'Lesley Castle' was preparing the way for *Sense and Sensibility*, where Mr and Mrs John Dashwood's sense is exposed early, and where certain kinds of sense prove more repulsive than any degree of Sensibility.

In all her novels she reacted against Smith's cosmopolitan settings, fanciful heroinely names, incursions into proletarian society and intrusive authorial presence. She read *Emmeline* when she was twelve, when her own need to write was growing on her, and when she was of an age to idolise Delamere.[11] The heroine and the anti-heroine of 'Catharine' reveal their respectively good and bad taste in a conversation about Mrs Smith and *Ethelinde*.[12] In the characterisation of John Willoughby[13] in her first published novel, *Sense and Sensibility* (1811), she defines her attitude to Smith, and especially to *Celestina*. *Sense and Sensibility* examines and rejects, often reluctantly, the Sensibility Smith encouraged her reader to admire: impulse and rashness, violent sexual feeling, a contempt for traditional forms. Smith created a fictional world against which Austen was to react sharply, the more so because it attracted her.

There are many reworkings of *Celestina* in *Sense and Sensibility*, such as Marianne's impulsive letters to Willoughby, her anxiety while waiting for a reply and, as Tompkins and Magee have noticed, the scene where Willoughby cuts Marianne at a party. Like Austen's, Smith's party scene shows the dislocation between private feelings and public manners:

> fixed to the place where [George Willoughby] stood unheeded, among some other idle people who were looking on, he remained gazing at her for several minutes. His legs trembled so, that it was with difficulty he supported himself, and his heart beat as if it would break. He debated with himself, whether he should speak to her, or retire unobserved; but while he yet argued the point, a smile and a whisper that passed between her and Montague Thorold, determined him to fly from the torments he felt, and which he found it almost impossible to endure another moment: he stepped hastily away to find his sister, and entreat her to go; but so deeply was he affected, that, weakened as he was by illness, he staggered, and might have fallen, had not the shame of betraying so much weakness, lent him resolution to reach a chair, where he sat a moment to recover breath and recollection. . .

> The agitation of poor Celestina could not be concealed, nor could she for a moment or two escape from the enquiring eyes of those who remarked it. As soon, however, as she could disengage herself from the throng, she sat down, hardly daring to enquire whether what she had seen was real or visionary. She had returned from Oxfordshire, with Lady Horatia, only the evening before, and knew nothing of

Willoughby's being in England; while, in addition to the amazement the sight of him occasioned, his apparent ill health impressed her with concern, and the displeasure with which he surveyed her, with terror. Montague Thorold, who had seen Willoughby, and whose eyes were never a moment away from Celestina, knew at once the cause of her distress. He followed her, little less affected than she was herself, to a sofa where she had thrown herself, and asked her, in a faint and tremulous voice, if he should fetch her anything? She answered – 'If you please', – so low, that he scarce distinguished what she said: but stepping a few paces from her, he took a glass of lemonade from a servant, and brought it to her. She took it, and carried it to her lips, almost unconscious of what she did, while Montague Thorold leaned over the arm of the sofa on which she sat, and watched the emotions of her countenance, with all the solicitude he felt strongly painted on his own.

At the same moment Willoughby appeared, leading Lady Molyneux through the room. The first objects that he saw as he approached the door, were Celestina and Montague Thorold: but having once seen them, he turned hastily from them; and seeming to give all his attention to his sister, he disappeared.[14]

Slander and misunderstandings separate Smith's hero and heroine in a novelistic cliché Marianne longs in vain to claim for her own case. George Willoughby suffers as much as Celestina, while Austen recognises how much more women had to lose by taking novels of Sensibility seriously, for Marianne suffers more than John Willoughby. Smith conveys the pressure of the social world, though Austen does this more dramatically as Elinor physically screens Marianne from the curiosity of the other guests. As well as using movement and gesture, Austen has more dialogue and more immediacy:

'But have you not received my notes?'cried Marianne in the wildest anxiety. 'Here is some mistake I am sure – some dreadful mistake. What can be the meaning of it? Tell me, Willoughby; for heaven's sake tell me, what is the matter?'

He made no reply; his complexion changed and all his embarrassment returned; but as if, on catching the eye of the young lady with whom he had been previously talking, he felt the necessity of instant exertion, he recovered himself again, and after saying, 'Yes, I had the pleasure of receiving the information of your arrival in town, which you were so good as to send me,' turned hastily away with a slight bow and joined his friend.[15]

At the end of *Sense and Sensibility* John Willoughby duplicates his predecessor's last minute race to the West Country and so almost, but not quite, re-establishes his claim to be the hero. The novel grew out of Austen's ambiguous response to *Celestina*, and to the kind of hero she liked in her teens, though it also bears traces of Jane West's *A Gossip's Story* (1796), a brightly conformist tribute to the claims of sense. Here the staid heroine's beautiful and absurdly romantic younger sister is called Marianne. By the 1790s, the sophisticated reader was able to follow the dialogue of ideas between one novel and another. This was part of the interest a new novel offered, which is why Austen preserved the two principal names, Marianne and Willoughby. *Sense and Sensibility* was taking shape in the nineties, though its late publication obscures Austen's dialogue with Smith.

In Smith's *Marchmont* (1796), published when Austen was twenty, there is a parallel with the scene in *Pride and Prejudice* where Mrs Reynolds shows Elizabeth Bennet over Pemberley. Such a scene is familiar in its Gothic version: Henry Tilney parodies it when he fantasises about the housekeeper Dorothy showing Catherine over Northanger Abbey. The *Marchmont* passages have interesting resemblances and contrasts with Elizabeth's visit, which have not been noticed before. Althea is taken through the rooms by Mrs Mosely, housekeeper to the previous owners, the Marchmonts. Althea has met and liked young Marchmont, and observes the house closely to learn more about him:

> Althea cast her eyes around this scene of former gaiety and splendour, now dreary and deserted.
>
> The ceiling had once been curiously stuccoed in large copartments; but the swallows had at present a colony among the cornices, and great projecting roses. The room was wainscoted, and ornamented with carving and gilding; now much defaced and broken. Around the chimney had been rich and massy festoons, of which enough was left to shew that they had originally been splendid and expensive. Of the furniture little remained: in one corner some heavy picture frames were piled together; and in a single frame which stood against the wall was a damaged picture, representing a lady in the costume of the court of Charles the Second. The countenance was remarkable pleasing, but pensive, and even dejected.[16]

As well as the family portraits Althea looks at several oval miniatures, as Elizabeth does at Pemberley. Unlike Darcy, the present Marchmonts cannot afford to have their portraits painted, but as Mrs Mosely praises Marchmont, he

> was at this moment so present to the memory of Althea, that she thought she really saw him leaning dejectedly on his desk. The place

seemed sanctified by the fortitude and filial piety of its former inhabitant.[17]

From the housekeeper's admiring description, Althea sees him vividly in her mind's eye as Elizabeth looks at Darcy's picture and thinks of him as she has seen him in the past.

At this point the action moves temporarily away from Althea, but a few months later, when we next see her, she is walking in the gallery. The two children of the caretaker, playing hide-and-seek, catch sight of a man hiding in the room where Althea has visualised Marchmont:

> Althea, holding by the baluster, looked up. She saw, standing on the top of the stairs, a figure, of which, as his back was to the light which came from the open door of the gallery, she could not distinguish the face. – She was now alone in the house (for the children were already out of hearing); and in a state of mind difficult to describe, she hesitated a moment whether she should stop to hear what this man had to say, or fly. It was evident that he knew her – his voice and manner were such as seemed not to indicate any evil design. Rapidly these ideas passed through her mind – while the person, perceiving that she wavered, approached her. – Althea still descending the stairs, though with less speed – he spoke to her again. 'Miss Dacres', said he, 'will not surely refuse to hear, for one moment, an unhappy man, whose life is perhaps in her power?'
>
> She now saw his face, and became riveted to the place where she stood; for through some change, which she was in too much confusion to consider, she recollected the features and voice of Marchmont.[18]

He has been hiding in a deserted wing of his former home to escape arrest for his family's debts.

In *Pride and Prejudice* Austen fully exploits Smith's emblematic house, adapting its representation to her own very different sensibility. Elizabeth's visit to Pemberley takes place in a safe and daylight world, and the estate is flourishing and in the right hands. For Austen there is much less to discard amongst the accumulated wisdom of the past. As Darcy says, 'I cannot comprehend the neglect of a family library in such days as these',[19] and no swallows fly in and out of the Pemberley library. He has been arrogant, but Mrs Reynolds reassures us that the upper classes are quite different once one gets to know them, and the taste apparent in house and grounds attests to the owner's character. Concern for the poor is not confined to those with radical views, and Mrs Reynolds praises his sense of social responsibility. Austen could see Burke's house alarmingly redeployed in *Desmond* and *The Old Manor House*, and created Pemberley, Mansfield Park and Donwell Abbey as stable and consolatory images.

English society has its abuses: the arrogance of a Lady Catherine, the servility of a Mr Collins. These two are serious threats, but they are powerless against Elizabeth. Her appreciation of England's best domestic architecture is briefer than Althea's brooding over its decay. She sees Darcy just as she leaves his house, and her embarrassment at his reappearance is more sharply conveyed than Althea's fear of Marchmont – inevitably, since Althea and Marchmont are insubstantial compared to Elizabeth and Darcy. The late publication of *Pride and Prejudice*, as of *Sense and Sensibility*, obscures Austen's comment on programmatic Smith scenes. She reasserts Burke, and her England, though not perfect, is well ordered and needs no change of ownership. Marilyn Butler initiated the discussion of the shift towards reaction in the nineties in her *Jane Austen and the War of Ideas*, but she underestimates Smith's political content, and her influence on Austen.

In *Mansfield Park* the character groupings of the visit to Sotherton and the emblematic layout of that estate owe much to Smith's handling of domestic space. Austen read the sexual coding of Emmeline's locked door and Orlando's entry to Monimia's room, and adapted these strategies in the symbol of the locked gate at Sotherton, for which Mr. Rushworth has no key. Mansfield Park itself is an emblem of a securer, an all-too-secure England: change in the fabric of this house is vandalism. Mrs Rayland and Sir Thomas Bertram are both authoritarian owners, but Sir Thomas' principles are represented with a greater degree of sympathy. *Mansfield Park* has important similarities to the plot of *The Old Manor House*: Monimia's progress from the isolated upper room to the state rooms where her merits are recognised is repeated by Fanny Price twenty-one years later. The aunts, Mrs Lennard and Mrs Norris, are similarly fierce and greedy, and a morally superior younger brother befriends and helps to educate the heroine. Philip Somerive the dissipated elder brother dies, enacting reformist hostility to primogeniture, but Tom Bertram merely falls ill, repents and recovers to inherit the estate, in keeping with Austen's narrative of a providentially ordered society.

A radical voice is scarcely heard in Austen's novels. Those who try to alter her houses are boorish like John Dashwood and Mr Rushworth, inconsiderate like Tom Bertram, or concerned to display fashionable taste, like Henry Crawford. The Crawfords are never allowed to argue a sceptical point of view in religion or politics, though to speak and act as they do, they would have to have one. Mary's comments in the Sotherton chapel, for instance, are the result of frivolity, not agnosticism. The radical voice in *Mansfield Park* is there only in the echo of Smith's narrative and in Inchbald's disruptive *Lovers Vows*, and perhaps Austen felt that that was voice enough. Yet though she rejects the old-fashioned radical politics of the nineties, her plot celebrates change and renewal. From the constricting Portsmouth house where a room looks like a passageway to somewhere better come William, Fanny and Susan to contribute to Mansfield Park's safety and comfort.

The battle of ideas continues as late as *Emma*. Critics have discussed the heroine as imaginist and failed novelist, but nobody has noted how political is the fiction-making in the novel. Though Emma Woodhouse is no Jacobin, the unwritten fictions she prefers are radical and Smithian. In Emma's fantasy, Harriet Smith's birth and lack of education will be no hindrance to a marriage with Elton or Frank Churchill. Emma is comfortably inconsistent in her radicalism, convinced that Harriet will prove to be the daughter of a nobleman and justify her patronage, just as Smith promotes Emmeline and Celestina to a higher status at the end of their novels. Emma acts like a courtship-novelist, making marriages and looking forward to the rolling complacencies of the happy ending, 'the comfortable fortune, the respectable establishment, the rise in the world which must satisfy'[20] Harriet's unknown relations. ·

Emma's thinking is dominated by literary models. Whether or not she reads the radical women novelists of the nineties is immaterial: by this time their ideas have permeated even provincial culture, and her judgement is, from Austen's point of view, tainted by them. In her fantasy about staying single to look after her father, she is influenced by the feminism of Wollstonecraft rather than by Smith's fictions. But radical writers such as Smith, Inchbald and Hays, who familiarise the young reader with extramarital sex by making it central to their narratives, encourage Emma to assume an intrigue between Jane and Dixon. She has a novelistic propensity to make rescues the indices of sexual attraction. When she learns that Dixon has saved Jane from drowning, her suspicions about them are confirmed. Like Gertrude Leicester's rescue by Sommerfeldt, Harriet's rescue by Frank from the gypsies must also, in Emma's judgment, lead to their marriage.

Influenced by Emma, however, Harriet has been indulging a grander rescue fantasy of her own after Mr Knightley's politeness at the dance, and he is now the hero of her private novel. Catherine Morland's mind had been full of the books she was reading, and Austen would not preempt a novel she still hoped to publish, though by 1815 she had more to say about the tyranny of the literary imagination. We never catch Emma reading a novel, yet her mind works in courtship narrative clichés. She is Maker rather than reader, a bad novelist and a parodic version of Austen herself: the book would have been impossible without a tradition sophisticated enough to produce such self-conscious works as *The Young Philosopher.*

Out of her shallow literary culture, Emma creates four radical love-fantasies: about Harriet marrying Elton, about herself refusing Frank, about Jane's intrigue with Dixon, and about Harriet marrying Frank. These narratives are potentially disruptive to an ordered, patriarchal society like Highbury in that they imagine cross-class marriage, women's independence and women's assertive sexuality. But though they are dangerous, they are safely contained within the conservative framework of a novel of education where the heroine learns the errors of such imagining.

Not only Emma and Harriet but other characters too try to take the story in different directions from the narrator. Mrs Weston's fantasy that Jane will marry Knightley is appropriate in an ex-governess, and has some novelistic credibility: Jane seems the perfect heroine in beauty, slight ill-health, musical gifts, family background – her father was killed in battle and her mother died of grief – and in her destined profession. As a sensible man Mr Weston knows the Churchills may still leave their money elsewhere, and if they do, Emma's £30,000 will be needed by Frank. Mr Elton's story is of marriage to that dowry. Mrs Elton creates splendid egotistical scenarios of impressing Highbury in Mr Suckling's barouche-landau. Mr Woodhouse, with his imagination of disaster, creates fictions where everyone stays single and falls ill. None of the characters' stories come true.

The narrator's main story of Emma and Knightley, engaging from the opening pages, falls into a popular fictional framework, the 'learning' framework where a faulty young heroine recognises her mistakes, adopts the standards of her older male mentor, and marries him, as in Burney's *Evelina* and *Camilla* (1796), though of course Austen's main plot transcends that framework. Emma's attempt to organise the Highbury material into radical patterns impedes but cannot change the narrator's ending. Her stories prove unworkable and ephemeral: the novel that is going to last will see it Knightley's way, guiding the heroine's individualism into an acceptance of marriage, hierarchy and more Christian conduct.

In contrast, the sourer of narrator's two sub-plots, the story of Frank and Jane, has the radical plotline of a Smith novel: a rich, domineering elderly relative, a hero prepared to lie and deceive though not to work, a poor heroine with secrets, and a happy ending which results from the old relative's long-awaited death. This is essentially an anti-authority plot. But though they sometimes threaten to take over, Frank and Jane remain subordinate hero and heroine. When they sing together, Jane's voice hoarsens and the duet with Frank is broken off, an emblem of their eventual marriage relationship, and they leave Highbury. *Emma* is a fiction about making fictions, and perfect fiction displaces from the centre such characters and their dubious plots. In her main narrative of Emma and Knightley, and in the ironically handled Harriet plot with its very small rescue by Robert Martin from a very unthreatening crowd at the end, Austen makes myths appropriate to her dominant social and religious ideals, while acknowledging competing ideologies in the other stories: in the anti-authority plot of Frank and Jane; in Emma's disruptive fantasies; and in the dissident or self-centred plots of all the other characters, who fail to see that Emma's money must go into the Donwell Abbey estate.

Almost every character is preoccupied with class in *Emma*, which ratifies an enlightened English feudalism, and wins its own narrative Waterloo against invasive Jacobin subplots. If we may assume the novel is set in the year it was written, 1814–15, then Emma's most confused days, those of the Hartfield word game, the strawberry-picking 'at almost midsummer'[21] and the visit to Box Hill, fall on or very near the three days of Waterloo. After that, the narrator's plot prevails. It is just possible Austen emended an earlier spring resolution to fall in the third week of June. The novel was finished by April, but negotiations with her publisher John Murray went on into the autumn, allowing time for alteration. That would account for her uncharacteristic error over the fruit trees at Donwell Abbey, still in flower long after they should be: she forgot to alter them. But this must remain speculation unless some new evidence appears. Nothing here is intrusive: the complicated structuring is so well absorbed, so apparently effortless, that we experience *Emma* primarily as a dance of personalities, not as a conflict of political ideas. It is none-theless driven by ideas.

The novel's conservatism is focused in the great estate and prosperous farm. At the strawberry picking Emma begins to see what the narrator sees. Most importantly, she sees Donwell Abbey in the foreground and behind it, in perspective, the Abbey Mill Farm, the picturesque vista held in the curve of hill and river:

> The considerable slope, at nearly the foot of which the abbey stood, gradually acquired a steeper form beyond its grounds; and at half a mile distant was a bank of considerable abruptness and grandeur, well clothed with wood; – and at the bottom of the bank, favourably placed and sheltered, rose the Abbey Mill Farm, with meadows in front, and the river making a close and handsome curve around it.[22]

The image rebukes Smith's grim symbolic Gothic and her Rousseauesque conviction that Nature is hostile to hierarchy. The sheltering lines of Austen's landscape lock together Donwell Abbey and the Martins' farm. This is an England that by 1815 Austen knew herself powerful enough to define and shape. Her construction of the good society has probably been a greater force for conservatism than that of any other English writer. In these two houses Emma and Harriet will eventually settle, half a mile apart, and through their children ensure the perpetuation of England's stable hierarchy into the future.

After Waterloo, however, when the Jacobin threat diminished, Austen was more open to the idea of change, and *Persuasion*'s Kellynch Hall needs new ownership as much as any Smith castle. Austen's last and Smith's first heroine each reject a cousin, William and Frederic respectively, the heir to the family title, and marry a naval officer, Frederick and William respectively. But the most intriguing question in this context is what to make of *Persuasion*'s Mrs Charles Smith. She married a feckless husband and moved in fashionable society, but the husband wasted all their money. She comes to Bath for her health, lives in cheap lodgings, is rheumatic, impoverished, and owed money from plantations in the West Indies but unable to gain access to it because of the dereliction of lawyers. There are large differences: *Persuasion*'s Mrs Smith is a childless widow, who occupies herself with small bits of haberdashery for charitable purposes rather than writing for a living. But Austen could not have forgotten a writer whose work she responded to so eagerly in her teens and twenties when she read Smith's attacks on the lawyers and accounts of the damage caused through loss of the children's legacies. It was a subject with which she could sympathise. *Persuasion's* Mrs Smith is Anne's friend and mentor at school, though Anne soon overtakes her intellectually. Smith was dead by the time Austen began to publish, but there may be some odd intertextual tribute here to a poet whose elegiac sonnets sometimes still blessed her memory as they blessed Anne's, and to a novelist on whose emblems and structures she had drawn. She may once have wanted to help the older author, personally unknown to her. She lets Frederick Wentworth do that, fictionally. We are used to seeing Austen's novels as located well above the detritus of the author's biography. But perhaps there are places where that impersonal artistry is fractured by a private tribute, a private joke even.

Other novelists of the nineteenth and twentieth centuries seized on Smith's house metaphor, though usually through Austen and without knowing where it originated. Comparison of the two novelists tempts towards unqualified contrast of the house images, suppressing Smith's traditionalism and Austen's dissent. But comparison will usually end in Austen's favour. Though an admirable stylist and a mordant wit, Smith was under financial pressure to write too much too fast, padded her volumes and had no time to revise. Since readers usually come to Smith by way of Austen's early parodies, they may come expecting absurdities. But in her novels the compromised, ultimately defeated radical ideals of the early nineties were beaten into romance form with forcefulness and originality. Austen was involved in a dialogue of ideas with Smith that interested her long after Smith had ceased to write. This could never have happened if Smith had not possessed a powerful mind and style. She was a formidable antagonist who helped the younger novelist to define by contrast her own emerging view of England in the 1790s.

7
Beachy Head

In the last five years of her life Charlotte wrote three more children's books and the poems that appeared posthumously as *Beachy Head*, but she published no more novels. She had complained often in the nineties about the burden of the novelist's wretched trade; her health was probably damaged by the years spent at her desk. Sir Walter Scott, weighing the demands of her career and some phases of his own, wrote in his *Lives of the Novelists* where Catherine's memoir first appeared:

> Nothing saddens the heart so much as that sort of literary labour which depends on the imagination, when it is undertaken unwillingly, and from a sense of compulsion ... If there is a mental drudgery which lowers the spirits and lacerates the nerves, like the toil of the slave, it is that which is exacted by literary composition when the heart is not in unison with the work upon which the head is employed. Add to the unhappy author's task, sickness, sorrow or the pressure of unfavourable circumstances, and the labour of the bondsman becomes light in comparison.[1]

Insufferably smug, as it seems now, in his Caucasian similes, Scott was generous in his sympathy with the effort her novel writing cost her over fourteen years, and in his appreciation of her work.

But her literary labour had not been always from compulsion; she had written since childhood and evidently needed to write. The partial disengagement from authorship that followed *The Letters of a Solitary Wanderer* was unfortunate. As Hays says in *British Public Characters*, even if it appears in her narrative of Charlotte's life that

> superior endowments exempt not the possessor from the accidents and calamities of life, or that even in some situations they add poignancy to the sense of those calamities, yet let it not be forgotten, that a cultivated imagination possesses in itself an independent source of peculiar and appropriate enjoyment, compared with which, in richness and variety, the pleasures of sense are mean and scanty. When wearied with the futility of society, or disgusted with its vices, it is the privilege of genius to retire within itself, to call up, with creative power, new worlds, and people solitude with ideal beings.

Charlotte's mental state deteriorated when she had no fictional worlds to absorb her, when she no longer peopled solitude with ideal beings, in Hays' words, or even with rogues like the ones she knew. She was happier as a full-time author than when she was working on Trust business in her fifties. Her last five years produced nearly eight hundred typescript pages of often intimate and self-analytical letters. Only a brief account of these last years can be attempted here.

She continued to correspond with Joseph Cooper Walker. A long letter of 14 April 1801 describes Harriet's return from India and the previous year's anxieties about Lucy and Lionel, while she was working on the first three novellas. Thomas Newhouse was ill, drinking and violent; he beat up Lucy, who returned to her mother pregnant with her two small children. Charlotte expected Lionel home in July 1800. Instead the Duke of Kent ordered him to take six hundred maroons across the Atlantic to Sierra Leone; he was assigned only a subaltern and forty soldiers to do this. Not surprisingly, maroons got into her text, though they are constructed with some sympathy in 'The Story of Henrietta'. Her fear increased when he did not return by Christmas, and she was almost hopeless by spring. She describes to Walker how she was combing through the papers and saw the arrival of his ship, the *Asia*, then a moment later he walked in. It is a scene for a novel of Sensibility, literary and self-conscious. She still uses her letters to turn all their lives into controllable stories. He went with her to interview Newhouse, whom they found dying and whom he and Lucy looked after in his last weeks. All this was disruptive to *The Letters of a Solitary Wanderer*, but she had written through worse times, and probably could have given the novellas a better ending had that been all.

Charles got permission to visit Barbados before he joined his regiment in Bermuda, to deal in person with debts to the plantations and queries hindering the sale of Gay's. He took an English servant, Bernard Maule, who contracted yellow fever soon after they arrived. Charles nursed him through the illness, caught it himself and died there in the early summer of 1801, aged twenty-seven. The news reached England two months later, though without details. No personal effects came back and Maule decided to stay in Barbados. Three years later Charlotte still suspected, with some reason, that Charles had been murdered, though eventually she learned enough to disprove that.

She was trying to finish the novellas in 1801. Even when Augusta died, she had gone on writing, while the news from Barbados left her unable to do more than cobble together an ending. Physical debility, *The Critical* review, the failure of *What Is She?* which would have been very public, may all have contributed to her inability to end the novellas well or engage with a new book. But though there is relatively little reference to Charles' death in the surviving letters, this is obviously chance, and she may have felt nearly as grieved as when she lost Augusta.

She was determined to settle – finally – the business of the Trust, with the help of Egremont and her brother. Once that was adjusted and her children provided for, she might return to authorship but without the pressure to make money. So her talent was distorted and wasted in Trust correspondence. Many of these letters are frantic and obsessed; the reader has to watch her on the edge of madness. Sometimes she loses all her habitual sense of self-respect and of the proper distance to maintain from Egremont and his associates. 'I wish I was dead rather than go through all this',[2] she writes, or, 'Would to God that the Earth would open and swallow me.'[3] But the letters to friends still show her, more often than one might expect in her circumstances, sane and sardonic, absorbed in new reading and ideas, planning new books.

George, the Normandy baby, grew into a pretty young fellow, his mamma considered. He joined the army at sixteen, taking over his dead brother's commission in the 47th Regiment in September 1801. The perpetual avowdson of St Mary's, Islington Charlotte long hoped would make a safe haven for one of her boys went to Richard Smith III, the son of Benjamin's elder brother, unexpectedly following his father's profession. It is not clear whether he had to pay Charlotte Mary for this, but she seems to have been slightly better off than her sisters. All the legatees were allowed a little money from the Trust, and Lucy Towers Smith may have left Charlotte Mary something in addition. She took lodgings in Islington when she came back from Berwick-on-Tweed, though she often saw her mother and helped her in Trust business. In recent years she and Charles had been perhaps the closest to each other of Charlotte's scattered family, and his loss may have affected her as much as her mother.

The delay in settlement had now, as Charlotte saw it, claimed the lives of two children, since she always believed Augusta might have recovered abroad, which was the view of many medical men of the time. The Trust money was inextricably involved with her feelings about the dead, and came to signify a hope of safety for the survivors. Her bereavements focused here. With money, Lionel and George could arrange postings in England away from the killing climate of the West Indies. When she died, Benjamin would remarry on her £7,000. Though he still cohabited with his housekeeper Mrs Millar and had a child by her niece, Mr Monstroso had also, she believed, become engaged to a Miss Gordon, whose wedding presents were bought before her family found out he was married. Unless she could arrange provision with the Trustees, Harriet would have only a pin-money allowance William made her, and Lucy would have no income at all, except small variable amounts from the yearly dividends which were quite inadequate to keep her and three children. The descent into keeping, then prostitution was all too easy and had happened to Elizabeth Inchbald's sister among her acquaintance.

At first her relationship with Egremont was excellent, and dealing with him a tremendous relief after John Robinson, who died in 1802. But she had already quarrelled with her brother over his power of attorney for her son Nicholas' Trust money, which she wanted to transfer to Lucy, with her son's approval. Egremont and Nicholas Turner were both annoyed by her insistence that Alexandre should share in the estate, however minimally. Nicholas had changed his mind about Alexandre, which Charlotte attributed to a mixture of bigotry and self-interest. The Boehms, Henchmans and Allens were deviously claiming more than they should, she thought, and the Allens were preparing a suit in Chancery. There was 'something in old Smith's money' she wrote, that acted 'as Rhodium does on rats.'4 She could not help writing with passion and authority; it was her trade. Egremont considered her letters merely diffuse declamation.

He, and his friend Hayley in his lower sphere, could both be patronising patrons; both had problems with women all their lives. The bluff, coarse streak that made him a good friend to J.M.W. Turner alienated him from Charlotte's mercurial sensibilities. The Petworth Maecenas had £52,000 a year and a genealogy deriving from Charlemagne; his radicalism was never very convincing. Though she used the appropriate forms of courtesy, he found it annoying that a female novelist no longer young or attractive and sometimes lacking a change of clothes to go out in addressed him at length on terms of near-equality. Soon he was refusing to answer her letters, handing them over to his steward, William Tyler. The loss of his friendship bewildered her and she felt too how it weakened her position in the eyes of everyone else. Tyler was loathed in Petworth and burned in effigy at least once; the tenants are said to have danced on his grave. Egremont could hardly have insulted her more than by this move.

Not long after she learned of Charles' death, Egremont asked her to Petworth to give Tyler the death dates of all the others.

He was apparently insensitive enough to suggest that her problems could be easily resolved if she lived with Benjamin again. Though many of her letters to him swing between humility and aggression, she sometimes had the strength to defend herself sensibly:

> Yr Ldship says that we none of us seem disposed to submit to our circumstances. Pardon me if I reply that I have submitted not only to give up my situation in society but to actual & very humiliating deprivations & personal hardships, as well as continual labour greatly beyond my strength.[5]

But she knew it was impossible for someone in his circumstances to understand hers. Twice during these years she was forced to meet Benjamin to discuss Trust business in the presence of lawyers, first in London in the autumn of 1801, then at Petworth in September 1803. The latter occasion was especially acrimonious.

After a long silence Egremont wrote an unexpectedly friendly letter, inviting her to the meeting, and she accepted providing Benjamin was not there. He was, however. One of Egremont's and the Trust's lawyers, Samuel Rose, wanted Lucy to depose that her father had treated her mother cruelly, presumably in case the separation had to be discussed in Chancery. It is not clear whether Lucy did so, but she was present in the house. Benjamin was furious with her and refused to recognise her when they met again. Charlotte was sorry that Lucy had been called, pointlessly since no court would accept evidence dating back twenty years to when she was still a child. With her sons abroad, she knew Lucy could have no protection from anyone except Benjamin when she died.

To Charlotte's surprise and distress, Samuel Rose confirmed that Benjamin should have £500 he had recently claimed, and keep the interest from her marriage settlement. As the law stood, there was no alternative to the latter award. No provision had ever been made for a separation, so the money was his. Egremont and Rose both thought she was extravagant, which was true in a way, though she was not as extravagant as Benjamin, and spent money mainly on the children. She was awarded half that year's dividend, not more than £100 as profits on the plantations were decreasing. Harriet and George would have £60 a year after her death, though Harriet would lose hers if she married, and Charlotte's expenses incurred in Trust business were paid. It was much less than she had hoped.

She bore Samuel Rose no grudge, however, and fell into a friendly correspondence with his wife Sarah. The Roses knew Hayley, the literary sisters Harriet and Sophia Lee, and many other friends of Charlotte's. Samuel had defended Blake at his treason trial, and even walked all the way to The Mitre at Barnet to spend the evening with Cowper, Mary Unwin, Cowper's 'Johnny of Norfolk' and the spaniel Beau when they were on their way to Eartham in August 1792, apparently to check that they were managing the journey. Sarah found Charlotte's letters very entertaining, and became an intimate and helpful confidante, though the two never found a chance to meet; so the Petworth fiasco had one good outcome.

But in every other way it was humiliating. Charlotte was very fat now from dropsy, and had difficulty getting in and out of a carriage. She was conscious of the Petworth servants laughing at her when she met Benjamin again; only Egremont's contempt could have made that possible, she knew. And the outcome ended her hopes of retrieving at least her own family money.

She continued to visit Bignor and London, and moved frequently in these years, from the Frant house near Tunbridge Wells which she sublet, to lodgings in Hastings, back to Frant again, to Brighton briefly, then in 1803 to Elstead and finally to Tilford, both close to Guildford and Stoke Place where her mother was buried, and where she wanted to be buried too. The physical business of living grew harder. She was concussed in a carriage accident, hurrying back home at the news that Harriet was taken dangerously ill again, and frightened by a gang of robbers in the neighbourhood of Frant who duly broke in and stole half her remaining china. She mourned the loss of Augusta to the end: 'Eleven years on Wednesday have dragged their slow length along since that time – yet my misery has never abated.'[6] She praised her lost love's beauty and sweetness in terms as much like a lover's as a mother's.

After long negotiation she sold her library of about 1,000 books collected since she was twenty, to pay her household expenses and to prevent Benjamin inheriting them; she always maintained that he could not read. She got only about £150 for them, and missed them acutely; it must have felt like the end of her career. But Hays' biography in *British Public Characters* kept up interest in her and perhaps helped to counteract the relative failures of *The Letters of a Solitary Wanderer* and her play. Richard Phillips had a strong line in educational books among his many publishing ventures, and commissioned a history book for girls which she struggled with for several years. It was particularly difficult to write without her library. Her *History of England, from the earliest records, to the peace of Amiens in a series of letters to a young lady at school* is composed of simple stories like Alfred's burning the cakes and Philippa's saving the burghers of Calais. She amused herself in the writing by directing shafts at lawyers wherever possible. And she refused to go beyond the end of the seventeenth century. She could not reduce recent history to puerile exempla. After much wrangling between herself and Phillips, the third volume was efficiently produced by Hays and the work published in 1806.

In spite of her grief and anxiety, there are sparkles of cheerful malice and sharp judgements on books and people in her letters still. Cadell and Davies refused to accept any other work from her, though they continued as publishers of *Elegiac Sonnets*, but Joseph Johnson at last became her publisher, partly through the good offices of the Roses, and suggested she collect together poems for a new volume, which she was working on in the last three years of her life. And he commissioned two more children's books, *A Natural History of Birds*, still of interest for its careful observation, and *Conversations, Introducing Poetry; chiefly on subjects of Natural History, for the use of children and young persons*. Catherine contributed poems to this, and was to publish her own successful children's work, *The Peacock at Home, and other Poems*, after her sister's death.

Charlotte's hostility to her brother brought her closer to Catherine again. The sisters evidently enjoyed planning the volume of poems and stories together, though Catherine's input was slight. Her memoir records a visit to Elstead early in 1804 when they were working on *Conversations*, which Charlotte

> occasionally wrote in the common sittingroom of the family, with two or three lively grandchildren playing about her, and conversing with great cheerfulness and pleasantry, though nearly confined to her sofa, in great bodily pain, and in a mortifying dependency on the services of others, but in full possession of all her faculties.

Her critical faculties were in greater supply than Catherine perhaps appreciated. Though the sisters were on better terms, Charlotte was still angry about the transfer of Bignor Park, and even more so when its sale was planned. She had probably hoped it would go to one of her sons eventually. Catherine's daughter Lucy, Charlotte wrote to Sarah Rose, had been praised to the skies throughout her teens, then at twenty-two this miracle of wisdom & wit chose to marry a Man who, if he is *not* old, appears enough so to be her grandfather. With four children & almost all his property depending on his life which, as he eats & drinks like twenty Aldermen, is supposed to be not worth two years purchase. By this Man who is in character extremely like a large [? swine] put up in a stye, she has had *two* children within the year. Her beauty is lost in absolute deformity from table indulgences, & her mind so changed that she is quite estrangd from her Mother who has sacrificed every thing to her! – & now poor Bignor is sacrificed because this fat hog did not think the living there good enough.[7]

In 1806, Catherine and the Frasers sold the house for £13,500 to John Hawkins, Oriental explorer and travel writer.

Charlotte's sociable cheerfulness at Elstead was a lifelong characteristic according to the memoir. Those who formed their ideas of her from her work or even from what she said about herself in moments of depression, Catherine says, concluded she was always melancholy, but

> nothing could be more erroneous. Cheerfulness and gaiety were the natural characteristics of her mind; and though circumstances of a most depressing nature at times weighed down her spirit to earth, yet such was its buoyancy that it quickly returned to its natural level. Even in the darkest period of her life, she possessed the power of abstracting herself from her cares; and, giving play to the sportiveness of her imagination, could make even the difficulties she was labouring under subject of merriment.

Catherine did not understand her sister's writing and was temperamentally unlike her. She probably was not as close as more intellectual friends like Henrietta O'Neill, Mary Hays, or Charlotte Bolingbroke. Some of her final remarks seem made only to deny any singularity or unorthodoxy in her sister, and to gloss over family disagreements as far as possible. But she is obviously accurate here. What she sees in a social context is evident in the letters and similar to what Hays most admires in *British Public Characters*, Charlotte's ability to cut off from the hostile present, or at least to distance herself in word-play or stories. She may have started doing this when Anna died.

The poems in *Conversations* are intended for memorising and recitation. They are quirky and unexpected, 'The Close of Summer' for instance catching the poetically unseasonal:

> The burning dog-star, and the insatiate mower,
> Have swept or wither'd all this floral pride;

And mullein's now, or bugloss' lingering flower,
Scarce cheer the green lane's parched and dusty side.[8]

The volume caters also for more advanced ecological interests. 'Flora' and 'Studies by the Sea' catalogue land and submarine plants and meditate on migration and currents. The prose narrative is less episodic than in her earlier children's books. Mrs Talbot is the teacher, looking back to her childhood among the Sussex beechwoods and overflowing cottage gardens. She encourages George and Emily to question blood sports and even such common pastimes as fishing and birdsnesting, and to recognise 'the inscrutable Being pervading and animating all nature.'[9] *Conversations* made about £125 and allowed her to pay debts to Frant tradesmen unsettled when she moved. It was very well reviewed, especially in the *Monthly*, and reissued in 1863, though with an anonymous introduction that imposes an orthodoxy largely absent in the book.

According to her Preface, she wrote it with a five-year-old in mind, a child who had just arrived from abroad and could speak no English, but who was particularly attracted to birds and insects, and whose teaching could begin by learning their names. Nicholas Smith had sent his daughter by his Persian lover to be educated by Charlotte, who thus introduces her to the reader as part of her family. The expense of supporting Luzena was beyond what Nicholas had any idea of, though this was perhaps because Charlotte planned on a large scale. To a modern reader sympathetic to the undoubted hardships she bore, the harrassment of duns and anxiety about tomorrow's food and coal, the constant alarms that she would end up in Horsham jail, it comes as a surprise to learn that a French governess was hired at once for Luzena. Poverty had different configurations then. Governesses of any nationality were cheap, however.

La Grande Maternité was not always to Charlotte's taste. After a few weeks in the cramped Frant house with Lucy's three, she decided no literary labour was as exhausting as small children under foot all day. She had never had to deal with that when she was young. But she was passionately fond of Luzena, whom she considered unusually intelligent. The early separation from her family and the voyage from India taken alone except for a servant must have left her mind undamaged, and Charlotte, discussing *Conversations*, did not care so much that she seemed set to finish her 'Parnassian tour', rather bathetically, 'in the respectable character of an affectionate grandmother.'[10] Nicholas, Charlotte imagined, doted on Luzena's little dark face, as she did herself. The dark complexion came not from her

Persian mother, who was fair, but from Nicholas, she added, who was quite black. It is possible that Richard or his first wife had black antecedents and that the colouring reappeared among the grand or great-grandchildren. Charlotte and Charlotte Mary shared Luzena; she was a new source of happiness to both.

The French governess proved useless, and Charlotte considered opening a school for young children, though this never happened. She was more than ever anxious to find some money for Harriet, who had met a young man she hoped to marry, William Geary. He was an ex-officer who had lost a leg in similar circumstances to Charles, and who resembled Charles in other ways too, Charlotte thought. She liked him. William was dependent on his family, who would not agree to his marriage with a woman quite unprovided for.

But she was by no means entirely absorbed in her children. 'Tis misery past compute', she wrote, parodying the playwright Richard Cumberland's otiose phrasing, 'to hear of books, & hunger & thirst after them without being able to get them.'[11] She wanted everything from Drayton's *PolyOlbion* to Jane West's new novel. She wanted the Swan's *Memoirs of the Life of Dr Darwin* especially, though when she eventually read it, she was reminded of a jackal at prey. Johnson, and Cadell and Davies who were to issue a reprint of *Elegiac Sonnets I & II* in 1806, sent what they could spare. Though she was half inclined to think of herself now among the previous generation of writers, she was working on her long topographical poem, 'Beachy Head' – which was why she wanted *PolyOlbion* – as well as some shorter pieces.

She was agreeably shocked by Sophia Lee's *The Life of a Lover*, which she thought quite risqué, especially from an unmarried author. She had known the Lee sisters for years; they kept a school in Bath and wrote plays as well as novels, sometimes jointly. She waited for the reviews with an eagerness thinly disguised as concern. To Sarah she contrasts Sophia's imagined sex scenes, ideal and sylphish, with her own real ones, which, she says, 'have been restricted to one who contrived to create only abhorrence and disgust.'[12]

Eighteenth-century women wrote about their own sex lives so seldom it may seem perverse to question this. Certainly many young women were led unsuspecting into marriages experienced as a series of rapes they could never escape or complain of. But except perhaps in Tottenham, her confidence and self-esteem make it hard to imagine Charlotte among this wretched company. Her sense of Benjamin's mental inferiority, less noticeable when she was fifteen and he was twenty-three, must soon have started to affect everything else. But perhaps there were better times that she preferred to edit out later. Benjamin seems to have had plenty of crazy charm, and men liked him too, until they lent him money. The importance she places on consensual sex in *The Old Manor House* and to a lesser extent in other novels seems incompatible with years of sexual revulsion. However, there is no way of knowing. All her comments on the marriage probably date from long after the separation and by this time she was so inveterate against Benjamin she would not have acknowledged any earlier affection.

Hayley she seldom saw, and their old friendship never revived. He was on Egremont's side in the Trust business, she thought, and she was hurt by a charge of querulous egotism, which he may have made directly or may have been something repeated back to her. She analyses herself and the way she appears to others frequently in the letters to Sarah. After thanking her for some immediate response to a request, Charlotte continues:

> There *are* moments when the bitterness of repeated disappoint-
> ments, the inconveniences of the present, and dread of the future (not
> for myself but for others) counteract every resolution I attempt to
> form to forbear complaint of every sort & not to harrass those who are
> still so good as to be interested for me, with what my *ci devant* friend
> Mr Hayley would call 'querulous egotism'. And I know not how
> wholly to refrain when I do happen to meet, as in you, with one who
> understands how difficult it is to stifle all complaint even when
> conscious of its inutility, & who has an *heart*, a thing much rarer and
> more wonderful than is generally imagined.[13]

Hayley had lost Thomas, Cowper and his estranged wife in one year; he evidently needed to make new friends. Charlotte wanted Sarah to find out if he was really to be married again, as report said. She recurs to him often, circling round the subject, reminiscing about times he had paid her compliments. Once, she said, she had considered becoming his secretary, to save his eyes; this would of course have entailed living at Eartham. But she comes no closer than that to whatever understanding they once had, and most of her comments about the Bard are mocking. She is always scathing about Blake, considering he should have been anything other than an engraver. She was far too jealous of his friendship with Hayley to acknowledge his genius.

But she was often entirely frank to Sarah about things that pained her. 'Bengal ships, though my eldest son is there, never bring me even letters', she wrote on 10 September 1804. And she reminisces often about her marriage, and the chance she had wasted:

> I sometimes think it is better for me that I did not love my husband, for if some of the children of such a Man are so dear to me as to wring my heart with anguish at this late period, what would have become of me if they had been the children of a Man such as one might have seen in ones minds eye – at eighteen, & have *par ci et par là*, had a shadowy *resemblance* of in the wilderness of the World. I think I am talking a little like our poor friend Sophia.[14]

Her letters remain vivid and rangey, conveying an extraordinarily strong sense of her presence, though Hayley's charge might be substantiated from some of them. When after a long illness Sarah's Samuel died, feeding their four boys sweets in an attempt to cheer them up while he did so, most of Charlotte's next letter – which hardly could be called a letter of condolence –is dreadful. She cannot understand Sarah's loss, and moves at once into her own woes. But then she suddenly redeems herself by a few direct and sympathetic sentences.

In the last two years she was often immobilised, only occasionally able to get into the garden in the warm weather. She was 'planted like a cabbage', as Charlotte Denzil foretold in *The Banished Man*, 'to grow white-headed'[15] – though not hard-hearted, as the sentence ends. And her mind was more active than ever. Her three servants stayed with her, though their work was demanding and their wages chancy. She needed a lot of support, suffering from pleurisy and an accelerated heartbeat that woke her in the night unable to breathe.

Unexpectedly, Benjamin predeceased her, dying on 22 February 1806, aged sixty four, while in prison for debt at Berwick-on-Tweed. *The Gentleman's Magazine* of 22 March got his first name wrong but identified him as 'husband of the justly celebrated Mrs Charlotte Smith.'[16] No softening of tone is detectable in Charlotte's comments about him afterwards. His death at last freed her £7,000 for herself and the children who most needed it. Lionel was a lieutenant-colonel now and still advancing in his profession. Though it was not one she cared for, this was a matter of pride and even of some boasting; she never forgot how abruptly it might end. The money could be divided between Lucy, Harriet and George.

Her remissions from pain were few and brief. Uterine cancer or some other severe disorder of the womb had set in earlier, perhaps as early as her letter to Hays about internal notices, certainly by 1803 when she moved to Elstead then Tilford to be near Stoke. She was bleeding, she wrote to Sarah, 'like a woman of five and twenty in perfect health',[17] but without cessation. Some pleasant trenchancies appear in her letters to the end, as well as the unflagging complaints to and about Egremont.

The manuscript of *Beachy Head, Fables, and Other Poems* was delivered to Johnson in May, though without the Preface she had promised. The poems of her last volume are much the most original, both in their ideas and technically. Beachy Head itself had multiple significances for her. It is where the Downs, the landscapes of her childhood, meet the sea. The word Beachy used to mark the end of a journey. As she describes in *Montalbert*, sailors and passengers coming up the Channel called out 'Beachy, Beachy' at the first glimpse of England. Apart from her two crossings to Dieppe, nothing is known of other voyages, but there may have been several. In *Desmond* Geraldine notes that her maid has never crossed the Channel before, while she, Charlotte's alter ego, evidently has. The American branch of Charlotte's family, descendants of her son Nicholas' legitimate daughter, even retained a legend that she and Benjamin went to India to import rare tulip bulbs, which were ruined by salt water on the way back. This does not sound likely, but then some of Charlotte's documented life does not sound likely either.

Beachy also meant death. It has been a notorious place for suicides since at least the seventh century, when St Wilfrid found the locals jumping off after a three-year drought. More to the point, the great cliff on the way to Dover is Gloucester's destination in *Lear*, a play never far from her mind. There he means to escape his suffering from the loss of a child and from his blindness. She constantly solicited Johnson's help and approval in the writing. She wanted to get to the end, and knew she would need no leading after that. Johnson, who was unwell himself and often ignored her letters earlier, gave this project more encouragement.

As in *The Emigrants*, she incorporates passages of personal reminiscence. Here too the speaker traces the growth of a poet's mind among the Sussex hills and the effects of exile in the City. As a child,

> To my light spirit, care was yet unknown
> And evil unforeseen! – Early it came
> And childhood scarcely passed, I was condemned,
> A guiltless exile, silently to sigh,
> While Memory, with faithful pencil, drew
> The contrast; and regretting, I compar'd

With the polluted smoky atmosphere
And dark and stifling streets, the southern hills.[18]

Recollection inspires an artist here, not a poet, but the analogy between drawing and poetry is the dominant metaphor of eighteenth-century criticism.

'Beachy Head' meditates on history, natural history, archæology, politics, geography and botany, on Sussex shepherds and a shepherd from literary pastoral, on fossils, shells and geology. The landscapes and seascapes are in her chiaroscuro manner, tracing effects of sun and moonlight. She defines in verse what Turner was painting, 'colours, such as Nature through her works Shows only in the ethereal canopy',[19] when the sun 'fires the clouds With blazing crimson'[20] and the early moon 'distinctly rising throws Her pearly brilliance on the trembling tide.'[21] Her friend Andrew Caldwell was among the first to recognise that 'he beat every other artist all to nothing.'[22] Turner had already exhibited seascapes at the Royal Academy, though this was before his most dazzling phase. She also observes the scientific particularity she had long been practising, and again the footnotes are part of the total effect. From the top of the cliff, the speaker can command great vistas towards London or the Isle of Wight, her far-sightedness implying the poet's moral authority and understanding of her country too. As she reflects on ancient and local histories, the fragility of successive human communities is seen against the great landmass.

She was eliminating the Miltonic and latinate qualities noticeable in *The Emigrants*; there is a catalogue of flowers, but without classical allusiveness, and the language is often that of everyday life. In another passage where the speaker looks back to childhood, for instance, only 'vagrant' is noticeably latinate. She used

> To climb the winding sheep-path, aided oft
> By scatter'd thorns: whose spiny branches bore
> Small wooly tufts, spoils of the vagrant lamb . . .
> While heavily upward mov'd the labouring wain,
> And stalking slowly by, the sturdy hind
> To ease his panting team, stopp'd with a stone
> The grating wheel.[23]

Elsewhere the manner shifts from conversational to academic to epic. Her account of Roman, Viking and Norman invasions ends with defiance of the French. The beacons on the Downs were ready to be lit again in 1806; she refutes once and for all the Jacobin charge, foretelling the inevitable battle, and incorporating the Bastard's patriotic last words from *King John*:

> But let not modern Gallia form from hence
> Presumptuous hopes, that ever thou again,
> Queen of the isles! shalt crouch to foreign arms . . .
> But thou, in thy integrity secure,
> Shalt now undaunted meet a world in arms.[24]

But her thinking could be as daring as ever. Speculation as to whether the Sussex cliffs split off from their opposite Normandy shores posits a gradual evolution of Europe's landmass rather than a once-and-for-all Creation, though she ascribes such changes to the Omnipotent. And her shells and fossils are also hot topics, attesting to an antiquity beyond Bible-based conceptions of time. The speaker asks:

> did this range of chalky mountains, once
> Form a vast bason, where the Ocean waves
> Swell'd fathomless? What time these fossil shells,
> Buoy'd on their native element, were thrown
> Among the imbedding calx: when the huge hill
> Its giant bulk heaved, and in strange ferment
> Grew up a guardian barrier, twixt the sea
> And the green level of the sylvan weald.[25]

The question is declared unanswerable, but that it is asked at all shows again the influence of Erasmus Darwin. He had made himself suspect in Lichfield by writing about plant and animal competition and the survival of the fittest. His verse implies that all species including the human may come from a common origin over millions of ages, ultimately from the sea. He even added, briefly, the motto *e conchis omnia*, everything from shells, to his coat of arms and had it painted on the side of his coach until the Swan's father, a Canon of Lichfield Cathedral, insisted he remove it. He could not afford to lose his practice, and his ideas went underground for a generation.[26] Charlotte's reflections on shells and fossils are nothing like so far developed. But as she knew and admired Darwin personally, she may have discussed the subject, his brush with the church and the attacks of the press. Writing just after his death, she wanted to perpetuate his ideas. Her speaker returns with apparent humility to the simple perspective of the peasant, which suggests indirectly that such speculation is the business of the educated.

The poem's consciousness goes out along the seaways to the

Empire and its cruel consumerism, to diamond mining and the pearl-diving of Ceylon:

> There the Earth hides within her glowing breast
> The beamy adamant, and the round pearl
> Enchased in rugged covering; which the slave,
> With perilous and breathless toil, tears off
> From the rough sea-rock, deep beneath the wave.[27]

In a note she adds, 'For the extraordinary exertions of the Indians in diving for the pearl oysters, see the account of the Pearl fisheries in Percival's *View of Ceylon*'. But it was probably to her lines rather than to Percival Keats was responding when he wrote in 'Isabella, or the Pot of Basil' of the two evil factory-owning brothers:

> For them the Ceylon diver held his breath
> And went all naked to the hungry shark,
> For them his ears gushed blood . . .[28]

It is the beginning of a massive literary reaction against industrialism. With her imaginative sympathy and long unease about Empire she strikes out lines her younger contemporaries transformed.

All but one of the shepherds in 'Beachy Head' are working men, unidealised, moving through the mist with their dogs, making a little money on the side by smuggling, staring half in envy and half in contempt as the rich pass by in their coaches. The Sussex shepherds and wedgecutters coexist with The Shepherd of the Hill, a lovelorn stranger who is the speaker of two elegiac lyrics and a survivor from a time when shepherds were more literary, though there is little eighteenth-century diction in his songs:

> And I'll contrive a sylvan room
> Against the time of summer heat,
> Where leaves, inwoven in Nature's loom,
> Shall canopy our green retreat . . .
>
> And when a sear and sallow hue
> From early frost the bower receives,
> I'll dress the sand rock cave for you,
> And strew the floor with heath and leaves,
> That you, against the autumnal air
> May find securer shelter there.[29]

But this fantasy can never come true. The 'real' and largely silent shepherds are more solid for being juxtaposed with a scholar-gipsy shepherd who speaks for Romantic interiority and loneliness. She contrasts two versions of pastoral here, both new. As Robert Mayo and others have noted, Wordsworth was less innovative than was once assumed; he and Charlotte were developing pastoral and paring down diction simultaneously.

He had continued to read her into the early years of the nineteenth century. On Christmas Eve 1802, Dorothy Wordsworth wrote in her Journal, 'Sara is in bed with the toothache, and so we are [?]. My beloved William is turning over the leaves of Charlotte Smith's sonnets but he keeps his hand to his poor chest . . .'[30] He was conscious of his debt to these sonnets and to her two blank verse meditations on the growth of a poet's mind among natural landscapes. He wanted Alexander Dyce to put her 'I love thee, mournful, sober-suited Night' into his anthology in 1827. And in a footnote to 'Stanzas Suggested in a Steamboat off St. Bees' Heads' composed on a walking tour in the summer of 1833, he adds that the form and

> something in the style of versification, are adapted from the 'St Monica', a poem of much beauty upon a monastic subject, by Charlotte Smith: a lady to whom English verse is under greater obligations than are likely to be either acknowledged or remembered. She wrote little, and that little unambitiously, but with true feeling for rural nature, at a time when nature was not much regarded by English Poets; for in point of time her earlier writings preceded, I believe, those of Cowper and Burns.[31]

Beachy Head like her *History of Birds* was published three months after her death at the beginning of February 1807, without the memoir and selection of letters Johnson hoped to receive from the family. Charlotte Mary, according to Andrew Caldwell,[32] intended to prepare these, but never did, or did not publish them. The title poem ends with a local legend the speaker remembers from her childhood about a parson called Darby who lived in a cave at the base of the cliff until he drowned.

Death by drowning is a recurrent theme in her writing, perhaps an image of the suffocation of biology, perhaps a frequent dream or escape fantasy. In *The Young Philosopher* for instance the poet Elisabeth Lisburne has committed suicide by drowning before we read her verses. Abandoned by a young man she calls Hillario, she waits a month, presumably confirming her pregnancy, in a fisherman's hut near Milford Haven hoping to hear from her lover. When he fails to return, she rows herself out to sea and drowns. Denied burial in the churchyard, she is buried by fishermen in a spot where 'beetling rocks, barren, cold, sullen, hung over a stone cave, and on all sides enclosed it, save where it opened to the sea.'[33] Like Laura's cave, this burial place is an emblematic dwelling, but representing a sterile society's hostility to the fallen woman that leaves no way out but death.

In 'Beachy Head' the legendary hermit of the cave lives on clams, listens to the weather and watches the changing colours of the sea, wading into the water on stormy nights to pull out the survivors of shipwreck or retrieve the dead for burial, until one night

> the bellowing cliffs were shook
> Even to their stony base, and fragments fell
> Flashing and thundering on the angry flood.
> At day-break, anxious for the lonely man,
> His cave the mountain shepherds visited,
> Tho' sand and banks of weeds had choak'd their way –
> He was not in it; but his drowned cor'se
> By the waves wafted, near his former home
> Receiv'd the rites of burial.[34]

Here too the outlines of the landscape are linked with human experience, though more dramatically now. The shaking cliffs suggest the shock and terror of dying, though as the body is washed out from its cave shelter, the lines that end the poem are more tranquil:

> Those who read
> Chiseld within the rock, these mournful lines,
> Memorials of his sufferings, did not grieve,
> That dying in the cause of charity
> His spirit, from its earthly bondage freed
> Had to some better region fled for ever.[35]

In his Advertisement to the volume Johnson declares that the title poem 'is not completed according to the original design',[36] the author's last illness furnishing a sufficient apology. I would guess that a short elegy or epitaph, to which 'these mournful lines, Memorials' refers, was to be added at the end. Instead the sense is that the whole poem is inscribed inside the empty cave. The life lived for a cause is over, the self-referential lines are chiselled inside a womb-like space, its opening choked with sand and weeds. The body gendered into neutrality as an old man floats out to sea and is retrieved for burial near its former home while the spirit, now free, vanishes to a better place. It is a vertiginous ending. She had five months left to add the elegy that would make it more rational, but was too ill, or simply decided the broken ending was more effective. Storm and sea, images of dysfunctional female physiology and folk legend combine to make a stoic and mysterious close. With the drive to self-presentation that had become second nature to her, she imagines and iconises her own death in this last verse-paragraph.

Some of the shorter pieces are accomplished metrically and think about Nature in new ways. In 'The Lark's Nest: a Fable from Esop', a dog eats the parent larks' eggs. They rear another brood in tremulous anxiety:

> But this took time; May was already past,
> The whitethorn had her silver blossoms cast,
> And there the Nightingale to lovely June
> Her last farewell had sung;
> No longer reigned July's intemp'rate noon,
> And high in heaven the reaper's moon
> A little crescent hung,
> Ere from their shells appeared the plumeless young
> Oh! then with how much tender care
> The busy pair
> Watch'd and provided for the panting brood![37]

This is quite unlike previous aphoristic bird fables. Her recognition of close resemblance across species is Darwinian in the sense associated with Charles' name. In her earlier poems the Linnaean and explanatory footnotes promoted, characteristically, international rather than specifically English naming and gestured towards an understanding that science would change the apprehension of Nature. But the latter concept was never clearly articulated, though one of the Augusta sonnets, 'Reflections on some drawings of plants', is interesting in its clashing models of Nature, benign and destructive. The shift away from Rousseau to encompass Darwin as philosophical base engaged more of her own experience and freed an always daring imagination. She already had the technical ability to express the new philosophy: a casual locution like 'But this took time' shows great confidence within the metrics of an Ode. She could only walk a few steps now, but from her window she could at last see her own struggle endlessly replicated in the natural world. Unlike the Romantics, she was learning how to register the cruelty and wastefulness as well as the beauty of Nature. Her voice was developing in distinctive ways.

She died five months after delivering *Beachy Head* to Johnson and was buried as she wished at St John's, Stoke-next-Guildford near Anna. George died of yellow fever six weeks earlier in Surinam, aged twenty-two, like his brother Charles on Trust business. It might be reckoned among Charlotte's few pieces of luck after her marriage that she was dead before the news reached England. The remaining children with her brother and sister had a tablet placed on the north wall of the chancel:

> Sacred to the talents and virtues of Mrs Charlotte Smith (eldest daughter of Nicholas Turner, Esq., late of Stoke Place) who terminated a life of great and various suffering on 28th October 1806. Also to the memory of Charles and George Frederic Smith, two of her sons, who met an early but honourable death in the West Indies, in the service of their country; – this tribute of gratitude and affection, of filial and fraternal love, is inscribed by the surviving family.

Though the omission of a mother's name was not unusual, it seems unlikely Charlotte had a hand in this, but somebody decided to omit Charles' second name, Dyer, and it was probably Catherine who gracefully transformed his death on Trust business into the service of his country.

Harriet married William Geary three months later, ignoring the usual period of mourning undoubtedly with her mother's blessing. At 24, she could not live alone, and a part of Charlotte's £7,000 fortune was now available for the couple. *Beachy Head* made £235; there may also have been some interim payments from the Trust in June 1807. No more is known of Lucy and her children. William and Nicholas prospered. The latter retired to Suffolk, leaving his Persian lover behind – or perhaps she was dead by now. He married happily and had a second family. Lionel's military exploits are told in the *Dictionary of National Biography* and need not be repeated here. He was knighted, and between 1833 and 1839 made Governor first of Barbados, then of Jamaica when slaves throughout the Empire were being freed. The planters tried to dodge the new law by charging rent for their ex-slaves' huts, ensuring that they still worked for nothing. Lionel's attitude to the West Indian oligarchy was not conciliatory, the *DNB* entry notes. He had absorbed his mother's reformist politics at their brightest before he left home in 1794, and set about Emancipation energetically, gaining the respect of the black population and the loathing of the whites. He was made a baronet on Victoria's Coronation, in a line that continues to the present. Charlotte Mary and her niece Luzena lived unmarried into old age.

On 22 April 1813 the Court of Chancery made the final settlement of Richard's estate. Charlotte's three remaining sons were abroad. Lionel was in any case ineligible, as was Harriet. For unknown reasons, Charlotte Mary and Lucy failed to appear in answer to the Court's summons. A little over £4,000, all that was left after thirty-

seven years of mismanagement and the lawyers' fees, went to a
retired major from Lymington, the husband of Mary Gibbs Smith
Allen, Richard's granddaughter by his elder son.

It was among the most famous eighteenth-century lawsuits.
Children had grown up and grown grey while it was debated among
learned legal jokes. Working at Doctors Commons in his teens,
Dickens would have heard the legend retold into the late 1820s. He
was to become very well read in the eighteenth-century novelists and
knew at least *The Old Manor House.* Joseph Bartolomeo shows convincing evidence of this in 'Charlotte to Charles: *The Old Manor House*
as a source for *Great Expectations*'. His England-houses derive directly from hers. *Desmond* may be one of the two sources he mentions
(the other is Carlyle) for the episode where Monseigneur in his coach
runs over a child in *A Tale of Two Cities.* In each novel an uncle and a
nephew exemplify contrasting aristocratic attitudes to the people's
rights. Dickens' interest in Charlotte's futile case with some contemporary examples of the law's asininities issued eventually as the
Jarndyce and Jarndyce suit of *Bleak House.*

Many of the places she knew have vanished or changed, though
there are continuities too. Her King Street birthplace was bombed in
the blitz. Stoke Place was demolished in the 1960s. Lys Farm, now
Brockwood, is an international school, remodelled and greatly extended but its landscapes and rare plantings probably deriving from
eighteenth century designs. Eartham too is a school. The smaller
village houses she rented have gone, but The Esplanade and Belle
Vue survive relatively unchanged from Weymouth's fashionable
1790s. Stourhead and its Claudean grounds are among the National
Trust's greatest attractions. Two family portraits have recently been
identified as Henrietta O'Neill's. They were originally listed as hers,
but the sitter's identity was lost in the nineteenth century. Perhaps
her taste for acting and opium or her association with Charlotte's
most revolutionary novel encouraged later owners to forget her
name. She stares rather dangerously back at the visitor there. Shane's
Castle burned down in the early nineteenth century with whatever
letters Charlotte wrote to her.

Woolbeding House is refaced and altered internally, and Tilford
House where she died is enlarged, though it was always the 'big
house' of Tilford. Bignor Park was rebuilt on the old site by John
Hawkins soon after he bought it, though walls and arches in the
garden may predate the present building. On a warm evening in the
late summer of 1996, an old poster in the village still invited the

neighbourhood to a fête in its grounds and the house seemed alive
with guests and cheerful au pairs getting ready to go out. Coming
back from a tour of sites I switched on the TV to find the four women
who wrecked an Aerospace Hawk destined for Indonesia acquitted
by the jury, a verdict that might have restored some of even Charlotte's faith in British justice. Only these four women could have the
right to blame her for her unsought complicity in the slave trade.

'I can say, I think truly, that it is the act of dying I fear & nothing
else, let come what will afterwards',[38] she wrote to Sarah. Her sonnets'
reiterated desire for oblivion, passages from her novels and letters
where death seems welcome, were not histrionic. She meant what
she said. At three she may have wanted to follow Anna. The immense
intellectual energy that kept her writing, the post-crisis returns to
laughter Catherine remembered, prevailed over the pull of death.
But as the pain got worse and her body gave up she could perhaps
look beyond the fearful act, as she does in 'Beachy Head', and face the
end without much regret. She had had some pleasure from authorship, from her lyre as she called it, using the ancient symbol for poetic
inspiration. She always valued her poetry highest. But she might
have considered her novels and even her children's books subsumed
into that symbol too, part of her identity as the celebrated Mrs
Charlotte Smith, part of the career that had helped to feed and house
her children and herself as long as she could hold a pen.

In retrospect it was hard to separate the strains of the life from the
strains of the lyre, to distinguish between self and self's book, in
Cowper's phrase.[39] 'In the stillness of the night, verses occur to me',[40]
she had written to Cadell and Davies in one of their battles. She was
trying to convince them she could not turn out poetry at will to suit
any occasion. Luckily, while she could still just trace the words on her
paper, verses occurred she knew would make her a suitably
gasconading, not at all awkward bow:

To My Lyre

Such as thou art, my faithful Lyre,
For all the great and wise admire,
    Believe me, I would not exchange thee
Since e'en adversity could never
Thee from my anguish'd bosom sever,
    Or time or sorrow e'er estrange thee.

Far from my native fields removed,
From all I valued, all I loved;
    By early sorrows soon beset,
Annoy'd and wearied past endurance,
With drawbacks, bottomry, insurance,
    With samples drawn, and tare and tret;

With Scrip, and Omnium, and Consols
With City Feasts and Lord Mayors' Balls,
    Scenes that to me no joy afforded;
For all the anxious Sons of Care,
From Bishopsgate to Temple Bar,
    To my young eyes seem'd gross and sordid.

Proud city dames, with loud shrill clacks,
The 'Wealth of Nations' on their backs,
    Their clumsy daughters and their nieces,
Good sort of people! and well meaners,
But they could not be my congeners,
    For I was of a different species.

Long were thy gentle accents drown'd,
Till from the Bow-bells' detested sound
I bore thee far, my darling treasure;
And unrepining left for thee
Both calepash and callipee,
    And sought green fields, pure air, and leisure.

Who that has heard thy silver tones –
Who that the Muse's influence owns,
    Can at my fond attachment wonder,
That still my heart should own thy Power?
Thou – who hast soothed each adverse hour,
    So thou and I will never sunder.

In cheerless solitude, bereft
Of youth and health, thou still art left,
    When hope and fortune have deceived me;
Thou, far unlike the summer friend,
Did still my falt'ring steps attend,
    And with thy plaintive voice relieved me.

And as the time ere long must come
When I lie silent in the tomb,
    Thou wilt preserve these mournful pages;
For gentle minds will love my verse,
And Pity shall my strains rehearse,
    And tell my name to distant ages.

Notes

INTRODUCTION

1. CS, to Joseph Cooper Walker, 9 Oct. 1793.
2. Cowper to Hayley in *Correspondence*, Vol. 4, p. 363.

1. EXILE

1. I have drawn on Geraldine's crossing the Channel in *Desmond* and on the Normandy scenes in *Emmeline* for these opening pages.
2. Page numbers for *British Public Characters*, *The Monthly Magazine* and Catherine Dorset's memoir will not be given as they are short pieces and easy to find one's way around in. This is from *British Public Characters*.
3. Sonnet 12 in *The Poems of Charlotte Smith*, p. 20. All line numbering and pagination of Smith's poems refer to this edition. There may be an allusion here to *Titus Andronicus*, III, i, 93–7.
4. Cora Kaplan, *Sea Changes: Culture and Feminism*, p. 78.
5. CS, *The Emigrants*, Book 2, in *The Poems of Charlotte Smith*, p. 160.
6. William Wordsworth, *The Prelude* (1805 version) Book 1, line 294.
7. CS, *Rural Walks*, Vol. 2, p. 104.
8. Jane Austen, *Northanger Abbey*, pp. 21–2.
9. CS, *Emmeline*, p. 209.
10. CS, *Emmeline*, p. 210.
11. CS, to Sarah Rose, 15 June 1804. CS' letters will be identified by date and name of recipient where known.
12. CS, *Emmeline*, p. 211.
13. CS, *Emmeline*, p. 212.
14. Lengths of coarse linen of a type originally made in Osnaburgh.
15. CS, *Celestina*, Vol. 2, pp. 255–6.
16. CS, *The Young Philosopher*, Vol. 2, pp. 124–5.
17. *Othello*, V, ii, lines 346–8.
18. Henry Austen's 'Biographical Notice' to *Persuasion*, ed. D. W. Harding.
19. I have been unable to trace this quotation.
20. *The Life of Mary Russell Mitford, related in a Selection from her Letters to her Friends*, ed. A. G. L. L'Estrange, Vol. 1, p. 209.
21. Quoted in James Austen-Leigh's Biographical Notice, added to Austen's *Persuasion* p. 390. Mary Russell Mitford herself is doubtful about the accuracy of her mother's memory here.

22. Hilbish, p. 83, citing a footnote to a letter by Andrew Caldwell in Nichols' *Illustrations*, Vol. 8, p. 35.
23. CS, *Celestina*, Vol. 2, p. 296.
24. CS, *Desmond*, Vol. 3, p. 166.
25. Sonnet 1, in *The Poems of Charlotte Smith*, p. 13.
26. The poems mentioned in this and the following paragraph may be found in Roger Lonsdale, ed. *Eighteenth-Century Women Poets: an Oxford Anthology*, OUP, 1989.
27. Sonnet 9, in *The Poems of Charlotte Smith*, p. 18.
28. Sonnet 11, in *The Poems of Charlotte Smith*, pp. 11-12.
29. George Crabbe, *The Borough*, 'Prisons', lines 31–2.
30. Sonnet 3, in *The Poems of Charlotte Smith*, p. 14.
31. Sonnet 2, in *The Poems of Charlotte Smith*, p. 13.
32. L'Estrange, *Life*, Vol. 3, p. 148.
33. Austen, *Persuasion*, p. 107.
34. Preface to *Elegiac Sonnets and Other Essays*.
35. Austen, *Persuasion*, p. 139.
36. Sonnet 23, in *The Poems of Charlotte Smith*, p. 28.
37. Sonnet 27, in *The Poems of Charlotte Smith*, pp. 30–1.
38. Stella Brooks, 'The Sonnets of Charlotte Smith', in *Critical Survey*, Vol. 4, 1, 1992, p. 15.
39. Thomas Gray, 'Elegy in a Country Churchyard', Epitaph.
40. Daniel E White, 'Autobiography and Elegy: the Early 'Romantic' Poetics of Thomas Gray and Charlotte Smith', a paper read at the Early Romantics Conference, Reading University, 7–8 Sept. 1995.
41. Alexander Pope, 'An Epistle to Dr Arbuthnot', line 44.
42. Richard Smith's will is reproduced in full with its codicils as an appendix to Hilbish's *Charlotte Smith: Poet and Novelist*.
43. See John Robinson's Life in *DNB*.
44. Hilbish, *Charlotte Smith: Poet and Novelist*, p. 574.
45. CS, *Emmeline*, p. 177.
46. CS, to the Earl of Egremont.
47. CS, *The Old Manor House*, pp. 348–9.
48. ibid., p. 345, footnote.
49. CS, to the Earl of Egremont, 8 Dec. 1791.
50. CS, *Ethelinde*, Vol. 5, p. 31.
51. Sonnet 31, in *The Poems of Charlotte Smith*, p. 34.
52. CS, to an unnamed recipient, 14–15 Oct. 1803.
53. Hayley, *Memoirs*, 1, p. 437.
54. *The Monthly Review*, 71, Nov. 1784, p. 368.
55. CS, *Manon Lescaut*, Vol. 1, p. 45.
56. L'Abbé Prévost, *Histoire du Chevalier des Grieux et de Manon L'Éscaut*, p. 34

2. WRITING TO LIVE

1. CS, *Montalbert*, Vol.. 2, p. 124.
2. Sonnet 32, in *The Poems of Charlotte Smith*, p. 34.
3. CS, *Manon Lescaut*, Preface, iiii.
4. Transcribed in Catherine Dorset's memoir.
5. CS, *The Romance of Real Life*, Preface, vi, Vol. 2, p. 144.
6. *ibid.*, Vol. 2, p. 144.
7. *ibid.*, Vol. 3, p. 28.
8. *ibid.*, Vol. 3, p. 67.
9. *ibid.*, Vol. 2, p. 71.
10. *ibid.*, Vol. 2, p. 96.
11. CS, to an unnamed recipient, 8 Dec. 1791.
12. CS, to Sarah Rose, c. August, 1805.
13. 'Thirty Eight', in *The Poems of Charlotte Smith*, p. 92.
14. CS, to the Earl of Egremont, 5 Nov. 1802.
15. CS frequently used this phrase, as in the letter of 22 August, 1789 quoted later in the chapter.
16. John Mullan, *Sentiment and Sociability*, p. 239.
17. CS, *The Banished Man*, Vol. 2, pp. iii–iv.
18. CS, *Emmeline*, p. 4.
19. *ibid.*, p. 37
20. *ibid.*, p. 27.
21. *ibid.*, p. 3.
22. Kate Ferguson Ellis, *The Contested Castle*, p. 92.
22. *Emmeline*, p. 19.
24. *ibid.*, p. 32.
25. Jane Spencer, *The Rise of the Woman Novelist*, p. 194.
26. Mark Madoff, 'Inside, Outside', p. 57.
27. *Emmeline*, p. 403.
28. Mary Wollstonecraft, *Works*, Vol. 7, pp. 26–7.
29. *ibid.*, p. 22.
30. Anna Seward, *Letters*, Vol. 2, p. 215.
31. *ibid.*, Vol. 2, p. 162.
32. *ibid.*, Vol. 2. p. 287.
33. Sonnet 40, in *The Poems of Charlotte Smith*, p. 39.
34. Walter Scott, *Miscellaneous Prose Works*, Vol. 4, p. 60.
35. CS, to Sarah Rose, c. August, 1805.
36. Cited by Mona Wilson, *The Life of William Blake*, p. 13.
37. Sonnet 44, in *The Poems of Charlotte Smith*, p. 42.
38. Oliver Goldsmith, *The Deserted Village*, lines 51–6.
39. *ibid.*, line 50.
40. CS, *The Emigrants* in *The Poems of Charlotte Smith*, Dedication, p. 132.
41. William Cowper, *The Task*, Book 3, lines 108–14.

42. *ibid.*, Book 5, lines 384–90.
43. *ibid.*, Book 5, lines 522–9.
44. CS, *Ethelinde*, Vol. 1, p. 56.
45. S. R. Martin, p. 276.
46. CS, *Ethelinde*, Vol. 4, pp. 268–9.
47. Scott, *Miscellaneous Prose Works*, Vol. 4, pp. 67–8.
48. 'An Unpublished Tour', in *The Prose Works of William Wordsworth*, Vol. 2, p. 308.
49. CS, *Ethelinde*, Vol. 1, p. 30.
50. *ibid.*, Vol. 1, p. 31.
51. *ibid.*, Vol. 1, p. 47.
52. *ibid.*, Vol. 1, p. 49.
53. *ibid.*, Vol. 1, p. 58.
54. Thomas Gray, *Journal*, Vol. 1, pp. 265–6.
55. *ibid.*, Vol. 1, p. 266.
56. CS, *Ethelinde*, Vol. 4, p. 263.
57. *ibid.*, Vol. 4, p. 299.
58. *ibid.*, Vol. 4, p. 250.
59. *ibid.*, Vol. 3, p. 21.
60. *ibid.*, Vol. 4, p. 31.
61. *ibid.*, Vol. 2, p. 201.
62. *ibid.*, Vol. 4, pp. 214–5.
63. *ibid.*, Vol. 2, p. 30.
64. *ibid.*, Vol. 1, p. 238.
65. *ibid.*, Vol. 5, pp. 172–3.
66. *ibid.*, Vol. 5, p. 43.
67. *ibid.*, pp. 56–7.
68. Mary Anne Schofield, *Masking and Unmasking*, p. 154.
69. *ibid.*, p. 153.
70. *ibid.*, p. 154.
71. *Ethelinde*, Vol. 5, p. 104.
72. *ibid.*, Vol. 2, p. 170.
73. Wollstoncraft, *Works*, Vol. 7, pp. 188–9.
74. CS, to Sarah Rose, 10 Sept. 1805.
75. William Hayley to Walter Scott on 15 Sept. 1811, cited by Morchard Bishop in *Blake's Hayley*, p. 65.
76. Hayley, *The Young Widow*, Vol. 1, p. 189.
77. *ibid.*, Vol. 2, p. 294.

3. GIRONDISM

1. Edmund Burke, *Reflections on the Revolution in France*, pp. 169–70.
2. James Boulton, *The Language of Politics in the Age of Wilkes and Burke*, p. 112.
3. Burke, *Reflections*, pp. 121–2.

4. *ibid.*, p. 152.
5. *ibid.*, p. 122.
6. Thomas Love Peacock, *The Misfortunes of Elphin*, p. 16.
7. CS, *Celestina*, Vol. 4, pp. 220–1.
8. *ibid.*, Vol. 1, pp. 153–4.
9. *ibid.*, Vol. 2, pp. 247–8.
10. Sonnet 49, in *The Poems of Charlotte Smith*, pp. 45–6.
11. CS, *Celestina*, Vol. 4, pp. 305–6.
12. *ibid.*, Vol. 1, p. 35.
13. *ibid.*, Vol. 1, p. 77.
14. CS, *Ethelinde*, Vol. 4, p. 6.
15. *The Critical Review*, 3 (Nov 1791): 323.
16. CS, Preface to 6th ed. *Elegiac Sonnets*, pp. 5–6 in *The Poems of Charlotte Smith*.
17. CS, Preface to *Desmond*, ii.
18. *Desmond*, Vol. 2, pp. 62–3.
19. Boulton, *The Language of Politics*, pp. 97–8.
20. Preface to *Desmond*, i.
21. Preface to *Desmond*, iii.
22. Judith Stanton, Charlotte Smith's Prose, p. 84.
23. *Desmond*, Vol. 1, p. 177.
24. Quoted in *Desmond*, Vol. 1, p.111.
25. Georg Lucacs, *The Historical Novel*, p. 15.
26. *Desmond*, Vol. 1, pp. 71–2.
27. *ibid.*, Vol. 3, p. 42.
28. *ibid.*, Vol. 1, pp. 216–8.
29. *ibid.*, Vol. 1. pp. 220–1.
30. *ibid.*, Preface, ix, quoting from memory and slightly inaccurately *Hamlet*, *III*, i, 70–1.
31. *ibid.*, Vol. 3. p. 19.
32. *ibid.*, Vol. 1. p. 169.
33. S. R. Martin, p. 329.
34. *Desmond*, Vol. 1, p. 173.
35. *ibid.*, Vol. 1, p. 176.
36. Diana Bowstead, Convention and Innovation, p. 253.
37. *Desmond*, Vol. 2, p. 67.
38. *The Critical Review*, 6 (Sept. 1792): 100.
39. Mary Wollstonecraft, *Works*, Vol. 7, p. 450.
40. Leigh Hunt, *Men, Women and Books*, p. 273.
41. see Hilbish, *Charlotte Smith, Poet and Novelist*, p. 227.
42. Hays is caricatured in Elizabeth Hamilton's novel, *Memoirs of Modern Philosophers*, published while she was writing her life of CS for *British Public Characters*.
43. Stanton, Charlotte Smith's Prose, p. 68.

44. Quoted by Morchard Bishop in *Blake's Hayley*, p. 165.
45. William Cowper, letter to Hayley of 6 April 1792 in *The Letters and Prose Writings of William Cowper*, Vol. 4, p. 51.
46. CS, to J.C. Walker, 25 March, 1794.
47. CS, *The Old Manor House*, p. 53.
48. *ibid.*, p. 248.
49. *ibid.*, p. 190.
50. Burke, *Reflections*, p. 121.
51. *The Old Manor House*, p. 17.
52. *ibid.*, p. 6.
53. *ibid.*, p. 7.
54. *ibid.*, pp. 250–1.
55. Anna Seward wrote to Eliza Hayley on 11 Jan 1789 (*Letters*, Vol. 2, p. 214): 'no intuitive strength of understanding, no possible degree of native sensibility, could have enabled [Emmeline] to acquire the 'do me the honour' language of high life, and all the punctilious etiquette of its proprieties'.
56. *The Old Manor House*, p. 230.
57. *ibid.*, p. 51.
58. *ibid.*, pp. 130–1.
59. *ibid.*, p. 360, note.
60. CS, *Ethelinde*, Vol. 4, p. 86.
61. *The Old Manor House*, p 5.
62. *ibid.*, p. 527.
63. Richard Gill, *Happy Rural Seat*, p. 239.
64. Bowstead, Convention and Innovation, p. 84.
65. *ibid.*, p. 85.
66. *ibid.*, p. 87.
67. *ibid.*, p. 83.
68. *The Old Manor House*, p. 181.
69. Gary Kelly, 'Jane Austen and the English Novel of the 1790s', p. 286.
70. *The Old Manor House*, p. 186.
71. *ibid.*, p. 186.
72. *ibid.*, p. 219.
73. *ibid.*, pp. 50–1.
74. *The Guardian*, 28 June, 1988, p. 16.
75. *The Old Manor House*, p. 14.
76. *ibid.*, p. 12.
77. *ibid.*, p. 317.
78. Bowstead, Convention and Innovation, p. 216.
79. *The Old Manor House*, pp. 41–2.
80. Anne Ehrenpreis, Introduction to *The Old Manor House*, xvii.
81. *The Old Manor House*, p. 29.
82. *ibid.*, p. 27.

83. Burke, *An Enquiry . . . into the Sublime and Beautiful*, p. 175.
85. *The Old Manor House*, p. 160.
85. M. H. Abrams, *Natural Supernaturalism*, p. 269.
87. *The Critical Review*, 8 (May 1793): 54.
87. CS, Dedication, *The Emigrants*, in *The Poems of Charlotte Smith*, p. 132.
88. *The Emigrants*, Book 1, lines 87–8.
89. *ibid.*, 1, lines 132–3.
90. *ibid.*, 1, lines 297–8.
91. *ibid.*, 2, lines 319–24.
92. *ibid.*, 2, lines 347–62.
93. George Eliot, *Collected Poems*, p. 84.
94. *The Emigrants*, Book 1, lines 155–6.
95. Dedication to *The Emigrants*, in *The Poems of Charlotte Smith*, pp. 132–4.
96. *Lear*, V, 2, 11–2.
97. William Cowper, *The Letters and Prose Writings*, Vol. 4, p. 308 (19 March 1793).
98. *ibid.*, Vol. 4, p. 371 (24 July, 1793).
99. *ibid.*, Vol. 4, pp. 411–2, (5–6 Oct. 1793).
100. *ibid.*, Vol. 4, p. 418 (26 Oct. 1793).
101. Simon Schama, *Citizens*, p. 655.

4. AN INTEREST IN GREEN LEAVES

1, *The Comedy of Errors*, II, 1, 98.
2. 'And truly, innovation has already cost this poor country so dearly (and I don't know if we have come to the end of it yet) that I have altogether ceased to support it.'
3. CS, *The Banished Man*, Vol. 1, pp. 1–2.
4. *ibid.*, Vol. 1, p. 224.
5. *ibid.*, Vol. 1, p. 150.
6. William Godwin, *Cursory Strictures*, p. 22.
7. *ibid.*, p. 40.
8. *The Banished Man*, Vol. 2, p. 231.
9. Stanton, Charlotte Smith's Prose, p. 172.
10. *ibid.*, p. 174.
11. *The Banished Man*, Vol. 4, p. 174.
12. *ibid.*, Vol. 4, p. 254.
13. *ibid.*, Vol. 4, p. 211.
14. *ibid.*, Vol. 4, pp. 254–5.
15. *ibid.*, Vol. 4, pp. 255–6.
16. *ibid.*, Vol. 4, p. 38.
17. S. R. Martin, p. 371.
18. *The Banished Man*, Vol. 3, p. 189.
19. *ibid.*, Vol. 3, p. 191, quoting *Lear*, V, iii, 307–8.

20. CS, *The Banished Man*, Vol. 3, pp. 234–5, and *The Poems of Charlotte Smith*, pp. 117–8.
21. *ibid.*, Preface, ix.
22. *The Critical Review*, 13 (March 1795): 276.
23. *The Analytical Review*, 20 (Nov. 1794): 255.
24. *The European Magazine*, 26 (Oct. 1794): 273.
25. CS, *Rural Walks*, Preface, iv.
26. Margaret Shaw, *Ideas of Women Writers*, p. 61.
27. *Rural Walks*, Vol. 2, p. 76.
28. *ibid.*, Vol. 2, p. 76.
29. *ibid.*, Vol. 2, pp. 74–5.
30. James Thomson, *The Poetical Works*, p. 17.
31. Richard Polwhele, 'The Unsex'd Females', lines 6–7, 9–10.
32. S.R. Martin, p. 55.
33. *Rural Walks*, Vol. 2, pp. 25–7.
34. Meena Alexander, *Women in Romanticism*, p. 146.
35. CS, *Rambles Farther*, Vol. 2, pp. 94–5.
36. Sonnet 68, in *The Poems of Charlotte Smith*, p. 59.
37. Stanton, *Charlotte Smith's Prose*, Preface, xi.
38. CS, *Montalbert*, Vol. 2, p. 69.
39. *ibid.*, Vol. 2, p. 116.
40. *ibid.*, Vol. 3, p. 218.
41. *ibid.*, Vol. 3, p. 310.
42. *ibid.*, Vol. 3, p. 324.
43. Patricia Meyer Spacks, *Desire and Truth*, p. 202.
44. Mary Anne Schofield, *Masking and Unmasking*, p. 9.
45. *The Analytical Review*, 22 (July 1795): 60.
46. CS, *A Narrative of the Loss of the Catharine*, p. 6.
47. *ibid.*, p. 21.
48. *ibid.*, p. 19.
49. *ibid.*, p. 34.
50. *ibid.*, p. 26.
51. Goldsmith, *The Deserted Village*, line 50.
52. CS, *Marchmont*, Vol. 2, p. 145.
53. *ibid.*, Vol. 2, p. 130.
54. *ibid.*, Vol. 2, pp. 70–1.
55. S. R. Martin, pp. 47–8.
56. *Marchmont*, Vol. 1, p. 134.
57. *ibid.*, Vol. 1, p. 178.
58. *ibid.*, Vol. 1, p. 198.
59. *ibid.*, Vol. 3, pp. 61–2.
60. *ibid.*, Vol. 4, p. 366.
61. *ibid.*, Vol. 3, pp. 154–5.

62. *ibid.*, Vol. 3, p. 159.
63. *Marchmont*, Preface, viii–ix.
64. Wollstonecraft, *Works*, Vol. 7, p. 485.
65. CS, to Cadell and Davies, 22 July, 1797.

5. THE GODDESS OF BOTANY

1. The Houyhnhnms, the talking horses in Swift's *Gulliver's Travels*, cannot say the thing that is not, ie. cannot lie.
2. 'The Dead Beggar' in *The Poems of Charlotte Smith*, p. 97.
3. Sonnet 91 in *Poems*, p. 77.
4. Sonnet 79 in *Poems*, p. 68.
5. Quoted from *Cymbeline*, IV, ii, 12–13.
6. *Lear*, IV, vii, 45–47.
7. 'The Forest Boy' in *Poems*, p. 116.
8. Preface to Vol. 2 in *Poems*, p. 9.
9. Sarah Zimmerman, 'Charlotte Smith's Letters', p. 60.
10. S. T. Coleridge in *Table-Talk*, Vol. 1, pp. 444–5.
11. CS, *The Young Philosopher*, Vol. 2, pp. 32–3.
12. ibid., Vol. 2, pp. 165–6.
13. *ibid.*, Preface, vi.
14. Robert Kiely, *The Romantic Novel in England*, p. 20.
15. Gary Kelly, 'Jane Austen and the English Novel of the 1790's', p. 287.
16. *The Young Philosopher*, Vol. 4, p. 219.
17. *ibid.*, Vol. 4, pp. 139–40.
18. *ibid.*, Vol. 4, p. 140.
19. Angela Carter, *The Sadeian Woman*, p. 46.
20. in *The Wrongs of Woman, or Maria*.
21. Bowstead, Convention and Innovation, p. 234.
22. *ibid.*, p. 234.
23. John Mullan, *Sentiment and Sociability*, p. 2.
24. *ibid.*, p. 165.
25. *The Young Philosopher*, Vol. 1, pp. 183–5.
26. Jean Hagstrum, *The Romantic Body*, p. 20.
27. *The Young Philosopher*, Vol. 1, p. 53.
28. Janet Todd, *Sensibility: an Introduction*, p. 28.
29. *The Young Philosopher*, Preface, v.
30. *ibid.*, Vol. 4, p. 166.
31. *ibid.*, Vol. 4, p. 228.
32. Wollstonecraft, *Works*, Vol. 4, p. 368.
33. William Godwin, *An Enquiry Concerning Political Justice*, pp. 144–5.
34. *The Young Philosopher*, Preface, vii.
35. Sonnet 12, in *Poems*, p. 20.
36. *The Young Philosopher*, Vol. 2, p. 139.
37. *ibid.*, Vol. 4, p. 343.

38. S. R. Martin, p. 116.

39. *The Critical Review*, 24 (Sept. 1798): 84.

40. CS, to Charlotte Mary Smith, 2 Feb. 1803.

41. See Austen's 'Catharine, or The Bower', in *Minor Works*. The elder of the Wynne sisters may have been intended for a prominent part in the story, as she helps Catharine construct her bower.

42. CS, to Joseph Cooper Walker, 23 June, 1799.

43. CS, to Egremont, 18 July, 1800.

44. CS, to Cadell and Davies, 16 Feb. 1797.

45. CS, to Cadell and Davies, 8 Oct. 1797.

46. CS, to Mary Hays, 26 July, 1800.

47. Robert Southey to Charles Danvers, in *Selections from the Letters of Robert Southey*, ed. John Wood Warter, p. 184.

48. CS, *The Letters of a Solitary Wanderer*, Vol. 2, p. 9.

49. *ibid.*, Vol. 2, p. 299.

50. *ibid.*, Vol. 3, p. 251.

51. *ibid.*, Vol. 3, p. 182.

52. *The Critical Review*, 32 (May, 1801): 35–2.

53. *The Letters of a Solitary Wanderer*, Vol. 4, Preface, viii.

54. *ibid.*, Vol. 4, Preface, v–vi.

55. *ibid.*, Vol. 4, p. 80.

56. *ibid.*, Vol. 5, pp. 135–6.

57. *ibid.*, Vol. 5, p. 244.

58. *ibid.*, Vol. 5, p. 298.

59. *ibid.*, Vol. 5, p. 72.

60. *ibid.*, Vol. 5, p. 67.

61. *The Critical Review*, 37 (Jan 1803): 54.

62. Walter Allen, *The English Novel*, p. 96.

63. *ibid.*, p. 97.

64. David Punter, *The Literature of Terror*, p. 409.

65. Lois Whitney, *Primitivism and the Idea of Progress*, p. 1.

66. R. F. Brissenden, *Virtue in Distress*, p. 21.

67. John Rae, *Life of Adam Smith*, p. 12.

68. William Leechman, Preface to Hutcheson's *A System of Moral Philosophy*, Vol. 1, xvi–xvii.

69. Leechman, *Sermons*, p. 27.

70. Laurence Sterne, *Works*, Vol. 3, p. 3.

71. *ibid.*, Vol. 3, p. 13.

72. 'Rasselas' in *Samuel Johnson*, ed. Donald Greene, p. 355.

73. R. F. Brissenden, *Virtue in Distress*, p. 52.

74. Louis Bredvold, *The Natural History of Sensibility*, p. 7.

75. In a letter quoted earlier, to Cadell Sr, 22 July, 1794.

76. CS, *Ethelinde*, Vol. 4, pp. 233–4.

77. Marilyn Butler, *Romantics, Rebels and Reactionaries*, p. 31.

6. JANE AUSTEN

1. Jane Austen, *Northanger Abbey*, p. 37.
2. William Magee, in 'The Happy Marriage', p. 120.
3. *ibid.*, pp. 125–6.
4. Diana Bowstead, Convention and Innovation, pp. 9–10.
5. *ibid.*, p. 298.
6. CS, *The Young Philosopher*, Vol. 2, pp. 188–9.
7. Austen, *Works*, Vol. 7, p. 101.
8. *ibid.*, Vol. 7, p. 183. See p. 347, note 55.
9. *ibid.*, Vol. 7, Introduction, p. 1.
10. *ibid.*, Vol. 7, p. 114.
11. Austen refers to Delamere in *Minor Works*, p. 144 and p. 147.
12. Austen, *Minor Works*, pp. 198–9.
13. The passage where Austen appears to parody Smith's Willoughby in his relation to his Uncle and Aunt Castlenorth is in *Minor Works*, pp. 169–70.
14. CS, *Celestina*, Vol. 3, pp. 250–6.
15. Austen, *Sense and Sensibility*, pp. 190–1.
16. CS, *Marchmont*, Vol. 1, pp. 294–5.
17. *ibid.*, Vol. 1, p. 306.
18. *ibid.*, Vol. 2, pp. 106–7.
19. Austen, *Pride and Prejudice*, p. 84.
20. Austen, *Emma*, p. 69.
21. *ibid.*, p. 352.
22. *ibid.*, p. 355.

7. BEACHY HEAD

1. Sir Walter Scott, 'Charlotte Smith', in *Miscellaneous Prose Works*, Vol. 4, pp. 68–9.
2. CS, to William Tyler, 7 April, 1802.
3. CS, to the Earl of Egremont, 17 Sept. 1802.
4. CS, to Egremont, 17 Feb. 1803.
5. CS, to Egremont, 5 Nov. 1802.
6. CS, to Sarah Rose, 26 April, 1806.
7. CS, to Sarah Rose, 10 Sept. 1805.
8. CS, 'The Close of Summer', in *The Poems of Charlotte Smith*, lines 13–6.
9. This quotation is not from *Conversations* but from *The Letters of a Solitary Wanderer*, Vol. 5, p. 88, but it sums up very well what CS tried to teach in her children's books.
10. CS, to Samuel Rose, 9 Feb. 1803.
11. CS, to Sarah Rose, 5 March, 1804.
12. CS, to Sarah Rose, 14 Feb. 1805.
13. CS, to Sarah Rose, 4 July, 1804. Coleridge had used the phrase of Sonneteers, including himself, in the Preface to his Poems of 1797, which

Hayley and Charlotte knew: the phrase may have had a long history between them.

14. CS, to Sarah Rose, 20 March, 1806.
15. CS, *The Banished Man*, Vol. 4, p. 220.
16. *The Gentleman's Magazine*, 76 (Mar 1806): 285.
17. CS, to Sarah Rose, 26 April, 1806.
18. CS, 'Beachy Head', in *The Poems of Charlotte Smith*, lines 285–92.
19. 'Beachy Head', lines 83–4.
20. *ibid.*, lines 94–5.
21. *ibid.*, lines 98–9.
22. Quoted in *Dictionary of National Biography* under J. M. W. Turner.
23. 'Beachy Head', lines 300–9.
24. *ibid.*, lines 143–53.
25. *ibid.*, lines 381–9.
26. See Desmond King-Hele on Erasmus Darwin in 'The Origin of the Specious' in *The Times Higher*, 11 July 1997, and his forthcoming book on E. Darwin.
27. CS, 'Beachy Head', lines 50–4 and note.
28. John Keats, 'Isabella, or The Pot of Basil', stanza 15.
29. CS, 'Beachy Head', lines 613–24.
30. Dorothy Wordsworth, in *The Grasmere Journal*, ed. Woof, p. 135.
31. William Wordsworth, *The Poetical Works*, ed. de Selincourt, Vol. 4, p. 403.
32. Andrew Caldwell quoted in John Bowyer Nichols, *Illustrations of the Literary History of the Eighteeth Century Consisting of Authentic Memoirs and Original Letters of Eminent Persons*, Vol. 8, p. 65.
33. CS, in *The Young Philosopher*, Vol. 3, p. 83.
34. CS, 'Beachy Head', lines 718–26.
35. CS, 'Beachy Head', lines 726–31.
36. Joseph Johnson in 'Advertisement' to 'Beachy Head' in *The Poems of Charlotte Smith*, p. 215.
37. CS, 'The Lark's Nest', in *The Poems of Charlotte Smith*, lines 65–75.
38. CS, to Sarah Rose, 10 Sept. 1805.
39. William Cowper, *Letters*, ed. King and Ryskamp, Vol. 1, p. 418.
40. CS, to Cadell and Davies, 20 Oct. 1797.

CS's Works in Chronological Order

1784   *Elegiac Sonnets and other Essays* (London: J. Dodsley). Published with additional poems in ten editions in CS' lifetime including subscription editions with illustrations in 1789 and 1797, the latter expanded to two volumes, the fifth and subsequent editions published first by Thomas Cadell, then by Thomas Cadell, junior and William Davies.

1785   *Manon Lescaut, or, The Fatal Attachment*, a translation of Prévost's *Manon L'Escaut*. 2 vols. (London: T. Cadell). Withdrawn.

1786   *Manon* published anonymously in one volume (London: T. Cadell).

1787   *The Romance of Real Life*, a translation of selected tales from Gayot de Pitaval's *Les Causes Célèbres*. 3 vols. (London: T. Cadell).

1788   *Emmeline, the Orphan of the Castle*. 4 vols. (London: T. Cadell).

1789   *Ethelinde, or the Recluse of the Lake*. 5 vols. (London: T. Cadell).

1791   *Celestina : a Novel*. 4 vols. (London: T. Cadell).

1792   *Desmond: a Novel*. 3 vols. (London: G.G.J. and J. Robinson).

1793   *The Old Manor House: a Novel*. 4 vols. (London: J. Bell).
       The Emigrants, a poem in two books (London: T. Cadell).
       (*D'Arcy*, sometimes attributed to CS., is clearly not her work.)

1794   *The Wanderings of Warwick*, a sequel to *The Old Manor House* (London: J. Bell).
       The Banished Man: a Novel. 4 vols. (London: T. Cadell, junior and W. Davies).

1795   *Rural Walks: in dialogues intended for the use of young persons*. 2 vols. (London: Cadell and Davies).
       Montalbert: a Novel. 3 vols. (London: Sampson Low).

1796   *Rambles Farther: a Continuation of Rural Walks, in dialogues intended for the use of young persons*. 2 vols. (London: Cadell and Davies).
       A Narrative of the loss of the Catharine, Venus and Piedmont Transports, and the Thomas, Golden Grove and Aeolus Merchant-ships near Weymouth, on Wednesday the 18th of November last. Drawn up from information taken on the spot by Charlotte Smith, and published for the Benefit of an unfortunate Survivor from one of the Wrecks, and her infant child (London: Sampson Low).
       Marchmont: a Novel. 4 vols. (London: Sampson Low).

1798   *Minor Morals, interspersed with sketches of natural history, historical anecdotes, and original stories*. 2 vols. (London: Sampson Low).
       The Young Philosopher: a Novel. 4 vols. (London: Cadell and Davies).

1799   *What Is She?* A comedy in five acts, as performed at the Theatre Royal, Covent Garden (London: Longman and Rees, published 1799).

1801   *The Letters of a Solitary Wanderer.* Volumes 1–3. (London: Sampson Low).

1802   *The Letters of a Solitary Wanderer.* Volumes 4–5. (London: Longman and Rees).

1804   *Conversations, Introducing Poetry; chiefly on subjects of natural history, for the use of children and young persons,* with an engraved portrait of Charlotte Smith, by J. Condé. 2 vols. (London: Joseph Johnson).

1806   *A History of England, from the earliest records, to the peace of Amiens in a series of letters to a young lady at school.* 3 vols. Volumes 1 and 2 by Charlotte Smith (London: Richard Phillips).

1807   *Beachy Head, Fables, and Other Poems* (London: J. Johnson).

      A Natural History of Birds, intended chiefly for young persons. 2 vols. (London: J. Johnson).

Editions of Works Cited

The Banished Man. 4 vols. 1st edition (London: Cadell and Davies, 1794).

Celestina: a Novel. 4 vols. 2nd edition (London: T. Cadell, 1791).

Conversations, Introducing Poetry: chiefly on Subjects of Natural History For the use of Children and Young Persons (London: T. Nelson and Sons, 1863).

Desmond: a Novel. 3 vols. 2nd edition (London: G. G. J. and J. Robinson, 1792).

Emmeline, the Orphan of the Castle, ed. with an introduction by Anne Henry Ehrenpreis (Oxford English Novels Series, O.U.P., 1971).

Ethelinde, or the Recluse of the Lake. 5 vols. 2nd edition (London: T. Cadell, 1790).

The Letters of a Solitary Wanderer. Vols. i–iii (London: Sampson Low, 1801).

The Letters of a Solitary Wanderer. Vols. iv and v (Microfilm of Yale University, New Haven, 1989).

Charlotte Smith's Letters, edited by Judith Stanton, are now at the University of Indiana Press, and are identified here by date and name of the recipient where known.

Manon Lescaut, or, the Fatal Attachment. (London: T. Cadell, 1786). Published without the names of CS or Prévost, 2 volumes bound as one.

Marchmont, a Novel. 4 vols. (London: Sampson Low, 1796).

Montalbert: a Novel. 3 vols. (London: Sampson Low, 1795).

A Narrative of the loss of the Catharine, Venus and Piedmont Transports, and the Thomas, Golden Grove and Aeolus Merchantships near Weymouth, on Wednesday the 18th of November last. Drawn up from information taken on the spot by Charlotte Smith, and published for the Benefit of an unfortunate Survivor from one of the Wrecks, and her infant child (London: Sampson Low, 1796).

A Natural History of Birds, intended chiefly for young persons. 1st edition (London: J. Johnson, 1807).

The Old Manor House: a Novel, ed. with an introduction by Anne Henry Ehrenpreis (Oxford English Novels Series, O.U.P., 1969).

The Poems of Charlotte Smith, ed. Stuart Curran (Women Writers in English Series. O.U.P., 1993).

Rambles Farther: a Continuation of Rural Walks. 2 vols. 2nd edition (Dublin: P. Wogan, P. Byrne et al., 1796).

The Romance of Real Life. 3 vols. (London: T. Cadell, 1787).

Rural Walks: in Dialogues intended for the use of young persons. 2 vols. 2nd edition (London: Cadell & Davies, 1795).

The Wanderings of Warwick (London: J. Bell, 1794).

What Is She? A Comedy (London: Longman and Rees, 1799).

The Young Philosopher: a Novel. 4 vols. 1st edition (London: Cadell and Davies, 1798).

Primary Sources

Akenside, Mark. *The Pleasures of the Imagination and other Poems* (London: John Walker, 1853).

Alger, John Goldworth. *Paris in 1789–1794: Farewell Letters of Victims of the Guillotine* (London: George Allen, 1902).

The Analytical Review, or History of Literature, Domestic and Foreign, 1788–1799, (Wollstonecraft's Reviews of *Emmeline, Ethelinde, Celestina* and *Marchmont* are collected in her *Works,* vol. 7).

Reviews of:

Desmond, 13 (Aug 1792): 428–5.

The Old Manor House, 16 (May 1793): 60–3.

The Banished Man, 20 (Nov. 1794): 254–5.

Montalbert, 22 (July 1795): 59–60.

A Narrative, 24 (July 1796): 102–3.

The Young Philosopher, 28 (July 1793): 73–7.

The Annual Register. Founded by J. Dodsley. Account of fighting in Susquehanna Valley (1779): 8–14.

Anthologica Hibernica (Dublin: Richard Edward Mercier, 1793) 2: 319–20 (Obituary of Henrietta O'Neill).

Austen, Jane.

Emma (1816), ed. with an introduction by Ronald Blythe (Harmondsworth: Penguin, 1966).

Lady Susan, The Watsons, Sanditon, ed. M. Drabble (Harmondsworth: Penguin, 1974).

Jane Austen's Letters, ed. Deirdre Le Faye (O.U.P. 1995).

Mansfield Park (1814), ed. Tony Tanner (Harmondsworth: Penguin, 1966).

Minor Works, ed. R. W. Chapman, vol. vi of *The Oxford Illustrated Jane Austen* (O.U.P., 1954).

Northanger Abbey (1818), ed. Anne Henry Ehrenpreis (Harmondsworth: Penguin, 1972).

Persuasion (1818), ed. D. W. Harding (Harmondsworth: Penguin, 1965).

Pride and Prejudice (1813), ed. Tony Tanner (Harmondsworth: Penguin, 1972).

Sense and Sensibility (1811), ed. Margaret Anne Doody (Harmondsworth: Penguin, 1990).

Austen, Henry. 'A Biographical Notice of the Author', in *Persuasion,* by Jane Austen, ed. with an introduction by D. W. Harding (Harmondsworth: Penguin, 1965).

Austen-Leigh, James. 'A Memoir of Jane Austen', in *Persuasion*, by Jane Austen, ed. with an introduction by D. W. Harding (Harmondsworth: Penguin, 1965): 271–372.

Bage, Robert.
Hermsprong, or Man As He is Not (1796), (London: Turnstile Press, 1951).
Man As He Is (1792), (New York: Garland, 1972).

Barbauld, Mrs Anna Laetitia (née Aikin).
Evenings at Home; or, The Juvenile Budget Opened. 2 vols. (London: Joseph Johnson, 1792).
Introduction to *The Old Manor House*, in *The British Novelists, with an Essay and Prefaces Biographical and Critical.* 50 vols., vols. 36 and 37 (London: Rivington, 1810).

Beattie, James.
Dissertations, Moral and Critical (1783), (New York: Garland, 1971).
The Poetical Works (London: William Pickering, 1853).

Beckford, William. *A Descriptive Account of the Island of Jamaica.* 2 vols. (London: T. and J. Egerton, 1790).

Blackett, M. D. *The Monitress; or the Oeconomy of Female Life* (London: n. p. 1791).

Blake, William. *The Complete Poems*, ed. Alicia Ostriker (Harmondsworth: Penguin Classics, 1977).

Bowles, William Lisle. *The Poetical Works of Bowles, Lamb and Hartley Coleridge*, ed. with an introduction by William Tirebuck (London: Walter Scott, 1887).

Breen, Jennifer, ed. *Woman Romantic Poets 1785–1832: An Anthology* (London: Dent, 1992).

British Journal of Medical Psychiatry. 'Self-mutilation', by A. Roy, 51 (1978): 201–3.

British Public Characters, ed. Richard Phillips. 'Mrs Charlotte Smith', vol. 3 (1800–01): 44–67 (Mary Hays).

Brooke, Henry. *The Fool of Quality; or, The History of Henry, Earl of Moreland.* 5 vols. (London: W. Johnston, 1767).

Brydges, Sir Samuel Egerton.
'Memoir of Mrs Charlotte Smith', in *Censura Literaria, Containing Titles, Abstracts and Opinions of Old English Books.* 10 vols. in 5. Vols. 7 & 8 (London: Longman & Co, 1815): 242–55.

Burke, Edmund.
A Philosophical Enquiry into the Origin of our Ideas of the Sublime and Beautiful (1757), ed. with an introduction by J. T. Boulton (London: Routledge and Kegan Paul, 1958).
Reflections on the Revolution in France and on the Proceedings in Certain Societies in London Relative to that Event (1790), ed. with an introduction by Conor Cruise O'Brien (Harmondsworth: Penguin, 1970).

Burney, Frances (Madame d'Arblay).
Camilla, or A Picture of Youth (1796), ed. with an introduction by

Edward A. Bloom and Lilian D. Bloom (Oxford English Novels Series, O.U.P., 1972).

Cecilia, or Memoirs of an Heiress (1782), ed. Peter Sabor and Margaret Anne Doody (World's Classics Series, O.U.P., 1989).

Evelina, or The History of a Young Lady's Entrance into the World (1778), ed. with an introduction by Edward A. Bloom and Lilian D. Bloom (World's Classics Series, O.U.P., 1968).

Selected Letters and Journals, ed. with an introduction by Joyce Hemlow (O.U.P., 1987).

Burns, Robert. *The Poems and Songs*, ed. James Kinsley (O.U.P., 1969).

Carlyle, Thomas. *The French Revolution: a History* (O.U.P., 1989).

Carter, Elizabeth. *Letters to Mrs Montagu 1755–1800*. 2 vols. (London: F. C. & J. Rivington 1808).

Cavendish, Georgiana, Duchess of Devonshire. *The Sylph* (London: T. Lowndes, 1779).

Chapone, Hester. *The Works of Mrs Chapone: containing Letters on the Improvement of the Mind Addressed to a Young Lady*. 2 vols. (London: J. Walter, 1773).

Chatterton, Thomas. *The Poetical Works*, ed. W. W. Skeat. 2 vols. (London: Aldine, 1891).

Cheyne, George. *The English Malady, or a Treatise of Nervous Diseases of all Kinds* (London: G. Strahan, 1733).

Coleridge, Samuel Taylor.
Poems, To which are added Poems by Charles Lamb and Charles Lloyd with a preface by S. T. Coleridge (Bristol: J. Cottle, 1797).
The Poetical Works of Samuel Taylor Coleridge, ed. with a biographical introduction by James Dykes Campbell (London: Macmillan, 1898).
Table-Talk. Recorded by Henry Nelson Coleridge and John Taylor Coleridge, 2 vols. (Princeton University Press, 1990).

Collins, William, Thomas Gray and Oliver Goldsmith. *The Complete Poems*, ed. Roger Lonsdale (London: Longmans, 1969).

Cowper, William.
The Complete Poetical Works, ed. H. S. Milford (O.U.P., 1907).
Correspondence, ed. Thomas Wright (London: Hodder and Stoughton, 1904).
The Letters and Prose Writings, ed. James King and Charles Ryskamp (Oxford: Clarendon Press, 1979).

Crabbe, George. *Tales, 1812 and Other Selected Poems*, ed. with an introduction by Howard Mills (O.U.P., 1967).

The Critical Review or Annals of Literature. By a Society of Gentlemen (London: A. Hamilton, 1756–1817).
Reviews of:
Emmeline, 65 (June 1788): 530–2.
Ethelinde, 3 (Second Series), (Sept 1791): 57–61.
Celestina, 3 (Nov 1791): 318–23.
Desmond, 6 (Sept 1792): 90–105.

The Old Manor House, 8 (May 1793): 44–54.
The Emigrants, 9 (Oct 1793): 299–302.
The Banished Man, 13 (March 1795): 275–8.
Montalbert, 20 (Aug 1797): 469.
The Young Philosopher, 24 (Sept 1798): 77–84.
The Letters of a Solitary Wanderer, vols. 1–3, 32 (May 1801): 35–42
vols. 4–5, 37 (Jan 1803): 54–8.
Darwin, Erasmus.
The Botanic Garden; a poem. Part I, containing the economy of vegetation. Part II. The Loves of the Plants: with philosophical notes (London: J. Johnson, 1790).
The Loves of Plants (London: J. Johnson, 1789).
A Plan for the Conduct of Female Education in Boarding Schools (London: J. Johnson, 1797).
The Temple of Nature; or, The Origin of Society: a poem with philosophical notes (London: J. Johnson 1803).
The Essential Writings of Erasmus Darwin, ed. Desmond King-Hele (London: MacGibbon and Kee, 1968).
Denham, Sir John. *The Poetical Works* (London: John Bell, 1793).
A Dictionary of National Biography, esp.
'Catherine Ann [sic] Dorset'.
'John Robinson'.
'Charlotte Turner Smith'.
'Lionel Smith'.
Dorset, Catherine Anne.
'Charlotte Smith', in Sir Walter Scott's *Miscellaneous Prose Works*, vol. 4 (Edinburgh: Cadell, 1834): 20–58.
The Peacock at Home and Other Poems (London: John Murray, 1809).
Think Before You Speak: or, The Three Wishes (Philadelphia: Johnson & Warner, 1810).
Dyce, Alexander, ed. *Specimens of British Poetesses* (London: T. Rodd, 1827).
Edgeworth, Maria.
The Absentee (1812), ed. with an introduction by W. J. McCormack and Kim Walker (World's Classics Series, O.U.P., 1988).
Belinda (1801), ed. with an introduction by Eva Figes (Mothers of the Novel Series, London: Pandora, 1987).
Castle Rackrent, Emilie de Coulanges and The Birthday Present (London: Nelson Classics, 1953).
Edwards, Bryan. *The History, Civil and Commercial, of the British Colonies in the West Indies*. 3 vols., 1793–1801 (Abridged. London: B. Crosby, 1798).
Eliot, George (Mary Ann Evans).
Collected Poems, ed. Lucien Jenkins (London: Skobl Books, 1989).
Middlemarch (1870), ed. David Carroll (Oxford: The Clarendon Press, 1986).
The European Magazine and London Review (London: James Asperne, 1782–1826).
Reviews of:
Emmeline, 14 (Nov 1788): 348–9.

Ethelinde, 17 (April 1790): 270.
Celestina, 20 (Oct 1791): 278.
Desmond, 20 (July 1792): 22–3.
The Emigrants, 24 (July 1793): 41.
The Banished Man, 26 (Oct 1794): 273–7.
Obituary: 50 (Nov 1806): 339–41.

Fenwick, Eliza.
The Fate of the Fenwicks; Letters, 1798–1823 (Mainly from E. F. to Mary Hays) ed. A. F. Wedd (London: Methuen, 1927).
Secrecy, or, the Ruin on the Rock (1795), ed. with an Introduction by Isobel Grundy (Ontario: The Broadview Press, 1994).

Ferrier, Susan Edmonstone
Marriage (1814), (London: J.M. Dent, 1928).
Memoir and Correspondence of Susan Ferrier, ed. John A. Doyle (London: John Murray, 1898).

Fielding, Henry. *The History of Tom Jones* (1749), ed. with an introduction by R. P. C. Mutter (Harmondsworth: Penguin, 1966).

Fordyce, Rev. James.
The Character and Conduct of the Female Sex (London: T. Cadell, 1776).
Sermons to Young Women. 2 vols. (London: A. Millar & T. Cadell, 1765).

The Gentleman's Magazine, 18 (March 1806): 285.

Gilpin, William. *Observations relative chiefly to Picturesque Beauty, Made in the Year 1772, On Several Parts of England, particularly the Mountains and Lakes of Cumberland and Westmorland* (London: R. Blamire, 1786).

Gisborne, Thomas. *An Enquiry into the Duties of the Female Sex* (London: Cadell and Davies, 1797).

Gissing, George.
New Grub Street (1891), ed. with an introduction by Bernard Bergonzi (Harmondsworth: Penguin, 1985).
The Odd Women (1893), ed. with an introduction by Margaret Walters (London: Virago Modern Classics, 1982).

Godwin, William.
Cursory Strictures on the Charge Delivered by Lord Chief Justice Eyre to the Grand Jury, on Oct 2, 1794 (London: D. I. Eaton, 1794).
An Inquiry Concerning Political Justice and its Influence on Modern Morals and Happiness (1793), ed. Isaac Kramnick (Pelican Classics Series, Harmondsworth: Penguin, 1976).
Memoirs of the Author of 'A Vindication of the Rights of Woman' (1798), ed. W.C. Durant (London: Constable and Co. 1927).
'Of Choice in Reading', in *The Enquirer. Reflections on Education, Manners and Literature* (London: G.G. & J. Robinson, 1797): 129–46.
St. Leon: A Tale of the Sixteenth Century. 4 vols. (London: G.G. & J. Robinson, 1799).
Things As They Are: or The Adventures of Caleb Williams (1794), ed. with an introduction by Maurice Hindle (Harmondsworth: Penguin, 1988).

Goethe, Johann Wolfgang von. *The Sorrows of Young Werther*, translated by William Rose (London: The Scholartis Press, 1929).

Goldsmith, Oliver. *Selected Writings,* ed. with an introduction by John Lucas (London: Carcanet, 1988).

Gray, Thomas. 'Journal in the Lakes, 1769' in *The Works of Thomas Gray in Prose and Verse,* ed. Edmund Gosse. 4 vols. (London: Macmillan & Co., 1884), vol. 1, 249–81.

Gray, Thomas, William Collins and Oliver Goldsmith. *The Complete Poems,* ed. Roger Lonsdale (London: Longman, 1969).

Gregory, John. *A Father's Legacy to his Daughters* (London: W. Strahan, T. Cadell and J. Balfour, 1774).

Hamilton, Elizabeth. *Memoirs of Modern Philosophers.* 3 vols. (London: G. G. & J. Robinson, 1800).

Hanson, Michele. 'Letting Out the Big Scream Inside', in *The Guardian* (Tuesday, 28 June, 1988): 16.

Hawkins, John. *I Am, My Dear Sir,* a selection of letters written to and by John Hawkins, ed. with an introduction by Francis W. Steer (W. Sussex County Council, 1959).

Hayley, William.
The Life and Posthumous Writings of William Cowper (Chichester: J. Johnson, 1803).
Memoirs of the Life and Writings of William Hayley, Esq., the Friend and Biographer of Cowper, written by himself, ed. John Johnson (London: Henry Colburn & Co., 1823).
A Philosophical, Historical and Moral Essay on Old Maids by a Friend to the Sisterhood. 3 vols. (London: T. Cadell, 1785).
The Young Widow, or the History of Cornelia Sedley in a Series of Letters (Dublin: L. White, 1789).

Hays, Mary.
Female Biography, or Memoirs of Illustrious and Celebrated Women. 6 vols. (London: R. Phillips, 1803).
Letters and Essays, Moral and Miscellaneous (New York: Garland, 1974).
The Love Letters of Mary Hays, 1779–1780, ed. A. F. Wedd (London: Methuen, 1925).
The Memoirs of Emma Courtney (1796), ed. with an introduction by Sally Cline (London: Pandora Press, 1987).
The Victim of Prejudice (1799) 2 vols., ed. with an introduction by Eleanor Ty (London: Broadview Press Ltd, 1994)).
'Mrs Charlotte Smith,' in *British Public Characters,* 1800–01, ed. Richard Phillips. Vol. 3: 44–67.

Haywood, Eliza. *The History of Miss Betsy Thoughtless* (1751), ed. with an introduction by Dale Spender (London: Pandora Press, 1986).

Holcroft, Thomas. *Anna St. Ives: A Novel* (1792), ed. with an introduction by Peter Faulkner (Oxford English Novels, O.U.P., 1970).

Household, Geoffrey. *Rogue Male* (London: Chatto and Windus, 1939).

Hume, David. *The History of England.* 8 vols. (London: A. Millar, 1754–63).

Hunt, Leigh.
Men, Women and Books (London: Smith, Elder & Co., 1876).
One Hundred Romances of Real Life (London: Simkin & Co, n.d.)

Inchbald, Elizabeth,
 ed. *The Modern Theatre; a Collection of Successful Modern Plays ...
printed from the prompt books, with biographical and critical remarks by
Mrs Inchbald*. 25 vols. (London: Longman et al, 1808–16) *What Is She?*,
vol. 10, no. 4. 1811.
 Nature and Art. 2 vols. (London: G. G. and J. Robinson, 1796).
 A Simple Story (1791), ed. J. M. S. Tompkins with an introduction by
Jane Spencer (World's Classics Series, O.U.P., 1988).

Ishiguro, Kazuo. *The Remains of the Day* (London: Faber and Faber, 1989).

Johnson, Samuel. *Works*, ed. Donald Greene (Oxford Authors Series, O.U.P.,
1990).

Keats, John. *The Complete Poems*, ed. with an introduction by John Barnard
(Harmondsworth: Penguin Classics, 1973).

Laclos, Choderlos de. *Les Liaisons Dangereuses* (1782), translated with an
introduction by P. W. K. Stone (Harmondsworth: Penguin, 1961).

The Lady's Monthly Museum, 'Mrs Charlotte Smith', 2 (May 1799): 336-41.

Lawrence, D. H. *Lady Chatterley's Lover* (Harmondsworth: Penguin, 1960).

Lee, Sophia. *The Life of a Lover in a Series of Letters*. 6 vols. (London: G. and J.
Robinson, 1804).

Leechman, William.
 'Preface', in Francis Hutcheson's *A System of Moral Philosophy*
(London: A. Millar and J. Longman, 1755).
 Sermons (Edinburgh: Balfour, Auld and Smellie, 1768).

Lennox, Charlotte. *The Female Quixote, or the Adventures of Arabella* (1752),
(Oxford English Novels Series, O.U.P., 1970).

Lewis, M. G. *The Monk* (1796), ed. with an introduction by John Berryman
(New York: The Grove Press, 1957).

Lightfoot, James. *Flora Scotica, or, A Systematic Arrangement, in the Linnaean
Method, of the Native Plants of Scotland and the Hebrides* (London:
J. Dickson et al., 1792).

Lloyd, Charles. *Edmund Oliver* (Bristol: J. Cottle, 1798).

Lonsdale, Roger, ed. *Eighteenth Century Women Poets: an Oxford Anthology*
(O.U.P, 1989).

Mackenzie, Henry.
 Julia de Roubigné, A Tale. In a Series of Letters. 2 vols. (London:
W. Strahan and T. Cadell, 1777).
 The Man of Feeling (1771), ed. with an introduction by Brian Vickers
(World's Classics Series, O.U.P., 1987).

Mackintosh, Sir James. *Memoirs of the Life of the Right Honourable James
Mackintosh*, ed. R. J. Mackintosh (Boston: Little, Brown & Co., 1853).

Macpherson, James. *The Poems of Ossian translated by James Macpherson*
(Edinburgh: John Grant, 1926).

Mathias, Thomas. *The Pursuits of Literature, or What You Will: a Satirical Poem*
(London: J. Owen, 1794).

Menninger, K. A. 'A Psychoanalytic Study of the Significance of Self-
Mutilation,' in *Psychoanalytic Quarterly*, 4 (1935): 408-66.

Milton, John. *Areopagitica,* in vol. 2, *The Complete Prose Works of John Milton* (New Haven: Yale Univ. Press, 1959).

Mitford, Mary Russell. *The Life of Mary Russell Mitford, Related in a Selection from her Letters to her Friends,* ed. A.G. L'Estrange. 3 vols. (London: Richard Bentley, 1870).

The Monthly Magazine or British Register (London: Richard Phillips, 1776–1826).
Obituary, 23 (New Series), (April 1807): 244–8.

The Monthly Review, or Literary Journal by Several Hands (London: R. Griffiths, 1749–1825).
Reviews of:
Elegiac Sonnets, 71 (Nov 1784): 368–369.
Manon Lescaut, 75 (Oct 1786): 315–6.
Emmeline, 79 (Sept 1788): 241–4.
Ethelinde, 2 (New Series), (May 1790): 161-5 (?Mrs Barbauld).
Celestina, 6 (Nov 1791): 286–91.
Desmond, 9 (Dec 1792): 406–13.
*The Old Manor House,*11 (May 1793): 150–3.
*The Emigrants,*12 (Dec 1793): 375–6.
The Young Philosopher, 28 (March 1799): 346–7.

Moore, Dr John.
The French Revolution: Moore's Residence in France. 2 vols. (London: G. G. & J. Robinson, 1793).
Zeluco: Various Views of Human Nature Taken from Life and Manners, Foreign and Domestic. 2 vols. (London: A. Strachan and T. Cadell, 1789).

More, Hannah.
Coelebs in Search of a Wife, comprehending observations on domestic habits and manners, religion and morals. 2 vols. (London: Cadell and Davies, 1809).
Strictures on the Modern System of Female Education. 2 vols. (London: Cadell & Davies, 1799).

Morrison, Toni. *Beloved* (London: Chatto & Windus, 1987).

Nichols, John Bowyer. *Illustrations of the Literary History of the Eighteenth Century: Consisting of Authentic Memoirs and Original Letters of Eminent Persons.* 8 vols. (London: J. B. Nichols and Son, 1831).

Opie, Amelia. *Adeline Mowbray, or, The Mother and Daughter: a Tale.* 3 vols. (London: 1805).

Ossian (James Macpherson). *The Poems of Ossian translated by James Macpherson* (Edinburgh: John Grant, 1926).

Otway, Thomas. *The Orphan* (1680), in *The Works of Thomas Otway.* 2 vols, ed. by J. C. Ghosh (Oxford: The Clarendon Press, 1932).

The Oxford Companion to English Literature ed. Margaret Drabble (O.U.P., 1985).

Paine, Thomas. *The Rights of Man* (1791), ed. with an introduction by Eric Foner (London: Penguin Classics, 1985).

Peacock, Thomas Love. *The Misfortunes of Elphin* and *Crotchet Castle*, vol. 4 of *The Works of Thomas Love Peacock*, ed. H. F. B. Brett-Smith and C. E. Jones (London: Constable & Co., 1924).

Percival, Robert. *An Account of the Island of Ceylon; . . . to which is added, the Journal of an Embassage to the Court of Candy* (London: C. and R. Baldwin, 1803).

Pitaval, Gayot de, *Causes Célèbres et Intéressantes avec les Jugements qui les ont Décidés*. 13 vols. (La Haye, 1735–9).

Polwhele, Richard. *The Unsex'd Females: a Poem Addressed to the Author of* 'The Pursuits of Literature' (London: Cadell and Davies, 1798).

Pope, Alexander. *The Poems of Alexander Pope*, ed. John Butt (New Haven: Yale Univ. Press, 1963).

Prévost d'Exiles, L'Abbé Antoine-François. *Histoire du Chevalier des Grieux et de Manon L'Escaut*, ed. Henri Coulet (Paris: Garnier-Flammarion, 1967).

Pye, Henry James.
The Spectre (London: John Stockdale, 1789).
'Faringdon Hill: a Poem' in *Poems*, ed. Anna Laetitia Aikin [Barbauld], (London: Joseph Johnson, 1773).

Radcliffe, Ann.
The Italian, or, The Confessional of the Black Penitents (1797), (O.U.P., 1968).
The Mysteries of Udolpho (1794), ed. with an introduction by Bonamy Dobrée (World's Classics Series, O.U.P., 1966).
The Romance of the Forest (London: Hookham and Carpenter, 1791).
A Sicilian Romance (1790), (Oxford: Woodstock Books, 1996).

Rae, John. *Life of Adam Smith* (London: Macmillan & Co, 1895).

Reeve, Clara. *The Old English Baron: A Gothic Story* (London: Edward and Charles Dilly, 1778).

Richards, George. 'Bamborough Castle' in *Poems*. 2 vols. (London: Cadell & Davies, 1804).

Richardson, Samuel.
Clarissa: or the History of a Young Lady (1747–8), ed. with an introduction by Angus Ross (London: Penguin, 1985).
Pamela, or Virtue Rewarded (1740) 2 vols., ed. with an introduction by M. Kinkead-Weekes (Everyman's Library, London: J. M. Dent, 1986).
Sir Charles Grandison (1753–4), ed. with an introduction by Jocelyn Harris (World's Classics Series. O.U.P., 1986).

Robinson, Mary Darby. *Vancenza; or, The Dangers of Credulity*. 2 vols. (London: Bell's British Library, 1792).

Roche, Regina Maria Dalton.
The Children of the Abbey (1798). 4 vols. (London: William Lane, The Minerva Press, 1797).

Rousseau, Jean-Jacques.
The Social Contract: an Inquiry into the Nature of the Social Contract, or Principles of Political Right (London: 1791).

The Confessions (1781–8), (Everyman's Library, London: Dent and Dutton, 1955).

Emile, or Education (1762), (Everyman's Library, London: Dent and Dutton, 1955).

Emilius and Sophia: or, New System of Education. Tranlated by W. Kenrick. 4 vols. (London: 1767).

Julie: or the New Eloisa. A Series of Original Letters, Collected and Published by Jean-Jacques Rousseau (1761). Translated from the French. 3 vols. (Edinburgh: J. Bell, J. Dickson and C. Elliott, 1773).

Savile, George, Marquis of Halifax. 'The Lady's New Year's Gift' (1688), in *The Complete Works*, ed. Walter Raleigh (O.U.P., 1912).

Scott, Sir Walter.
The Antiquary (1816), (Everyman's Library, London: Dent and Dutton, 1955).
'Charlotte Smith', in *Miscellaneous Prose Works*. Vol. 4 (Edinburgh: Cadell, 1834) : 58–70.
Waverley (1814), ed. with an introduction by Andrew Hook (Harmondsworth: Penguin, 1972).

Seward, Anna.
Letters of Anna Seward, written between the years 1784 and 1807. 6 vols. (London: Longman, Hunt and Rees, 1811).
Original Sonnets on Various Subjects, and Odes Paraphrased from Horace (London, G. Seal, 1799).
Memoirs of the Life of Dr Darwin (London: J. Johnson, 1804).

Shakespeare, William. *The Complete Works* (Riverside Edition).

Shelley, Percy Bysshe. *Selected Poetry and Prose*, ed. with an introduction by Kenneth Neill Cameron (Chicago: Holt, Rinehart and Wiston, 1957).

Sheridan, Frances. *The Memoirs of Miss Sidney Bidulph* (1761), (London: Pandora Press, 1982).

Smith, David Nichol, ed. *The Oxford Book of Eighteenth Century Verse* (Oxford: The Clarendon Press, 1926).

Smith, James Edward, MD. *Memoir and Correspondence*, ed. Lady Pleasance Smith (London: Longman, 1832).

Smollet, Tobias. *The Adventures of Ferdinand, Count Fathom* (1753), ed. with an introduction by Paul-Gabriel Boucé (London: Penguin, 1990).

Southey, Robert. *Selections from the Letters*, ed. John Wood Warter, 2 vols. (London: Longman et al., 1856).

Steevens, George ('Scourge'), quoted by Catherine Dorset in Sir Walter Scott's *Miscellaneous Prose Works*.

Sterne, Lawrence. *Works*. 4 vols. (London: J. Johnson, 1880).

Thackeray, William Makepeace. *Vanity Fair: a Novel Without a Hero* (1847), ed. with an introduction by John Sutherland (World's Classics Series, O.U.P., 1983).

Thomson, James. *The Poetical Works*, ed. Rev. George Gilfillan (Edinburgh: James Nichol, 1853).

Thompson, E. P. *Whigs and Hunters* (London: Allen Lane, 1975).

Turner, Thomas. *The Diary of Thomas Turner of East Hoathly (1754–65)*, ed. Florence Maris Turner (London, 1925).

Voltaire (François Marie Arouet). *Candide and Other Stories* (1759), translated with an introduction by Roger Pearson (World's Classics Series, O.U.P., 1990).

Walpole, Horace.
The Castle of Otranto (1765), in *Shorter Novels of the Eighteenth Century* (Everyman's Library, London: Dent and Dutton, 1967).
The Letters of Horace Walpole, Earl of Oxford, ed. Mrs Paget Toynbee (O.U.P, 1903).

Warton, Thomas *The Poetical Works of Goldsmith, Collins and T. Warton: with Lives, Critical Dissertations and Explanatory Notes* (London: J. Nichol, 1854).

West, Jane. *A Gossip's Story* (London: T. N. Longman, 1796).

Willliams, Helen Maria.
Julia: a Novel (1790), (London: Routledge, 1995).
Letters From France, ed. with an Introduction by Janet Todd (London: Scholars' Facsimiles and Reprints, 1975).
A Farewell for Two Years to England; A Poem (London: J. Johnson, 1791).

Wollstonecraft, Mary. *Works*, ed. Janet Todd and Marilyn Butler, Assistant Editor Emma Rees-Mogg. 7 vols. (London: William Pickering, 1989).

Wood, Mrs Henry. *East Lynne* (1861), ed. with an introduction by Stevie Davies (London: J. M. Dent, 1988).

Wordsworth, Dorothy. *The Grasmere Journals*, ed. Pamela Woof (O.U.P., 1991).

Wordsworth, William.
The Poetical Works, ed. Ernest de Selincourt and Helen Darbishire. 5 vols. (O.U.P., 1959).
The Prose Works of William Wordsworth, ed. W. J. B. Owen and J. W. Smyser. 3 vols. (Oxford: The Clarendon Press, 1974).

Yearsley, Ann. *Poems on Various Subjects* (1787), (Oxford: Woodstock Books, 1994).

Young, Edward. *The Complaint: or, Night Thoughts on Life, Death and Immortality*, ed. Rev. George Gilfillan (Edinburgh: James Nichol, 1853).

Secondary Sources

Abrams, Meyer Howard. *Natural Supernaturalism: Tradition and Revolution in Romantic Literature* (New York: W. W. Norton & Co., 1971).

Adams, M. Ray. *Studies in the Literary Backgrounds of English Radicalism with Special Reference to the French Revolution* (Pennsylvania College Press, 1947).

Alexander, Meena. *Women in Romanticism: Mary Wollstonecraft, Dorothy Wordsworth and Mary Shelley* (Women Writers Series, London: Macmillan, 1989).

Allen, Walter. *The English Novel : A Short Critical History* (London: Dutton and Co., 1954).

Alter, Robert. *Partial Magic: the Novel as a Self-Conscious Genre* (Berkeley: Univ. of California Press,1975).

Altick, Richard. *The English Common Reader: A Social History of the Mass Reading Public* (Univ. of Chicago Press, 1953).

Altieri, Joanne. 'Style and Purpose in Maria Edgeworth's Fiction', in *Nineteenth Century Fiction*, 23 (Dec1968): 265–78.

Armstrong, Nancy. *Desire and Domestic Fiction: a Political History of the Novel* (O.U.P., 1987).

Auerbach, Nina. *Communities of Women: An Idea in Fiction* (Cambridge: Harvard Univ. Press, 1978).

Backscheider, Paula, Felicity Nussbaum, and Philip Anderson. *An Annotated Bibliography of Twentieth-Century Critical Studies of Women and Literature, 1660–1800* (New York: Garland, 1977).

Baine, Rodney. *Thomas Holcroft and the Revolutionary Novel* (Athens, Georgia: Univ. of Georgia Press, 1965).

Baker, Ernest A. *The History of the English Novel*, vol. 5, *The Novel of Sentiment and the Gothic Romance* (London: H. F. and G. Witherby, 1934).

Banfield, Ann. 'The Influence of Place: Jane Austen and the Novel of Social Consciousness', in *Jane Austen in a Social Context*, ed. David Monaghan (London: Macmillan, 1981): 28–48.

Barrell, John. Review of Anne Janowitz's *England's Ruins: Poetic Purpose and the Natural Landscape* (*T.L.S.*, (28 Sept 1990): 1043.

Bartlett, Andrew Hollis. Birth Secrets: Violence and Inheritance in Four Eighteenth Century Novels. Ph.D. Thesis. York Univ., 1996.

Bartolomeo, Joseph F. 'Charlotte to Charles: *The Old Manor House* as a source for *Great Expectations*', in *Dickens Quarterly*, vol. 8, no. 3 (Sept. 1991): 112–20.

Bate, Walter Jackson.
  The Stylistic Development of Keats (London: Routledge and Kegan Paul, 1958)
  'The Subversion of Romance in *The Old Manor House*', in *Studies in English Literature, 1500–1900*, 33, 3 (Summer 1993): 645–57.

Battestin, Martin C. *The Providence of Wit: Aspects of Form in Augustan Literature and the Arts* (Oxford: The Clarendon Press, 1974).

Beer, Gillian. 'Our Unnatural No-Voice: the Heroic Epistle, Pope and Women's Gothic', in Leopold Damrorsch, ed. *Modern Essays in Eighteenth Century Literature* (O.U.P., 1988).

Beers, Henry A. *A History of English Romanticism in the Eighteenth Century* (New York: Henry Holt & Co., 1899).

Bender, John.
  Imagining the Penitentiary: Fiction and the Architecture of the Mind in Eighteenth Century England (Chicago: Univ. of Chicago Press, 1987).
  Review of J. David Grey, ed. *Jane Austen's Beginnings: The Juvenilia and Lady Susan*, in *T.L.S.*, 10th August 1990.

Benkowitz, Miriam. 'Some Observations on Woman's Concept of Self in the Eighteenth Century', in *Women in the Eighteenth Century and Other Essays*, ed. Paul Fritz and Richard Morton (Toronto: Hakkert, 1975): 37–54.

Berryman, John.
  Introduction to *The Monk* by M.G. Lewis (New York: The Grove Press, 1957).
  The Tale of Terror: a Study of the Gothic Romance (London, Constable & Co., 1921).

Birkhead, Edith. 'Sentiment and Sensibility in the Eighteenth Century Novel', in *Essays and Studies by Members of the English Association*, 11 (1925): 92–116.

Birley, Robert. *The English Jacobins from 1789–1802* (O.U.P., 1924).

Bishop, Morchard. *Blake's Hayley: The Life, Works and Friendships of William Hayley* (London: Victor Gollancz, 1951).

Bissell, Benjamin. *The American Indian in English Literature of the Eighteenth Century* (New Haven: Yale Univ. Press, 1925).

Blackburn, Robin. *The Making of New World Slavery: From the Baroque to the Modern, 1492–1800* (London: Verso, 1997).

Bloom, Harold. *The Anxiety of Influence: A Theory of Poetry* (O.U.P., 1973).

Bogel, Frederick V. 'Structure and Substantiality in Later Eighteeenth Century Literature', in *Studies in Burke and his Time*, 15, 2, no. 49 (Winter 1972–3): 143–154.

Boulton, James T. *The Language of Politics in the Age of Wilkes and Burke* (London: Routledge and Kegan Paul, 1963).

Bowstead, Diana.
  'Charlotte Smith's *Desmond*: The Epistolary Novel as Ideological Argument', in *Fetter'd or Free? British Women Novelists, 1670–1815*, ed. Mary Anne Schofield and Cecilia Macheski (Athens, Ohio: Ohio Univ. Press, 1986): 237–263.

Convention and Innovation in Charlotte Smith's Novels. Ph.D Thesis. City Univ. of New York, 1978.

Bradbrook, Frank W. *Jane Austen and her Predecessors* (O.U.P., 1966).

Brailsford, Henry N. *Shelley, Godwin and Their Circle* (O.U.P., 1951).

Braudy, Leo. 'The Form of the Sentimental Novel', in *Novel*, 7 (1973): 5–13.

Bray, Matthew.
Sensibility & Social Change: Charlotte Smith, Helen Williams and the Limits of Romanticism. Ph.D. Thesis. Univ. of Maryland, 1994.
'Removing the Anglo-Saxon Yoke: the Francocentric Vision of Charlotte Smith's Later Works', in *The Wordsworth Circle*, 24, 3 (Summer 1995): 155–8.

Bredvold, Louis I. *The Natural History of Sensibility* (Detroit: Wayne State Univ. Press, 1962).

Brewer, John. *The Pleasures of the Imagination: English Culture in the Eighteenth Century* (London, Harper Collins, 1997).

Brissenden, Robert Francis. *Virtue in Distress: Studies in the Novel of Sentiment from Richardson to Sade* (London: Macmillan, 1974).

Brody, Miriam. 'Mary Wollstonecraft: Sexuality and Women's Rights', in Dale Spender, ed. *Feminist Theorists* (London: The Women's Press, 1983): 40–59.

Brooks, Peter. *The Novel of Worldliness: Crébillon, Marivaux, Laclos, Stendhal* (New Jersey: Princeton Univ. Press, 1969).

Brooks, Stella. 'The Sonnets of Charlotte Smith', in *Critical Survey*, vol. 4, 1 (1992): 9–21.

Brown, Laura. *Ends of Empire: Women and Ideology in Early Eighteenth-Century Literature* (Cornell Univ. Press, 1993).

Brown, Marshall. *Pre-Romanticism* (Stanford Univ. Press, 1991).

Brownstein, Rachel M. *Becoming a Heroine: Reading About Women in Novels* (New York: The Viking Press, 1982).

Bushnell, Nelson S. 'Artistic Economy in *Jane Eyre*: a Contrast with *The Old Manor House*,' in *English Language Notes*, 5 (1967–8): 197–202.

Butler, Maida. 'Mrs Smith and Mr Cadell', in *The Sussex County Magazine*, 30 (1956): 330–4.

Butler, Marilyn,
ed. *Burke, Paine, Godwin and the Revolution Controversy* (C.U.P., 1984).
'Introduction', in R.W. Chapman, ed. *Jane Austen: Selected Letters* (O.U.P., 1985): ix–xxvii.
Jane Austen and the War of Ideas (Oxford: The Clarendon Press, 1975).
Romantics, Rebels and Reactionaries: English Literature and its Background, 1760–1830 (O.U.P., 1981).

Bygrave, Stephen. *Coleridge and the Self: Romantic Egotism* (London: Macmillan, 1986).

Byrd, Max. 'The Madhouse, the Whorehouse and the Convent', in *Partisan Review*, 44 (1977): 268–78.

Carter, Angela. *The Sadeian Woman: an exercise in cultural history* (London: Virago Press, 1979).

Cary, Meredith. *Different Drummers: A Study of Cultural Alternatives in Fiction* (London: Scarecrow Press, 1984).

Castle, Terry.
Introduction to *Northanger Abbey, Lady Susan, The Watsons and Sanditon* (World's Classics Series, O.U.P, 1990).
Masquerade and Civilization: The Carnivalesque in Eighteenth Century English Culture and Fiction (Stanford Univ. Press, 1986).

Chew, Samuel C. 'The Nineteenth Century and After (1789–1939)', in *A Literary History of England*, ed. Albert C. Baugh (New York: Appleton-Century-Crofts,1967).

Chodorow, Nancy. *The Reproduction of Mothering* (Berkeley: Univ. of California Press, 1978).

Christ, Carol P. *Diving Deep and Surfacing* (Boston: The Beacon Press, 1980).

Christiansen, Rupert. *Romantic Affinities: Portraits from An Age, 1780–1830* (London: Penguin Sphere Books, 1988).

Christie, Ian R. *Wars and Revolutions: Britain 1760–1815* (New History of England Series, London: Edward Arnold, 1982).

Colby, Vineta. *Yesterday's Women: Domestic Realism in the English Novel* (New Jersey: Princeton Univ. Press, 1974).

Conway, Alison. 'Nationalism, Revolution and the Female Body: Charlotte Smith's *Desmond*', in *Women's Studies: An Interdisciplinary Journal*, 24, 5 (1995): 395–409.

Copeland, Edward.
'What's a Competence? Jane Austen, her Sister Novelists and the 5%s', in *Modern Language Studies*, 9 (1979): 161–68.
Women Writing about Money: Women's Fiction in England, 1790–1820 (C.U.P., 1995)

Cross, Wilbur L. *The Development of the English Novel* (London: Macmillan, 1899).

Curran, Stuart,
ed. *The Poems of Charlotte Smith* (O.U.P., 1993).
Poetic Form and British Romanticism (O.U.P., 1986).
'Romantic Poetry: the "I" Altered', in Anne K. Mellor, ed. *Romanticism and Feminism* (Bloomington: Indiana Univ. Press, 1988).

Darnton, Robert. *The Literary Underground of the Old Regime* (Cambridge: Harvard Univ. Press, 1982).

Davies, Norman. *Europe: a History* (O. U. P, 1996).

Davidson, Cathy N. and E. M. Broner, ed. *The Lost Tradition: Mothers and Daughters in Literature* (New York: Frederick Ungar, 1980).

Derry, Stephen. 'The Ellesmeres and the Elliotts: Charlotte Smith's Influence on *Persuasion*', in *Persuasions: Journal of the J. A. Society of North America*, 16, 12 (Dec. 1990): 69–70.

Diamond, Arlyn, and Lee R. Edwards. *The Authority of Experience: Essays in Feminist Criticism* (Amherst: Univ. of Mass. Press, 1977).

Doody, Margaret.
'Deserts, Ruins and Troubled Waters: Female Dreams in Fiction and

the Development of the Gothic Novel', in *Genre*, 10 (1977): 529–72.

'English Women Novelists and the French Revolution', in *La Femme in Angleterre et dans les colonies américaines aux XVIIe et XVIIIe siècles* (Univ. of Lille, France, 1976).

A Natural Passion: A Study of the Novels of Samuel Richardson (Oxford: The Clarendon Press, 1974).

Introduction to *Sense and Sensibility* (Harmondsworth: Penguin, 1990).

Duckworth, Alistair.

The Improvement of the Estate: a Study of Jane Austen's Novels (Baltimore: Johns Hopkins Press, 1971).

'Jane Austen's Accommodations', in *The First English Novelists: Essays in Understanding*, ed. J. M. Armistead (Knoxville: Univ. of Tennessee Press, 1985): 225–67.

Duckworth, Alistair and David C. Streatfield. *Landscape in the Gardens and the Literature of the Eighteenth Century: Papers Read at a Clark Library Seminar*, 18 March 1978 (Los Angeles: Univ. of California, William Andrews Clark Memorial Library, 1981).

Duncan-Jones, E. E. [E. E. Phare]. 'Lydia Languish, Lydia Bennet and Dr Fordyce's Sermons', in *Notes and Queries*, 11 (1964): 182–83.

Dussinger, J.A. *The Discourse of the Mind in Eighteenth Century Fiction* (The Hague: Mouton, 1974).

Eagleton, Terry. *The Rape of Clarissa: Writing, Sexuality and Class Struggle in Richardson* (Oxford: Blackwells, 1982).

Ehrenpreis, Anne Henry.

'Charlotte Smith', in *The Novel to 1900: Great Writers Student Library*, ed. James Vinson (London: Macmillan, 1980): 265–6.

ed. *Emmeline*, by Charlotte Smith (Oxford English Novels Series, O.U.P., 1971).

'Northanger Abbey, Jane Austen and Charlotte Smith', in *Nineteenth Century Fiction*, 25 (Dec. 1970): 343–8.

ed. *Northanger Abbey*, by Jane Austen (Harmondsworth: Penguin, 1972).

ed. *The Old Manor House*, by Charlotte Smith (Oxford English Novels Series, O.U.P., 1969).

Elliot, Pat. 'Charlotte Smith's Feminism: a Study of *Emmeline* and *Desmond*' in *Living By The Pen: Early British Women Writers*, ed. Dale Spender (N. Y: Teacher's College Press, 1992).

Ellis, Kate Ferguson.

'Charlotte Smith's Subversive Gothic', in *Feminist Studies* 3 (1976): 51–5.

The Contested Castle: Gothic Novels and the Subversion of Domestic Ideology (Urbana: Univ. of Illinois Press, 1989).

Elwood, Anne K. *Memoirs of the Literary Ladies of England*. 2 vols (London: Henry Colburn, 1843).

Epstein, Julia. *The Iron Pen: Frances Burney and the Politics of Women's Writing* (Madison: Univ. of Wisconsin Press, 1989).

Erdman, David V. *William Blake, Prophet Against Empire: A Poet's Interpretation of the History of his Own Times* (New Jersey: Princeton Univ. Press, 1954).

Figes, Eva. *Sex and Subterfuge: Women Writers to 1850* (London: Macmillan, 1982).

Finney, Claude. *The Evolution of Keats' Poems* (Cambridge, Mass: Harvard Univ. Press, 1936).

Fitzpatrick, Martin. 'Charlotte Smith', in Janet Todd, ed. *British Women Writers: A Critical Reference Guide* (London: Routledge, 1989): 623–6.

Flanders, W. Austin. 'An Example of the Impact of the French Revolution on the English Novel: Charlotte Smith's *Desmond*', in Carla E. Lucente, ed. *The Western Pennsylvania Symposium on World Literatures, Selected Proceedings: 1974–1991* (Greensburg PA: Eadmer, 1992).

Fleenor, Juliann E., ed. *The Female Gothic* (Montreal: The Eden Press, 1983).

Fletcher, Loraine.
'Charlotte Smith's Emblematic Castles', in *Critical Survey*, vol. 4, 1 (1992): 3–8.
'Emma: the Shadow Novelist', in *Critical Survey*, vol. 4, 1 (1992): 36–44.
'Four Jacobin Women Novelists', in *Writing and Radicalism*, ed. John Lucas (London: Longman, 1996)
Satire and Sensibility in the Novels of Charlotte Smith. Ph.D. thesis, Birkbeck, 1993.

Forbes, Joan. 'Anti-Romantic Discourse as Resistance: Women's Fiction 1775–1802', in *Romance Revisited*, ed. Jackie Stacey and Lynne Pearce (New York Univ. Press, 1995).

Foster, James R.
'The Abbé Prévost and the English Novel', in *P.M.L.A.*, 42 (1927): 443–64.
'Charlotte Smith, Pre-Romantic Novelist', in *P.M.L.A.*, 43 (1928): 463–75.
The History of the Pre-Romantic Novel in England (O.U.P., 1949).

Foucault, Michel. *Madness and Civilisation*, trans. by Richard Howard (London: The Tavistock Press, 1977).

Françoise, Albrecht. 'Charlotte Smith and Rousseau: De l'Emile au Jeune Philosophe', in *Le Continent et Le Monde Anglo-Américain aux XVXIIe et XVIIIe Siècles* (Reims: P. U. de Reims, 1987).

Frank, Frederick S. *The First Gothics: A Critical Guide to the English Gothic Novel* (New York: Garland, 1988).

Fry, Carroll Lee.
Charlotte Smith, Popular Novelist. Ph.D. Thesis. Univ. of Nebraska at Lincoln, 1970.
Charlotte Smith (N.Y: Twayne Publishers Ltd, 1997).

Frye, Northrop. 'Towards Defining an Age of Sensibility,' in James L. Clifford, ed. *Eighteenth Century English Literature: Modern Essays in Criticism* (O.U.P., 1959).

Fulford, Tim. *Landscape, Liberty and Authority: Poetry, Criticism and Politics from Thomson to Wordsworth.* (C.U.P., 1996)

Fuss, Diana. *Essentially Speaking: Feminism, Nature and Difference* (London: Routledge, 1988).

Gilbert, Sandra M. and Susan Gubar.
   The Madwoman in the Attic: The Woman Writer and the Nineteenth Century Literary Imagination (New Haven: Yale Univ. Press, 1979).
   The Norton Anthology of Literature by Women: The Tradition in English (New York: W. W. Norton, 1985).

Gill, Richard. *Happy Rural Seat: The English Country House and the Literary Imagination* (New Haven: Yale Univ. Press, 1972).

Gilson, David. 'Jane Austen's Books', in *The Book Collector*, 23 (1974): 27–39.

Girard, René. *Deceit, Desire and the Novel: Self and Other in Literary Structure*, trans. by Yvonne Freccero (Baltimore: Johns Hopkins Univ. Press, 1976).

Gledhill, Peggy Willand. The Sonnets of Charlotte Smith. Ph.D. Thesis. Univ. of Oregon, 1976.

Glen, Heather. *Vision and Disenchantment: Blake's Songs and Wordsworth's Lyrical Ballads* (C.U.P., 1983).

Goldschmidt, Mary Louise. A Genealogy of the Subject of Feminism in the Works of Mary Wollstonecraft, Mary Hays and Charlotte Smith. PhD. Thesis. Emory Univ., 1993.

Goodridge, John.
   ed. *The Independent Spirit: John Clare and the Self Taught Tradition* (The John Clare Society and the Margaret Grainger Memorial Trust, 1994).
   Rural Life in 18th Century English Poetry (C.U.P, 1995).

Graham, Kenneth W. *Gothic Fictions: Prohibition/Transgression* (New York: A. M. S. Press, 1989).

Grainger, Margaret, 'Some Literary References: Charlotte Smith and Gilbert White' in *The Nightjar: Yesterday and Today*, ed. Paul Foster (Bishop

Green, Katherine Sobba. *The Courtship Novel, 1740–1820: A Feminized Genre* (Univ. Press of Kentucky, 1991).

Gregory, Allene. *The French Revolution and the English Novel* (London: G. P. Putnam's Sons, 1915).

Gregory, P. The Popular Fiction of the Eighteenth -Century Commercial Circulating Libraries. Ph.D Thesis. Univ. of Edinburgh, 1984

Grey, J. David, ed. *Jane Austen's Beginnings: The Juvenilia and Lady Susan* (Ann Arbor: Univ. of Michigan, 1990).

Gross, Harvey. 'The Pursuer and the Pursued', in *Texas Studies in Literature and Language*, 1 (1959): 401–11.

Grundy, Isobel.
   Introduction to *Secrecy, or, the Ruin on the Rock*, by Eliza Fenwick (Ontario: The Broadview Press, 1994).
   Women, Writing, History 1640–1740 (London: Batsford, 1992).

Hagstrum, Jean H.
   The Romantic Body: Love and Sexuality in Keats, Wordsworth and Blake (Knoxville: Univ. of Tennessee Press, 1985).

Sex and Sensibility: Ideal and Erotic Love from Milton to Mozart (Chicago: Univ. of Chicago Press, 1980).

Hall, K. G. The Exalted Heroine and the Triumph of Order: Class, Women and Religion in the English Novel. Ph.D. Thesis. Univ. of Edinburgh, 1981.

Hardwick, Elizabeth. *Seduction and Betrayal* (New York: Random House, 1974).

Hardy, Barbara. *A Reading of Jane Austen* (Univ. of London: Athlone Press, 1979).

Harris, Jocelyn. *Jane Austen's Art of Memory* (C.U.P., 1989).

Heilman, Robert B. *America in English Fiction 1760–1800* (Baton Rouge: Louisiana State Univ. Press, 1937).

Hemlow, Joyce.
'Fanny Burney and the Courtesy Books', in *PMLA*, 65, 2 (1950): 732–61.
The History of Fanny Burney (Oxford: The Clarendon Press, 1958).

Hilbish, Florence May Anna. *Charlotte Smith, Poet and Novelist, 1749–1806* (Philadelphia Univ. Press, 1941).

Homans, Margaret. *Bearing the Word: Language and Female Experience in Nineteenth-Century Women's Writing* (Chicago Univ. Press., 1986).

Honan, Park. *Jane Austen: Her Life* (London: Weidenfeld and Nicolson, 1987).

Honour, Hugh. *Neoclassicism* (Harmondsworth: Penguin, 1977).

Horner, Joyce. 'English Women Novelists and their Connection with the Feminist Movement, 1688–1797', in *Smith College Studies in Modern Languages*, 11, nos 1, 2 and 4 (Northampton, Mass:Smith College Press, 1930).

Howells, Coral Ann. *Love, Mystery and Misery: Feeling in Gothic Fiction* (Univ. of London: Athlone Press, 1978).

Hufton, Olwen.
The Poor of Eighteenth-Century France 1750–1789 (Oxford: The Clarendon Press, 1974).
Europe: Privilege and Protest (London: Fontana, 1985).
Women and the Limits of Citizenship in the French Revolution (Univ. of Toronto Press, 1992).

Humphreys, Jennett. 'Dorset, Catherine Ann [sic] ?1750–1817', in *DNB*, 15 : 253.

Hunt, Bishop C., Jr. 'Wordsworth and Charlotte Smith', in *The Wordsworth Circle*, 1 (1971): 85–103.

Husbands, Hilda Winifred. The Lesser Novel, *1770–1800*. M.A Thesis. Univ. of London, 1922.

Imig, Barbara Linnerson. Shooting Folly as it Flies: a Dialogic Approach to Four Novels by Charlotte Smith. PhD. Thesis. Univ. of Nebraska, 1991.

Jacobus, Mary. 'Cowper's *The Task*: the Poetry of Introspection', in *Pre-Romanticism in English Poetry of the Eighteenth Century*, ed. J. W. Watson (London, Macmillan,1989).

James, C. L. R. *Black Jacobins: Toussaint L'Ouverture and the San Domingo Revolution* (London: Allison and Busby, 1984).

Janowitz, Anne. *England's Ruins: Poetic Purpose and National Landscape* (Oxford: Blackwell, 1990).

Johnson, Claudia. *Jane Austen: Women, Politics and The Novel* (Univ. of Chicago Press, 1988).

Johnson, R. Brimley. *The Women Novelists* (New York: Chas. Scribner's Sons, 1919).

Jones, Ann H. *Ideas and Innovations: Best Sellers of Jane Austen's Age* (New York: AMS Press, 1986).

Jones, Kathleen. *A Passionate Sisterhood: the sisters, wives and daughters of the Lake Poets* (London: Constable, 1997).

Jones, Vivien, ed. *Women in the Eighteenth Century: Constructions of Femininity* (London: Routledge, 1990).

Kamm, Josephine. *Hope Deferred: Girls' Education in English History* (London: Methuen, 1965).

Kaplan, Cora.
  Salt and Bitter and Good: Three Centuries of English and American Women Poets. With original portraits by Lisa Unger Basken (London: Paddington Press, 1975).
  Sea Changes: Culture and Feminism (London: Verso,1986).

Kavanagh, Julia. *English Women of Letters: Biographical Sketches.* 2 vols. (London: Hurst and Blackett, 1863).

Kelly, Gary.
  English Fiction of the Romantic Period 1789–1830 (London: Longman, 1989).
  The English Jacobin Novel, 1780–1805 (Oxford: The Clarendon Press, 1976).
  Introduction to *Mary* and *The Wrongs of Woman* by Mary Wollstonecraft (O.U.P., 1976): vii–xxi.
  'Jane Austen and the English Novel of the 1790s' in *Fetter'd or Free? British Women Novelists 1670–1815*, ed. Mary Anne Schofield and Cecilia Macheski (Athens, Ohio: Ohio Univ. Press, 1986): 285–306.
  Revolutionary Feminism: The Mind and Career of Mary Wollstonecraft (London: Macmillan, 1992).

Kelly, Linda. *Richard Brinsley Sheridan: A Life* (London: Sinclair-Stevenson, 1997).

Kelley, Paul. 'Jane Austen, Charlotte Smith and "An Evening Walk"', in *Notes and Queries*, 29, 3 (1982): 220.

Kermode, Frank. *The Sense of an Ending: Studies in the Theory of Fiction* (O.U.P., 1967).

Kiely, Robert. *The Romantic Novel in England* (Cambridge Mass: Harvard Univ. Press, 1972).

King, James. 'Charlotte Smith, William Cowper and William Blake: Some New Documents', in *Blake: An Illustrated Quarterly*, 13 (1979): 100–1.

King-Hele, Desmond. 'The Origin of the Specious', in *The Times Higher Education Supplement*, 11 July, 1997. See also King-Hele's forthcoming book on E. Darwin.

Kinsley, James and Gary Kelly. 'Introduction', in Mary Wollstonecraft, *Mary* and *The Wrongs of Woman* (O.U.P., 1976): vii–xxi.

Kirkham, Margaret. *Jane Austen, Feminism and Fiction* (Brighton: The Harvester Press, 1983).

Kowaleski–Wallace, Elizabeth. *Consuming Subjects: British Women and Consumer Culture in the Eighteenth Century* (Columbia Univ. Press, 1997).

Kraft, Elizabeth, ed. *The Young Philosopher* (Lexington: Univ. of Kentucky Press, Forthcoming).

Labbe, Jacqueline M.
'Every Poet Her Own Drawing Master', a paper given at the Early Romantics Conference, Reading University, 8 Sept, 1995.
'Selling One's Sorrows: Charlotte Smith, Mary Robinson and the Marketing of Poetry', in *The Wordsworth Circle*, 25, 2 (Spring 1994): 68–71.

Lascelles, Mary. *Jane Austen and Her Art* (Oxford: The Clarendon Press, 1939).

Lee, Elizabeth. 'Smith, Charlotte, 1749–1806,' in *DNB*, 43: 27–9.

Legates, Marlene. 'The Cult of Womanhood in Eighteenth Century Thought', in *Eighteenth Century Studies*, 10 (1976): 21–39.

Lessenich, Rolf P. *Aspects of English Preromanticism* (Koln; Wein: Bohlan Verlag, 1989).

Litz, A. Walton. *Jane Austen: A Study of her Artistic Development* (London: Chatto and Windus, 1965).

London, A. Landscape and the Eighteenth Century English Novel. PhD. Thesis. Univ. of Oxford, 1980.

Lonsdale, Roger, ed. *Eighteenth-Century Women Poets: An Oxford Anthology* (O.U. P. 1989).

Lovell, Terry. *Consuming Fiction* (London: Verso, 1987).

Lucacs, Georg. *The Historical Novel*, translated by Hannah and Stanley Mitchell (Harmondsworth: Penguin, 1969).

Luria, Gina, and Irene Taylor. 'Gender and Genre: Women in British Romantic Literature', in *What Manner of Woman*, ed. Marlene Springer (New York Univ. Press, 1977).

MacAndrew, Elizabeth. *The Gothic Tradition in Fiction* (New York: Columbia Univ. Press, 1979).

MacCarthy, Bridget. *The Female Pen: The Later Women Novelists, 1744–1818* (Cork: Cork Univ. Press,1941).

Macheski, Cecilia, and Mary Anne Schofield, ed. *Fetter'd or Free? British Women Novelists 1670–1815* (Athens, Ohio: Ohio Univ. Press, 1986).

Madoff, Mark S. 'Inside, Outside, and the Gothic Locked-Room Mystery', in Kenneth W. Graham, ed. *Gothic Fictions: Prohibition/Transgression* (New York: A.M.S. Press, 1989): 49–62.

McKeon, Michael. *The Origins of the English Novel, 1600–1740* (Baltimore: John Hopkins Press, 1987).

McKillop, Alan Dugald.
'Allusions to Prose Fiction in Jane Austen's "Volume the Third"', in

Notes and Queries, 196 (Sept 1951): 429.
'Charlotte Smith's Letters', in *The Huntington Library Quarterly,* 15 (1951–2): 237–55.

Magee, William. 'The Happy Marriage: the Influence of Charlotte Smith on Jane Austen', in *Studies in the Novel,* 7 (1975): 120–32.

Martin, S. R. *Charlotte Smith, 1749–1806, A Critical Survey of her Works and Place in English Literary History* . Ph.D. Thesis. Univ. of Sheffield, 1980.

Mayo, Robert D.
'The Contemporaneity of the Lyrical Ballads', in *P.M.L.A.,* 69 (1954): 486–522.
The English Novel in Magazines, with a catalogue of 1375 magazine novels and novelettes, 1740–1815 (O.U.P., 1962).

Mellor, Anne K., ed. *Romanticism and Feminism* (Bloomington, Univ. of Indiana, 1988).

Miller, Nancy K.
'Emphasis Added: Plots and Plausibilities in Women's Fiction', in *P.L.M.A.,* 96 (Jan 1981): 36–47.
The Heroine's Text: Readings in the French and English Novel, 1722–1782 (New York, Columbia Univ. Press, 1980).

Millett, Kate. *Sexual Politics* (London: Abacus Press, 1970).

Moers, Ellen. *Literary Women: The Great Writers* (New York: Anchor Books, 1977).

Moi, Toril. *Sexual/Textual Politics: Feminist Literary Theory* (London: Methuen, 1985).

Moler, K. L. *Jane Austen's Art of Allusion* (Univ. of Nebraska Press, 1968).

Molyneaux, Maribel Waldo. *Women and Work: On the Margins of the Marketplace.* Ph.D Thesis. Univ. of Pennsylvania, 1988.

Morgan, Susan. *In the Meantime: Character and Perception in Jane Austen's Fiction.* (Univ. of Chicago Press, 1980).

Morris, David B. 'Gothic Sublimity', in *New Literary History,* 16 (1985): 299–320.

Mudrick, Marvin, *Jane Austen: Irony as Defense and Discovery* (New Jersey: Princeton Univ. Press, 1952).

Mullan, John. *Sentiment and Sociability: the Language of Feeling in the Eighteenth Century Novel* (Oxford: The Clarendon Press, 1988).

Murdoch, Iris. *Sartre: Romantic Rationalist,* Studies in Modern Thought Series, ed. E. Heller (Cambridge: Bower and Bower, 1953).

Napier, Elizabeth R. *The Failure of the Gothic: Problems of Disjunction in an Eighteenth-Century Literary Form* (Oxford: Clarendon, 1987).

Needham, Gwendolen Bridges and Robert Palfrey Utter. *Pamela's Daughters* (London: Macmillan 1936).

Newey, Vincent. 'Cowper, Wordsworth and Nature', in *Pre-Romanticism in English Poetry of the Eighteenth Century,* ed. J. R. Watson, 1989.

Nicoll, Allardyce. 'Late Eighteenth Century Drama, 1750–1800', in *A History of English Drama 1660–1900* (C.U.P, 1955).

Nokes, David. *Jane Austen: A Life* (London: Fourth Estate, 1997).

Nussbaum, Felicity. *The Autobiographical Subject: Gender and Ideology in Eighteenth-Century England* (Baltimore: Johns Hopkins Univ. Press, 1989).

O'Donoghue, D. J. *The Poets of Ireland: a Biographical Dictionary* (London: The Paternoster Steam Press, 1892).

O'Flinn, Paul. 'Man As He Is and Romanticism as it ought to be', in *Critical Survey*, vol. 4, 1 (1992): 28–35.

Papashvily, Helen Waite. *All the Happy Endings* (New York: Kennikat Press, 1972).

Parnell, Paul E. 'The Sentimental Mask', in *P.M.L.A.*, 78 (Dec. 1963): 529–35.

Pascoe, Judith.
'Female Botanists and the Poetry of Charlotte Smith', in *Re-Visioning Romanticism: British Women Writers 1776–1837*, ed. Carol Shiner Wilson and Joel Haefner (Philadelphia: Univ. of Penn. Press, 1994).
Romantic Theatricality: Gender, Poetry and Spectatorship (Ithaca: Cornell Univ. Press, 1997).

Paulson, Ronald. *Emblem and Expression* (London: Thames and Hudson, 1975).

Perry, Ruth. *The Celebrated Mary Astell: an Early English Feminist* (Chicago: Univ. of Chicago Press, 1986).

Pinion, Frances B. *A Jane Austen Companion: A Critical Survey and Reference Book* (London: Macmillan, 1975).

Piorkowski, Joan L. Revolutionary Sentiment: a Reappraisal of the Fiction of Robert Bage, Charlotte Smith and Thomas Holcroft. Ph.D. Thesis. Temple University, 1980.

Platt, Constance McCormick. Patrimony as Power in Four Eighteenth Century Women's Novels: Charlotte Lennox, *Henrietta*; Fanny Burney, *Evelina*; Charlotte Smith, *Emmeline*; Ann Radcliffe, *The Mysteries of Udolpho*. Ph.D. Thesis. Univ. of Denver, 1980.

Pollin, Burton R. 'Keats, Charlotte Smith and the Nightingale', in *Notes and Queries*, 211 (1966): 180–1.

Ponting, K. G. *Wiltshire Portraits* (London: Moonraker Press, 1975).

Poovey, Mary. *The Proper Lady and the Woman Writer: Ideology as Style in the Works of Mary Wollstonecraft, Mary Shelley and Jane Austen* (Univ. of Chicago Press, 1984).

Pratt, Annis. *Archetypal Patterns in Women's Fiction* (Bloomington: Univ. of Indiana Press, 1981).

Preston, John. *The Created Self: The Reader's Role in Eighteenth Century Fiction* (London: Heinemann, 1970).

Prickett, Stephen. *England and the French Revolution.* (Basingstoke: Macmillan Education Ltd, 1989).

Proper, Coenrad Bart Anne. *Social Elements in English Prose Fiction Between 1700 and 1832* (Amsterdam: H. J. Paris, 1929).

Punter, David. *The Literature of Terror: A History of Gothic Fiction from 1765 to the Present Day* (London: Longman, 1980).

Rendall, Jane. *The Origins of Modern Feminism: Women in Britain, France and the United States 1780–1860* (London: Macmillan, 1985).

Renwick, W. L. *English Literature 1789–1815*, vol. 9 of *The Oxford History of English Literature*, ed. F. P. Wilson and Bonamy Dobrée (Oxford: The Clarendon Press, 1963).

Reynolds, Myra. *The Treatment of Nature in English Poetry Between Pope and Wordsworth* (Univ. of Chicago Press, 1909).

Riley, Esther Powell. Resisting Writers: Four Eighteenth-Century Women Writers in Search of a Voice (Aubin, Davys, Lennox, Smith). PhD. Thesis. Univ. of Tennessee, 1993.

Roberts, Bette B. *The Gothic Romance: Its Appeal to Women Writers and Readers in late Eighteenth-Century England* (New York: Arno Press, 1980).

Roberts, Warren. *Jane Austen and the French Revolution* (London: Macmillan, 1979).

Rogers, Katharine M.
Before Their Time: Six Women Writers of the Eighteenth Century (New York: Ungar, 1979).
'The Contribution of Mary Hays', in *Prose Studies* 10, 2 (Sept 1987): 131–42.
'Dreams and Nightmares: Male Characters in the Feminine Novel of the Eighteenth Century', in *Women and Literature*, 2 (1982): 9–24.
Feminism in Eighteen Century England (Urbana: Univ. of Illinois Press, 1982).
'Inhibitions on Eighteenth Century Women Novelists: Elizabeth Inchbald and Charlotte Smith', in *Eighteenth Century Studies*, 11 (Fall, 1977): 63–78.
'Romantic Aspirations, Restricted Possibilities: The Novels of Charlotte Smith', in *Re-Visioning Romanticism: British Women Writers 1776–1837*, ed. Carol Shiner Wilson and Joel Haefner (Philadelphia: Univ. of Penn. Press, 1994).

Russ, Joanna. *How to Suppress Women's Writing* (London: The Women's Press, 1984).

Sadleir, Michael. 'The Northanger Novels', in *The Edinburgh Review*, 264 (July 1927): 91–106.

Sage, Victor, ed. *The Gothic Novel, A Casebook* (Basingstoke: Macmillan Education Ltd, 1990).

Schama, Simon. *Citizens: A Chronicle of the French Revolution* (London: Penguin, 1989).

Schofield, Mary Anne and Cecilia Macheski,
ed. *Fetter'd or Free? British Women Novelists 1670–1815* (Athens, Ohio: Ohio Univ. Press, 1986).

Schofield, Mary Anne,
ed. *Marchmont* (N. Y: Scholars' Facsimile Press, 1989).
ed. *Montalbert* (N. Y: Scholars' Facsimile Press, 1989).
'The Witchery of Fiction: Charlotte Smith, Novelist', in *Living By The Pen: Early British Women Writers*, ed. Dale Spender (N. Y: Teachers' College Press, 1992).

Masking and Unmasking the Female Mind: Disguising Romances in Feminine Fiction, 1713–1799 (Newark: Univ. of Delaware Press, 1991).

Shaw, Margaret Elizabeth. Ideas of Women Writers on the Education of Young Children in the late Eighteenth and early Nineteenth Centuries. M.Ed Thesis. Univ. of Hull, 1984.

Simons, Judy. *Fanny Burney* (London: Macmillan, 1987).

Sitter, John. *Literary Loneliness in Mid-Eighteenth Century England* (Ithaca: Cornell Univ. Press, 1982).

Smith, Bernard, and Peter Haas. *Writers in Sussex* (Bristol: Redcliffe, 1985).

Smith, Warren Hunting. *Architecture in English Fiction* (O.U.P., 1934).

Southam, Brian.
  ed. *Critical Essays on Jane Austen* (London: Routledge and Kegan Paul, 1968).
  Jane Austen's Literary Manuscripts: A Study of the Novelist's Development through the Surviving Papers (O.U.P., 1964).

Spacks, Patricia Meyer.
  The Adolescent Idea: Myths of Youth and the Adult Imagination (New York: Basic Books, 1981).
  Desire and Truth: Functions of Plot in Eighteenth Century Novels (Univ. of Chicago Press, 1990).

Spector, Robert Donald. *The English Gothic: a Bibliographic Guide to Writers from Horace Walpole to Mary Shelley* (Westport, Connecticut: The Greenwood Press, 1984).

Spencer, Jane.
  'Charlotte Smith', in *A Dictionary of British and American Women Writers 1660–1800*, ed. Janet Todd (Totowa, New Jersey: Rowman and Allanheld, 1985): 287–9.
  The Rise of the Woman Novelist: From Aphra Behn to Jane Austen (Oxford: Blackwells, 1986).

Spender, Dale.
  ed. *Living By The Pen: Early British Women Writers* (New York: Teachers' College Press, 1992).
  Mothers of the Novel: One Hundred Good Women Writers Before Jane Austen (London: Pandora, 1986).

Springer, Marlene, ed. *What Manner of Woman: Essays on English and American Life and Literature* (Oxford: Basil Blackwell, 1978).

St. Cyres, Viscount de. 'The Sorrows of Mrs Charlotte Smith', in *The Cornhill Magazine*, 15 (1903): 683–96.

Stanton, Judith Phillips.
  'Charlotte Smith's Literary Business: Income, Patronage and Indigence,' in *The Age of Johnson: A Scholarly Annual*, 1 (1987): 375–401.
  Charlotte Smith's Prose: A Stylistic Study of Four of Her Novels. Ph.D.Thesis. Univ. of N.Carolina at Chapel Hill, 1978.
  Introduction to *The Old Manor House*, by Charlotte Smith (World's Classics Series, O.U.P, 1989).
  'Mr Monstroso', a Paper delivered to the British Society for Eighteenth Century Studies, London, 6 Jan 1990.

Staves, Susan.
'Don Quixote in Eighteenth-Century England', in *Comparative Literature*, 24 (1972): 193–215.
Married Women's Separate Property in England 1660–1833 (Mass: Harvard Univ. Press, 1990).

Steeves, Harrison R. *Before Jane Austen: The Shaping of the English Novel in the Eighteenth Century*. With Contemporary Illustrations (London: Allen and Unwin, 1965).

Stevenson, Lionel. *The English Novel: a Panorama* (London: Constable & Co, 1960).

Stone, Lawrence. *The Family, Sex and Marriage in England 1500–1800* (London: Weidenfeld and Nicolson, 1977).

Sulloway, Alison. 'Emma Woodhouse and *A Vindication of the Rights of Woman*', in *The Wordsworth Circle*, 7 (1976): 320–32.

Summers, Montague. *The Gothic Quest: A History of the Gothic Novel* (London: The Fortune Press, 1938).

Tanner, Tony. *Jane Austen* (Macmillan, London, 1985).

Taylor, Irene, and Gina Luria. 'Gender and Genre: Women in British Romantic Literature', in *What Manner of Woman*, ed. Marlene Springer (New York: Univ. Press, 1977).

Tillyard, Stella. *Citizen Lord: Edward Fitzgerald, 1763–1798* (London: Chatto and Windus, 1997).

Todd, Janet,
ed. *A Dictionary of British and American Women Writers 1660–1800* (London: Methuen, 1984).
ed. *A Dictionary of British Women Writers* (London: Routledge, 1989).
Feminist Literary History (New York: Routledge, 1988).
'Message Overlooked', a review of Patricia Meyer Spacks' *Desire and Truth*, in *T.L.S.* (Sept 7, 1990): 953.
ed. *New Perspectives on Jane Austen* (New York: Holmes & Meier, 1983).
Introduction to *The Old Manor House* by Charlotte Smith. Mothers of the Novel Series (London: Pandora Press, 1987).
Sensibility: An Introduction (London: Methuen, 1984).
The Sign of Angellica: Women, Writing and Fiction 1660–1800 (New York: Columbia Univ. Press, 1989).

Tomalin, Claire.
Jane Austen (London: Viking, 1997).
The Life and Death of Mary Wollstonecraft (London: Weidenfeld and Nicolson, 1974).

Tompkins, Joyce Marjorie Sanxter. *The Popular Novel in England 1770–1800* (London: Constable & Co., 1932).

Tripathi, P. D. *The Doctrinal English Novel (Later Eighteenth Century): Middle Class Consciousness in England during the American and French Revolutions* (Calcutta: K. P. Bagchi & Co., 1978).

Turner, James. *The Politics of Landscape: Rural Scenery and Society in English Poetry 1630–1660* (Oxford: Basil Blackwell, 1979).

Turner, Rufus Paul. *Charlotte Smith 1749–1806: New Light on her Life and Literary Career.* Ph.D. Thesis. Univ. of S. California, 1966.

Ty, Eleanor Rose.
'Ridding Unwanted Suitors: Jane Austen's *Mansfield Park* and Charlotte Smith's *Emmeline*' in *Tulsa Studies in Women's Literature* 5, 2 (Fall 1986): 327–8.
'Romantic Revolutionaries: Women Novelists of the 1790s'. Ph.D Thesis. McMaster University, 1987.
Unsex'd Revolutionaries: Five Women Novelists of the 1790s. Wollstonecraft, Hays, Inchbald, Williams, Smith. (Toronto: Univ. of Toronto Press, 1993).

Utter, Robert Palfrey, and Gwendolen Bridges Needham. *Pamela's Daughters* (London: Macmillan, 1936).

Varma, Devendra P. *The Gothic Flame: being a history of the Gothic Novel in England* (London: New York: Russell & Russell, 1957).

Wagenknecht, Edward. *Cavalcade of the English Novel* (New York: Holt, Reinhart & Winston, 1954).

Watson, R. J, ed. *Pre-Romanticism in English Poetry of the Eighteenth Century: A Casebook* (London: Macmillan, 1989).

Watt, Ian, *The Rise of the Novel: Studies in Defoe, Richardson and Fielding* (London: Chatto and Windus, 1957).

White, Daniel. 'Autobiography and Elegy: the Early 'Romantic' Poetics of Thomas Gray and Charlotte Smith', a paper given at the Early Romantics Conference, Reading University, 7 Sept, 1995.

Whiting, George W. 'Charlotte Smith, Keats and the Nightingale', in *Keats–Shelley Journal*, 12 (1963): 4–8.

Whitmore, Clara. *Women's Work in English Fiction from the Restoration to the Mid-Victorian Period* (New York: G. P. Putnam & Sons, 1910).

Whitney, Lois. *Primitivism and the Idea of Progress in English Popular Literature of the Eighteenth Century* (Baltimore: The Johns Hopkins Press, 1939).

Willey, Basil. *The Eighteenth Century Background: Studies on the Idea of Nature in the Thought of the Period* (London: Chatto and Windus, 1940).

Williams, Raymond.
Culture and Society, 1750–1950 (London: Dent, 1958).
The Long Revolution (Harmondsworth: Penguin, 1975).

Williamson, Karina, 'Mundanity in Women's Poetry', a paper given at the Early Romantics Conference at Reading University, 7 Sept, 1995.

Wilson, Mona. *The Life of William Blake* (London: The Nonesuch Press, 1927. Revised, Rupert Hart-Davies, London, 1948).

Wolff, Cynthia Griffin. 'The Radcliffean Gothic Model: a Form for Feminine Sexuality', in Juliann Fleenor, ed. *The Female Gothic* (Montreal: The Eden Press, 1983): 207–23.

Woodward, Lionel. *Une Anglaise Amie de la Révolution Française: Hélène Maria Williams et Ses Amis* (Paris: Librarie Ancienne Honoré Champion, 1930).

Wordsworth, Jonathan.
The Bright Work Grows: Women Writers of the Romantic Age. Revolution

and Romanticism Series (Poole: Woodstock Books, 1997).

ed. *Elegiac Sonnets* 1789, by Charlotte Smith. Facsimile. Revolution and Romanticism Series (Poole: Woodstock Books, 1992).

Introduction to *The Letters of a Solitary Wanderer* (Poole: Woodstock Books, 1995).

Wright, Walter Frances. *Sensibility in English Prose Fiction 1760–1814: A Reinterpretation* (London: Russell and Russell, 1937).

Yamanouchi, Hisaaki. The Mind's Abyss: A Study of Melancholy and Associated States in Some Late Eighteenth Century Writers, and in Wordsworth and Coleridge. Ph.D. Thesis. Univ. of Cambridge, 1975.

Zimmerman, Sarah MacKenzie.

'Charlotte Smith's Letters and the Practice of Self-Presentation', in *Princeton University Library Chronicle*, 53, 1 (1991): 50–77.

Romantic Lyricism and the Rhetoric of Actuality: Charlotte Smith, Dorothy Wordsworth, and John Clare. Ph.D. Thesis. Univ. of Princeton, 1993.

Index

The following abbreviations have been used:
CS Charlotte Turner Smith
BS Benjamin Smith (husband)
RS Richard Smith (father-in-law)
CS's children are indexed under her entry.
In general, fictional characters are not indexed.